Rapture Advent of the Last Days

Rapture Advent of the Last Days

Jocolby Phillips

Elm Hill

A Division of
HarperCollins Christian Publishing

www.elmhillbooks.com

Rapture Advent of the Last Days

Published in Nashville, Tennessee, by Elm Hill, an imprint of Thomas Nelson. Elm Hill and Thomas Nelson are registered trademarks of HarperCollins Christian Publishing, Inc.

Elm Hill titles may be purchased in bulk for educational, business, fund-raising, or sales promotional use. For information, please e-mail SpecialMarkets@ThomasNelson.com.

Library of Congress Cataloging-in-Publication Data

Library of Congress Control Number: 2019936950

ISBN 978-1-400325719 (Paperback)
ISBN 978-1-400325733 (eBook)

To my Savior, Jesus Christ; I dedicate this book to you. You transformed my life that many, including me all too often, judged and destined for failure and disgrace. I am now a person whose life is filled with boundless potential and success, and I thank you. Through my tears of pain and the questioning of the value my life held; you've waited and welcomed me despite my doubts of you. Whatever I've needed in any moment of life; I realize now you've provided: mother, father, doctor, friend, counselor, and so much more. I still feel unworthy when thinking of the mercy and grace I find in my life, but I am grateful that you love me unconditionally. I am humbled to be a vessel for your message in these trying days. May you and your eternal kingdom receive all the praise and glory of this book and the books that follow.

Return soon, King Jesus. Love, J.P.

Chapter 1

While Major Christopher Barrett had long ago stopped trusting or believing in God, he could not shake the feeling that God was trying to get his attention over the career he loved. He had desired at several points and for various reasons throughout his life to establish a relationship with Him. However, he carried deep emotional scars from a painful childhood—a childhood for which he blamed God daily, making trust impossible in his mind. The major felt God had been absent in his life when he had needed Him most, so he had stopped looking for His presence. The Army, and special operations in particular, provided the major with a sense of reliability and trust in himself over any faith he might have in God.

He always felt uneasy on missions where the absinthe-colored light provided by his night-vision goggles was required, but something about tonight's mission made the feeling different, worse. His years of experience as a special forces officer demanded poise in this situation, but he felt he was wrestling with that "still, small voice" that his estranged wife Erin identified as the Holy Spirit. That voice had made it a practice of late to blare like a foghorn in his head. As a result here he was on one of the most significant missions of his military career, debating whether the Holy Spirit was battling him for his mind and soul.

Christopher had prepared for this mission mindlessly, which was admittedly out of character. The green glow of his goggles quickened his apprehension about this operation as his team approached the target location along the banks of the Tigris in Mosul, Iraq. General Amir bin Waleed, commander of the Mosul District Iraqi Army Commandos, had made recommendations on saving a French journalist, but in his opinion far too many of those recommendations had been followed when creating the rescue plan.

General Waleed insisted that the Americans take the Tigris to the ISIS stronghold, while his commandos secured the perimeter around the target to prevent escape. Though it seemed harmless enough, Christopher knew it potentially left his team vulnerable, yet here he was in the midst of Waleed's plan with his unit. Very little intelligence on General Waleed's unit had been provided to him, and the major knew enough not to place his men with Waleed's, as first suggested by the sketchy Iraqi general. He had a strong feeling that he was missing something, but he couldn't put his finger on what it was.

It was too late for second-guessing now. The abrupt change in the din of the rigid inflatable boat's high-powered engine pulled Major Barrett into the moment as the vessel rounded the last river bend before the target. One minute was called across the radio as the dark silhouette of the Bash Tapia Castle dominated the horizon. Per the plan, his twelve-man "A Team" would land behind the compound and split into two six-man elements, converging on the estimated location of the journalist. As the major steeled his mind for the fight ahead, all that mattered now was saving the journalist and bringing his men home alive.

As the two boats made shore below the fallen rear wall of the castle, the quiet stillness of the night was deafening; it seemed even nature was holding its breath. The exhale that broke the silence came with the sharp report of a DShK Russian heavy machine gun. Without speaking a word the team separated and began assaulting the castle, the team sergeant and his crew moving up the west side as Christopher and his team breached the eastern side.

His men worked their way along an ancient rock wall to a point where the incoming rounds of the DShK sounded like buzzing bees. He could hear the spent machine-gun brass cartridges hitting the ground as the air around him snapped from near misses. Two hand-grenade explosions silenced the machine gun raining lead on his team, providing a momentary lull. He should've received a situation update from his team sergeant's crew by now, so the silent radio and the crack of an explosion in the distance were not reassuring.

Sergeant Major Jackson Williams shook his head in shock after the grenade explosion. The smell of his own heat-singed face and cauterized skin forced him back into the reality that Rev and two others were dead. He radioed a brief situation update to Christopher. "Three men down, continuing to move to the target." Knowing there was still a job ahead and nothing he could do for Rev and the others at the moment, he told the two soldiers left in his element to form up. The three men formed an inverted triangle, clearing the remaining ISIS fighters from the corridor leading into the interior stateroom of the castle.

Jackson's first situation report confirmed Christopher's fears: men down. He fought the urge to try to salvage the situation. He knew Jackson well, and if he was continuing the mission then the soldiers were gone. More pressing, the path in front of Christopher quickly escalated into a crisis as his group approached the great room adjacent to the hostage. He was sure that some of the figures firing AK-47s at them were General Waleed's commandos.

The battle was short-lived given the poor accuracy of the enemy, but the fight proved to him that Waleed and his men had betrayed his team.

Four of the dead men wore the uniform of the Mosul District commandos. It took all of Christopher's willpower to remain focused, blaming himself for not seeing Waleed's betrayal due to his distraction with the "voice" in his head. Even worse, some of his men had paid the ultimate price for his error. The scene of carnage and the ever-increasing tug on his soul were too much at the moment. He wanted to give in to his emotions, fall to the floor, and scream like a lost child. Instead he came to rest on one knee, seeming to the others to be preparing his equipment for the final assault.

The major's mental war raged in the midst of this real battle. *What is wrong with me? Why so much emotion?* He heard himself say aloud, "Get it together, Barrett." The still, small voice seemed almost audible in his mind. *"You will not fear the terror of night, nor the arrow that flies by day, nor the pestilence that stalks in the darkness, nor the plague that destroys at midday. A thousand may fall at your side, ten thousand at your right hand, but it will not come near you."* He knew the words were from Psalm 91, which Rev often quoted to all of them.

He braced himself for the fight he was sure was awaiting him on the other side of the two massive wooden doors blocking access to the journalist. "Let's go," was all the major could muster to say as he radioed his people and led the charge into the stateroom.

The ancient grandeur of the stateroom lingered with old tiled murals dotting the walls, accented by a vaulted and buttressed ceiling, all of which seemed misplaced given the savagely brutal display before him. There was little doubt in Christopher's mind about the journalist's fate at the hands of ISIS. The low light provided by the old candelabra ceiling lights gave off just enough light to reveal that they were too late; he didn't need his hi-tech goggles to see that she was dead. Half clothed, gagged, and bound at the ankles with her hands pulled behind her, she sat in a plush ottoman where the chair's seeming comfort belied the horrific scene. The team medic rushed over only to confirm what everyone already knew.

Strangely no fighters were guarding the journalist, though a large part of Christopher wished someone was left so justice could be doled out for this crime. Instead a horrible, crushing sense of failure filled him as he looked at the disheveled and matted brunette locks of hair covering the victim's face. *So much loss of life tonight*, he thought, consumed with rage and disappointment. *And I know one more person set to expire tonight...General Amir bin Waleed,* the major thought as he ran alone toward the castle entry where Waleed was supposed to be positioned.

Jackson held up a single fist to his remaining two soldiers, signaling them to halt as he tried to establish radio contact before entering the stateroom, but his attention was captured by a lone figure darting out of the room and down the adjacent hallway. "Barrett, this is Williams, over." Nothing returned across the radio. "Barrett, this is Williams." Still no answer. "Any green element, any green element, this—" the sergeant major was cut off by a reply on the radio."Hey, Green 9, we are in the stateroom with the target. You're clear to approach."

"What the…?" Jackson could not even finish his sentence as he walked toward the men clustered around the lifeless woman. He knew from her body position that she was gone. Trying to break the hold that the strikingly beautiful deceased victim held over the men, the sergeant major screamed, "Barrett is where?"

The medic responded, "He's right…well, Sarge, he was right over there." He pointed near the hallway where Jackson had seen the running figure.

The sergeant major grabbed the nearest man and barked, "Take charge. Recover the journalist's body and the bodies of our brothers." He turned his attention to the two men who had fought through the castle with him. "You two, with me," he ordered as he began running after Major Christopher Barrett.

The crisp fall night air and the star-filled sky were a refreshing reprieve from the stagnant castle. As Christopher flipped on his night-vision goggles, he quickly recognized his vulnerability and the foolishness of letting his emotions lead him out here alone—always a dangerous position. He spotted the command vehicle of General Waleed and noted the absence of commandos securing the perimeter. *Did Waleed kill the journalist, try to destroy our team, and then flee into the Mosul night?* he wondered.

As he approached the vehicle with his M4 carbine rifle at the ready, the answer became clear. General Waleed and his security detail were dead. He, like the major, had missed the infiltration of ISIS fighters into the ranks of the Mosul commandos. Unfortunately it was too late for General Waleed, but his death vindicated him of betrayal in Christopher's mind.

The familiar voice of Sergeant Major Jackson Williams filled Christopher's earpiece. "Green 6, this is Green 9. What's your location?"

"Green 9, I see you. Keep walking to your twelve o'clock."

Jackson didn't know whether to punch Christopher or hug him. Instead he chose a passive-aggressive question. "Are you okay?"

"Yeah, I'm okay," the major stated flatly. "I take that back. I am far from okay. This night has been a colossal disaster, and I am at fault."

"Look, we don't have the time, nor is this the place, for a pity party. I've already got guys securing Rev and the other casualties. I suggest we load up the journalist and our guys on the back of that five-ton truck and convoy back to Camp Marez," Jackson said, pointing to an abandoned cargo truck near Waleed's command vehicle.

Hearing Rev's name as a casualty was like a devastating punch to Christopher's gut. Rev was his best soldier and dear friend. He could only mutter numbly, "Yeah, that's fine."

"Fine? Look, Barrett, get it together," Williams demanded loudly.

Christopher, while grateful to his mentor and friend for handling the situation, bristled outwardly before turning abruptly to walk toward the men loading the fallen soldiers and the journalist, not trusting himself to respond. He felt alone, despite being surrounded by chaos and some of the people he knew best in the world. He had endless questions about why the night had played out as it had. If God was trying to reach him, the major was tired of receiving the call. Tonight's operation just reinforced that God was not to be trusted when he needed Him most.

As Christopher watched the truck carrying the bodies of his men and the French journalist leave the Bash Tapia Castle, the voice returned. *"I will never leave you, nor forsake you. So say with confidence, The Lord is my helper; I will not be afraid. What can mere mortals do to me?"* The voice seemed to refute the major's thoughts that God had been absent from his life tonight. *Am I going crazy? Is this real?* he thought. *Is God really challenging me, using my own thoughts?*

With the team settling back in at their headquarters at Camp Marez on the outskirts of Mosul, Major Barrett called the group together. "We will hold a short memorial in an hour for Rev and the other men who gave their lives tonight."

The sergeant major separated himself from the group and began walking toward a solitary berm at the end of the compound that overlooked the rest of the camp. His abrupt departure caught Christopher's eye as Jackson's figure was consumed by the darkness. He slowly followed the team sergeant to the edge of the berm, lit only by a single moth-encircled floodlight, and sat down gingerly next to his long-time mentor, hoping to find solace.

"You call her yet?" Jackson asked, staring at the endless Mosul night sky.

Christopher nervously chuckled. "No, I haven't contacted Erin. I see you remember my post-mission habit." Jackson let the comment hang in the air and fade away without replying, purposefully forcing the major to break the awkward silence. "So what's on your mind, Jackson?"

"Rev is on my mind," Jackson responded without turning to face Christopher. "More importantly, Rev's last Bible study is uppermost in my mind right now."

"His Bible study?" The words had come out more sarcastically than the major intended, and he could see the offense on Jackson's partially illuminated face as he briefly turned toward Christopher.

"Yeah, the Bible study! I mean, this young man had such a passion for his beliefs. How can you not be curious to know more about what drove his desire? I mean, with all we just went through tonight, the real question is, how are you not curious about God?"

Christopher didn't want to get into a religious debate or reveal to Jackson the spiritual battle in his own mind of late, especially given how raw their emotions seemed at the moment. Standing, he shot back, "You're not the only one dealing with the loss of good men here. I am sorry I let the team down tonight and, yeah, I remember that Bible study and all the ones you missed."

Jackson ignored Christopher and tried to recall Rev's last Bible study as he relished the chill of the night air. He knew it was wrong not to acknowledge Christopher's departure, but he wanted to cherish his few memories of Rev, the man who had made God seem real to him. It was only the chattering and gathering of soldiers near the dining facility that pulled Jackson back from his thoughts and into the present. He stood and rubbed his sweat-matted brown hair while stretching his stiff and aching frame, realizing that the year he had spent behind a desk at Special Operations Command Headquarters, commonly called SOCOM, in Tampa Bay had done him no favors for fieldwork. For a man of average build in his early forties, Jackson was proud of the way he had held up during the operation tonight. He was still strong and felt he had a few good years of service in the Army left in him.

As Jackson walked toward the memorial service, it was a sobering fact that Rev was gone, but Jackson could not deny the impact Rev had made on his life in such a short time. He promised himself he would explore what Rev had called the gift of salvation. It was the least he could do to honor the man.

Christopher began the memorial as Jackson joined the group in the back. The major's firm tone contradicted the endless emotions with which he had wrestled over the last few days. He focused heavily on his handwritten notes to steady his shaky composure. He began with administrative data, fighting a wave of panic and nausea as he announced, "The team will be heading back to the States at 0300 tonight." Gaining strength, he went on to say that their fallen teammates were being flown back to Dover Air Force Base, Delaware, in about an hour and funeral details would follow shortly. He paused longer than he intended before he was able to continue with the memorial by making some comments regarding the men who had lost their lives that night. He started by briefly recounting anecdotes about the two other men on his team, trying to build up to discussing Rev. Finally he could delay no longer. "Brett Councilman was an outstanding brother-in-arms."

"Who's Brett Councilman?" a single voice shouted from the rear of the gathering, providing the major a respite of levity and causing most of the men to laugh.Christopher said, "Brett Councilman, *aka* Rev, was not only one of the greatest special operations soldiers I've ever seen but also one of the best men I've ever known." As the tears streamed down his cheeks and dripped onto his notes, he stopped speaking momentarily to compose himself. It was in this momentary pause that the still, small voice spoke once again in his heart: *"Blessed are those who mourn, for they shall be comforted."*

Christopher seemed buoyed by the voice and finished his remarks on Rev in a manner that emphasized his impact on the team. He eulogized Rev as a man of unshakeable faith and principle. "Rev cared for you whether or not you believed his views. I know he has impacted all of us profoundly, and his trust in God defined him as his often-quoted favorite verses of scripture highlight.

"I am sure anyone who knew Rev could recite the verses from Psalm 91: 'He who dwells in the secret place of the Most High shall abide under the shadow of the Almighty. I will say of the Lord, He is my refuge and my fortress; My God, in Him I will trust.'" Christopher concluded the memorial by saying, "Rev's trust in God made him a man of conviction. Let us all live our lives with such confidence in honor of the man we called Rev."

Jackson took a detail of soldiers to Rev's quarters to box up his personal effects. As the men were placing his clothes and other items in boxes, Jackson was drawn to Rev's makeshift nightstand that was littered with looseleaf paper, a journal of some sort, and a worn Bible.

"Hey, Sarge, we're done. You coming?" a soldier asked Jackson, who remained sitting on Rev's bed.

"No, you guys head out. I'll catch up in a few minutes," Jackson replied. He became enthralled by Rev's study journal and his Bible that was tabbed and highlighted, seemingly on every page. Turning off the single light in the room, he thought, *There is no better way to honor Rev than to study what made him so passionate about God.*

After a routine but uncomfortable military flight out of Mosul, Christopher was glad to be in a secluded airline lounge with a few hours to relax before taking a commercial airline back to Washington, D.C. He always loved people watching, and as many times as he had flown out of Kuwait City International Airport, this particular view never grew old. The clashing of Western and Middle Eastern cultures was intriguing.

The major watched his team of elite soldiers, now dressed in casual attire, seamlessly blend into the backdrop of businessmen and women in various forms of clothing, from skintight to traditional suits. It was a sign of the times and how things had changed in the ten years since Christopher had been traveling the world and visiting business lounges, where he saw a group of young adults wearing T-shirts, hoodies, and jeans—likely software engineers, given away by their nonconformist "Silicon Valley uniform." All of this was in contrast to the view outside the lounge, emphasized by a group of Islamic women wearing niqabs as a statement of their modesty.

As Christopher watched an American businessman and his presumed spouse kissing, he thought about how he missed his wife Erin. Over the last year she had become so demanding about his attending church with her. In fact she had pressed him so hard to "mend his relationship with the Lord" that he had left their shared Alexandria, Virginia, townhome six months ago to live with a group of old Army buddies in the D.C. area.

Erin returned to her family's farm near Harrisonburg, Virginia, a few months after he left, placing their future as a couple in question. Christopher loved Erin dearly but found her zeal and unquestioning trust in Jesus Christ overbearing and unattractive; she was the one who had put God first in their relationship, leaving him feeling like a third wheel. He felt Erin had caused their rift and wished they could go back to the days when she relied on and trusted him more than she did God.

Christopher pulled out his cell phone, and sure enough Erin had left him a message—typical for her when he was away on a mission. He sighed and checked his watch. Two in the morning in Kuwait City made it six in the evening in Virginia. He placed the call.

Erin answered halfway through a sentence or two. "Yes, Mom, it's him. I am sure it's him. I've got it…hello," she said then offered a laugh.

Christopher should have known she would answer like that, but he chuckled all the same. "Hello, Erin."

Erin told him how worried she had been and how things had been going with her parents, knowing she could not share his professional life—a fact she had begrudgingly accepted years ago. She just focused on what she could talk about—his welfare.

"Well, it'll be good to get back to D.C. I am looking forward to a few days' off," Christopher confessed.

"I have been praying for you…" A pause, and then she continued and said, "For us. Maybe you can come down when you get back so we can talk."

Christopher only heard Erin say "praying," which caused him to sigh aloud. "I see you're still a Bible thumper."

Erin's voice seemed thick as she said, "I asked you not to call me that or to make fun of my faith."

Christopher instantly felt his stomach turn and, trying to apologize, began saying, "Erin, I—" But she cut him off. "Chris, I understand why you think God is not real and that He has been absent from your life. I get it. However, I don't comprehend how someone so bright and perceptive could miss how much God has done for you." Feeling a surge of courage to stand up for her faith, Erin continued. "You have completed countless high-risk missions and walked away to tell the tale, acknowledging that you shouldn't have made it out alive on more than one occasion. Just think back to Israel three years ago. How can you not see that the possibility of God's active presence in our lives is more than credible?

"I love you, Chris. I pray you begin to understand and trust God above yourself before God has to put you through some experience that brings you to your knees in order to bring you back to Him." Erin, sobbing now, pleadingly added, "Don't miss your opportunity to receive God's gift of salvation." And with those words Christopher's phone went silent.

I wish I could tell Erin how much she means to me. Why did I have to treat her faith so callously? Why do I let it anger me so profoundly when someone places their trust in God? I know she has a point about trusting God over myself, but I just can't buy into having to submit myself to God.

Christopher, catching his reflection in a mirrored wall in the lounge, barely recognized himself as he gazed at the image through bloodshot brown eyes. Now in his mid-thirties, his six-foot-tall athletic frame, defined by years of rigorous exercise, seemed fragile. The stress of a failed mission, his crumbling marriage, and the raging war for his soul being played out between that still, small voice and his mind made him look ten years older.

As the boarding announcement for his team's flight back to Washington came across the PA system, Christopher watched Jackson approach with a pensive look on his face.

"You look older than me tonight, boss," Jackson remarked with a small smile.But the major didn't bite on the attempt at humor, instead responding, "What's up?"

Jackson wanted to ask Christopher the same but thought better of it. He instead conveyed the message sent by Colonel Delmar with the debriefing schedule attached. "There's going to be a full day of questions about what went wrong. Colonel Delmar said to expect some heat."

Christopher replied flatly, "Great. Well, there goes my few days off, but I expected some blowback."

"You're not going in there alone. I'll delay my trip back to Tampa until after the debriefings," Jackson responded.

Christopher smiled tiredly. "You know, you caring about people is going to get you into trouble one day."

Jackson laughed. "Man, I know. You're a terrible influence on me. And before you ask, I gave the rest of the team seventy-two hours off." After a short pause, he started again. "Hey, about blowing up at you about the Bible study and Rev—"

Christopher cut him off. "Don't worry about it, Jackson. I could see from the first time you met Rev that you were impressed with him far beyond his soldiering skills."

Jackson thanked him with a smile as the boarding announcement was made for their flight. The two men left the lounge and headed toward the gate for the long trip to Washington, D.C.

CHAPTER 2

As Christopher and his team made their way onto the U.S.-government-chartered 787, he felt the dismissive glances and whispers of the State Department personnel seated in the premium cabin. He knew the look—a look that viewed his team as a tool that was dirty and unrefined, like a toilet brush. Most of the government outside of the Department of Defense saw his team as a necessity, but not something worthy of acknowledgment. He was glad to find the State Department flight relatively empty, allowing him to have a three-seat row to himself. As the jet climbed effortlessly into the night sky, leaving the trouble of the Middle East behind for another day, Christopher fought to flush the thought of the doomed mission out of his head.

Erin's last words over the phone seemed destined to make this an even longer flight. "Don't miss the opportunity to receive God's gift of salvation." Rev had said something similar in his last Bible study. Christopher, if he was honest with himself, thought that a lot of what he had experienced over the previous several years were perhaps God providing him opportunities to accept His salvation. None stood out more than the Russian-led invasion of Israel, which should have pushed him to God like Erin had suggested. Yet as his eyes closed, he felt no closer to God tonight than he did after visiting Israel three and half years ago. Though it likely appeared to others that Christopher sank into a restless sleep, in reality the Israel mission began to play in his mind like a mid-flight movie.

Christopher asked the seemingly harmless question of why his team was being called on to protect the SecDef in Israel. "Isn't that a job for the Pentagon Force Protection Agency?"

Colonel Delmar swore before barking, "Barrett, I think I know the role and mission of Omega Group as its commander."

Christopher liked pushing Delmar's buttons but acknowledged his task with a simple, "Yes, sir."

"Now, if there are no more interruptions," Colonel Delmar continued, glancing at Christopher who raised his hands in a gesture of mock surrender, "I will tell you the details of the mission. The president feels like this conflict in Israel may not be over, but wants to get to the bottom of why Israel can still be found on a map this morning. Omega is the best at getting an individual or a group out of situations that seem impossible, hence the reason you boys are taking this little vacation to the Middle East.

"You will be traveling to view the destruction that the Israelis leveled against the Russian-Iranian alliance two days ago. The Intelligence Community has convinced the president that the reports coming out of Jerusalem are wrong and that the Israelis have a new superweapon. Your job is to protect the SecDef as he tours the country to see the battlefield firsthand.

"Christopher, your team will embed into the SecDef's security detail, just in case things go sideways while the SecDef is on the ground. If needed, you'll get the SecDef safely out of the country. Additionally I want you, Christopher, to provide an assessment of what occurred. You will depart from Andrews Air Force Base at 1800."

Colonel Delmar concluded the meeting, but as staffers and members of Christopher's team headed out to prepare, Delmar stopped Christopher. "Barrett, keep your head on a swivel. Something strange happened over there. No telling what you'll find."

Christopher found it odd for the unemotional Colonel Delmar to express concern, but he chalked it up to stress as he watched Delmar proceed down the hall yelling at some hapless staff officer before leaving the Pentagon for yet another unique mission.

Christopher designated six men from the twelve-man Omega Group for the trip, with Rev serving as his second-in-command. As Rev and Christopher were discussing potential alternative evacuation routes in the executive terminal at Andrews Air Base, a bulky over-cologned man approached the two of them.

He asked, "Which one of you is in charge of the military guys?"

"That would be me," Christopher replied.

"Look, you guys just stay out of the way, and this will be an easy few days for all of us," the protection agent demanded.

"Hey, officer," Christopher said, purposefully demoting the power-obsessed protection agent, "we are here to do a job and do it professionally. And by the way, it's *Major* Barrett."

"*Major* Barrett, is it? It's not *officer*, but Special Agent in Charge Dewberry, and I don't want any loose cannon hero types screwing up, so just toe the line. Remember, Barrett, I have the ear of the SecDef."

Christopher took a step toward Special Agent Dewberry, but Rev grabbed his arm, saying, "We got it, Special Agent Dewberry, you're in charge. Have a great day." Dewberry paused as if to respond, but left in true Hollywood fashion: walking away abruptly as he raised a hand to his earbud and loudly replied that he copied some order.

"Wow, what was that guy's deal?" Christopher wondered aloud.

"Who knows? You know people always get uptight when military guys wear suits and are 'helping' with security." In a low voice Rev added, "Forget him. Aren't you excited to be heading to the Holy Land?"

Christopher was not in the mood for a sermon. "No, I am just ready to get this trip done quietly."

Rev, undeterred and as giddy as a child before Christmas morning, began to describe what he saw as the reason for Israel's overwhelming victory as the men left the terminal to board their flight to Israel.

Christopher had a momentary reprieve from Rev's latest sermon as the two climbed the stairs of *Nightwatch*, the code name of the SecDef's plane, and the engines roared to life. Unfortunately, as soon as Rev and Christopher found their seats near the rear of the aircraft, the sermon continued.

Christopher laughed. "You know, I shouldn't have chosen *you* for this mission! What was I thinking to bring a preacher to Israel?"

"You need me for one, and two, what better tour guide of the Holy Land than me?" Rev replied with a chuckle.

Christopher laughed as he buckled up. "Okay, Rev, let's hear your theory on what happened."

Rev, seated adjacent to Christopher, grew solemn and stared out into the cabin before replying, "Are you sure you want to listen to this message?"

"Yeah, I want to understand your take on what occurred. It seems everyone has a theory, so why would I refuse to listen to yours?"

"You would resist my perspective if it centered on God," Rev replied without turning to face Christopher.

"Rev, you're right. It's hard for me to believe anything dealing with God. However, I am also open to hearing your thoughts. Besides, if the reports are even half accurate regarding what happened a couple of days ago, I would say God is back."

"He's always been here, Christopher. You're the one who has yet to accept His presence," Rev retorted, evidently failing to see the humor in Christopher's last comment.

"My apologies. I know you're serious about your faith," Christopher said, feeling a bit embarrassed.

"Apology accepted. There's so much to tell you about this incident, but I'll spare you the dissertation."

Christopher wanted to say thanks but realized his humor might not go over well once again. Instead, silent and attentive, he listened as Rev proceeded.

"The Bible foretold of an event that bears a resemblance to the recent Russian-led invasion of Israel in the book of Ezekiel. The event is called the War of Gog and Magog." Rev laid out his outline of the invasion as the *Nightwatch* rocketed off the Atlantic seaboard toward Israel. "The timing and nations involved in this were all foretold in the Bible, Christopher. And this war could be a significant step toward the start of the tribulation. This is really an exciting time to be alive."

"I am excited and all ears for the next fourteen hours," Christopher responded.

"I wish you were less mouth," Rev shot back. "Okay, the major players in the biblical battle are likely Russia and Iran," Rev explained.

"Wait, why do you say *likely* Russia and Iran? We know they were the leaders in the event from a few days ago," Christopher questioned.

"I say likely because in *Ezekiel 38:2*, Russia and Iran are not explicitly named. We have to do some homework to discover who those two nations are. While I believe what happened in Israel a few days ago was the Ezekiel 38 War of Gog and Magog, it's not clear-cut until we can confirm some things on the ground.

"The Bible says the attack will be led by Gog. He is described as a military and political leader who establishes a coalition to destroy Israel. Russia's dictator fits that bill, but really it's the spirit behind his actions that are significant. That spirit comes from Satan, in yet another attempt to destroy the people of God, but I digress. It's also likely that Russia's leader is the Gog of Ezekiel 38, due to Flavius Josephus, the first-century Roman historian, detailing in his seminal book *The Antiquities of the Jews* that Magog was a land filled with people whom the Greeks called Scythians. The Scythians settled in the areas north of the Black Sea in the former Soviet satellites and current Russia.

"Now for Iran, Ezekiel 38:5 depicts Persia as the chief ally to Gog, whom I've established is most likely Russia. Persia, as you know, is now called Iran, and we both know how close Tehran is to Russia. That's why I believe the invasion of Israel led by Russia and Iran was the fulfillment of the first War of Gog and Magog," Rev concluded.

"Why do you say first war? Is there a second one coming?"

"Yes, there is. Revelation 20:7–10 speaks of another War of Gog and

Magog that will occur at the end of Jesus' millennial kingdom reign. In both cases of the War of Gog and Magog, the nations coming against Israel and at the end of the millennial kingdom, against Jesus Himself, are driven by the same evil spirit."

"Okay, I am lost. Continue with the recent crisis."

"Last part to understand is the motive. The Bible helps paint the picture of why the invasion we witnessed took place. In Ezekiel 37:4–8, the physical restoration of the Jewish state was the first domino to fall for several key prophecies, including the event that occurred a few days ago. When we put together the announcement by the Israelis about a year ago of finding one of the world's largest untapped gas reserves in their borders and their supplanting of Russia in the EU energy market, we get a motive to match the actions.

"The Bible decrees in Ezekiel 38:8 two conditions that seemingly are in line with what occurred before the recent attack. First, Israel must be living securely in the land, which, given the strength of the Israeli Defense Forces, cannot be easily dismissed. Next, ahead of the War of Gog and Magog, Israel would have some prosperity that this coalition would seek to plunder as outlined in Ezekiel 38:12 and manifested with the gas-reserve find. I see only one conclusion: that the Russian-Iran-led attack came about as the Bible predicted thousands of years ago," Rev finished.

Christopher awakened sweating from his haunting vision of Rev detailing the War of Gog and Magog, relieved to find himself still on a plane bound for the U.S. He looked around only to see Jackson's cabin light glowing in the darkness of the plane, and it looked like he was studying for something. Christopher didn't want to sleep, much less remember a potential missed opportunity to realize the power of God, but he felt his eyelids growing heavy as his mind traveled back to Israel.

"Hey, wake up! Look out your window," Rev shouted to Christopher as they entered Israeli airspace.

"Huh…? What…?" Christopher slurred.

"Look at those fissures and the destroyed tank and armored vehicle columns."

Christopher wiped the sleep from his bloodshot eyes and saw the dawning light of the new day illuminating the Central Hills and Jordan Rift Valley regions of northern Israel aglow with many burning and destroyed pieces of military hardware.

"Oh man, did God do a number on them," Rev exclaimed.

"I'm not sure that's exactly what happened, Rev, but we will have some better answers shortly," Christopher assured him as he listened to the announcement of the final approach into Ben Gurion International Airport.

As *Nighthawk* finished taxiing to a secured area of the airport, Christopher watched as several black sedans approached the plane, escorted by Israeli Defense Forces (IDF) military vehicles. He could see countless minions setting up a receiving line marked with well-dressed soldiers holding Israeli and U.S. flags along a red carpet. At the end stood the Israeli Minister of Defense and General Benjamin Havid.

General Havid was a legendary figure in the special operations community, known the world over as the tougher-than-nails officer who had been a distinguished commander in both the Kidon and Unit 269, also known as Sayeret Matkal. Christopher knew the drill. The SecDef and his immediate entourage would proceed, and he and the rest of the "support" folks would wait until they had made their way down the receiving line before moving to their vehicles.

As Christopher walked down the red carpet, he could see his guys climbing into random vehicles and Rev jumping into a car near him.

"Hey, Major Barrett, you're riding here," Agent Dewberry instructed, pointing to a waiting sedan. "Remember to keep a low profile. The Israelis don't know we have military embeds."

"Got it, Agent Dewberry," Christopher said as he entered his "assigned" luxurious but obviously up-armored sedan. Christopher craned his neck to see Agent Dewberry arguing with someone and wondered who it was. When he finally saw the face, his first thought was, *Nah, it couldn't be...*

"I will sit wherever I wish, young man. Now go with your principal," shouted the Israeli officer.

"Hello, I am General Benjamin Havid, and your name, young man?" General Havid closed the sedan door and turned to Christopher, who sat next to him.

"Good morning, sir. I am Christopher Barrett. I am security—" Christopher was summarily cut off by the General.

"I can spot a warrior a mile away. I was watching you proceed along the receiving line. Why do you think I wanted to ride in the car with you?" General Havid asked.

"It's an honor, sir. Your reputation precedes you," Christopher replied, almost struck dumb by his good fortune.

"I would be right to assume you're with Omega Group, yes?"

"Sir, I don't want—" General Havid cut him off again.

"No need to answer. Your response—or lack thereof—tells me what I want to know. Are you an officer or a soldier," General Havid pressed.

"I'm an officer."

"Ah, then that would make you at least a major. Well, Major Barrett, now that we are acquainted with each other, what shall we talk about today?"

Laughing, Christopher replied with the question that was uppermost in his mind. "What happened, sir?"

"That is easy. God defended His people. Do you believe me, Major?" General Havid asked.

"I don't know, sir," Christopher replied honestly.

General Havid laughed as the caravan of sedans began to move toward the Valley of Jezreel. "Major Barrett, by the end of the day, you will, I assure you."

As the vehicles made their way through Israel toward one of the most significant sites of the invasion force's destruction, the Valley of Jezreel, Christopher was struck that he could see no signs of conflict or damage to anything dotting the Israeli countryside. While there were numerous jets downed along the route to the Valley of Jezreel, it seemed as though they had crashed "purposefully," landing in vacant lots and fields.

"It is amazing. We have yet to receive one report of any loss of life here in Israel," General Havid said, noticing the bewilderment on Christopher's face as he stared out his window.

"That *is* amazing considering the size of the force that came against you," Christopher responded.

"The invasion occurred so quickly that we did not have a chance to get more than a few intercept jets into the air to meet the inbound fighters. Momentarily you will see an example of what our ground forces found as they rushed to meet the hordes pouring across all our borders. I've never seen anything like this in my more than thirty years of military service," General Havid asserted.

It was hard for Christopher to comprehend the destruction his eyes were seeing as the vehicles stopped at a scenic overlook that had been prepared for the SecDef's visit. The Valley of Jezreel was covered as far as you could see with all forms of modern military hardware, everything from destroyed tanks and artillery pieces to troop carriers and support vehicles. It was clear to him that this was not an invasion as a punitive measure for stealing gas revenues. No, this force aimed to wipe the nation of Israel from the face of the Earth.

"This is something all right," Rev remarked, surveying the battlefield as he joined Christopher and the others at the edge of the overlook.

"I am at a loss for words. I mean, what kind of weapon could have produced this type of damage? It looks as if everything was targeted all at once, including the jets," Christopher replied.

"You mean to tell me you can't see the evidence of God's hand all around you?" Rev questioned loudly in shocked disbelief.

"Your soldier is right, Major Barrett," General Havid chimed in. "God did this. No man-made weapon could have come close. I am sure you already know that we didn't even have time to consider what response was appropriate before the attackers had crossed into Israel."

"Look at the wide fissures in the ground that swallowed whole divisions. Ground force commanders submitted reports that massive hailstones, the size of small vehicles, fell from the sky, crushing the enemies you see here. We are still trying to determine what happened with the jets, but our pilots noted, and I quote, 'rolling waves of lightning sweeping the skies, engulfing the enemy planes.' I tell you, Major Barrett, God was fighting for Israel," General Havid concluded, walking away from Rev and Christopher to go speak with the SecDef and the Israeli Minister of Defense.

Christopher pondered the scene before them. He dared not attribute the victory so clearly to God in the report he had to provide to Colonel Delmar, given how he had never seen God do anything so significant in his own life. However, he would say that something supernatural had occurred.

"It seems that your SecDef is now convinced that Israel has no new weapons, but like you, Major Barrett, the SecDef is struggling to articulate what his eyes are telling him. We are heading back to Tel Aviv for the night. Tomorrow, you will depart for the U.S.," General Havid remarked as he returned to stand near Rev and Christopher.

"Just a few other things, sir, if you don't mind," Christopher said.

"Yes, please ask," General Havid answered.

"First, who are all of those people in the valley wearing the bio-suits?"

"We have mobilized the entire nation to begin the cleanup before any disease can spread. You can already see scavenger birds and animals are racing our crews for the remains. However, it will take us months to rid the land of the dead. The Russian coalition has made no attempt to secure their fallen troops, so we have designated the Valley of Passengers near the Dead Sea for burning the bodies. What's your next question, my bright young friend?" General Havid asked.

"Sir, I also see what looks like crews stripping off components from the vehicles and fallen enemy troops."

"Yes, we are 'improving' our own military inventories. A small fraction of the cowardly invaders escaped, but we are taking advantage of what was left behind. The fuel alone will take years for us to burn through given the size of our military."

"Let me guess…you're estimating about seven years to complete the cleanup," Rev opined.

"Why, I believe that is one of the initial estimates I've been presented. How did you arrive at that number of years?" General Havid queried, his curiosity naturally piqued.

"The prophet Ezekiel described what we are seeing. Well, he described the scene in the best way someone of his era could have," Rev said proudly.

"I believe you have the answers for your report, Major Barrett. The living God of Israel defended the nation, as He always has and will," General Havid concluded.

"Sir, how did you know I was writing a report?" Christopher said, shocked by the general's shrewdness.

The barrel-chested General Havid erupted in a booming laugh as he replied with a smile. "You don't get to where I am in life without knowing the game that is played. I assumed your SecDef was not just going to give a speech to your president and leaders. My last piece of advice for you is, don't deny the significance of *God* allowing you to witness His power. There is a reason beyond the report."

Christopher awoke in a cold sweat, troubled by the lingering dream of reliving the Israeli mission, or the War of Gog and Magog as Erin and Rev described the event. He stared wide-eyed out his window into the darkness, wondering if God was trying to reach him. Perhaps General Havid was right; maybe there was something beyond the report he had given. Perhaps God was providing opportunities through the profession Christopher loved to receive His salvation. Christopher didn't want to give God any credit for trying to connect with him because that felt like he was letting God off the hook for the pain of his childhood. However, what he had experienced recently in Iraq and previously in Israel left him confused about where he stood with God.

Jackson glanced at Christopher and couldn't help but notice him fitfully sleeping a few rows across from him. Jackson worried about him. In Mosul he had been distant and distracted. Christopher impressed Jackson the first time they met with his dedication to the profession, his men, and each mission Christopher completed, which made his recent behavior the more concerning. Jackson hoped getting back to the States would settle Christopher's mind before it cost him his life or career. He held the man in high esteem, and Jackson planned on confronting Christopher about his troubled mind when they got back to D.C.

Jackson had envisioned his "out to pasture" job as a covert operative was destined to be something like building slides for the morning update brief at SOCOM. Jackson had made the decision to retire from the military so he could get to know the family he had for years placed second to helping strangers. He had overachieved within the U.S. special operations community but hardly knew how to relate to his wife Sarah and two small daughters Katie and Sadie. So Jackson unhappily accepted that his final days were going to be spent as a staff advisor. When the call from Christopher came asking for his help, after losing his team sergeant to an emergency appendectomy, Jackson had jumped at the chance for fieldwork. He loved helping others and serving a calling more significant than himself, which is why he loved being a Green Beret so dearly.

Now he was the team sergeant for Omega Group. It was an awesome feeling for Jackson serving as Christopher's team sergeant yet again. He and Christopher had served together for six years in "the Legion," when Christopher was a newbie commander. They had grown close over the years, with Christopher being like a little brother to Jackson.

Three days ago, in Iraq ahead of the mission, was Jackson's first time meeting the team, and he was grateful the integration went seamlessly.

Jackson found the dynamic of the team functional but unique all at the same time. In particular, the religious sentiment that ran through this elite special forces team was intriguing given Christopher Barrett's expressed distrust of the things of God.

At the moment, the things of God was exactly what filled Jackson's mind. His thoughts spun with an ever-growing curiosity about God. Jackson had never grown up going to church or hearing about God, but he couldn't shake Rev's last Bible study. Jackson believed that he was a good person, but felt in his heart that he was missing something after hearing the Bible study. Rev, a nickname earned due to his constant preaching, had been the bond of this team and, without question, the leader of its spiritual movement. But Jackson had found that Rev was just as keen in his marksmanship as he was in quoting the Bible. He smiled as he thought back to the contest Rev had set up to lure him into last night's Bible study.

"Pick a weapon, distance and target, and I'll bet I can outshoot you," the Logan, Ohio, native told Jackson.

"Don't chase this rabbit," Christopher warned his team sergeant.

"Come on now, sir, don't get upset because you can't outshoot me." Rev picked up an M4 assault rifle, switched the selector to full automatic, and proceeded to hollow out the center of a watermelon at 150 meters, watermelons being the team's favorite practice target. He then coyly looked over the rim of his sunglasses at Jackson. While Jackson hit his melon, his accuracy didn't equal Rev's, and as the shots rang out across Camp Marez, Iraq, Jackson was impressive but no match for the preacher man.

"Well, you're a solid shot for an old man," Rev teased.

"Watch it, baby breath. This old dog still knows a few tricks. So what do I owe you, Rev?" Jackson had asked as the men cleaned up the weapons range and prepared to head back to the team's makeshift headquarters.

"That's easy. You just got to show up to my Bible study tonight."

"What? Really? I've never been to a Bible study, especially in a place like this," Jackson replied, apparently puzzled.

"It might help your shooting," Rev suggested boldly.

Christopher laughed as he teasingly drawled in his best imitation of Jackson's Southern accent. "I told you to be careful, Alice! That white rabbit there is trouble."

Jackson had let out a hoot and responded, "I'll be there."

Jackson's vision blurred with tears as he recalled memories of Rev, making him realize that sleeping was going to be a challenge. He figured he could quench his curiosity about God and perhaps even lull himself to sleep by reading Rev's journal that he had taken while helping pack up his personal effects for transport home. Rev had done a great job of explaining what he saw going on in the world and how it was all leading to Jesus Christ returning to claim His "bride," the Church. Now whether Jackson believed him or not was another question, but what he could not do was easily dismiss the argument laid out in Rev's notes.

As Jackson started reading the typed Bible study notes from yesterday, he could feel the passion Rev carried through the words he had written. Rev almost pleaded with the entire team to accept, as he put it, the "gift of salvation." It became more and more evident to Jackson as he read Rev's notes that the man had been more at home in this environment than with his "day job."

Jackson's mind drifted back to the Bible study as he read Rev's opening prayer note. Jackson felt a flush of shame as he remembered that he had been people watching instead of praying, taken by the genuine sincerity of those attending.

The more he read of Rev's Bible study notes, the more he wanted to know about what Rev had said yesterday, and sleep became a distant memory. Jackson continued to pore through the Bible study, trying to digest Rev's message, making further notes of what Rev had said beside Rev's written comments in the journal.

As Jackson began reading the passage dated yesterday in Rev's journal, he was transported once again in thought back to Rev's last Bible study. Jackson pictured himself sitting in a small folding chair in the Omega Team dining facility on Camp Marez the previous evening, mesmerized by the passion Rev exuded regarding the Bible. As he studied the journal this remarkable man called Rev had left behind, he could almost hear Rev's voice as he had said, "There is an ancient saying amongst sailors and fishermen: Red sky at morning, sailor take warning. Red sky at night, sailor's delight. Jesus quoted that proverb to the religious elite of His day, and it is recorded in Matthew 16: 2-3: 'He replied, When evening comes, you say, 'It will be fair weather, for the sky is red,' and in the morning, 'Today it will be stormy, for the sky is red and overcast.' You know how to interpret the appearance of the sky, but you cannot interpret the signs of the times.'"

Jackson noticed that Rev had scribbled a note in the margin of yesterday's entry that said, *"If people missed the signs that Jesus Himself presented, which announced him as the Messiah, what might we be missing that is announcing the approach of the final season, or bluntly stated, the end-times?"*

Leafing through Rev's journal with a pen in his mouth and Rev's open Bible in the adjacent seat, Jackson looked like a college student cramming for finals. He scribbled in the journal margin that Rev had been covering the segment of history known as the end-times, which the Bible says culminates with the second coming of Christ Jesus.

Grabbing the Bible, he tabbed Matthew 24–25, which Rev called Jesus Christ's "Olivet Discourse," Jesus' sermon to His disciples on the end-times. In this passage of the Bible, Jesus answered the question of what "signs" mark the last days.

Jackson began writing down his own translation of Rev's message in simple terms that he could visualize. He wrote, *"Jesus told the disciples that the end-time was not immediate and that the start would be decided by the Father alone. However, in Matthew 24:8, he compared the signs of the end-time to a woman going through birth pains, meaning we should see an increasing frequency of the end-time signs as the start to this final season draws near."*

Jackson remembered the soldier sitting next to him lifting his hand. When all eyes turned toward the man, it seemed to Jackson that everyone was looking at him, since everyone knew he didn't believe in God, and he remembered how his face grew warm under the imagined scrutiny. The soldier asked, "I am confused, Rev. If only the Father knows when the end-time will begin, as outlined in Matthew 24:36, then why does Jesus tell us to watch and be ready? What am I supposed to be ready *for* exactly?"

As Jackson shifted his attention back to the notes in his hand once again, he realized Rev had prepared for just such a question. Jackson followed Rev's notes as they transitioned to a passage of Scripture in Matthew 24, where Jesus outlined the entire end-times period; Rev had also noted that the opening act and final scene are two watershed moments in human history. He had written that Jesus' second coming to Earth would serve as the capstone to the last seven years of history and would also mark the start of the millennial kingdom. Jackson wrote question marks next to *millennial kingdom* so he could figure out later what that meant. Undeterred, Jackson tabbed several Scriptures in the Bible that Rev had used as sources for his notes, including Daniel 7:13–14, Zechariah 14, and Revelation 19:11–15.

It seemed to Jackson that what Rev had referred to as the "opening act" to the end-times was central to the notes for his last Bible study. Jackson wrote in the margin that the answer to the soldier's question was that Jesus was telling us to be vigilant regarding the indications of the rapture. *"We are to be watching for evidence that Jesus' rapture of faithful Christians is drawing near."* Jackson saw another note that Rev had penned in the margin: *"Knowing that the rapture is imminent should make Christians live in a way that brings people to the comfort that salvation in Jesus Christ provides."*

Rev noted in his lesson that Jesus' rebuke about the religious elite having a better understanding of the weather than discernment for the advent of the Messiah was a subtle warning to Christians in our day. Rev's challenge to both Christians and nonbelievers like himself leaped from the pages of the journal as he silently read, *"We should live each day with the knowledge that the rapture could happen today, right now... that our friends, loved ones, and the world must come to accept Jesus, for we are not promised tomorrow in this life. As Jesus says in Matthew 24:43: 'Therefore you also be ready, for the Son of Man is coming at an hour you do not expect.'"*

Jackson smiled as he read over a note Rev had made for himself that hinted at his sharp wit. He remembered Rev covering this very point.

"Yes, I know that the word *rapture* is not in the Bible. However, it is the proper word to describe this event. *Rapio* is the Latin base for our English word *rapture* where *rapio* means *to seize or snatch from one location to another,*" Rev had told them.

Jackson, afraid that he would miss the point Rev was trying to make speaking through the journal, brought his mind back to the present and jotted down his own definition of the rapture. "The rapture means Jesus will suddenly and with force take the Church out of this world to be with Him."

While the Bible study and the Bible, in general, were foreign to Jackson, he was captivated by Rev's message. He carefully examined the rest of Rev's detailed notes on the last days, savoring the way this written message filled him in a way that he had never experienced.

He wrote underneath Rev's notes on the rapture: *"The rapture will affect the entire world, believers and nonbelievers alike."* Rev had scribbled, *"Those who have accepted Jesus Christ's salvation, collectively known as the 'Church,' will be ushered off to what the Bible describes as the Marriage Supper of the Lamb."* Jackson wrote, *"Look up"* by this statement, realizing more and more his ignorance about the topic.

Jackson read that the occurrence of the rapture means the unbelieving world will begin the final seven years of human history, which the Bible calls the tribulation.

"Would you like anything else?" Jackson startled as the flight attendant spoke, dismissing him with the wave of someone who was deep in thought. Jackson drew a box around one of Rev's sentences, which stated that *"God the Father declares the moment along the road of time and history when the end-times are to start; however, Jesus has provided us roadsigns to know when the exit is drawing near."* Rev had journaled that the Church (those accepting Jesus Christ's gift of salvation) will be "raptured" from Earth to be forever with Jesus, just as He promised in John 14:3.

Grateful was the best word Jackson could come up with to describe how he felt about finding Rev's journal. As complex as it was, it provided a wealth of detail. Jackson found notes on the end-times all way to a point described as the "Glorious Appearance of Jesus." He assumed Rev had meant to teach the team more about the end-times in other Bible studies. Jackson followed Rev's written guidance to *"see Matthew 25,"* thumbing through the man's worn Bible to find the chapter. Jackson was confused by the story he read there, but he drew from the notes that Jesus was describing in the passage how we are to be watchful for His return using an example Rev called a "parable."

Jackson rewrote the story in a way he could understand. He noted that the parable of the ten bridesmaids described five who were watchful (a symbol of the Church) and ready for the groom's return (referring to Jesus) and five who were sleeping (symbolizing the unbelieving world). Rev had noted that *"Jesus calls us to always live with a prepared mentality because His return will happen swiftly and unexpectedly for the world at large—but this is not to be the case for the bride (Church) awaiting her groom."*

It was here again that the notes threw Jackson back to the Bible study as he remembered one of the communications support soldiers challenging Rev. The soldier blurted out, "Bad things have always been happening. What makes Jesus' claims about these events significant?" He recalled that Rev had handled the test masterfully, like a seasoned trial prosecutor cross-examining a flawed witness. Jackson smiled as he remembered the sly grin he had observed on the range the previous day slide across Rev's face just before he answered the belligerent kid. Rev, seemingly savoring the challenge, first asked the soldier, "How do you know Major Barrett is in charge of this unit?"

The communications expert responded, "Because his actions demonstrate the authority the Army has given him over this group."

Jackson knew Rev was drawing the young man into his snare. He was, at this point, on the attack as he asked his next question. "I assume you would follow Major Barrett's orders if given by someone else in the unit because of his authority?"

The soldier, growing slightly uncomfortable with all the attention, replied in the affirmative.

Rev sprung his trap. "Then you understand power stems from someone's position and actions." Just like an expert prosecutor, Rev did not give the young man a chance to answer. Instead he offered the answer himself. "Jesus' authority came to Him from the position and actions of being the Son of God. Jesus fulfilled forty-four prophecies announcing Him as the Messiah."

As Jackson glanced at the section of the journal highlighting the exchange between Rev and the soldier, he once again forced himself back to his present study of the notes. Based on what he was reading and what he had witnessed, it was apparent that Rev had anticipated a challenge to Jesus' authority. Jackson unfolded an underscored section torn from the book *Science Speaks* that was taped to Rev's notes. The page detailed the statistical improbability of one man, whether accidentally or deliberately, fulfilling just eight of the prophecies Jesus fulfilled. The statistical probability is 1 to 10^{17} power, and that would be like trying to find one silver dollar in a place the size of Texas covered with silver dollars. Jackson remembered that he and the others at the Bible study had been floored by those statistics when Rev had shared them.

Jackson pulled the simple truth from Rev's notes that Jesus' reference to the end-times or any other matter would be significant, due solely to the unique authority he holds as the Messiah—a fact that was described in the Bible before He was born in Bethlehem, just as the last days have been explained before they occur.

Jackson realized that Rev was trying to drive home in the study that the authority that identified Jesus as the Messiah before His arrival had also described signs leading up to the end of time. Rev wrote that *"Jesus drew His power from God the Father, guided by the Holy Spirit, and He demonstrated His authority throughout His life as recorded for us in the Bible. The nation of Israel and their religious elite failed to recognize the deity of Jesus and the signs that pointed to the source of his Messiahship."*

Rev's voice continued before Jackson as he read. *"The signs Jesus illuminates in Matthew 24 have continued gaining intensity since Jesus' ascension from the Mount of Olives over two thousand years ago. The fact that Jesus Christ's birth, ministry, crucifixion, and resurrection were all announced in the Bible before they ever took place make Jesus' statements on the end-times critical to understand."*

A bit of turbulence and a call over the intercom to buckle seat belts interrupted Jackson's focus on his crash course in biblical end-times prophesy. As he glanced about the dark plane cabin, Jackson saw that his reading light had become a single beacon in the vast economy section.

Returning his thoughts to the notes, Jackson realized he had never had someone articulate something so utterly incomprehensible and implausible, yet at the same time so simple and straightforward as clearly and passionately as Rev had done in his journal. While he still found it hard to believe in the existence of God, he was intrigued to know that daily events were perhaps not a mere coincidence, but maybe part of a message described thousands of years ago to warn humanity of dark days ahead.

Jackson contemplated recent world events, recalling the numerous theories, some of which seemed to have a biblical connection that stemmed from the invasion of Israel by a Russian-led coalition a few years ago. The attack came after Israel's announcement of finding the world's largest natural gas reserves within its borders, and its deal to supply the European Union with natural gas over Russia and Middle Eastern energy leaders. He began highlighting Rev's examples of current-day events that illuminate the birth pains described in the Bible.

Rev pointed out that terrorism was not a new phenomenon: *"Terror's global spread and growing ties to religion provide a modern example of Jesus' message in Matthew 24 regarding intensification of old troubles."*

Jackson highlighted Rev's declaration on climate change in the journal, which said, *"Climate change or any issue facing humanity is not a simple black-and-white issue, but contains a spiritual component as well. I acknowledge humanity's sinfulness and failure to steward the Earth as God intended, which enhances climatic problems. However, the Bible decrees in Romans 8:22 that we know that the whole creation has been groaning as in the pains of childbirth right up to the present time, meaning even the Earth is anticipating Jesus' return to set things back into proper order."*

The conclusion of the study notes served as a mirror for Jackson; he saw himself as one of the lost of the world that Rev was desperately imploring to receive God's gift of salvation. He was beginning to realize that being a decent person was not enough…that God's gift of salvation was Jesus Christ, and that the offering of His only Son to die for the sins of the world—for each one of us—was a gift without price. Jackson thought on Rev's challenge to the team to understand the view that Jesus offered about the events of today, a perspective that was written thousands of years ago, an assessment that said the events of the world serve as a proclamation to receive Jesus as the gift of salvation before it's too late.

The final notes of the Bible study brought a chill to Jackson's frame, and a shiver ran down his spine as he read it. Rev boldly appealed to his listeners that *"the end-times, announced by the rapture of the Church, could happen at any time. The signs that Jesus provided for His disciples and all that have followed over the last two thousand plus years lead to the inevitable climax of humanity's history. I urge all of you who have been attending these Bible studies to review the notes provided, seek to understand the message of Jesus Christ, and make the decision to accept His gift of salvation before it's too late. While there may be some who come to find Jesus as their Lord and Savior during the final years of humanity's history, it will come at a tremendous cost, which will likely be your life."*

Jackson felt a tightness in his chest as he read the last paragraph Rev had written: *"I don't want to scare anyone, but I do want to leave you with an authoritative description of what the end of time will be like for those who choose to ignore God's warnings and are left in the wake of the rapture. Jesus has this to say about the latter days: 'If those days had not been cut short, no one would survive, but for the sake of the elect those days will be shortened' (Matthew 24:22)."*

Jackson had no idea what to make of what he had read and heard over the last day, but he would be lying to himself if he didn't acknowledge that Rev's message did stir within him something he didn't yet understand. As the plane made its final approach and landing, Jackson promised himself that he would study Rev's Bible and notebook and come to a decision about God sooner rather than later.

Chapter 3

"Hello? Hey, we are downstairs outside the hotel waiting for you, so hurry up. Let's not make the day any worse by being late," Jackson growled through the phone into Christopher's ear.

"Oh man, I'll be down in ten minutes," Christopher promised, surfacing from a deep sleep. He was glad that he had put his dress uniform together last night before crashing into a coma-like sleep. Christopher ran through the lobby, slowing only long enough to grab a cup of black coffee before heading out to the waiting standard black government SUV. The soothing aroma of the coffee almost pushed from Christopher's mind the feeling that this day would be one to remember.

"Well, hello, sleeping beauty. I am glad you could join me for the festivities today," Jackson razzed.

"Listen, old man, I am trying to get through this day without killing anyone, and why are you so chipper?"

"I am chipper because I am the supporting cast in this drama, not the lead. I also know that most of the anger is coming your way, so how could I not be happy?"

"Thanks, Jackson, that's really hilarious. I am so glad you're here," Christopher returned sarcastically as he sipped the black coffee. "Joe Cunningham! You're still working for the Executive Support Office. Great to see a decent person this morning," he greeted as he took notice of the driver.

"Glad to be with you again, sir. I hope you have been giving all these terrorists some justice."

"Joe, business has been a little rough lately. Have you met Jackson?"

"Yes, sir, while we were waiting…" Joe didn't finish the sentence as Jackson started to chuckle.

"I see you know my comic relief," Christopher responded. "So where is our first stop today, Joe?"

"Sir, we are off to the Pentagon to meet with Colonel Delmar, then to the Eisenhower Executive Office for meetings with the National Security Advisor and some folks from the Intelligence Community."

"Hey, could you turn that off or change the station?" Christopher directed, suddenly taking exception to Joe's selection of Christian radio.

"Oh, sorry, sir. Sure. Praise and worship music just helps me get through the day driving with this D.C. traffic."

"That's great, Joe, but I would like some peace and quiet before this day starts."

Jackson shot a glance at Christopher, who was now staring out the window, but he knew he had to figure out his own struggles with God before helping someone else.

As the black SUV wheeled into the north parking lot of the Pentagon, Christopher's government-issued cell phone beeped with an incoming message. *"Meet me at Ground Zero,"* the text from Colonel Delmar read.

"Well, this can't be good. Instead of meeting Colonel Delmar in his office, he wants us to meet him at Ground Zero," Christopher relayed to Jackson.

Jackson scurried out of the SUV, scrambling to keep up with a hurried and unsettled Christopher. "Hey, wait up a second."

"Not now, Jackson. You know how Colonel Delmar gets."

"Well, that's even more reason to collect yourself before meeting with him," Jackson replied, stepping in front of Christopher. "What is the best way to handle a near-side ambush?" He posed his question in an attempt to quiet Christopher's mind.

"That's easy—assault through."

"Well, in this case, don't go into the meeting thinking you're being ambushed and set the colonel off by trying to defend yourself and assaulting him. Perhaps the colonel just wants to help us get through the day outside of a formal setting."

"I doubt it, Jackson, but I'll do my best."

"Your best today should be exciting," Jackson remarked with raised brows.

Christopher rolled his eyes as the two of them entered the Pentagon.

As Christopher and Jackson moved through the Pentagon security point and toward the open area at the center of the complex, colloquially called Ground Zero, that still, small voice popped up unexpectedly to reinforce Jackson's advice. *Listen to advice and accept discipline, and at the end, you will be counted among the wise.* It first struck him that the voice sure did seem to speak up at opportune moments. Before Christopher dismissed it as nerves, Colonel Delmar waved them over to a bench.

Colonel Roberto Delmar greeted the men with his usual barrage of swearing. "Well, I am glad to see you boys. But I am madder than my mother leaving a wedding without *capias*."

"Well, sir—" Christopher began, but Colonel Delmar cut him off with another barrage of expletives liberally sprinkled among his assertions that "they"—*they* being policymakers—didn't know how to use Omega Group.

"Gentlemen, I'll cut to the heart of what you're facing. The target for your mission was not an ordinary French reporter but rather the niece of the French prime minister. It has gone from a military operation to political fodder."

"Wow, and that little golden nugget was withheld from me why, sir?" Christopher queried.

"It had zero relevance to rescuing her, Christopher. The more significant problem is the National Security Advisor wants your heads. Making matters worse is the French going on about how we screwed up and, well, it's become a political issue." Colonel Delmar stood and swore again as he berated political leadership.

"I see, sir. I can explain," Christopher began, but Jackson coughed loudly in an attempt to signal him that silence should be his option of choice right now.

"Christopher, there is no need to explain to me," Colonel Delmar said, placing a large hand on his shoulder. "I have been in your shoes as a warrior, as a tool for policymakers who are willing to get us dirty, but who are slow to keep us clean. So go and meet these stuffy 'leaders' and, no matter what, Christopher, hold your head high," Colonel Delmar exclaimed before heading toward the entrance to the Pentagon.

"Wait, so you just wanted us to come by here for a pep talk before we get slaughtered? Should I say thanks, sir?"

Colonel Delmar wheeled around to meet Christopher face-to-face. "You have a lot of attributes, young man, but trust is not one. You're in no position, Major Barrett, to argue how the mission's failure was not your fault. You screwed up, and your Texas-born and -sized ego can't handle it. The fact that you even have an audience with the National Security Advisor should tell you that people have your back. *I have your back*, Major!"

"Sir, I won't—"

Colonel Delmar cut him off. "Stop, Christopher, and think before you say another word."

Jackson touched the major's shoulder in an attempt to steady him and slow the dialog between the colonel and him. Colonel Delmar finished the one-sided conversation. "The fact remains a well-connected journalist died because your team was unable to save her. If you took a second to look beyond yourself, you would see that everyone standing here and a few who are not here will make sure you get through this. Let me remind you, it was me who supported you after you turned in the report that all but claimed God Himself destroyed the Russian-led invasion of Israel a few years ago."

"Sir—"

"Not another word, Major Barrett. Get out of my sight. I will follow up with you on your career path after your meeting with the National Security Advisor."

The sergeant major pushed the seething Major Christopher Barrett toward the entrance of the Pentagon, saving the man from himself.

"Hey, what the heck is your problem?" Christopher demanded as he was pushed into an empty meeting room. He wheeled around to face the sergeant major, shouting, "Get your hands off me! Let's not forget who outranks who here!"

"That's funny, Christopher, because that colonel you just pissed off out there was trying to help you, but you're so stuck in your little world that you missed that very pertinent fact!"

"Look, I don't need this stuff from you, Jackson. I am not just going to sit back and have people say I can't lead this team…that I got Rev and that journalist killed."

"Who said you got those guys or the journalist killed? So that's your problem? You think you got our guys and that journalist killed?"

The major slammed his hands on a desk that stood between them. "No, I am just the fall guy. God let our guys down—including Rev who loved Him. That's my issue—God forgot to show up yet again."

"Look, I am the last one to argue with you about God, but what would Rev tell you right now?" Jackson asked. "Look me in the face and tell me how Rev would want you to handle this situation."

The major dejectedly replied, "I don't know, man. I just feel like God hates me and has been at war with me all my life."

"I can't imagine that feeling, Christopher, but I think Rev would tell you that bad things happen to saints and sinners alike. Look, you can't blame yourself for who dies in our line of work. We all signed up knowing the risk. The first step in becoming a Green Beret is to volunteer, so stop beating yourself up," Jackson said, slapping Christopher on the back. "Okay, let's roll. Don't forget who you are...the Omega Team leader."

Major Barrett erupted into a loud guttural laugh. "Wow, you sound like a cheesy military movie character."

"Hey, man, I am trying to find my sensitive side."

Christopher squeezed Jackson's outstretched hand and gave him an embrace, quietly saying, "Thanks, brother. You always have my back, and I can't tell you what that means to me."

"Yeah, well, just know I expect compensation for all this free counseling I am giving you," Jackson retorted as they exited the Pentagon.

The major definitely felt uneasy as they arrived at the Eisenhower Executive Building and headed inside. He imagined this was the same sensation a convicted man had on his way to the gallows. As they passed through security, they were met by the National Security Advisor's executive assistant. The young man told the major and the sergeant major that the meeting would be held in the Diplomatic Reception Room and that National Security Advisor Markeson was running a little late.

"Well, at least we will have a few moments to collect ourselves before the meeting starts. My suggestion to you, Christopher, is to remain calm. Yes, this meeting is to scapegoat us, but just try to remember that Colonel Delmar already said you're going to be all right at the end of this process," Jackson reminded.

"That's not what I remember him saying, but sure, I will attempt to not freak out like I did this morning."

Christopher tried to size up his "jurors and executioners" as they entered the stately Diplomatic Reception Room. He didn't recognize anyone, but the place cards at the table told him that the heavy hitters from the Intelligence Community were represented—the National Security Agency, the National Geospatial Agency, the Defense Intelligence

Agency, and of course the Central Intelligence Agency. The latter representative had not arrived.

"Now what's your deal? What's with the primping like a teenager heading out to prom?" Jackson asked. "Christopher?" It took only one glance up from heckling Christopher for Jackson to notice a head-turning, petite, olive-skinned, raven-haired thirty-something woman who walked in with National Security Advisor Markeson. "Who is…?"

"That's Gabriella Teresa Smith-Costa," Christopher said, answering Jackson's unfinished question.

"Oh, I see you and Miss Gabriella have a little history. Why haven't I heard stories about her?"

"Quiet, we can talk later," Christopher said, elbowing Jackson.

Mr. Markeson set the tempo for the proceedings from the start. "We are here today because we failed one of our most trusted and long-standing allies a couple of days ago. You're all here to help us discover what went wrong and how we ensure this does not repeat itself in the future. I've brought in the Omega Group commander to help us from the ground perspective."

"No, sir, we have the Omega Team leader," Gabriella said, unflinchingly correcting the National Security Advisor.

"She is a firecracker," Jackson remarked, whispering louder than Christopher was comfortable with.

"Yes, of course. Thanks, Gabriella. The Omega Team leader and… you are who, sir?"

"I am, umm, I am the team sergeant major, sir," Jackson answered, flushing instantly as it seemed he was being called out.

"Excellent," Mr. Markeson said. "Let's get down to business, shall we? Gabriella, the floor is yours."

"Thank you, sir. Good afternoon, ladies and gentlemen. For those who are unfamiliar with me, let me briefly acquaint myself. I am Dr. Gabriella Costa. I serve as the associate director for Military Affairs at the CIA. In this role, I oversee the sharing of critical intelligence related to military operations around the world. Today we will attempt to determine if Omega Group had all the relevant information required to achieve a successful outcome. There seems to have been a breach between the intelligence Omega Group received and what was available."

"Well, Gabriella, let's not be too hasty in our conclusion," Mr. Markeson chimed in. "It seems to me that it was weak operational tactics that led to the demise of the French prime minister's niece."

Despite an elbow from Jackson, Christopher said, "Sir, there were many oddities in our operation, but I accept responsibility for the outcome."

"Well, I did not expect to receive such objective sincerity from a Department of Defense official, but the fact remains, Mr. Barrett."

"That's Major Barrett, sir."

"Yes, excuse me, Major Barrett. I have always worked within the diplomatic architecture of our government and still err with military protocol occasionally. In any case, *Major* Barrett, I have my doubts that your organization should even exist. Perhaps if the president and the Secretary of Defense had entertained my original solution for diplomatic talks with the extremists, then we might not be here today."

"Sir, perhaps we should conclude the briefing before we begin a debate," Gabriella suggested.

"Pardon me, Gabriella, please excuse my *faux pas*."

Gabriella continued without acknowledging the National Security Advisor. "Major Barrett, could you please provide us a brief rundown from a previous mission where data from the Intelligence Community ran contradictory from your assessments."

"Well, is there a particular mission you want me to discuss?" Christopher sensed that Gabriella was trying to lead the meeting, and him, to a specific destination.

"Yes, the Israel mission from three and a half years ago would do just fine."

"Israel…okay, the bottom line was that something supernatural occurred, with no signs that the Israelis had produced a secret weapon that could have decimated the sizeable invasion force they faced."

"Supernatural? The report all but said it was God that had defeated the Russian-led invasion. I remember as I was the then chargé d'affaires at the embassy in Jerusalem," Mr. Markeson inserted.

"Mr. Markeson," Christopher began, purposefully avoiding the use of *sir*, "in my report, I made no mention of God doing anything. I merely stated that one of the dominant views, even held by some of the Israelis, was tied to God and religion. General Benjamin Havid, the then Israeli chief of the general staff and now the Israeli defense minister, is the source of the religious sentiment found in my report. General Havid believed that the God of the Jewish people had decimated the Russian coalition."

Christopher continued before Markeson could interrupt. "Furthermore, the Intelligence Community assessment of a neutron device was unsubstantiated by my findings on the ground. There were no radiological indicators of a neutron event, nor did any nation with the means to detect nuclear explosions describe anything abnormal occurring during the invasion. Heck, the Israelis didn't even have time to get a complete fighter squadron off the ground before the assault was pouring across its borders.

"The invasion forces were decimated in the air by something yet to be discovered, while ground forces were consumed by massive chasms opening in the Earth and hailstones the size of small vehicles. General Havid said it was as if the sky and Earth were fighting for Israel; he had never seen anything in his thirty years of military service so terrifying. If that is not supernatural, sir, then please provide me a better definition."

Mr. Markeson, bereft of a response, said nothing.

"Thanks, Major Barrett. Your recounting of the invasion of Israel clarifies some of the questionings of your character and ability for critical thinking," Gabriella said.

"What…does?"

Gabriella pressed Christopher before he could shoot himself in the foot. "Please provide us with your understanding of the insider threat within the Mosul District commandos before the recent rescue mission."

Christopher hesitated as he tried to remember the threat intelligence update the day before the mission. “The brief hardly touched on insider threats. It was more focused on the ISIS stronghold at the Bash Tapia Castle.” Now feeling more assured of what he had received from the Omega Group intelligence staff, he continued. “I read a report that said ISIS sympathizers had infiltrated certain Iraqi forces units, but I had no indications that the Mosul commandos contained ISIS fighters. Ultimately General Waleed, my men, and the journalist paid the price.”

Gabriella projected several reports with timestamps onto a large screen at the center of the room. “Well, Major Barrett, the problem is that the fact remains that each agency represented here had passed knowledge to Omega Group that the Mosul commandos were infiltrated by ISIS.”

“Well, I never received confirmation or direct revelation of those reports,” Christopher challenged.

Gabriella ignored Christopher’s response and turned her attention back to the National Security Advisor. “As you can see, sir, the problem is not entirely the tactics of Omega, but rather the dissemination of intelligence to the operatives. I believe my recommendations presented to the director of National Intelligence and the president will ensure the mitigation of future failures of this nature.”

“Hey, you know we are still here,” Christopher asserted loudly.

“Yes, Major, I know you’re still here, and the fact that you’re here and not peeling potatoes in the farthest outpost of the U.S. military is only because of Gabriella’s and the SecDef’s influence with the president.” The National Security Advisor, relishing placing a military leader in his place, continued. “If I had my way, your entire group of trained killers would be discharged from the military and handed over to the French. So, Major Barrett, effective immediately, Omega Group will stand down until an operational review headed by the National Security Council is concluded. Dr. Costa will become the deputy and intelligence director for Omega Group upon its potential reinstatement. As for you and your men, I, unfortunately, have no say in your fate.”

Markeson, with an almost twinkle in his eye, concluded the meeting and departed.

Christopher swore aloud and pushed himself back from the beautiful conference table, causing all who remained in the room to stare at the disgraced man.

"Well, that sucked. I wonder where they are going to assign us?" Jackson asked.

"Gentlemen, if you would follow me," Gabriella said, directing Christopher and Jackson into an adjacent smaller room.

"Well, I wish I could say it was great to see you, Gabriella, but maybe I should just stick to calling you 'Boss' now," Christopher remarked sharply.

"Real mature, Chris. I saved your angry and ungrateful butt back there. You should know better than most that non-Defense Department folks are leery of you guys at best and hate you more than likely. Markeson wanted you kicked out of the military, but a few of us that know and care about the Omega mission, and you, were able to win over the president."

"Yeah? Then why, Gabriella, does it feel like I just got beat down?"

"Well, Chris, that's because you don't trust people and you love punishing yourself when things don't go your way. Should I continue?"

"No, I think we got it," Christopher responded tartly.

"Ma'am? Gabby, right? It's a pleasure," Jackson said, extending his hand.

"First, let's get something straight, Sergeant Major Williams. Don't call me Gabby. I am not your cute little something waiting at home, impressed that you're in special operations."

"Ma'am, I didn't mean—"

"Next, you can call me Gabriella or Doc or even something crude if I am not around, but drop the Ma'am and Gabby. I work just as hard as you do."

"It's so sweet to see that you're still setting the world on fire with your charm, Gabriella," Christopher taunted.

"Okay, enough, smart guy. I was very sorry to hear about Rev. He was a fantastic soldier and man. Listen, I've got to run, but trust me when I say you're not going anywhere and neither is Omega. Expect a call from Colonel Delmar tonight. Good-bye, Sergeant Major Williams."

"Wow, I think I am in love," Jackson said, almost laughing, as he watched Gabriella walk toward the West Wing of the White House.

Christopher chuckled. "Gabriella would eat you alive. I met her when I first got to Omega, and we were sent to Syria when that crisis kicked off. She was the lead country analyst within the CIA at the time. Gabriella was the only woman on the ground but made sure we all understood she was definitely not weak or fragile."

As the two men walked back to the SUV where Joe Cunningham waited, Christopher told Jackson that the hazel-eyed Gabriella had been a love interest of his before Erin.

"Yeah? What happened?"

"Nothing. I never even got the chance to tell her how I felt. It was as if Gabriella could sense my interest, and she rebuffed me one day after a meeting on Russian troop movements in Damascus. She told me we could never work. I was so shocked I couldn't even say anything. Gabriella said that we both loved what we did too much to love someone else. You know, she is the only woman outside of Erin that calls me Chris."

"Yeah, I could tell something had been between you at some point in the past, but, man, what a woman," Jackson said admiringly.

As they stepped out into the fall afternoon, Christopher finished up the topic of Gabriella, giving Jackson further insight into her background.

"Gabriella is the daughter of an Italian vineyard heiress and an Air Force fighter pilot who flew with the president during the Gulf War. She is Ivy league educated—Columbia undergrad and Princeton for her masters and doctorate, and as you saw, brilliant at her job."

"Yeah, I get she can take care of herself."

"Well, I see you're still alive," Joe remarked cheerfully as Christopher and Jackson climbed back into the SUV. "Where can I take you, gentlemen?"

"Just drop us back at our hotel in Crystal City. There is no need to fret about the future as it seems we are going to have at least a few days off," Christopher responded.

"Man, I know just what we need tonight—crab cakes and beer, and I even know the place," Jackson said enthusiastically.

"I'm in, and thanks again for being here for me today. I wouldn't have made it without you," Christopher replied.

Jackson smiled and said, "Man, that's what brothers are for. We have survived worse. This day was too easy."

Chapter 4

As the SUV passed by the Lincoln Memorial, Christopher stared out his window, feeling defeated. For as long as he could remember, he had prided himself on being reliable and trustworthy, things he found impossible to believe outside of himself. Now he had cost his men their jobs and the credibility of the Omega Group because he had allowed himself to fall into the trap of entertaining God's "voice" in his life.

That still, small voice—which, despite Christopher's attempts to deny it, he knew was the Holy Spirit—had bombarded him over the last month, warning and pushing him to look beyond his job. For what? This? Just more pain and suffering. How could he trust God after this? How could he let God back into his life? Christopher's thoughts flashed to Erin and her insistence that he start making an effort to trust God.

As the SUV made the turn onto the Arlington Memorial Bridge, Christopher noticed Joe's praise and worship music was on again. A familiar tune from his childhood was playing on the vehicle's speakers. "Hey, Joe, is that song 'Everything Is Going to Be Alright'?"

"Yes, sir…"

"Joe!" Christopher screamed, but in an instant the car was pilotless and careening over the Memorial Bridge and into the Potomac River below. The impact and rush of water were shocking, as Christopher felt the stinging pain of a cut across his right leg.

"Jackson, are you all right? Jackson, answer me!" Christopher could see that Jackson was passed out, with water already up to his chest. He noticed a deep cut on Jackson's head with blood pouring out. Christopher quickly reached for the window-break tool, grateful that the government had gotten something right in its bureaucratic method of purchasing vehicles. He broke his window and waited for the water to fill the SUV. He was momentarily glad that Jackson hadn't put on his seatbelt as he pulled the limp man out of the window and toward the surface.

As Jackson and Christopher reached the surface, Christopher glanced toward the sinking SUV, half wondering if he had only imagined he saw Joe Cunninghman disappear before the crash. He got his bearings and swam toward the D.C. shore along West Potomac Park, towing Jackson behind him.

When he reached land, he found Jackson was breathing, but unconscious and bleeding profusely. Christopher, who always carried a knife, cut off a portion of his dress shirt to make a temporary bandage. With Jackson's wounds taken care of, Christopher quickly inventoried himself and cut off the remainder of his shirt to tie around the gash in his thigh that was deep enough to need stitches.

Christopher had to fight to keep from going into shock as he took an assessment of what was going on around him. He found himself immersed in chaos. It was as if the whole world had been stopped and shaken like an enormous snow globe. The noise of car horns blaring from being pressed by deceased drivers, panicked drivers, and accident damage was unbelievable. Christopher felt like he was in New Delhi during rush hour. People everywhere were screaming incoherently from what Christopher could make out. His only thought was that D.C. had been struck by some terrorist act.

Moments later, the life-draining roar of a jumbo jet that seemed about to land on top of them slammed Christopher to the ground; he instinctively covered Jackson with his body. The plane slammed into the nearby Lincoln Memorial Reflecting Pool, causing a loud explosion and more screams. Christopher's instincts kicked in as he limped toward an empty sedan near the Memorial Bridge on-ramp. He opened the passenger door but immediately fell back at the sight of a woman's clothing and what looked like metal dental work in the driver's seat. He was startled by what seemed to be what was left after the driver just stepped out of everything and headed off to who knows where.

The mystery woman's car had crashed into oncoming traffic, killing the other driver. Christopher pushed the woman's clothes and fillings out of the driver's seat and drove over to a still-unconscious Jackson. He strained as he carefully laid Jackson across the rear seat. As he buckled the center seatbelt around Jackson for safety, he laughed ironically since his lack of a safety belt is what had allowed Christopher to easily save him from their sinking vehicle at the bottom of the Potomac. Christopher knew he had to get Jackson to an area hospital as quickly as possible, which, according to signage on the Memorial Bridge, was George Washington University Hospital.

Christopher turned on the radio to get some idea of what was going on. Instead of information, he was greeted with the piercing noise of the public alert system, but with no instructions following. He picked up the cell phone in the cupholder and tried to dial the Pentagon operations center, but received an error message that the system was overloaded. He drove through the park grounds surrounding the Lincoln Memorial and Reflecting Pool, attempting to avoid the ever-expanding gridlock on every road in sight. However, it was apparent that driving was not going to get him far once he left the grassy knoll of the park.

Everywhere he looked, people were in need of some form of emergency assistance as he rocketed around the Lincoln Memorial grounds, nearly hitting several waves of panicked and fleeing tourists. Christopher's senses were overwhelmed. The blaring sirens announcing the approach of first responders seemed to be coming from multiple directions. Yet the realization of such a massive casualty event like this meant that the sirens would be like a mirage in the desert to a thirsty soul—salvation would be only an illusion for thousands.

The wall of people and wrecks at Consitution Avenue ended Christopher's demolition derby. As he grabbed Jackson from the back in a fireman's carry, streams of fire emanating from the leg wound raced up and down Christopher's body. But he was determined to get Jackson and himself to the hospital—now over ten blocks away—on foot.

"Hey, what happened?" Jackson questioned.

"Oh man, I am glad you woke up! You're heavy. I don't know, but I think we're under attack—planes are down, comms are down, and there are a ton of accidents," Christopher said, propping Jackson up against a wall.

"Was it a nuke attack?"

"Nah, I didn't see a mushroom cloud, but who knows? If the blast was far enough away, I suppose it could have been—in which case, you already know our prognosis."

"Yeah, we're dead men walking. But what happened to Joe?"

Christopher had a thousand-yard stare, and Jackson decided he might be in shock.

"Hey, what happened to Joe?" Jackson demanded once again.

"He's gone…just disappeared, man. I don't know what happened or what's going on, but we've got to get to a hospital," Christopher said, forcing himself to focus on a tangible person versus the ghost Joe had become.

"Do you think you could walk?" Christopher asked.

"Can a duck quack?" Jackson replied.

"I will take that as a Southern yes."

Christopher's thoughts whirled as he tried to understand a scenario where this much damage was done that was not a military attack. The carnage around them was beyond any war zone even a seasoned veteran could have imagined. Just in this small area of D.C. where they found themselves, it was easy to see that the death toll would reach the tens of thousands. Fires were raging out of control, vacated cars caused gridlock, and people lay dead or dying on the streets, not to mention the screams of those grappling with the apparent disappearance of many people.

Jackson leaned on a shell-shocked Christopher, afraid to ask what fears were running through his mind, but knowing it was likely the same that were in his own. His throbbing head and senses were overcome by the endless sirens and explosions in the distance, probably due to the unchecked fires raging around the city. The silence between the two men persisted due to fear on his part, but it was the voices of the nameless people they passed on the way to the hospital that fueled his worries. The conversations from the multitudes wandering the streets turned into a single cry of sheer agony that terrified him. They passed a man sitting on the curb crying into his hands as he wailed, "She's gone! She's gone!" And they saw that same scene repeated over and over again with increasing frequency as they drew closer to the hospital. People all around them were frantically searching and screaming for loved ones and collapsing in inconsolable grief when they couldn't find them.

Jackson had witnessed something similar before, but in a war-ravished country where endless masses tried to escape the fighting; they were lifeless zombies dead to the world around them and the war that caused their pain. Now in his own country, that same look of desperation and despair had hit home. Jackson thought American society had been decimated by a not-yet-named nation or terror group, that war had once again breached America's shores.

The scene at George Washington University Hospital was anarchy materialized. People were piled almost on top of each other in the emergency waiting room, and some looked like they were dead. The screaming people seeking lost loved ones or friends out on the streets were pouring into the emergency room waiting area in hopes of locating the lost. A frail older man who looked like he might be a security guard tried to maintain some semblance of order, but he was being shouted down and physically overwhelmed by the mob.

The stern but calm voice of a nurse blared loudly through a bullhorn: "LISTEN UP, I KNOW YOU'RE ALL HERE LOOKING FOR HELP AND ANSWERS, BUT WE ARE SHORTHANDED. THE FEW

NURSES AND DOCTORS WE HAVE WILL BE COMING THROUGH TO TRIAGE THE MOST URGENT NEEDS AND ANSWER QUESTIONS. START FORMING FOUR LINES."

Christopher and Jackson stood in a long line where people were pushing and shoving to get to the young woman running triage. It seemed every available nurse and doctor was working on multiple people, with more and more patients joining the queue every minute.

Jackson instructed, "Look at that," as he directed Christopher's gaze to a pile of scrubs.

"Yeah, those are the people that disappeared, and how bad are you two hurt?" The same haggard nurse who had used the bullhorn earlier had made her way down the line to Christopher and Jackson. Her nametag said RUTH.

"My friend has a pretty big gash on his head and maybe a concussion, and I am in need of a few stitches," Christopher responded.

"Ma'am, I will be fine, and I can see you folks are in need of some extra medical assistance. If you could just direct me to a treatment room, I could sew up my friend and myself, and I'll even stick around to help you," Jackson offered.

"Huh, you think I fell off the turnip truck yesterday, young man? You're not stealing drugs out of this hospital. Now find a place out of the way and wait like all the rest of the lower priority folks," Ruth ordered tersely.

"Ruth, Jackson is telling the truth. We are Army special forces soldiers and Jackson's career field is general medicine. He's basically a physician's assistant," Christopher said, assuring her.

"Actually, I am considered a doctor in most countries around the world," Jackson quipped.

"Well, let me see some identification, 'Doctor,' because I've never seen a 'soldier doctor' with such calloused hands, a dirty uniform, and a half-naked friend," Ruth ordered, directing that last remark to the shirtless Christopher.

Jackson pulled out his identification card and vouched for

Christopher, whose wallet and phone were undoubtedly somewhere in the Chesapeake Bay.

"Well, I guess you two are soldiers. Follow me," Ruth instructed.

"Hey, why are they getting treated?" a lady from the line protested.

"Ma'am, I'll be right back to check on you," Jackson promised as he winked at her with a blood-crusted eye, causing the woman to wince in revulsion.

Ruth spoke as the men entered treatment room one. "Okay, hop up on that table, Doc. Let's see if you have a concussion. Sir," she added, pointing Christopher to a chair, "strip down to your undies so I can fix you up next."

"Ma'am, Ruth, I am okay," Christopher protested.

"Look, I don't have time for this. If the doctor here can help me, then that's what's about to happen. So strip down like I told you. I can see the bloodstains on your pants. Take off that uniform, too. It looks disgraceful in its current state. Put on a pair of scrubs, in the closet behind you."

Christopher felt like a child at his grandmother's house as he mustered a defeated, "Yes, ma'am."

"Ruth, I am really okay," Jackson told her.

"Really, let's see," she responded as she ran Jackson through a series of cognitive tests. "How many fingers am I holding up?"

"Two."

"Okay, what's today?" Ruth asked.

"The worst freaking day ever," Jackson proclaimed.

"You're well enough, and your attitude seems intact as well. Sir, hand me the gauze and that suture needle in the drawer next to you," Ruth said, directing Christopher.

As Christopher handed Ruth the items, he asked, "So what do you know about what's happened here in D.C.?"

"Oww..." said Jackson, scowling.

"Oh, hush up. You're just a big baby," Ruth scoffed as she continued stitching up Jackson's head. "I don't know much, but I will never forget talking in the nurse's lounge when people just disappeared." She shuddered as she spoke.

Another cry erupted from Jackson. "Ouch!"

"Shush! I'm all but done," Ruth instructed as Jackson wriggled under her strong hands and will. "I am the head nurse on shift here—"

"No kidding," Jackson quipped before letting out another yelp as Ruth tugged his wound closed, likely harder than necessary due to his wisecrack.

"So what happened?" Christopher asked again.

"That young nurse you saw out front came running up to me saying that her lead just disappeared." Ruth explained that the young triage nurse was brand new and had been shadowing a veteran nurse. "Today is her first day. I thought the nurses were playing games, which I don't tolerate," she assured them.

"I can imagine," Jackson said, smarting off again.

"Anyway, I followed her to a patient's room, and sure enough, all of her lead nurse's clothes were in a pile. It freaked me out so bad, I just told her to head back up front. Well, about that time, the alarm for a maternity floor security breech starting going off, so per protocol we head for assigned exits. As I was running to the ER front entrance, I notice two more clothing piles at my nurse's station and…" Ruth's tough exterior cracked.

"It's okay, Ruth, you don't need to talk about this," Christopher murmured.

"No, I do need to because I feel like I am going crazy. Once I was at the ER entrance, a security guard ran up to me along with another nurse friend. They both said all the babies and children had disappeared."

"What did you say about children?" Jackson asked in a strange voice.

"You heard me. Every single baby, born or unborn, is gone, and many of the children in this hospital are gone as well. Several mothers were already in active labor when it happened—the labor stopped and the infants vanished. One mother had a heart attack from the shock and died. The maternity floor is still on lockdown after her husband took the gun of a security guard and killed himself. The hospital administration is trying to contain the distraught parents until counselors can be provided."

"What kind of terror attack could do this, Christopher?" Jackson questioned.

"I am not sure, my friend, that it *was* a terror attack," Christopher said grimly as he pulled out the cell phone he'd acquired and tried to call the Pentagon operations center again...nothing.

"Hey, let me use that thing while Florence Nightingale here stitches you up real quick," Jackson said.

"Watch it, Doctor Jackson. You might be a soldier, but this old lady can take you," Ruth threatened.

Christopher tossed the cell phone to Jackson and winced as Ruth unapologetically began cleaning and treating the gash on his leg.

Jackson tried to call his wife Sarah but couldn't get through, so he attempted a text knowing that data sometimes goes through when voice calls don't. *"I'm alright will call later love ya,"* was his quick message. "Hey, Christopher, I'm gonna stick around here and help Ruth. Once comms are reestablished, I will meet you at the Pentagon. I am guessing they will have a need for us sooner than expected."

"Yeah, okay. I need to get to Erin," Christopher replied as he read the first news reports rolling across a television screen: *"Millions missing and millions more dead in a global catastrophe."*

"Well, there's my answer. This is something worse than a terror attack. Seems like the whole world experienced this. Godspeed to you, brother. I know how to get to you if something happens. Just check on Erin," Jackson said.

"Thanks. I hope Sarah and the girls are okay."

"I am sure they are, but thanks, man."

"Ruth, can you please find me a change of clothes?" Christopher asked.

"One second," Ruth said, disappearing from the room and returning a minute later with a set of scrubs, a sweatshirt, and a slightly too big pair of sneakers.

"This is all I could find that might fit you," Ruth said.

"Thanks, you two. I am heading for Harrisonburg now. Let Colonel Delmar and Gabriella know once you get back up on the net, Jackson," Christopher instructed.

Ruth suddenly buried her head into Jackson's shoulder as her shoulders heaved with a quiet sob. Jackson nodded, but he heard Ruth's muffled admonition. "Please be safe. Who knows who will disappear next?"

But Christopher didn't think anybody else was going to disappear, which was why he needed to see if Erin was still here.

Gabriella had just entered the West Wing after the meeting with the National Security Advisor and Omega Group when she heard screams. "Show me your badge, *now*," said an aggressive Secret Service agent, his gun trained on her to prevent Gabriella from proceeding farther into the White House.

"Wow, is that necessary?" she asked as she pulled her badge out of her jacket.

"You're clear," the agent said, and with that he ran toward the Oval Office.

Gabriella's heart was racing not only from the unexpected and violent encounter with the Secret Service agent but also due to the screams echoing throughout the White House. *Has the president been assassinated?* she wondered, horrified by the mere thought. As Gabriella neared the office of the National Security Advisor, she noticed several staffers gathering outside the office, and several were crying. "Hey, *what* is going on?" she asked.

A teary-eyed staffer answered that Estelle, the long-standing secretary of the National Security Advisor's West Wing office, had disappeared.

"What do you mean *disappeared*?"

"Where have you been? Millions of people are being reported

missing all over the world, and the president is about to declare martial law," the staffer informed Gabriella.

Gabriella felt like someone had just sucker punched her as she collapsed onto a plush lounger outside the National Security Advisor's office to keep from landing on the floor—her legs refused to support her. "How many have been affected in the White House?"

The staffer, apparently in shock, answered, "Estelle, and some of the cooking staff according to reports I've heard, but that's it."

"Oh, thank goodness, Gabriella! At least you weren't caught up in this attack," National Security Advisor Markeson said, gasping, as he came out of his office.

"Sir, *what* attack?" Gabriella asked.

"Cindy, get these people back to work and away from my office. We are in the middle of a global crisis, and crying is not going to help. Did you hear me? Move!" Markeson yelled at the staffer who had been telling Gabriella what she knew of the situation.

Gabriella watched as Cindy shooed the other onlookers away from Markeson's office while picking up Estelle's clothes like a mother picks up a newborn.

"Gabriella, please come with me to the Oval Office," ordered Markeson as he all but pulled her to her feet.

President Glen Rodgers, the no-nonsense Gulf War veteran fighter pilot, looked nervous and at a loss for words as Gabriella and Mr. Markeson entered the room full of staffers and advisors who were briefing him on the disappearances. He spoke in a shaky and rushed tone as he next asked for a situation report from his chief of staff.

"Sir, the initial reports indicate every country in the world has been affected by this event. The missing persons count is approaching hundreds of millions based on initial tallies across the globe. Panic is widespread, and rioting and looting have already begun in many locations around the world.

"Additionally we recommend you approve an already-drafted executive order rescinding the Posse Comitatus Act and declare defense readiness condition level 2 immediately. The Defense Department has yet to provide the numbers of military personnel missing or dead, but we anticipate a loss of some military capabilities, especially the longer we wait to raise the DEFCON level.

"Lastly, Homeland Security is reporting that every major city has critical shortages of first responders and key infrastructure staffing. We are facing absolute pandemonium throughout the nation," the chief of staff concluded.

President Rodgers asked, "What about the First and Second ladies?"

"Sir, in the last communication the White House Situation Room received from Executive One Foxtrot, the plane was sending out a distress signal, reporting that two of the pilots were taken in the disappearances."

President Rodgers ran his fingers through his salt-and-pepper hair, saying, "God help us!" He strode solemnly over to a window before speaking. "Okay, I approve all of those recommendations. Get as many troops and resources as possible out on the streets to mitigate the loss of life. Declare martial law and price control the economy. What bread costs today, it better cost tomorrow. If you get reports of some company trying to turn a profit off this thing, let me know and keep me updated on how the rest of the world is handling this."

He turned his attention to Gabriella. "I understand that you have been named the new deputy of Omega Group, is that correct, Gabriella?"

"Yes, sir." Markeson answered the question.

"I wasn't talking to you," the president said dismissively.

"Yes, sir, I am the new deputy of Omega Group," Gabriella confirmed as Markeson watched helplessly.

"Then I need you to get to the Pentagon as soon as possible and have Omega get to Brasilia to determine the fate of the First Lady, my daughter, and the Second Lady," the president ordered.

"Yes, sir," Markeson replied, interrupting again, declaring that he would ensure that the first families would be returned safely.

President Rodgers ignored Markeson, addressing the room in

general. "What do we have available regarding aircraft to get Gabriella across town if traffic is as bad as you guys are telling me?"

A rustle of papers and a few clicks on laptops were heard before the president's chief of staff responded, "There is a Blackhawk helicopter at Andrews Air Base we could get over to the South Lawn, but the availability of a crew may take a while due to the widespread communications issues."

"Well, get started!" the president barked. "Everyone, let's get back to work. A lot of people need us to figure this thing out." That last order from the president sent staffers scurrying out of the Oval Office like rats deserting a sinking ship.

"Gabriella, if I could have a word alone with you?" asked President Rodgers.

"Sir, would you like me to stay?" Markeson inquired, interrupting again.

"No. Go find something to do," the president scolded, apparently irritated by the obnoxious man.

Gabriella watched as Markeson sulked his way out of the Oval Office, closing the door behind him.

"Gabriella, what do you think just happened?" the president inquired gravely.

"Sir, I have no idea—perhaps some complex terror attack?" she posited.

"No, I don't think so. I think my wife of thirty years would call this event the rapture."

"The *rapture*, sir?" Gabriella asked, beginning to seriously question the president's reasoning capabilities.

"Yes. Are you familiar with the term?"

"I am. My mom took me to church all the time when I was as a child—at least, it seemed like all the time."

President Rodgers laughed. "Yeah, I know the feeling. My wife grew up in the Bible belt and has always fussed over my daughter and me, telling us that this day would come. She said it would be a terrible day not just due to the loss of life, but due to the missed opportunity to avoid what was to come."

"I see, sir. But if I may ask, what does this have to do with me?" Gabriella queried, clearly confused.

"Gabriella, I am telling you this for two simple reasons. First, she was right. The guilt of dismissing her beliefs and helping my daughter make the same decision is overwhelming right now, and I needed to tell someone. Second, it's important that Omega not expect to find the First Lady since, if she is correct, she will be safe—though missing. My daughter and the Second Lady are my primary concern. I don't want to place those men in greater danger by having them search for someone who isn't going to be found."

"How do you know she won't be found, sir? She could still be in Brazil."

The president turned to look out a window in his office once again before saying with dead certainty, "Gabriella, you can't be married to someone as long as I have been without instinctively knowing certain things about your spouse. Trust me when I say my wife is in Heaven."

Just then the president's chief of staff burst into the Oval Office, saying, "Dr. Costa, we have a helicopter en route to the White House South Lawn estimated to arrive in ten minutes."

"Thank you, and, sir, don't worry. We will bring them all back."

"No, Gabriella, you won't. But please bring back my daughter if she is alive. There is much I need to discuss with her…and, Gabriella, your dad would be proud of you, as am I," President Rodgers concluded.

As Gabriella strode across the South Lawn of the White House with her high heels in one hand, escorted by the Secret Service agent who had nearly shot her, she felt unsure of herself for the first time in a long time.

"Ma'am, are you ready?" came the voice of the lone pilot across Gabriella's headset.

"Yes, let's go," Gabriella instructed.

The results of the disappearances made for a horrific view from the air. The Washington, D.C. metro area seemed more like a smoldering parking lot than a bustling capital. Cars lined the streets, unmoving. Fires were raging across the metro area, and she knew that the disappearances had created a significant shortage in every sector of public service, which would make responding to the needs of so many impossible. It was a sad reality that many would die tonight. Hordes of people had begun walking across bridges, heading toward home or at least away from the carnage of D.C. toward the unknown trials that awaited them at their destinations.

Gabriella felt the warm sting of tears in her eyes as she witnessed humanity and disaster interacting hundreds of feet below her. President Rodgers's take on the disappearances stirred in her a notion she had long ago dismissed—God.

Gabriella had started challenging the concept of God in her teens, as her promising intellect put her at odds with her mother's devotion to the Church in general and, in particular, her mother's "relationship with Jesus," as she put it. Gabriella saw the Church as a fantasy world of promises for a better life for people who believed in Jesus Christ as their personal savior. Instead she trusted in the possibilities of the human mind working to make the wrongs of the world right with tangible technologies and science versus hope and prayer. Gabriella couldn't understand how people could believe in God or religion when so much was wrong in the world that God supposedly loved and created.

She could hear her mother's voice in her head now. *"Science demands adherence to principles that are bound by the limitations of human intellect, Gabriella. A belief in God is not a condemnation of science, but rather an acknowledgment of the power behind science and nature. The intellectual world makes humanity its god, while Christianity places God above man. My belief in Jesus Christ allows me to have hope and provides a sense of purpose that life is more than an accident, that we are not just born to live and die only seeking our own purposes."* This dogma was her mother's standard rebuttal speech when Gabriella would berate Christianity.

Gabriella was forced to attend church until her teenage years, when, with the help of her show-me-evidence-and-I-will-believe-it father, she became militant regarding anything dealing with religion in general, but especially toward Christianity. She always accused her mother of being narrow-minded and bigoted for thinking that Jesus was the only way to Heaven, and that became even truer after her mother was diagnosed with terminal breast cancer in her junior year of high school.

Gabriella remembered asking her mom on her deathbed how she could love a God who was destroying her body and her family. Remembering her mom's words evoked a sob from somewhere deep inside that she thought was long barren of any feeling. "My dear Gabby, I love God because His promises to love and care for my family and me won't end with my life. God never wastes the pain life brings us. We just need to let go of the pain of life and give it to Him. God is always faithful to see us through to a better day."

As Gabriella watched the sun begin to set behind the Pentagon, she wondered if this day had been orchestrated by God. She had little doubt that her mom would believe that to be true. Perhaps God did have a plan for the world that her mother had known and she had overlooked.

Chapter 5

Christopher had to know if Erin had disappeared. If she was still here, then in some strange way he felt everything would be okay. If she was gone he feared what might come next. As he left the George Washington University Hospital, he realized that dusk had fallen, changing the atmosphere from bleak to grim.

The endless hordes trying to get into the hospital were developing a mob mentality, and sporadic fights erupted as folks waited for care or came seeking information about missing loved ones. Christopher knew widespread violence was one shove away, based on the swearing and jostling in the crowd. He looked out over the formerly upscale and sophisticated Foggy Bottom neighborhood, which now resembled a riotous cityscape. Men and women in business attire and day laborers and waiters, people who only hours before had no visible similarities, began banding together to pillage abandoned cars and businesses, either seeking gain or exploiting the chaos for future survival. Christopher sensed that any shred of compassion within society was rapidly giving way to savagery. The disappearances had exposed the true nature of each individual who had been left behind.

Christopher knew he had to get out of D.C. before martial law was declared. He started toward the Francis Scott Key Bridge with the goal of reaching I-66 and ultimately Erin in Harrisonburg. Though every kind of vehicle from exotic luxury cars to large SUVs were available for

Christopher's choosing, the problem was finding something that could navigate through the endless parking lot of abandoned and wrecked cars littering the roads. He was looking for a motorcycle. It seemed like he rambled for miles looking for one, finally crossing into Virginia. He was about to give up and head for the Pentagon to link up with Jackson when the still, small voice echoed in his heart. *"And my God will supply every need of yours according to his riches in glory in Christ Jesus."* It was at that very moment that Christopher noticed a parking lot with a couple of street bikes near a hotel. Hearing the Holy Spirit convinced him he was probably crazy, but he mustered a hollow, "Thank you, God," as he ran toward the hotel parking lot.

It seemed his salvation chariot had belonged to a disappearance victim. Christopher found a pile of clothes on the bike, along with a Gaelic cross, which only fueled his nightmarish fear that this event was indeed the rapture of the Church. He was grateful to put on the previous owner's riding jacket and pants over the thin hospital scrubs, despite them being a little large. It was nine o'clock at night. While Harrisonburg was only two and a half hours from his present location in Rosslyn, Virginia, in nonapocalyptic conditions, he feared that tonight's trip would take much longer.

Christopher fired up the machine, noticing that the traumatized crowds of people around him didn't even appear to acknowledge the loud rumble of the performance bike—instead they all seemed to be in shock. As he pulled onto I-66 to determine the truth of the day's events for himself, he realized that martial law must have been declared—police vehicles were closing off the Key Bridge.

Jackson had just finished setting a young man's broken arm when Ruth came into the treatment room.

"How are you doing?" she asked.

"I'm alive, just tired—but glad to have my mind focused on a task rather than trying to decipher what's going on. It seems plenty of theories are floating around but nothing solid." Jackson pointed to the now continuous news coverage on the television about the unparalleled disappearances. "Consuming too much fast food, leading to spontaneous combustion has been my favorite theory yet."

"Too much fast food, huh? That's a good one, but I think it will fall short in the end. Thanks for your help, but you can head out of here. We have rounded up a bunch of freaked-out medical students from the dorms and are putting them to work."

"Sounds like a solid plan, placing the inmates in charge of the prison," Jackson sassed.

"Young man, I will miss you and that attitude. However, these are beyond desperate times and staying busy provides a much-needed outlet for these students. Just leave them to me," Ruth said confidently. "Before you go, take this. It belonged to one of the nurses who's gone, and I figured you could use it." She handed him a cell phone.

"I can't thank you enough, Ruth. I appreciate it more than you know. Listen, here is the number to the Pentagon operations center. You can reach me there in a pinch, but expect me to contact you with my personal number soon. If you need anything, Ruth, you just give the old doctor here a shout."

"Boy, you're a mess. But thank you, Jackson, for all you did, and take care of yourself out there."

Jackson began the "short" three-mile walk to the Pentagon, physically weak and emotionally wrecked. It seemed like every person he had treated and encountered tonight was searching for the same answer he was: "What comes next?"

The emerging theories about what had happened ranged from ridiculous to terrifying. The argument that stood out to Jackson came from a priest being interviewed by a local news channel as part of a panel of "experts." When he had been asked for his take on the day's events, he had replied confidently, "It is easy to answer your question about what has happened. God has raptured His Church ahead of His judgment on the world." When the reporter questioned the priest about why, if that were true, he remained on Earth, the man began crying as he sorrowfully answered, "I never had a relationship with Jesus. I never really believed." Jackson remembered Rev mentioning in his last Bible study the need to have a personal relationship with Jesus and not to rely on individual assessments of being an upright person.

He felt so helpless, immersed in a disaster with no idea what to do or, even worse, what the next day would hold. The suffering that people were experiencing was hard to reconcile as somehow being a part of God's plan for the world. Rev had said God was merciful, but just; gracious, but holy. Perhaps the events of today illustrated just and compassionate all at the same time. Jackson was grateful that he had survived this long when so many had died in the immediate aftermath of the disappearances. *Yes, perhaps this is divine compassion. Yet so many others died seemingly for no reason. What had they done to merit such judgment?* He was so confused. As he walked along the Potomac River, Jackson wondered if the sirens blaring across the city would ever stop and if his world would ever be the same again. He felt that if there ever was a time to pray to God, today was that day. But the thought of praying to God brought only deep sobs because he did not know how to pray. What he needed was a guide, and he knew Rev's Bible and journal were the best guides available. He promised himself that he would return to his hotel for some soul-searching after checking in with Omega.

He pulled out the cell phone Ruth had given him and tried to call Sarah once again—still no voice connection. Jackson was not one for worrying, but the fact that children across the globe were reported missing made his blood run cold. He was scared, his fear so palpable that it drew his mind back to the fear he had felt in his childhood due to his father's alcohol-fueled abuse. He could only hope that Sarah and his two young daughters had somehow been spared from whatever caused the disappearances.

As Jackson crossed over the George Washington Parkway and into the Pentagon's north parking lot where his day had begun hours earlier, he was repulsed that he felt such comfort in seeing the Pentagon and all that it represented. Jackson had dedicated his life to serving strangers over his family, and now he wasn't even sure if he would ever see his wife and children again.

Gabriella was growing concerned since it was now nine o'clock at night, martial law had been declared, and ninety percent of the Omega Group was unaccounted for and presumed missing or dead.

"Ma'am, are you the deputy of Omega Group?" a senior airman for the Pentagon operations center inquired.

"Yes, I am."

"The SecDef left a message for you." The airman handed Gabriella a sealed envelope and left the room as she tore it open. The message read, *"Gabriella, Colonel Delmar was found in his car with a gunshot wound to the head, an apparent suicide, after finding out his two young children had disappeared. You are, effective immediately, the commander of Omega Group. Omega is fully reinstated, and the priority is the Brazil mission."*

Gabriella sat down and buried her head in her hands, overcome with emotion. The tragedy of this day seemed like it would never end. She had started the day with a plan to keep Omega Group going, but now its survival rested squarely on her shoulders, or at least it felt that way at the moment. As she stood to begin the hurried search for Christopher Barrett and his team, she was startled by a knock at her door. "Come in," she called.

"Good evening, ma'am. I figured I better check in before you folks turned off my pay," Jackson said.

Gabriella did not even try to hide her elation that Jackson had just stepped through her door. “Sergeants Major Williams, I can’t remember the last time I was so excited to see someone.”

“I would have never guessed you’d say that about me, but I’ll take it. Hey, listen, could you do me a favor and just call me Jackson? All this sergeants major stuff makes me feel like I can’t trust you.”

“You’ve got a deal, Jackson. By the way, you look like you’ve been in World War Three. Are you okay?”

“Yeah, I’m fine, but it’s a real nightmare out there. I am in desperate need of a change of clothes and some sleep.”

“The view from the air and the reports I’ve been getting all evening show that the damage and casualty counts may take weeks to officially total. I can help you with a change of clothes, but sleep will have to wait. Jackson, where is Chris—I mean, Major Barrett? He didn’t disappear, or something worse, did he?”

“Chris…he is alive and likely getting near Harrisonburg by now, trying to figure out if his wife Erin is still with us.”

Gabriella felt a surge of confidence and purpose from seeing Jackson and hearing that Chris was still alive. “Listen, Jackson, I want you to get cleaned up in the Omega Team room and then meet me in the group briefing room. We have a mission to plan and a leader to pick up. You feel like taking a helicopter ride?”

“Sure. I’ll meet you in the conference room in fifteen minutes, and we can make plans to pick up ‘Chris.’”

Gabriella laughed softly, saying, “Yes, he means a lot to me, but don’t read too much into the ‘Chris’ thing. I am glad to see you’re as snarky as ever. One more thing before you go. Please accept my apology for freaking out on you for calling me Gabby. It’s just that name has a particular and intimate meaning for me.”

“No need for apologies. I like a fiery woman,” Jackson declared, chuckling.

“Go get cleaned up, funny guy,” Gabriella responded.

Christopher was grateful that darkness had consumed the Shenandoah Valley as he rode along Skyline Drive. He didn't even want to imagine what the light of day would unveil. The motorcycle had proven to be a wise choice for moving around as the four-lane I-66 had become a minefield of debris. The drive had taken longer than Christopher had anticipated given the slowdowns for emergency crews attempting to clear the two-lane westbound section of I-66 and the countless masses of humanity stuck along the roadways. He was exhausted after six hours on the bike but still had about an hour to go before he reached Erin's family farm.

Almost an hour later he heard the cycle begin to sputter. He should have expected to run out of gas, but he had been foolishly optimistic that a gas station would be available if needed. As the motorcycle coasted to a stop, Christopher pulled off the road and ditched the bike among a collection of deserted vehicles. Thankfully his miscalculation would cost him only a five-mile walk to the farm.

As he crested the hill that served as the northern boundary to his in-laws' farmland, he had a feeling of passing into the last remaining semblance of the old world he had known. A wave of panic struck, and he suddenly found it difficult to walk toward the rustic farmhouse that lay below. The rising sun provided rays of hope as he spotted smoke rising from the farmhouse chimney about two hundred yards away—hope that his in-laws were warming the house before heading out to tend the farm. He slogged through the plowed rows of red-clay Virginia dirt, sweating from both effort and trepidation.

Christopher's hopes were crushed as he walked out of the fields to a farm in disorder, which he knew his in-laws would never allow. The sight of chickens running loose across the property and the open barn doors brought on a wave of nausea and fear. He ran into the house, screaming, "Erin! Erin! Please…anybody?" When he saw the pile of clothes in the chair near the well-worn needlework basket of his mother-in-law and the smoldering remains of logs in the fireplace, he burst into tears. He turned to run upstairs to Erin's room, but halted in his tracks at the sight of coffee spilled on the kitchen floor and what looked like a leg. As he moved into the kitchen he realized that his father-in-law was gone, too, leaving behind only the lingering bittersweet smell of coffee and his overalls.

Christopher collapsed on the stairs, trying not to vomit as he felt his stomach heave while mustering the courage to climb up to Erin's bedroom, to whatever fate awaited him there. He stood, taking each stair one at a time, wanting to delay the confirmation of his worst fear—the fear that God was real. He paused at the top of the stairs in front of Erin's room, closing his eyes to the evidence before him that God had returned to claim those who had trusted Him. Christopher would now have to face the trials and judgment of God, starting with opening Erin's door. As he pushed open her door, the smell of her perfume dominated the tiny room, bringing painful old memories to the surface of his mind and fresh tears to his eyes.

Erin's clothes were in a pile on the chair and floor around her desk. The faint glint from her wedding ring caused Christopher to lose the battle with his heaving stomach. He vomited then collapsed onto her bed, weeping and moaning uncontrollably. Christopher should have told Erin when they last spoke of his love for her, but it was his thoughts of God, not Erin, that had caused his outburst. A part of Christopher that he had been trying to suppress for the last month realized that no matter how vast the chasm was between God and him, the fact staring him in the face was that Erin had been right. The only hope he had to see her again was to trust God and attempt to survive the days ahead.

Yet as he pondered the thought of trusting God at this moment—surrounded by memories of Erin and her glaring absence—his jaw clenched. He thought bitterly, *And here is just one more example of pain caused by God!* That thought replaced any momentary idea of putting his trust in God. A belief began to grow in Christopher's mind that he could overcome any judgment God could throw his way. *I still don't need You, God.* Christopher's sobs and wails became primitive as he refused to surrender his pain to God. He kicked the small desk where Erin had been sitting, shattering it into two pieces as it hit a wall, as he screamed, "Where are You? Why do You hate me?" Christopher challenged the God of the universe to explain the pain, much as Job had done thousands of years before him.

The distinct chop of air caused by a Blackhawk helicopter interrupted Heaven's answer to Christopher's challenge. He picked up Erin's wedding ring and walked down the stairs, shaking and sweating from his encounter with the truth of God. As he closed the farmhouse door and walked toward the Blackhawk in the tilled fields of his former in-laws, he refused to look back because he knew the old world was gone, and the unknown world in front of him demanded his full and immediate attention.

A few hours before Christopher was to be picked up, Gabriella had gathered the Omega Group intelligence staff and was outlining the Brazil plan when Jackson entered the Omega briefing room.

"Glad to see you looking better, Jackson," Gabriella said by way of greeting.

"I do clean up pretty, don't I?" Jackson quipped in return.

"Sure, Jackson, you look ready for the prom. Anyway, let's go over the big picture of the plan, and then you can head out to pick up Major Barrett, hopefully in Harrisonburg."

"Okay, lay it on me."

Gabriella directed an intelligence officer to proceed.

"Good morning. Recent reports indicate that the executive targets are likely being held by a separatist faction of the Brazilian military that is trying to take power in the chaos of the disappearances. No official demands have been made by the group holding the executive targets. Additionally little is known about the number of hostiles, but we do have confirmation of their location at the *Residência Oficial do Torto* or

Granja do Torto, which is the presidential ranch retreat of Brazil," the intelligence officer reported.

"Thank you," Gabriella said. "I will take it from here." She laid out a large map of the *Granja do Torto* on the briefing room table. "The disappearances have created havoc in Brazil with the elected government losing its ability to govern. The first and second ladies along with the president's daughter were en route to Brasilia, Brazil, for a global women's conference when their plane went down during the final airport approach after two of the pilots disappeared. The U.S. Embassy in Brasilia sent a vague report indicating the possibility that at least the president's daughter had been taken to a ranch."

"This will be tough…we won't be able to move in until we can confirm the number of hostiles and the location of our targets," Jackson commented.

"You're right. We have your team set up with a country liaison in Brasilia via the embassy, which is where you guys will stage for the rescue. The team will also have access to an MH-47 Chinook helicopter and a C-40B military business jet for the mission. I figured the MH-47 can extract your team and the targets from the mission site straight to the airport, and the C-40B makes for a smooth ride home."

"That was good thinking, Gabriella. I think moving by air is going to be the best option we have in this situation," Jackson confirmed.

"Now for the bad news. The disappearances have stripped Omega down to a skeleton crew. There are only four original members left, and that's including Christopher and you."

"So where are we getting the other half of the team?"

"I have replacements from the Joint Special Operations Command inbound. I just need you to pick up the Omega Team leader. I sincerely hope he's mentally able to execute this mission. We don't need any mistakes and distractions like the French journalist operation. Your team will depart for Brasilia on the C-40B this evening."

"I'm sure Christopher will be ready to go, no matter what he found in Harrisonburg. We will meet you at Andrews Air Base later today," Jackson promised.

As Christopher climbed aboard the helicopter and watched Erin's family farm disappear, his tears flowed like the rain falling from the leaden sky over his in-laws' farm. He heard Jackson's voice over his headset.

"I am sorry, man. I know you're hurting, but we will get to the bottom of where these folks went."

"I already know where Erin and her family are. They're in Heaven, and we are about to go through hell."

"What are you talking about?"

"The rapture has occurred, Jackson, just like Rev said it would…just like Erin talked about."

"How do you know?"

"I've heard about this scenario enough from Erin to recognize the truth that all of us who are left have missed the chance to avoid the judgment that will follow the rapture."

"So what now?" Jackson asked, surprised to feel his heart in his throat.

"I don't have that answer. The only thing I know for sure is that things are gonna get rough."

"Well, thanks for the pep talk, but I know we can make it. I just feel it."

"How're Sarah and your kids?"

"I don't…" Jackson's voice trailed off.

"Hey, brother, no matter what you may believe or not believe right now, hang on to this thought for all it's worth. Your children are safe. Just believe that your children are safe."

Jackson found himself unable to respond as the tears streamed down his cheeks. As the helicopter banked toward the nation's capital, the light of the new day revealed out of Jackson's window that there was no place left untouched by the instantaneous disappearance of millions from Earth.

"Stop focusing on the disaster down there. The world as we knew it is gone. Tell me about our next mission," Christopher demanded.

"Before I get to the mission, do you actually believe that God took His Church and all the young children out of this world so He can judge the rest of us?"

"Yes, a part of me believes it. Truthfully, I am having a hard time seeing beyond my own pain to accept God. But this," Christopher replied, pointing out his window to the destruction below, "is part of a plan I've heard Erin and others speak of many times. What we see today and what lies ahead started with the fall of Adam and Eve in the garden of Eden, and according to Rev will end with Jesus' second coming. We missed the free gift Jesus Christ offered us to escape the troubles to come."

"Then how can you sit there and know that with such certainty and still not accept God? It seems to me that we need Him now more than ever," Jackson asserted.

Christopher couldn't answer because he hadn't been able to answer that question for years. He only knew that he trusted himself and not God right now. "Look, I am here for you, but I am still working things out with God, so give me some details on the mission."

"Fair enough, but I know I am going to figure out God because I have no reason to doubt His existence from what I see. The mission is to rescue the president's daughter, and possibly the first and second ladies from a separatist faction of the Brazilian military. They are likely being held at the Brazilan president's ranch retreat outside Brasilia. We fly out from Andrews Air Base at 1900 tonight."

"So what else did Colonel Delmar have to say?"

"He's dead, a suicide. Gabriella is the commander of Omega Group and will meet us ahead of our departure at Andrews."

Christopher was shocked to hear the news about Colonel Delmar, but he knew that the tragedy of missing the rapture was only the beginning of sorrows. He realized that many around him would likely die before the return of Christ, maybe even himself. The two of them sat in silence for the remainder of the trip, pondering the days ahead.

"The car heading to Andrews will meet us here at 1600, so I will meet you in the hotel lobby then. I'm heading up to my room for some sleep," Christopher told Jackson.

Yeah, that'll work. I'll see you at 1600," Jackson replied.

"Good day, Mr. Williams. Glad to see you weren't caught up in the disappearances," the hotel receptionist greeted him.

"I don't know how good it was to be left out," Jackson commented drily.

"Excuse me, sir?"

"Nothing. Can I have a key to my room, please? I just need to sleep for a few hours."

"I am sorry, sir. We thought you had disappeared so your belongings were collected and the room cleared. Please wait one second, and I will get your things," the hotel receptionist promised before disappearing through a door behind the desk and returning a moment later. "Okay, sir, I will bring the rest of your luggage up to your room in a few minutes, but here is your backpack."

"Look, ma'am, if you bring out my suitcase, I will lug it up to my room. I understand everyone is shorthanded right now. I promise I won't report you to the management."

"Thank you so much, sir," the receptionist said gratefully as she left again to retrieve Jackson's bag from an overflowing luggage room. "Here you go. You're all set."

"Thanks," Jackson responded. What he was most anxious to do besides sleep was read through Rev's journal about the topic of salvation and what he could expect next.

Jackson threw his backpack on the bed and pulled out Rev's Bible and journal. He was grateful that Rev kept such detailed notes, and he quickly found a section on "getting saved." He noted that Rev had outlined four parts to receiving the gift of salvation, paid for by Christ Jesus. The overview started in a blunt and upfront manner, conveying Rev's personality throughout his notes.

Jackson began reading in an attempt to end his confusion and satisfy his longing to know God. Rev had seemingly styled his notes in a manner especially suited for a critic or unbeliever like Jackson.

Rev started by explaining what salvation was: *"Salvation is being acquitted from the righteous judgment of God for our sins. The answer is, 'Yes, you are!' Because I know you're likely thinking, 'Well, I am a virtuous person and do good things for others, so I am a not evil or a sinner.' But you are! You are wondering how God could punish good people like you, but God does not compare us to people around us. We like to compare ourselves to our friends or loves ones or the people on the news, while God compares all of us to His standard—the standard of His own perfect holiness. God is entirely just; He is wholly moral and righteous in all He does and applies that standard to all of us, which we all fall short of each day."* Rev's words caused Jackson to feel uncomfortable as he thought about his own life.

He continued reading. *"We have all sinned at some point in our lives, and thus can never on our own meet the perfect standard of God's holiness."*

Jackson was starting to realize that his standard of seeing himself as a good, moral man had always been short of the mark. At this moment, reading Rev's words, he felt condemned and hopeless about ever being able to receive Jesus Christ as his savior.

He continued reading Rev's exposition on why humanity needed redeeming from the curse of sin. *"We are all sinners in God's eyes."* It was like Rev was sitting next to Jackson in the hotel room as the journal text answered his questions almost as soon as they entered his mind.

"You may ask why God views all of humanity as sinners with such cold objectivity. The reason is that all of us, every person who has ever followed our first parents Adam and Eve, inherited a deadly condition

called a sin nature, or a proclivity to commit sins. When God told Adam if he ate of the fruit from the Tree of the Knowledge of Good and Evil in the garden of Eden that he would die, yet he spared Adam and Eve, that is our first recorded example of His mercy and love for all humanity. He rightly could have killed Adam and Eve; instead He commuted their physical death for hundreds of years. However, spiritually they remained dead. Spiritual death, which is being separated from the provision and presence of God, required a remedy that God knew humanity was unable to provide by our own merits. The disobedience of humanity's progenitors Adam and Eve created a 'sin genetic marker' in all their descendants and the environment around humanity."

Jackson chuckled at the follow-up question and the answer Rev had provided. *"So where does our understanding that sin is a part of everyone and cannot be removed through our actions and goodness leave us? The answer is, it places us in a position to accept that God loved us so much that instead of destroying the human species and starting over, He implemented a plan to redeem us and our relationship with Him. While you as a critic or unbeliever may not like God's plan to save us and the relationship with Him that was lost, remember that we're the created beings, not the Creator. He is not seeking our approval of His plan for redemption. We are not God, and His ways are not our ways. All God asks is for you and me to place our trust in Him and what He has already done to save us from sin. God's holiness demands a perfect atonement plan to cover the sin of humanity. For generations following Adam and Eve, animals were brought to God as an appeasement to His judgment, but these were imperfect substitutes for man's sins. We needed a perfect sacrifice, a sacrifice that had lived and struggled as we do in facing the temptations of life. We needed a sacrifice that, despite living daily in a sin-filled environment, overcame everything we face in life so that the perfect Holiness of God could be met and humanity could be reconciled back to God."*

Overwhelmed with the story of salvation, Jackson could not stop the tears from flowing as he continued reading the notes. *"The overarching story of the Bible is a love story between a Holy God and His broken and beloved children, to save us from the judgment God's justness demands for sin. God so loved us that He allowed His only Son to lower Himself to live as one who was created, which is the greatest mystery in the story of humanity. God the Son, Jesus Christ, was born, lived, and died as a man in divine perfection, willingly sacrificing His life for every person who has lived or ever will live, thus ensuring the broken relationship between God and humanity was restored for those willing to place their hope and trust in Jesus."*

The journal entry continued. *"Christianity is like no other religion because its core centers on a relationship between God and humanity. We need to understand that it is what God did for us, not anything we can do in this life to garner God's love, that brings us into fellowship with God and each other. The Bible says in Romans 5:8: 'But God demonstrates his own love for us in this: While we were still sinners, Christ died for us.' The fact that Jesus hung suspended between Earth and Heaven on a wooden cross, suffering and dying in our rightful place, without making any requirements of us—like demanding a pilgrimage or spending a certain amount on the poor or any other prerequisites—for His sacrifice, tells us the value each of us has in God's economy. Jesus died knowing that many of us would never accept His sacrifice, that many people would never live a life aimed at pleasing Him. Yet He still died to give every person the opportunity to be saved from judgment someday."*

Tears soaked Jackson's T-shirt as he read on through Rev's guide to salvation. *"So many people wrongly view God as the angry grandfather-figure playing whack-a-mole with all of us. This mischaracterization of God leads many to feel that there is no way they could ever be forgiven by God because of the lives they have lived. We too often mistakenly judge God by our human perceptions of fairness, not realizing that God loves us beyond description within the bounds of His unwavering holiness. The Bible tells us clearly that there is nothing God is unwilling to forgive, besides not accepting His offer of salvation. If we accept the gift of salvation that Christ Jesus offers, Romans 8:1 says, 'Therefore, there is now no condemnation for those who are in Christ Jesus.'"*

As Jackson approached the last paragraphs of Rev's notes on being saved, he not only realized his need for Jesus as His Savior but also had a better appreciation for how much God loved him.

He continued reading. *"Now that you understand what salvation is, what we are saved from, who redeems us, and for what purpose, you're ready to receive and live out God's gift of salvation for your life. Remember, salvation resides in Jesus' efforts and life, nothing else. Salvation is graciously given as a priceless gift that is unmerited, but made so simple to obtain that even a child cannot fail to understand."*

As Jackson read the call to salvation that Rev had written, he rolled off the bed and onto his knees, reading aloud, "If you're ready to accept God's mercy and plan to bring you back into a loving relationship with Him, no matter what you've done or said, repeat this prayer after me. 'God, I confess that I am broken, having lived a sinful life. I am asking for and in need of Your forgiveness and merciful restoration. I confess with my mouth that Jesus died on the cross for my sins, and Jesus rose from the grave having authority over death, the grave, and Hell, which gives me eternal life through Him. I ask You to be the Lord over my life, and in Jesus' name, I pray to You, Father, Amen. (See Romans 10:9–10.)" With that, Rev's salvation notes concluded.

Jackson felt compelled to add to his prayer, saying, "And, God, please help me, and help others in the days ahead. Amen."

Jackson could not describe the sensation that overtook his body, but a tremendous sense of peace invaded him. It felt like he had just apologized to and been forgiven by an estranged friend. He wiped the tears from his eyes and showered. As he laid down for some much-needed sleep, he drifted off with one thought running through His mind. *Thank you, Jesus.*

Christopher was awakened by the new cell phone that Jackson had provided him, the usual Pentagon operations center number flashing across the display. "Hello."

"I am sorry to wake you, but I needed to relay something to you ahead of us meeting up at Andrews," Gabriella said.

"Nah, it's okay. So what's up?"

"There is no easy way to say this…Jackson's wife and daughters are dead."

"What? How do you know that?" Christopher demanded, sitting up on the bed.

"The staff and I are starting to get into a rhythm here. I had the intelligence folks scrubbing hospital admittance records and transportation manifests to confirm the disposition of the other team members, considering the team was on a seventy-two-hour pass when the disappearances hit. Long story short, Jackson's wife Sarah and his five- and eight-year-old girls Sadie and Kate were on a flight bound for D.C. that crashed halfway between Tampa and here," Gabriella stated flatly.

"Well, at least Jackson's daughters are in a better place."

"What, how can you say that, Chris?"

"I just have a feeling that they were taken with the other children who are missing from all around the world."

"Yeah, but no one is sure where all these people have gone."

"Gabriella, there is a plausible answer. God raptured the Church, including those that were mentally incapable of deciding if they wanted to have a relationship with Him or not—like young children and those with special mental needs."

"I've heard that theory, but I'm not sure I understand it or even want to accept it. It seems you have."

"I am comfortable with it because it's the closest explanation to the reality I see all around me. I lost some folks that literally staked their lives on believing in God. I am working toward trusting Him," Christopher returned in a matter-of-fact tone.

"Well, it is logically a theory worth me exploring, but not now. Look,

I think you are best suited to break the news to Jackson. Just let me know if we need to pull him from the mission."

"I'll tell him, but I would be shocked if he wouldn't want to be on the mission. We will see you in a couple of hours."

CHAPTER 6

Christopher called Jackson and asked him to meet downstairs a little early. He was a little concerned that Jackson agreed so quickly, saying he had to tell Christopher something unbelievable. Christopher wondered if it was possible that someone else had broken the news about his family to him already.

About an hour later, Jackson met Christopher in the hotel lobby. "Hey there, bossman. Ready for another adventure?"

"I am ready for saving the Omega Group name. But, Jackson, I need to tell you something first."

"Well, before you dump a downer on my day, let me tell you some great news first. I got saved."

"What?"

"You heard me right. I asked Jesus to save me. I am a fully certified believer in Jesus Christ, just a day too late it seems, but better late than never, right, brother?" Jackson perceived the raised eyebrows and pursed lips of Christopher as disapproval of his admission. "I thought you would be more happy for me, even if you're struggling with accepting God right now."

"It's not that, Jackson. That *is* great news, man. I am happy for you. It just makes what I have to tell you that much harder."

"Look, man, bad news doesn't get better with time, so just hit me with it," Jackson said stoically.

"Sarah and your girls were on a flight bound for D.C.—likely to surprise you—but the plane went down during the disappearances. There were no survivors. Gabriella found your family's names on the downed flight's manifest. I am so sorry, Jackson," Christopher murmured softly.

Jackson pulled his ball cap down over his face and Christopher watched helplessly as his shoulders heaved with brokenhearted sobs. The few folks in the lobby took little notice of the scene—it seemed that tears and pain were just becoming the new normal.

"God, help me understand. I have put my trust in You, so please help me through this," Jackson prayed quietly.

"Jackson, I don't know anything to say that I think will help. Just know I am here for you, whatever you need," Christopher promised.

"I am grateful the news came from you. I wish I could have said good-bye, but I know that at least my daughters are in Heaven, but Sarah…" Jackson's voice trailed off sadly.

"Jackson, as you just found out, all it takes is a prayer to be saved no matter what we have done. Just think about what you did in your hotel room. When you get a chance, look at the story of the thief on the cross next to Jesus. All he ever did in his life that mattered was asked to be saved, and Jesus said, 'This day you will be with me in paradise.' Sarah could have prayed for salvation in the last moments. Just hold on to that."

"Thanks, bro. I am new to this whole God thing, but I have no place else to turn. I'm going to believe I will see them all again one day," Jackson said, his chest heaving as he drew in a deep breath as though to fortify himself to go on. "Christopher, I know you're not ready to mend your fences with God, but it seems to me you're trying to keep your pain as a badge of honor. You seem to know at least enough about God to accept Him in your life as your savior, but instead you want to deny God like it's hurting Him instead of you. I am sorry, man, but I just want you to be okay."

"Thanks, Jackson. I mean really, I appreciate your thoughts, but…" Christopher couldn't even muster the words to argue.

"Look, I get it. You don't have to say anything else. Brother, I don't know what else to do right now besides work, so let's get to it," Jackson said, rising to his feet.

Gabriella waited nervously for Christopher and hopefully Jackson to arrive at the executive terminal lounge at Andrews Air Base. She was grateful to see both men walking toward her. "Hey, guys. It's good to see you both. Jackson, please know that your family, and you, are in my thoughts. Let me know if there is anything I can do for you."

"Thanks, Gabriella," Jackson replied. "I am holding on to the hope that they're in a much better place now."

"In any case, I just wanted to provide you all a few coordinating details and see the team off," she explained. Then she called a group of eight men who had been conversing with the other two members of Omega. She introduced the men in turn to their new team leader and team sergeant.Jackson interrupted the last introduction, saying flatly, "John Barnes."

"Hey, Jackson," John replied. "It's been a long time."

"Yep, just not long enough," Jackson said through clenched teeth.

"Okay, glad to see that everyone knows each other—even if awkwardly. Christopher, could I speak with you alone for a moment, please?" Gabriella pointed to an empty corner of the lounge. "We just need to discuss a few final details about this mission."

When they were out of earshot of the others, Gabriella began. "First, the president is convinced like you that the rapture has occurred. He has directed that Omega make no attempt to explore the crash site searching for survivors, in particular, the First Lady. He's certain she is in Heaven. The other thing is, the president will observe the rescue operation from the Situation Room at the White House."

"Thanks for the heads up, but what about the Second Lady?" Christopher questioned.

"We have satellite images of the crash site. *If* they are alive, they will be at the presidental ranch. If you establish a pattern of life of either leading lady or the president's daughter, then the mission will proceed. In the absence of any executive target, the mission will be aborted and you will be brought home. The last thing we need is to look like we are supporting the wrong side of a military coup."

An overworked flight manager stuck his head in the door of the lounge to loudly holler, "All the soldiers need to get on the plane *now.*"

"Well, that's our cue. Don't worry. We'll bring everybody home," Christopher assured Gabriella.

"Good luck."

As the military business jet taxied to a stop at Presidente Juscelino Kubitschek International Airport in Brasilia, Christopher watched steam rising from the tarmac after a late-afternoon tropical deluge. The State Department already had SUVs waiting as the staircase was lowered and the sweltering humidity of the Brazilian spring invaded the jet.

"Welcome to Brazil. You must be Barrett," a young bureaucrat said to Christopher.

"I'm guessing you're the country liaison, whose name is…?" Christopher asked.

"Sorry, I am Nick Lacroix."

"So, Nick, let's get off this very public tarmac and back to the embassy for the rest of the pleasantries. You can update me on where we stand along the way. Jackson, ride with us."

"Yeah, that sounds great," Nick replied. "I just was going to suggest we get moving." Jackson asked, "So how bad was it for you guys? The disappearances, I mean."

"We lost about ten people, the most important our deputy ambassador Charles Smith," Nick answered. "He was a very kind man, and charitable. He never made those like me feel out of place."

"What does that mean—'those like you'?" Christopher queried.

"I mean my sexual orientation. I knew the deputy ambassador was a Christian. He always spoke of his faith and even invited me to attend the embassy church services. However, he was different than most Christians I've encountered," Nick stated thoughtfully.

"How so?" Jackson asked.

"I never felt that he was judging me. He was honest about the fact that he believed my lifestyle was a 'sin,' but he expressed that in a way that was loving, if that makes sense. Mr. Smith always made it clear that Jesus hated the sin, not people. He said that if more Christians just loved people like Jesus did and met them where they were in life, it would be easier for people to see the sin in their lives and change, or something like that..." Nick trailed off.

Jackson was moved by Nick's story of a Christian man leading by the example Christ had set, meeting sinners where they were in life. He spent the rest of the drive to the embassy setting up a plan with Christopher and Nick to recon the Granja Torto Ranch later that night.

"Hey, Jackson, come here for a minute," Christopher called, pulling Jackson away from the other men prepping for the reconnaissance of the target location.

"What's up?"

"Tell me the backstory on John Barnes. You gave him a decidedly chilly reception."

"You noticed that," Jackson responded.

"I'm sure everyone did. So what's the story?"

"Long and bad. But to make the story short, I'll just say that guy's moral compass does not exist. I don't trust him," Jackson stated flatly.

"Should he even be here then?" Christopher asked.

"Hard times have come and we are short in men, but I plan to watch him. If he makes one wrong move, he's got to go," Jackson asserted unequivocally.

"Fair enough. I'll take him and two other guys for the recon tonight."

"What? Did you not just hear a word I said?" Jackson sounded shocked.

"Yeah, Jackson, I heard you. But I need to figure out what this guy—heck, all these new guys—are made of, so trust me."

"Understood. You're the boss, but make sure you listen to that still, small voice if it pops up this time."

It was a perfect night for a recon—well, almost. The humidity made everything wet, including Christopher. Thankfully as his small team approached the presidental ranch, the Brazilians had the place lit up like Carnavale.

"Okay, listen up. Here's the plan," the major instructed as John Barnes and two other men knelt in front of him. "John, I want you two," he ordered as he gestured to John and the team medic, "to move through the tree line toward the front of the complex near the tennis courts. When you get there, launch the drone and hover at fifty meters AGL. Try to identify the pattern of any roving patrols, guards, and quick ground-egress points. Keep radio traffic to a minimum. Only come up on the net in the event you make contact or to notify me of your return to the rally point here at the lake. You have an hour. I'll head out with the sergeant to cover the rear of the ranch. We'll try to identify the location of the executive target or targets and the number of hostiles guarding them. Are there any questions?"

"No, sir," Barnes answered.

"Okay, move out."

Christopher was uneasy given the gravity of the targets being held, but also due to the distrust Jackson held for John Barnes and his decision-making abilities. He hoped that he had not made a mistake in taking Barnes on this recon mission.

"Green 6, this is Green 3, mission complete," came the call from Barnes on the radio.

Christopher checked his watch—the first thing that came to his mind was, *Forty-five minutes. That was quick.* He decided to dismiss his concern due to the small size of the complex. He had yet to identify any facility at the compound that held the executive targets. The team was running out of time, and it looked like the mission would need to be aborted.

"Look," the communications sergeant whispered to Major Barrett.

Christopher used a night scope to zoom in on a female who looked like the president's daughter based on the dossier pictures he had studied. Unfortunately he also saw a big problem. She was bracing herself on crutches, with what looked like a cast on one leg. It seemed like they were keeping her in the large villa near the pool. A cigar-smoking man stood speaking with her, likely the rogue Brazilian general.

Christopher signaled to the sergeant that their time was up. He had the confirmation required to proceed with the mission.As Christopher linked up with John Barnes, he asked, "That was a quick recon. Is everything covered?"

"Yeah, I got it," Barnes assured him tersely.

"Okay, let's head back and discuss what we saw with the rest of the team," Christopher ordered.

"Welcome back. Good to see you still know how to execute a recon without being detected," Jackson ribbed.

"Oh ye of little faith, I can recon with the best of them, and your friend John was solid," Christopher assured him.

"That's good to know on all counts," Jackson replied.

Christopher called the team together, along with Nick and the embassy intelligence officer, to finalize the plan for the following night. He quickly outlined his plan for the others. "Okay, after watching the drone footage, we should go with a ground assualt force for the extraction. The complex is surrounded by high-speed avenues of approach and is lightly defended, about ten men guarding the place, plus the target is on crutches. The president's daughter was the only executive seen. The first and second ladies are presumed deceased."

"That doesn't make sense. You should have seen four times that number of hostiles. Over forty men were guarding that complex—which you've now confirmed holds the president's daughter—yesterday afternoon. Take a look at these images," the embassy intelligence officer said, pushing the images across the table to Christopher.

"I take it back," Jackson stated. "You *don't* know how to recon."

"Whatever, Jackson. Barnes, tell me, did you see any other buildings that could possibly have housed the other hostiles?" Christopher asked pointedly.

"No," Barnes replied firmly. "I saw no roving patrols and just a few guys milling about the complex."

Christopher pored over the images again, torn about whether to conduct a ground assault or helicopter extraction. The team debated for another thirty minutes with Gabriella weighing in via phone.

"It seems to me that helicopter extraction will be the safer option. You could take the president's daughter straight to the airport," Gabriella suggested.

"Noted, but there's an open field between the ranch and the helicopter pad, and remember, she can't run or walk," Christopher responded.

"Your call, but just make sure you look at all angles and consider all advice. We will be watching back here," Gabriella reminded him.

"Okay, team, we are going with a ground assault. I think with the other hostiles unaccounted for, it will be better to get the target into secure transportation as quickly as possible, considering the mobility limitations. We'll keep the helo in a holding pattern about five miles away. If needed, they can reach us in about fiveminutes," Christopher said.

"Five minutes is a lifetime in a firefight," Jackson cautioned.

"I get it, Jackson, but getting the president's daughter into something secure is my biggest concern," Christopher replied.

As the rest of the team left the conference room, Jackson lingered to talk with Christopher.

"Hey, listen, I will follow you anywhere, but the Spirit is telling me we should just use the helicopter. The fact that we don't know the location of the other hostiles could put the president's daughter at risk, not to mention us. There seem to be a lot of unknowns here," Jackson concluded uneasily.

"Look, I get it. You've put your trust in God, and now you feel led by Him, but we are going with a ground extraction. I trust my instincts here, and I was on the recon, not you. Just help me out by executing the orders given instead of trying to get me to 'trust the still, small voice.' I refuse to have that distraction again." Christopher's tone indicated the discussion was over.

"Got it." Jackson exited the room, his concerns not the least bit relieved.

Jackson sat in one of four Humvees on loan from the embassy security detachment that comprised the ground assualt force, sweating profusely. He listened to the radio and heard Christopher and the rescue element calling off checkpoints as they stalked through the woods to get closer to the target. Thankfully it was a starless night, making their approach easier; the guards seemed more willing to sleep than patrol. He couldn't stop his left leg from bouncing in anticipation of the message that the package was received, signaling the assault force to storm the main gate.

"All hostile guards down, package received," Christopher said into his radio transmitter.

Jackson heard only the sharp retort of gunfire on the radio and sirens as the ranch complex lit up like Paris at night. "Drive, now!" Jackson yelled at the soldier behind the wheel of his Humvee.

As the ground assault force raced toward the main entrance to the ranch, Jackson saw a large cargo truck carrying at least twenty Brazilian soldiers barreling across the road toward the main gate. "Ram that truck!" Jackson ordered. He watched the eyes of the cargo truck driver grow large with fright in the ultrabright headlamp beams right before the monstrous collision. The heavy combat vehicle cut through the cargo truck like a hot knife through butter, throwing out the troops in the back like spaghetti spilling from a bag.

The three Humvees behind Jackson instinctively fired their weapons at the overturned cargo truck, before turning toward the Brazilian presidental ranch to continue the mission.

"Are you all right?" Jackson quickly tossed the question toward his driver, his eyes scanning ahead.

"Yeah, Sarge, I'm okay," the driver replied. "But I think the Humvee snapped its front axle."

"Throw a thermite grenade on it, and let's get into this fight," Jackson ordered. He and the driver abandoned the now-useless Humvee and headed toward the villa on foot after the detonation. *At least it won't fall into enemy hands*, he thought ruefully as he watched the Humvee explode in flames.

"Anybody hit?" Christopher questioned, still reeling from the gunfight he found himself in.

"No, we're good," Barnes and the others replied.

Christopher quickly switched to the MH-47G Chinook helicopter's radio frequency. "Angel 6, this is Green 6, request immediate air extraction. The LZ will be hot and marked by a green laser."

"Green 6, this is Angel 6. We are inbound, ETA five minutes."

"Barnes, get the drone up. We need eyes for egress and a hostile count—and where is that ground assault force?" Christopher wondered aloud.

John Barnes pulled a small drone from his assault pack and initiated its flight sequence; the drone brought up a high-resolution picture on Christopher's wrist monitor, showing his team pinned down by fifteen Brazilian soldiers advancing toward the main villa as well as Jackson's ground assault team heading toward them.

"Green 9, this is Green 6, we have fifteen hostiles advancing on our position. We are going to lay down some smoke and move toward the air extraction point. Cover us and ground convoy back to the airport," Christopher ordered as he slung his rifle over his back and picked up the president's daughter in his arms. His small element immediately began making their way toward the helipad outside the presidental ranch under a hail of gunfire.

"Understood, we will cover your egress," Jackson responded as he ran to the villa.

The soldiers in the other three Humvees were monitoring the radio traffic, and Jackson heard them open fire on the unsuspecting Brazilian hostiles. He caught up to the three Humvees and instructed the team to throw thermite grenades into the lavish main villa of the presidental ranch, which started a raging fire.

"Load up," Jackson ordered. "We are heading to the air extraction point. They may need our help."

President Rodgers stood tensely in the White House Situation Room, watching Omega Team attempt to rescue his daughter from a deranged Brazilian general. He was grateful he couldn't hear what was going on, but as a former fighter pilot he knew from what he could see through Christopher's helmet cam video that the team was fighting against some terrible odds.

"Sir, the helicopter is being moved for air extraction, the team has your daughter, and the Brazilian presidental ranch is being reported on fire with additional Brazilian military units en route," Gabriella relayed as she received intelligence updates from the Pentagon.

"How did that gunfight start? Everything was going so smoothly," President Rodgers questioned.

"I don't know, sir, but Omega will get your daughter home safely," Gabriella assured him.

"I pray they all get home safely, Gabriella," President Rodgers murmured.

Gabriella just hoped that Chris had made the right decisions and had not been distracted as the fact that this mission appeared to be on the edge of failure seemed to indicate.

Christopher, the president's daughter being carried unceremoniously in his arms, and his element had just arrived at the helipad outside of the Brazilian presidental ranch when he saw what looked like three military cargo trucks heading toward them.

"Angel 6, this is Green 6, what's your ETA?" he asked urgently.

"Green 6, this is Angel 6, ETA one minute," the MH-47 pilot responded.

"Barnes, start marking the helipad with the laser," Christopher ordered. "Get down and stay down," he instructed as he pushed the president's daughter to the ground. His arms and legs were burning from carrying the svelte young woman, but he didn't have time to focus on his pain. He rallied the other men behind a berm to prepare to defend against the looming assault from the separatist Brazilian military. "Green 9, this is Green 6, we have three trucks of hostiles coming our way, I need you to cover us, over." Christopher waited for his radio to crackle with acknowledgment from Jackson. Instead he watched as three Humvees broke out of the citrus grove surrounding the presidential ranch, stopping the advance of the cargo trucks with fiery streaks of lead streaking from the miniguns atop the Humvees.

"Green 6, this Green 9, I got you covered. I'll see you folks at the airport," Jackson acknowledged, finally.

The whirl of dust and wind from the MH-47 landing drowned out any attempt Christopher made to thank Jackson over the radio.

"We need to go," Barnes yelled, urging Christopher to board the chopper.

As they lifted off, Christopher looked across the highway as Jackson and his team sped away from the overturned cargo trucks and the flaming Brazilian presidental ranch, grateful that Omega had overcome his mistakes tonight.

Nick Lacroix had the C-40B military business jet running hot as the first group from Omega poured into the airport. He watched as the president's daughter was loaded onto the plane, and two figures walked out of the darkness toward him in the empty hangar.

"Where's the ground team?" Christopher wondered aloud, concern evident in his voice.

"They should be here any minute," Nick assured him.

The screeching of Humvee tires and the muscular figure of Jackson Williams almost jumping out of his vehicle confirmed the ground team's arrival.

"What happened? Where did that firefight come from?" Jackson questioned tersely.

"I shot a guard," Barnes replied. "I thought he was going to compromise us."

"You did what?" Jackson exploded, grabbing Barnes's uniform top and pinning him to the wall.

"Hey, get your hands off him, Jackson," Christopher ordered firmly.

"You're still a freaking killer! You're still just a loose cannon, Barnes.

You could have gotten all of us killed tonight, not to mention the president's daughter," Jackson accused sharply.

"Shut up, Jackson. I was protecting everyone," Barnes answered hotly.

"Enough! Jackson, head to the plane, now." Christopher's tone brooked no argument.

Everyone watched as Jackson swore and threw his helmet across the tarmac on his way to board the plane.

"Gentlemen, I hate to interject, but the airspace will likely close shortly due to tonight's adventure, so please board and leave Brazil now," Nick Lacroix urged forcefully.

"Thanks for everything, Nick," Christopher said as he pivoted and headed for the tarmac. "This is not over, John," he warned as they jogged side by side out to the waiting plane that would take them home.

"I haven't sweated that much since my first sortie over Baghdad with your dad, young lady," President Rodgers exclaimed to Gabriella in the White House Situation Room as senior cabinet members celebrated Omega's deliverance of his daughter.

"I am very proud of Omega Group—from the support staff to the operatives. Complete team victory tonight, sir," Gabriella responded, her relief evident.

"Listen, Gabriella, after those boys get a few hours of sleep, I want you to send them over to see me. Let's make it early evening tomorrow after my official press conference on the disappearances. Most of the world leaders will be speaking in the next twenty-four hours, minus the EU president. He's scheduled a media event the following day," President Rodgers remarked thoughtfully.

"I wonder why the EU president feels the need to speak separately from the heads of state?" Gabriella queried.

"Who knows? You know he's always been lavish in his

announcements, even before he got into the political arena," President Rodgers commented with a roll of his eyes.

"Do you plan to announce to the world that the rapture has occurred, sir?" Gabriella asked tentatively.

"I have half a mind to do just that, but I can't completely wrap my mind around the fact, despite my wife not being in Brazil. I am going to our canned line that we continue to explore many possibilities but have ruled out any foreign attack or terrorism. It's a safe answer that will buy us a little more time."

"I am sorry that your wife is gone, but time for what, sir?"

"You don't need to be sorry, Gabriella. I've told you, I believe she is better off than we are. Time is needed for the world and me to figure out if it was God or just bad luck for hundreds of millions of people," President Rodgers responded wearily.

Gabriella liked the president's approach to the situation. If it were just bad luck, then things would turn around, and answers would become evident. On the other hand, if it was indeed God behind the disappearances, then she was fearful of the days ahead.

"You just don't get it, do you? You can't do everything in this world. You had better start trusting the people God has sent into your life before you wake up one day and find yourself dead!" Jackson was as angry as Christopher had ever seen him.

"Spare me the new Christian fire, Jackson. I am the first to admit that things went south tonight, but I see little evidence that God saved us!" Christopher yelled right back.

"Are you serious, Christopher? I told you that Barnes was trouble. Your recon missed over twenty hostiles due to piss-poor execution. Gabriella told you to use the helicopter, and so did I. It was only through divine grace that we didn't all die back there."

"I made a call. That's what leaders do," Christopher stated flatly.

"Exactly, you made the call—a bad call—despite having sound advice to the contrary! Your failure to trust is going to cost not only your life but the lives of others. Heck, at this rate, it might even cost your soul," Jackson spat.

"Look, I said I accept responsibility for the op getting dicey, and I even thanked you for covering my back out there. What more do you want from me, Jackson? I am done with this conversation."

"Brother, I just want you to stop acting like you can do everything all by yourself. I want you to stop trusting only yourself instead of relying on the collective strength around you."

Christopher moved to the front of the plane, leaving Jackson in the back and the rest of the team looking on wide-eyed as the two Omega Team leaders ended a tense mission with a heated argument.

Christopher knew Jackson was right, even if he couldn't admit that to his friend. As he settled into his seat for the long flight home, he shook out of a fear that his belief in himself was becoming a liability. He wondered if it was possible God was watching over him. He needed some time to figure out this God-versus-him thing, but the world only seemed to be speeding toward what felt like his demise.

Chapter 7

Christopher felt out of place after the president honored the Omega Team for the rescue of his daughter. It was not just the pomp and circumstance of being celebrated that made him uneasy, but the realization that his actions had been counter to the success of the mission, or so it felt. Jackson argued that the real hero was God, but Christopher struggled to give God credit for anything, especially in his career, which he felt was built on his talents alone. God came across to Christopher as erratic and unreliable in comparison to himself. Perhaps the days ahead would solidify a path toward his relationship with God, preferably without costing Christopher or someone close to him their lives.

"Listen, Christopher…sorry, man, I didn't mean to startle you." Jackson felt bad for apparently shocking Christopher out of deep thought. "I need to apologize for being so critical. I have no room to judge your relationship with God."

"I understand that you just want the best for me, and I am thrilled that you're building a great relationship with God, so let's just focus on that." Christopher needed to make things right between the two of them. He was thankful Jackson had made the first move.

"That's gracious of you, but I don't want to be overbearing in my zeal over finding God."

"Nah, I remember Erin having that same eagerness to see everyone around her be saved, too…" Christopher's voice trailed off as thoughts of

Erin flooded his mind. A moment later, he felt glad that Gabriella jumped into the conversation, saving him from breaking down among the numerous guests dotting the White House Rose Garden reception.

"So what did you guys think about President Rodgers's official announcement on the disappearances?" Gabriella asked, eyes narrowing as she looked closely at both men.

"I think it was a lie. The rapture occurred, and we should be looking out for the Antichrist," Jackson responded bluntly.

"Okay, so you're just dismissing any logical scientific explanation instantly, Jackson?" Gabriella asked incredulously.

"No," Jackson said. "I would accept a scientific explanation for what occurred, but there isn't one that makes sense—unless natural evaporation due to overeating counts. There is also the fact that the Bible made a significant declaration thousands of years ago this very scenario would take place."

"Christopher, please tell me that you don't see God in the works, too," Gabriella begged.

"I agree with Jackson that it's hard to find another answer that fits. I don't know what to believe besides what I see, which screams something supernatural. It seems to me that judgment is coming," Christopher replied.

"I've heard that my whole life, and I refuse to accept that I am a bad person and now my judgment has arrived. There is a lot of buzz surrounding the EU president's statement. Draven Cross has a brilliant mind and is a proven advocate for peace," Gabriella explained.

"Yeah, that's what worries me about old Mr. Cross. The Bible warns us that a man will appear to claim peace, but peace will be far from him. Anybody pushing peace as the answer to all the world's problem right now, well, that man will be the Antichrist in my book," Jackson asserted unequivocally.

"I don't even have the words to respond to that, Jackson. Look, I need you guys to follow me to the Oval Office. President Rodgers wanted to discuss something with us," Gabriella replied.

"What, right now? Why do I have the feeling we are about to head off for something else dangerous?" Jackson said, lacing his fingers together behind his head as they exited the room.

Laughing, Christopher ribbed, "I sometimes wonder how you got through basic training, much less special forces selection."

"What? Is it too much to ask to have more than a day off before heading out to God only knows where?" Jackson countered, sounding decidedly aggrieved.

"Let's go, you two babies. The president is waiting," Gabriella called, walking off ahead of them to the Oval Office.

Christopher quirked an eyebrow at Jackson, almost laughing.

With a hearty laugh, Jackson said, "Do you think it was too much? Seems like the Antichrist bit sent her over the edge." He was still chuckling under his breath as they followed Gabriella down the hallway.

President Rodgers looked like a middle-aged father about to explain the birds and the bees to his children as he sat in his office chair, which had been placed opposite the couch where Christopher, Jackson, and Gabriella all sat together.

"First, I can't say thank you enough to each of you for your part in saving my daughter down there in Brazil. You have given me the chance to right the wrong of misleading her about God all these years. Thanks are inadequate for that gift, but it's all this old man knows how to say," President Rodgers told them humbly.

"No need to ever say thanks, sir," Christopher replied. "We're just doing our jobs."

"I appreciate your humility, Major, and your relentless professionalism—because I need your expertise yet again. The rapture has opened Pandora's box. We've got fewer people to deal with an increasing number of critical national-security issues, none more significant right now than stopping the proliferation of weapons-grade fissile material from Pakistan."

Christopher shot Jackson and Gabriella a side-eyed look at the president's description of the disappearance of millions. Jackson met Christopher's gaze, while Gabriella seemed unfazed by anything she had heard.

"What is it, guys?" President Rodgers queried. "You seem puzzled."

"Well, sir. I just never would have guessed you would describe the event from a few days ago as the rapture. You being a politician and all, sir," Jackson explained carefully.

Chuckling aloud and with a small smile, President Rodgers remarked, "Well, I am still saying it only in select company, but I feel more and more like I should make my real views on what happened public."

"I hate to derail this meeting about that special material going missing in Pakistan, sir, but could you please tell me why you think it was the rapture?" Jackson said, flushing red.

"No, son, I don't mind at all," the president replied. "You see, it's simple. I've already told Gabriella this, but it boils down to my wife Janet. She led a life dedicated to God. She lived with honor, dignity, and servanthood despite all of my failings. She always loved me with what she called the love of Christ. If we fought, Janet was the first to say sorry, always aiming to reconcile our relationship even though I was wrong. It would make me mad because it made me feel all the more guilty because she loved me when I was unworthy of her love. Janet told me that's how God loves us. It apparently doesn't matter how much we reject Him or disavow Him. He still loves us, so much so that He allowed His Son to be sacrificed for all of us.

"So, you see, now that I believe with all of my spirit and might that God loves me, it has become easy to see God's impact on this world. I understand that God is doing exactly what He predicted in taking believers like Janet out of this world a few days ago, ahead of His justified judgment on a planet that for millennia has rejected His offer of reconciliation through Christ Jesus."

Christopher was shocked to see both Jackson and Gabriella in tears. He had to admit, even if only to himself, that hearing the most powerful man in the world speak of God's love in such personal terms stirred his own emotions powerfully. A part of Christopher intensely longed to have that type of relationship with God but feared the cost, namely, letting God off the hook for some painful events in his life.

"I apologize for being so emotional, but it is the most honest way I know to answer your question, Sergeant Major. And what I've said to you here this evening also affirms to me that I will need to, sooner rather than later, make my belief public," President Rodgers said firmly. "However, we have a pressing matter regarding national security to deal with presently. Dr. Muhammad Jafari, director of the Pakistani Atomic Energy Commission, relayed a message through the International Atomic Energy Agency that an ISIS-sympathizing nuclear scientist named Adeel Zardari has stolen several nuclear pits. Our most recent intelligence report..." he handed each of them a manila folder, "...indicates that Zardari is likely heading to Tajikistan to meet up with interested buyers."

"Have we been able to detect and trace the fissile materials with Zardari?" Gabriella asked.

"Yes, we have," President Rodgers confirmed. "He's has been in the village of Ishkashim, Afghanistan, for the past twelve hours. Human intelligence reports indicate he is supposed to link up with his buyers in Khorog, Tajikistan, in two days. Omega's mission is to intercept Zardari in Afghanistan before his meeting with the buyers in a couple of days."

"That's not a lot of time, sir. We need to start making our way there in the next few hours if we are going to have a shot of intercepting him before he makes that drop," Christopher said.

"You're right, Major," the president replied. "That's why I have the latest and greatest military business jet waiting for your team at Andrews. The C-39XER was built for getting guys like you and stuffy execs somewhere in a hurry. With over 7,000 nautical miles of range and cruising just a smidge below supersonic, there are not many places I can't get you boys in a hurry. It even has a galley and service crew for this trip, ensuring comfort for your team. Shoot, this thing makes me want to fly again."

"You're more than welcome to come with us, sir," Christopher offered.

"I'm tempted, but I also know that you men can do things this old pilot never dreamed of doing. I'll leave this to the professionals," President Rodgers said regretfully, slapping a big hand across Christopher's back. "Gabriella, we will bring the usual select cabinet members and members of Congress into the Situation Room tomorrow evening to watch the mission unfold. Let me know if you need anything from me," he added in dismissal as he moved behind his desk.

"Yes, sir, I'll finalize the details and let you know if we need any additional support," Gabriella confirmed.

"I hope you boys don't get stage fright," President Rodgers said hopefully.

"No, sir, we'll be ready, and we won't let you down," Christopher promised this man who appeared to be carrying a large weight on his shoulders.

"Good hunting and I will be praying for you," President Rodgers replied.

"Thanks, sir. Your prayers and support are greatly appreciated, more than you know," Jackson said before closing the Oval Office door behind him.

The near-transonic C-39XER delivered on President Rodgers's hype, and Christopher was grateful. The same trip flying in a "normal" airplane would have taken sixteen hours or more, but was completed in just over ten hours. Being back in Afghanistan brought back a flood of memories for Christopher as he gazed at the snow-covered Hindu Kush mountains surrounding Bagram.

As the aircraft taxied to a stop at Bagram Airfield, Christopher couldn't help but think about the perils hidden behind the stark beauty of this land. Anxious not to miss a detail in planning the upcoming mission, he knew all too well that distractions in Afghanistan led to disastrous outcomes. It was almost ten years ago, during his last deployment as a conventional soldier in the 82nd Airborne Division, where Christopher saw soldiers in his company pay for the sins of their company commander. Little change had taken place here over the past decade, where the sounds of war had become routine. He hoped that Omega's time in this beautiful but brutal land would be short.

A rush of cold air filled the plane and drew everyone's attention to the now open main cabin door.

"Gentlemen, if I could have your attention, please. I am Senior Airman Montana, the flight ops manager here. We are shorthanded due to the disappearances, so you will need to unload your own gear and then follow me to Stone Guard where you will be lodging."

"Huh, what's going on? Somebody turn off that A/C!" a disoriented Jackson yelled.

"How can you sleep so soundly?" Christopher asked with a chuckle.

"Easy, because I know you're not going to let me get any sleep anytime soon," Jackson retorted.

As the Omega Team quickly pulled their gear off the plane in an attempt to escape the frigid early morning air, Christopher felt a tug on his thoughts. *"It is better to trust in the LORD than to put confidence in man,"* was the crystal-clear thought that entered his mind from the familiar and uncomfortable still, small voice of the Holy Spirit. He hadn't heard from the Holy Spirit since the night of the French journalist mission. He said aloud, "What does that mean?"

"Are you okay?" Jackson asked, looking around. "Who are you talking to?"

"No one. I'm okay. I just thought I heard somebody say something," Christopher responded.

"Hey, check it out," Jackson said, directing Christopher's attention toward a television screen where preparations were being made to broadcast the EU president's address on the disappearances. "I wonder what this guy is going to say that's different from everybody else."

"Who knows? But we've got planning to do for tonight," Christopher answered firmly. He tried to hide the worry on his face. If the Holy Spirit was reaching out to him ahead of this mission, what was awaiting them in Ishkashim?

Stone Guard was the nickname of the area on Bagram used by the special operations elements for staging their clandestine missions. The most important part of the supporting cast was the 160th Special Operations Aviation Regiment, commonly known as the Nightstalkers, greeted Christopher upon his entrance as they awaited final guidance.

"Hello, sir. I am CW4 Mercer. I was 'Angel 6,' from the Brazil mission. It's good to be working with you guys again, although I wish it were not so soon."

"Yeah, great to see you again, Chief, and call me Christopher. I agree a few more days or even weeks of rest would have been awesome. Hey, let's get down to planning, so we can wrap this thing up and head home."

"Sure thing, Christopher, but before we start, let me introduce the lead pilot for the second bird for tonight. This is CW3 Watson, radio call sign Angel 64," Angel 6 related quickly.

"Nice to meet you. Guys, this is my team's sergeant major, Jackson Williams," Christopher replied.

"Nice to meet you, fellas. I am hoping for a smooth flight tonight," Jackson responded.

"We will do our best," Angel 6 promised.

As the leaders of the Omega Team and the 160th SOAR sat around a conference table with a large map laid across it to hear the intelligence brief, Christopher was struck with a sense of uneasiness. The Holy Spirit continued speaking into his mind. "*Some trust in chariots, and some in horses: but we will remember the name of the LORD our*

God. Christopher, don't trust in your plan; trust in God. There is always another way."

"Christopher! Earth to Christopher, are you ready for the brief?" Jackson asked, clearly puzzled.

"Oh, yeah, go ahead," Christopher murmured, focusing on the intelligence officer and not the eyes of the men gazing at him from around the room.

"Good morning, gentlemen. Adeel Zardari remains in Ishkashim but will likely be leaving for Khorog, Tajikistan, in the predawn hours, based on recent reports from the Pakistani government. We continue to detect a low-level radiation signature, which we assess means the fissile material remains with Zardari. We also have uncorroborated human intelligence reports that state the local residents of Ishkashim were forced out of town, and Zardari is being protected by at least fifteen armed men. Lastly, for tactical level intelligence, we have reports that some of the men possess Russian Verba man-portable air-defense systems. We consider air insertion the fastest, but a high-risk option. I will be followed by Omega HQ."

Christopher and the other men watched as Gabriella appeared before the group on a secure-video teleconferencing screen.

"Oh, here we go. Miss Sassy Pants herself," Jackson teased.

"Shhh," Christopher mouthed.

"Good morning, everyone. I don't have much more to add to the tactical-level intel. We have seen no movement in or out of Ishkashim since the fleeing of villagers right after Zardari arrived about a day ago. We are providing radiation shielding cases...did they make it?" Gabriella asked the previous intelligence briefer, who acknowledged with a thumbs up. "Those cases will ensure safe transport of the fissile material back to the States, where Department of Energy officials will take possession upon your return.

"Finally, we will notify the Tajiks only if Zardari escapes into Tajikistan with the fissile materials. Dushanbe is in disarray in the wake of the disappearances, with some reports that the Tajikistan president was assassinated. President Rodgers feels that letting the Tajiks know about the mission too early could compromise your team. I agree after hearing about the advanced Russian antiaircraft systems being in the area. It would seem Zardari is well connected. Good hunting," Gabriella concluded as the video screen went black.

"Angel 6, is the risk too great to fly us in tonight?" Christopher questioned.

"It's a risk for sure. Those antiaircraft systems will challenge our avionics. The best hope is to get you guys on the ground before they even know what's happening. That will mean a nap-of-the-earth flight for two straight hours. You guys up for that?"

"So much for a smooth flight, but we're ready to rock and roll," Jackson responded, knowing that the terrain-hugging flight would be rough, but also their best bet for avoiding detection on the way in.

Laughing, Angel 6 spoke again. "We need to finish up some flight planning and get some sleep, so we're going to head out. We'll be ready to take off at 0100 tonight. Let us know if the plan changes."

"Thanks, we will," Christopher replied. "But if you don't hear anything, plan on us loading out for a 0100 takeoff." Christopher watched as Angel 6 and his men left the conference room, still feeling hesitant. The still, quiet voice of the Holy Spirit had reiterated throughout the intelligence briefing the same message. *"Christopher, don't trust in your plan. Trust in God."* He felt trapped. *It's not like it's my plan,* he thought in frustration. *It's what the terrain and mission demand to get the job done. We have to fly in. What other choice do we have?*

"Hey, bossman, I am not going to argue with you like I did in Brazil, but just hear me out. I think flying in is too big of a risk—though the 160th boys would never tell you that. I think if we start ground convoying out of here in the next few hours, we could get up to Ishkashim around 2300, get set, and hit the objective around 0100. Longer haul, but less risk," Jackson asserted with confidence.

"I appreciate the solid recommendation, but there are many unknown risks of driving so far in such a small element. We don't know the IED pattern between here and Ishkashim, and our signature will be known well before we get to Zardari. I like the flying approach for the speed and surprise. Those helicopters will get us through," Christopher replied with a confidence he didn't really feel.

Jackson's faced showed his disagreement, but all he said was, "I hope you're right, bossman. I hope you're right."

"It will be okay. Trust me. I believe in this plan. Gather the guys up here in the conference room. I want to go over the mission and then have everyone start a rest cycle."

"You got it," Jackson said, leaving Christopher alone in the conference room.

The Holy Spirit, who had been all but yelling throughout the intelligence briefing, was now silent.

"Nothing more to say, huh? I don't get you, but I do understand me," Christopher said quietly, openly questioning the Holy Spirit's message.

As Jackson had the Omega Team settle in for the operation plan, Christopher's bravado switched to desperation as thoughts of losing Rev in a mission flashed into his mind. He wished the Holy Spirit would say something to him, but he heard only silence in his mind.

"Okay, guys, pretty straightforward mission," Christopher began. "We will split into two six-man elements on two birds. I will lead the primary assault team and will be flying with Angel 6. Once over the target location in Ishkashim, my team will fast rope down onto the roof, capture Zardari, and secure the loose fissile materials. I don't want to kill this guy, unless he puts us in that position, as he may have hidden the nuclear pits. If he did, we'd need him to lead us to them.

"Jackson will be leading team two and will fly with Angel 64. Your task will be to prevent Zardari from escaping across the border into Tajikistan. I want you to set up an ambush at the international border market on the northwest side of Ishkashim. There are only fifteen men assessed to be guarding this guy, but remember Brazil and be prepared for anything.

"Lastly, men, this could be a tough one, so I want you all to get some rest. Make sure you double up on your combat load of ammo and be ready to fight. We are going into a high-risk area for air defense so it will be a gut-turning nap-of-the-earth flight the whole way. We will have QRF support from the 101st Airborne, but they will delay an hour after our departure tonight and stage Zebak in case we need them."

"How far is Zebak from us?" one of the soldiers asked.

Christopher hesitated to answer, but he could see the question reflected on the face of every Omega Team member. "It is a forty-five-minute flight once we call them." He paused then added, "Okay, let's gear up and do what we do best." The men left the room, conversing among themselves, leaving him alone in the conference room. He was hoping for either some assurance about or condemnation of his plan from the Holy Spirit, but there was again nothing but silence in both the room and his mind.

Gabriella was exhausted both mentally and physically. The last few days were a blur of pain, elation, and more sadness. As she prepared the White House Situation Room with dossiers and executive summaries on the second Omega mission under her leadership, she felt an emptiness she could not comprehend. While Draven Cross's speech was inspiring and plausible, his assertion that religion, and Christianity in particular, was at fault for the disappearances did not sit well with her. Gabriella agreed religion had been divisive at times throughout history, but people like her mother had found so much comfort and hope in Christianity. She felt no closer now to a resolution of the struggle between her analytical perspective on the world around her and the possibility that God existed than she had felt a few days ago.

"Ah, Gabriella, why am I not surprised to find you here first? I sometimes wonder if you sleep. I picture your apartment with a single folding chair under a lightbulb, a refrigerator filled with spoiled Chinese takeout, and an air mattress. I am close, right?" President Rodgers asked with a smile.

"You've got me pegged, sir," Gabriella admitted. "The poster child for overachieving workaholics."

"I am kidding, dear. I appreciate your determination. I assume you watched Cross's speech today."

"Yes, sir, I did. It was rousing but…" she hesitated.

"But it came across as a not-so-veiled attack on religion, or better said, on Christianity. That's what you were going to say, isn't it?"

"No, not exactly what I was going to say. I was going to say his speech leaves me confused about a lot of things, not the least of which is God."

"God is easy to understand, Gabriella, once you allow yourself to see His presence all around you. I could have been the leader of the show-me-and-I-will-believe-it thought brand. It only took two minutes of being briefed on what the world was facing a few days ago for me to realize I just needed to see the world as it was, instead of how I wanted it to be."

Gabriella was glad that the cabinet members and the congressmen began filling the Situation Room. She did not know how to fend off the president's piercing indictments of the conflict between her reasoning and the growing tug to accept the reality that God exists.

"Okay, how close are we to wheels up?" President Rodgers questioned.

"Sir, the Omega Team should be wheels up from Bagram Airfield at any moment. I will put Major Barrett's and Sergeant Major Williams's locator beacons on the display screen here. This will allow us to track them in flight and once they've reached their respective objectives. We will have video from Major Barrett's helmet cam once they're in Ishkashim," Gabriella reported.

"Godspeed to those men. I pray it goes smoothly tonight," President Rodgers remarked, his voice full of emotion.

"I have the same hope, sir," Gabriella agreed.

As Christopher watched Jackson and his team load up on their MH-47G Chinook helicopter, he wanted a message from God to confirm that everything was going to be all right tonight. He was looking for something that would give him the chance to trust. Unfortunately he heard nothing but the howling, cold wind and the *chop* of the Chinook blades in the Afghanistan night.

"Green 6, this is Angel 6, we're clear to depart. Angel 64 has reported his team is loaded and ready," came the digitized voice of Angel 6 into Christopher's headset.

"Angel 6, this is Green 6, let's roll," Christopher said.

It was a cloudy night with snow falling throughout the Panj River valley as the two Chinooks flew perilously close to the valley walls at breakneck speeds. Nap-of-the-earth flights always tested Christopher's nerve for the job and his stomach's ability to stay in its proper location. His hatred for the green look of everything through his night-vision optics was validated again tonight and didn't help the sensations produced in his gut by the ground-hugging flight.

"Ten minutes to target," Angel 6 reported, breaking the long silence that filled the Omega Team's headsets.

"Green 6, this is Green 9. Is it too late for me to tell you I need to use the restroom?" came Jackson's familiar voice.

The soldiers of Omega all laughed, grateful for Jackson's levity in the situation, as the constant banking and maneuvering from the flight induced high levels of stress.

"Green 9, this is Green 6, just know if you poop on yourself, we will never forget it," Christopher returned, laughing loudly into his headset.

"Five minutes," Angel 6 said.

The smile on Christopher's face quickly faded as he saw the bright flash of red against the pitch-black backdrop of the horizon and the streaking red tracer racing toward Jackson and the Omega members aboard Angel 64's bird.

"We've been radar locked, inbound missile," Angel 64 shouted frantically across the radio.

The explosion blinded Christopher temporarily as his night-vision optics reset to protect his eyes from the intense light. He felt the heat of the antimissile flares Angel 6 released to protect their helo from being targeted. He watched helplessly out the opened back ramp of his Chinook as Angel 64 fought to keep his helicopter from hitting the valley below.

"We're hit. This is Angel 64. We are going down. I say again, we are going down." Christopher heard Angel 64 calling out grid coordinates and then a loud crash.

"Go, go, go, get down there," Angel 6 screamed at Christopher as they were now over the target location.

In mere seconds Christopher had fast roped the sixty feet down to the flat earthen rooftop as he looked up to see Angel 6 popping flares and lifting off into the void of the night. He didn't have time to think of what happened to Jackson and the others as shots from the street below began ringing across the rooftop.

"Move," Christopher shouted to the five other men on the roof with him. He switched on the thermal identifier mode on his night-vision optics and called out, "Thermals on," over his radio to ensure everyone was in the proper setting.

As they made their way to the safety of a staircase leading to the main level below, Christopher's augmented-reality eye-protection glasses provided a heads-up display of the radiation levels in the surrounding environment. The last thing they needed was to get overexposed and succumb to radiation poisoning. "Barnes, get the quick reaction force spun up and heading our way," he ordered. "We're going to need them." He was fighting panic with all his might. He told himself over and over again, *Focus on the task at hand. There is nothing you can do for Jackson but finish the mission.*

"The quick reaction force is en route," Barnes reported. "ETA forty-five minutes."

"Okay, form up and let's get this dirtbag for our teammates," Christopher ordered.

As Christopher's team started down the staircase to the main level, two men holding AK-47s appeared as bright silhouettes in his night-vision optics. Christopher's point man called out "two targets down" over the radio as he watched the men fall to the ground. Two questions remained: Where was Zardari? And where were the nuclear materials? Christopher only hoped Zardari had not fled.

Entry to the main floor of the target house was blocked by a thin wooden door, but it seemed to be barricaded by something on the opposite side. Breaching the door was required.

"Breacher up. I want you to blow that door open, and we will clear the room." Christopher directed the soldier who was moving past the stacked-up team on the stairwell toward the door.

"Roger," the breaching soldier acknowledged.

"Two targets street side," came a shout across the radio, followed by two suppressed M4 rifle shots from soldiers stacked along the wall with Christopher.

"Get us inside now!" Christopher shouted.

A loud crack and a flash of white light came from the bottom of the stairwell. Christopher and his team flowed through the expanded doorway like water pouring into a cup. As Christopher entered the room as the last man in the stack, he saw six armed men on the ground, having given their all in defense of Zardari.

"Form up, and let's clear the ground floor," Christopher directed, watching his trained team prepare to make their way down a short set of stairs to an open family room.

The quiet that filled the pitch-black house as Omega moved was broken only by a distant dog's barking somewhere in the village. The family room was empty but had a small alcove across from the staircase. Christopher saw from his integrated thermal optics that the point man had identified a significant heat signature in the nook. Christopher signaled to clear the room, watching three soldiers creep toward the alcove entrance across a sizeable Persian rug.

"Allah!" was the shout of the man who ran out of the alcove. Several well-aimed shots dropped him to the ground before he could take another step or say another word.

"Okay, go white light, check the bodies for Zardari," Christopher ordered. "The centigray levels are higher in this area, but safe for now. So quickly look for some semimetallic-looking spheres, which will likely be the nuclear material." He accessed his comms and, hoping against hope for a reply, shouted, "Green 9, Green 9, do you hear me? Over. Jackson, answer me. Jackson, do you hear me?" The hush over the radio nearly broke Christopher's psyche. Had his trust in his plan cost the lives of good men? He fell against a wall and slid to the floor, exhausted. In the last week, it seemed all he held dear had been stripped from him. Aloud he pleaded, "I need something, God. Please give me something to work with."

"Gabriella, are you seeing any movement from Sergeant Major Jackson's personal locator?" President Rodgers's low-voiced question sounded very loud in the quiet of the White House Situation Room.

"No, sir… I don't think…" Gabriella was overcome with emotion. The thought of losing Jackson and five other members of Omega was too much to comprehend.

The president's fighter pilot training kicked in. "I understand your feelings, but we still have boys in the fight. What about Major Barrett? It seems they are exploiting the target location right now. How's that going? What about the 101st quick reaction force? What is their ETA?" President Rodgers pushed Gabriella to refocus on what could be done. She said grimly, "Sorry, sir. The quick reaction force should be in Ishkashim in fifteen minutes. From the readings I am getting from Christopher's sensors, the nuclear material is somewhere near them. I am picking up some movement with Jackson's locator beacon. I just hope it's not the enemy."

"Okay, let's prepare to get more assets in that area," President Rodgers commanded. "Those boys have likely stirred up the hornet's nest."

Jackson's face stung as he felt the warm flow of blood down his left cheek. It hurt to breathe, but other than a raging headache and likely having a hard time getting out of bed tomorrow, he was okay. He murmured, "Thank you, Jesus. I don't know why You kept me alive, but I am grateful and will honor You." He turned to the semi-crushed fuselage of the Chinook helicopter and shouted, "Hey, anybody still with me?"

"Sarge," was the muffled cry from two other soldiers pinned by a fallen jump seat row.

"Hold on, boys. I'm coming," Jackson replied. As he half stood, he cried out due to the pain in his right side. Broken ribs for sure, but there was nothing he could do about it right now. He crawled over to the pinned-down soldiers and used the end of his rifle as leverage to lift the jump row off their legs. The pain from his efforts almost made him pass out. "You guys all right?" he asked through clenched teeth, his breathing labored.

"I think my left leg is broken," his weapons sergeant replied.

"I feel dizzy, and my back hurts, but I'll make it," replied the other soldier.

"Good news, you're both going to live. Bad news, we need to move away from this crash site and figure out how to get into the fight," Jackson said.

One look toward the cockpit and Jackson knew without a doubt that Angel 64 and his copilot were gone. The right front side of the helicopter was half buried in the earth. Three of his other soldiers were missing from the aircraft, meaning they likely had been thrown from the open ramp during the rotation to the valley floor. It's a miracle Angel 64 was able to gain enough control to pilot the machine into its current position instead of doing a complete nosedive.

"Green 6, this is Green 9, over." Nothing. "Green 6, this is Green 9, over," Jackson repeated into his radio handset. Silence persisted over the radio with every call he made to Christopher. "My comms are acting up.

Well, let's move down to the bottom of this." He pointed to a creek bed below the crash site. "That way, if trouble shows up looking for us, we can at least be hidden and maybe get the jump on them."

As Jackson limped along, helping his "able-bodied" soldier carry their weapons expert with a broken leg, the still, small voice came to him, saying, *"A thousand may fall by your side and ten thousand at your right hand, but it shall not come near you."*

"Thank you, Lord," Jackson responded. "I am grateful."

"What's that, Sarge?" the two soldiers asked in response to Jackson's utterance.

"Nothing, boys. I am just glad we're alive. We're gonna make it. Trust me."

Christopher pulled himself off the ground, knowing Jackson would want him to soldier on. He may have been physically standing, but mentally he was sucking his thumb in the corner, analyzing the actions that led to the disaster tonight. *Why can't I trust God? Why do I associate the pain of my childhood so closely with God? I cost Jackson and those men their lives tonight.* Then in an effort to pull himself back into the current situation, he mentally shouted at himself, *Enough!*

"Hey, I think we've identified Zardari. He was the guy running at us from the little nook. We're searching for the nuke stuff now," Barnes reported.

"Okay, let me know if you get something. Any word on the quick reaction force?" Christopher replied.

"ETA is fifteen minutes."

"Thanks. Let's find those nuclear pits and then head over to the crash site. We should be able to navigate there using the coordinates from Jackson's personal locator. We will have the quick reaction force meet us there and help with recovering the fallen members of our team to take home."

"Sounds good," Barnes said before leaving Christopher to continue the search for the nuclear pits.

Jackson was glad he had decided to move away from the crash site because, like moths drawn to a flame, he watched a "jingle truck" with at least three heat signatures in the back heading their way. He had helped the weapons sergeant put in two claymore mines at the top of the bank that led to their position. If trouble wanted a piece of him tonight, it was going to get all it could handle and then some.

"Okay, guys, we're gonna hunker down and wait," he directed. "If we see people up top, I will pop off the claymores, and you boys light up anything that comes down that hill or gives you a clean shot, got it?"

"Roger, Sarge," the Omega soldiers replied.

Jackson prayed for strength and courage to fight bravely to the end, if necessary, as he heard the truck come to a halt and saw the glow of flashlights and heard men speaking as they searched through the wreckage. He felt a chill as he watched a white light heading for the creek bank and heard voices growing louder. He didn't hesitate to set off the two claymores when he saw two faces staring down at him and his men. The claymores cracked off, followed by brief screams before silence invaded the valley once again.

"Hey, Smith," Jackson told his teammate with two working legs, "let's get up this hill and make sure nothing's waiting for us."

Jackson "ran" up the hill—which someone watching would have said looked more like a duck waddling than a man running—ready to bring justice to anybody waiting for him. What he found was destruction and relief, knowing he and his soldiers were at least temporarily safe. Now he needed to let the rest of Omega know their location and situation. He put out the call again. "Green 6, this is Green 9, over." Christopher was outside of the target house, heading for a chicken coop from where the most energetic radiation signature was emanating, when his radio crackled with a familiar voice.

"Green 6, this is Green 9, over." The weak but undeniable voice of Jackson Williams rang in Christopher's ears, and his knees almost buckled in relief.

"Jackson, I hear you. How are you?" Christopher asked.

"Well, that sucked, and I don't need to go to the bathroom anymore," Jackson responded.

With a grin, the major replied, "Hang tight, you old dog. We're about to pick up the nuke pits then head your way."

"Green 6 or any green element, this is Bandit 6, commander of the quick reaction force, we're five minutes out. Please provide coordinates to the LZ."

"Bandit 6, this is Green 9, coordinates to follow," Jackson responded.

"We're loading the pits into containers now. We'll see you guys soon," Christopher promised.

"Just make sure you leave trouble over there," Jackson commented. "I've had enough for one day."

President Rodgers had long abandoned sitting as he watched the Omega Team once again accomplish the impossible. However, the cost was steep to prevent the spread of nuclear weapons. Two great pilots and three special ops soldiers had paid the ultimate sacrifice in service to their nation and the world tonight—a sacrifice that billions of people would never even know about.

"Gabriella, I'll be at Dover when those men are flown home. I want you to know that the Omega Group has yet again gone above and beyond the call of duty," President Rodgers commended.

"Thanks, sir, I am…it's been a long day, sir. I'm heading to my apartment—or the place that holds my air mattress, according to you—to get some sleep," Gabriella said.

"Well earned, and again, great job," President Rodgers replied.

Gabriella left the White House in the soft glow of a late fall sunset, knowing that her team was well into the early hours of the next day and on their way home. While she was glad that Jackson had survived and the loose nuclear material had been recovered, she realized that the chaos of the last few days seemed to be the new normal. She wrestled with herself, thinking that perhaps her suffering was at her own hands, arrogance in her own intelligence, missing the fact that God never wanted her to go through any of this. She found herself wishing desperately for some tangible evidence that God was real, that the new world around her was part of some plan.

Chapter 8

As Satan observed the nations of the world from a favorite vantage point, he contemplated the news he'd received a few days ago—a message he had feared for millennia. The final countdown to his demise had begun, with God rapturing His beloved Church. Satan awaited a report from his longtime lieutenant Strife. "Is He ready? It seems God has finally made His move," Satan asked.

"Yes, my lord, He is ready, and we are ready," Strife responded bitterly.

"Then we shall make God's precious Earth and humanity suffer. We will make the next seven years with my chosen leaders the worst the world has ever witnessed. Leave me," Satan commanded grimly.

As Strife left his master to prepare the "appointed leader," he thought back in his mind to the circumstances that led to his master and all his followers being bound to the cursed Earth. He could still vividly picture the moment from time immemorial when his master's loathing for humanity was born.

Strife remembered a time and place before he was Strife, when his name was Harmony…

Lucifer was standing on a luminous gold-and-ivory balcony, watching over an angelic chorus preparing for the celebration commemorating God's completion of His masterpiece, Earth. He looked across Heaven feeling a tremendous sense of accomplishment. Lucifer, as the chief of praise and worship to God, orchestrated continuous music illuminating the glory of God, but he also had power over the air and heavens, providing celestial displays that demonstrated the anointed cherub's creative gifts.

Harmony remembered, however, that Lucifer had begun to sense that his handiwork as a creator wasn't fully appreciated and wondered why there was such fuss over the creation of yet another planet, one so small in comparison to many found in the vast cosmos. As Lucifer's deputy and a leader among Heaven's innumerable angelic host, he was the fateful messenger who delivered the pronouncement that would spark his boss's war on humanity.

The deputy's words had come fast, resonant with both excitement and uncertainty.

"Harmony, what is it, old friend?" Lucifer questioned.

Harmony had exclaimed that he knew why the celebration over Earth was demanding such extravagance.

"Well!" Lucifer said in a harsh tone. "I am sorry, Harmony, but there is much to do before the grand finale of the Earth celebration."

"Earth was created to house God's greatest creation, called *man*."

"Man? What is *man*?" Lucifer asked suspiciously.

"God created *man*, male and female, in His image and only a little lower than the angels. *Man* is designed to praise God and bring glory to Him. *Man* will have a unique relationship with God, to be His children."

Harmony's next question was an attempt to end the awkward silence on the balcony overlooking the golden court, where the chorus of angels now sang, "Glory to God in the Highest." How could he have known the eternal ramifications of what would follow? He asked, "What is our role now with *man* worshipping God?"

Lucifer was in such a state of shock that he heard little of what Harmony had said after the disclosure of *man*'s purpose, his face puckered in thought and heat flushed over him. He spat out, "The thought of this thing called *man* being created to replace me as the center of praise and worship in the universe is a slight too far. I will not be taken for granted, and God will answer for this disgrace!"

Harmony noticed the change first, as Lucifer's heart was filling with pride. "Lucifer! Your countenance is falling." Lucifer had been deaf to Harmony's words, murmuring and becoming more consumed with each passing moment with how much he had done for God—how he had arranged and created so much glory. Harmony remembered the devastating effects he witnessed as Lucifer's heart was overtaken by pride, displacing the Holy Spirit from his being and changing his visage. Lucifer, overcome with anger and pride, glanced at his hands and finally heard Harmony, who was now trembling as he shouted, "Lucifer, you're changing!"

Lucifer, seeing his once bright body now void of the ever-present light of God's Spirit, screamed with such ferocity that the choir below paused momentarily. He had turned to Harmony, demanding, "Are you with me or against me? God is not worthy of our praise. Worship me, Harmony, and we will rule the Heavens and Earth. I, Lucifer, am fit to be your Lord as I am an equal creator with God and will place my throne above the Highest."

Harmony thought back to the terror that had filled him as the beauty and majesty that had defined his beloved leader and friend became displaced by a sense of emptiness and distance that he had never experienced. Lucifer seemed to be out of the presence of God. Harmony knew what Lucifer suggested was wrong, but he felt Lucifer was justified in being angered by God's creation of man. Harmony knew better than most all Lucifer had created and done to praise God. He remembered feeling every fiber of his being resisting his movement as he dropped slowly to his knees in front of the seething Lucifer and bowed his head. And he promised, "I swear my allegiance to you, my lord."

In the same instant, Harmony felt disdain for the ever presence of God that occupied Heaven. Lucifer didn't even acknowledge Harmony's act, only commanding his first follower to convert as many of the angels as he could to their cause.

"Move quickly, as time is against us," Lucifer ordered.

As Harmony raced through Heaven, recruiting whom he could, Lucifer advanced toward the Great Throne of God. Michael, the archangel of Heaven's army, stopped Lucifer's advance.

"Lucifer, end this rebellion and repent of your sin against God," Michael emphatically implored the anointed cherub.

"You're a fool, Michael, always at the beck and call of your Master. You have free will but act like a slave. Bow to me now, and I will find a place for you in my kingdom," Lucifer promised.

Harmony remembered watching Michael give up on reasoning with Lucifer, knowing that his heart was given over to his rebellious actions. The archangel prepared the army of Heaven for battle, drawing flaming swords. Harmony stood behind Lucifer with a vast army of angels arrayed in the outer courts of the Temple of Heaven against Michael and the faithful of God.

"Heaven and the universe are ours to take," Lucifer had declared to his forces, which drew flaming swords to begin the assault on the Throne of God.

The battle that raged between once-united servants of God for mere seconds ended with an authoritative voice. The Son of God, the commander of Heaven's armies, spoke and all of Heaven ceased moving.

Lucifer, Harmony, and the angels who followed them fell to their faces, still blaspheming the names of God even while overcome by the power of the God of the Universe. God removed the titles and privileges associated with the names of Lucifer and his angels. Lucifer was given a new name—Satan, or adversary—forever to be known as an enemy of God. Harmony was renamed Strife for his actions in the brief War of Heaven. Each angel who aligned with Satan faced direct judgment from God the Father, doomed to ultimately suffer eternal punishment and separation from His presence in a dreadful dominion called Hell.

Michael and his angels gathered Satan and his followers and cast them to the Earth. Harmony remembered that as his new lord fell to the Earth like lightning, Satan swore that his forever purpose would be corrupting the Earth and separating God from His most loved creation, man.

Strife shuddered with renewed anger against humanity as he recalled his disgraceful fall. As he prepared the son of perdition, nothing was left to do but bring as many humans with them to Hell as possible in the short time remaining.

As the disappearance of millions occurred, Draven Cross was awakened by what seemed like a shout saying, "It's time." It was then that he heard the sirens and turmoil rising up to his third-story home in Knightsbridge, London. He reached for the phone, which dialed his executive assistant Gemma Sutherland, and said, "Tell me what is happening."

"Sir, it seems that some sort of global catastrophe has occurred. Millions are being reported missing around the world."

"Fine. When will the other world leaders make announcements?"

"Sir, no one has announced anything. The crisis is still so raw. I don't know of any plans for anyone to speak publicly yet."

"You are worthless, aren't you? How can you not know? I pay you plenty to *know* in matters like this. Make the world aware that I will speak on this matter in two days, and ensure I am the only world leader speaking that day."

"Yes, sir, I will make—" But Gemma spoke only to a dial tone.

Draven felt strangely invigorated by the news of millions disappearing. Instead of being shocked, he was only eager for the chance to speak to the world—it seemed as if he was destined for this very moment. He knew sleep was gone, so he woke up his senior EU cabinet members to strategize ways to maximize the crisis to his advantage. The ideas for leading the world seemed to be pouring into his mind faster than he could write them down, and he did not want to waste this opportunity sleeping.

A few days later, as the Omega Team was preparing to stop a nuclear weapons proliferator half a world away, Gemma found herself yet again on the short side of Draven's temper just moments before he took the world stage at the famed Westminster Hall. If it had been any other person, she would have said the nerves of the moment had gotten the best of him, but with Draven pettiness was a sport.

"Gemma, I dare ask the question only to hear your ridiculous answer. Why would you pick a navy suit for today's announcement? The world is waiting for 'the' answer and way forward after the loss of millions, and you want me to look like I am announcing the latest worthless smartphone. Just get out of my sight."

"Sorry, sir," Gemma replied in a subdued tone. Her mind drifted as she watched the six-foot-three-inch tall Draven Cross, in a black suit, stride confidently toward a lectern in the famed Westminster Hall. The duality of his personality never ceased to amaze her. It often caught her by surprise that a man so loved for his business savvy, charitable efforts, and love of peace was also such a cruel and detestable person. His split personality was an enigma. She knew the world would be clamoring for him after this morning's speech. He had told her as much. She just feared what Draven might do once he had the world under his control.

Gemma was unimpressed by the wild applause for Draven. She had witnessed this show hundreds of times. The response the tailored and undeniably handsome man drew was always the same. He made every piece of clothing look like it was cut to fit his youthful frame. At forty, his sun-kissed skin and chiseled face complemented by perfect jet-black hair radiated sex appeal and vigor. Gemma never liked talking to him face-to-face for long because of the mesmerizing effect of his emerald green eyes, and the control they exerted extended to everyone, not just her.

Draven allowed the roaring ovation to die down before he began to speak, feigning that he was overcome by the welcome. He had been told last night in a vivid dream by his spirit guide, the "Prince of This World," as the guide referred to himself, that he would provide Draven the words for this speech. This Prince had long promised Draven riches and fame if he only worshipped him above all others. All that remained for Draven to acquire was control of the world itself, which this Prince also promised.

The fanfare that the elite of British politics provided struck Draven as odd, considering he was the leader of a political organization from which the United Kingdom had chosen to distance itself years ago. However, he had long ago realized the power within himself to captivate men and women alike. He could manipulate people to get what he wanted, which allowed him to build his wealth and political influence to levels that provided him opportunities like today.

"Good morning to this august group of ladies and gentlemen. I was honored by your invitation to speak not only on behalf of the EU but also as an ambassador for all of humanity. The tragedy we all experienced days ago will live with us for years to come. I have been personally tormented the last few days by hearing stories from around the globe of the millions who are longing for their missing loved ones.

"In my own sphere, my dearly loved long-time assistant lost her entire immediate family in the disappearances. Like you, I have heard the countless theories about where our loved ones have gone and what has caused this unprecedented event in human history to occur. While I believe that many brilliant minds greater than mine..." Draven savored the outburst of laughter that remark caused before he continued. "These great minds have established a few theories that are plausible.

"I will expand today on what I believe is the best explanation and touch on the cause for why only select individuals were taken. Today marks the start of a journey that will allow us to overcome challenges of the past for a better future.

"The EU took a hard look at the disappearances from a scientific standpoint. We believe a physical explanation must exist for millions of people dematerializing without a trace. The best scientific answer we were able to formulate was...we don't know what happened."

A burst of almost nervous laughter erupted once again, but Draven continued his speech.

"The lack of a scientific answer forced my team of top scientists and advisors to search beyond the tangible. It was in this expanded search that we discovered we are not alone. The theory of alien visitation causing millions to vanish is, in my humble estimation, the most plausible answer.

"While alien visitation to Earth has been reported throughout history and increasingly in the last century by nations around the world—even the esteemed United States Department of Defense released files detailing unexplained encounters—this event almost a week ago was the first indisputable proof of a force beyond our world. At the time the disappearances were reported, the EU space consortium detected an overwhelming ray of light emanating from deep space and enveloping Earth, leading us to the conclusion that the vanishings have alien origins.

"Now, before you run me out of this revered hall, understand that I am not saying little green men stole our friends, coworkers, and loved ones." He paused as laughter erupted again. "No, I believe this is an alien-like power, or better said, a greater power that lies outside our boundaries of time and space.

"Now to answer the deeper meaning of this tragedy as I see it, I view religion as the greatest enemy of peace, and peace was the catalyst for this removal of millions from our world. Yes, I know this may seem to be a harsh statement in such a tragic time. I want to say for the record that I see nothing wrong with people finding balance, harmony, or self-guidance for growth through a spiritual medium that may come in the form of religion. Religious expression by an individual is a universal right of all humanity. However, when one religion espouses that it is the only way to spiritual enlightenment and mandates the private lifestyles of individuals are wrong, history illuminates the sorrow religion has brought the world in such cases.

"Religions like Christianity predicate judgment of others and have critically labeled science as wicked where it proves their beliefs wrong, and individuals outside of its dogma as 'sinners.' Humanity has been plagued by warfare and ethnic genocides and denied scientific advancement all in the name of human-created gods. Unified humanity working in peaceful harmony has more ability to produce greatness in this world than all of the well-meaning, but human-derived, religions could ever dream of having.

"It is humanity, not a distant and arbitrary God, that has solved the challenges the universe has presented. We evolved to be the dominant species on this planet because all of us, not just the religious elect, are endowed with divine greatness, intellect, and beauty that are without comparison to a fabricated God. Throughout history, it has been repeatedly demonstrated that God was either willfully neglectful or, more accurately stated, unable to help us due to the fact that he doesn't exist.

"I believe we have been given a glimpse in the last few days of a power superior to humanity—spiritual in the sense that this power is beyond our comprehension, but more real than any imaginary God from human-created religion. I speak of what I view as the real Power of This World that helped humanity evolve and discover many of our greatest scientific and philosophical advances throughout our long existence.

"The achievements of antiquity, like the Great Pyramid, that defy our understanding in how they were contemplated and then built provide evidence of this supreme power that has been watching our world from the shadows of time. This entity, for reasons we have yet to fully comprehend, decided mere days ago to reappear to the modern world and remove persons deemed to be currently under the delusion of religion as well as those who would one day fall under that spell—and this Revelation was provided to me by the real power of this world in such vivid clarity that I almost dared not share the message with the world. To be honest, I feared being perceived as mentally ill."

Laughter rose once again, but Draven proceeded.

"Humanity has missed the mark before, failing to appreciate all the peace this power had to offer. Instead we yielded to the feeble trappings of human-derived religion. Every great civilization and generation before us have all missed the message of peace that our benevolent hidden friend from beyond our universe has presented. However, I have humbly received this message from our peace-loving friend, as an ambassador for all of humanity.

"Peace is the only way for humanity to exist. Peace is the only way for us to evolve beyond the pettiness of ethnic and nationalist divisions. Peace has always been at war with humanity's insistence on religion setting the moral compass in our society. Yet time and time again, religious leaders used their power to manipulate and use the masses for their own selfish desires, even to the point of starting wars. It was religion and the division that religion creates in a society that ultimately led to the demise of many of our greatest civilizations.

"We have the opportunity ahead of us to change the course of humanity. I sincerely believe that this great and powerful force could no longer sit idle as humanity struggled with the division's religion created. I offer that we put religion, the desire of producing weapons of war, and ethnic and nationalist hatreds behind us once and for all. I urge us, the leaders and people of the world, to lead from this tragedy with the mind-set of seeking *peace* above all other political objectives. We have the ability and power within us to rule this world with unity and in one accord. Thank you for your time, and may *peace* reign on Earth."

Gemma watched as Westminster Hall erupted in thunderous applause. Reporters and TV cameramen rushed the lectern to get the perfect picture of the man of the hour. It was sickening to watch Draven humbly bowing while knowing he was pridefully relishing the swooning of the world leaders in response to his appeal for unity and peace. She didn't want to answer her phone, which was ringing nonstop with calls from celebrities and political leaders around the globe, nor did she want to see the social media sites alight with praise for Draven Cross. As she watched him appear to wipe what she knew to be nonexistent tears from his eyes—solely for the benefit of the cameras—as he left Westminster Hall, bile rose to her lips.

"Gemma, I expect the world will be calling any moment. Ensure you're ready," Draven ordered as he walked past her.

Christopher was grateful that securing the stolen nuclear materials had turned out as well as it had, considering that he had watched Jackson's helicopter crash and also lost three of his men as a result. Thinking over the last few weeks and in particular the latest mission, his experiences were starting to resonate as he began paying attention to the mounting evidence of God's pursuit of him.

While the gap between Christopher's pain and God's relentless efforts to reach him were closing, he knew the filler was trusting everyone outside himself, including God. He regretted that he had not listened to the Holy Spirit or Jackson before the mission. He sensed that if he had trusted God, perhaps things would have turned out differently.

After spending the first night in his new corporate apartment, Christopher sipped a soothing cup of coffee while watching the sun from his sixth-floor apartment balcony in Crystal City. Gratitude filled his heart. He was awed by the place the Executive Support Office had found for him, despite being extremely short-staffed. Christopher's new home was a nice pick-me-up, which Gabriella likely had a hand in setting up after a hectic week.

"Hey, man, thanks for letting me stay here in your new apartment," Jackson said as he slid into a recliner next to Christopher on the balcony.

"Good morning, and it's no problem. I couldn't let you keep living in that hotel. Plus I didn't want to live alone."

"You afraid of the dark?" Jackson joked.

"Yep, and now I'll have to kill you because you know my secret," the major responded with a laugh. Then his face became serious. "Actually, I just feel like you can help me get through the days ahead," he added soberly, pouring Jackson a cup of coffee from a stainless steel carafe.

"Thanks for the confidence that I'll be helping you, but I think we will be helping each other. The road ahead of us is long and treacherous, I'm afraid," Jackson asserted grimly, standing to look out from the balcony. "I slept last night, but it sure doesn't seem like it. I feel like somebody put me in a sack with a bunch of cats and rolled me down a hill. I think the only thing that helped me get a few hours of rest was the pain meds for my cracked ribs."

"Cats and sacks and a hill…that sounds painful," Christopher said with a smiling grimace. "I was wondering how you slept last night—now I know. But even if you're in pain, I'm just glad you're here, man. I thought I had lost you…"

"Christopher, I would be lying if I said I didn't think I was a dead man when that chopper started down. Yet here I am, bruised but alive. I remember waking up inside the bird, and after getting my bearings, just thanking God because, for the first time ever in my life, I realized that every day, every moment is a precious gift God gives us to use for either good or bad. I walked out of that crash site committed to honoring God with this new life I've been given."

Christopher had to admit to himself that he was impressed with the passion and determination Jackson had put into seeking God's direction and purpose for his life since his recent conversion. However, the light that God was shining into Jackson's world also made Christopher's war with God even more pronounced. He got up and went to start breakfast in an attempt to avoid the topic of God. "You hungry? Seems like Gabriella had the support office fully stock this place for us."

"I don't have much of an appetite right now, but thanks," Jackson replied, moving to a plush sofa and turning on the sixty-five-inch flat-screen television that dominated the modest-sized living room. "Look at this guy! He's a piece of work. He's very well put together, but I am telling you, Christopher, this guy is the Antichrist," he said confidently as he watched a rerun of the televised remarks from Draven Cross regarding the disappearances.

"He's a politician. That's what they all look like in these moments. What did you expect, for him to give the speech from a couch wearing a flannel shirt and some tactical pants while sipping a beer?" Christopher called back as he fried bacon and cracked eggs into a bowl in the kitchen.

Laughing, Jackson answered, "Well, if he had done that, I would have said he was a good ole Southern boy like me and not the devil."

Christopher rejoined Jackson in the living room to watch Draven Cross's speech, carrying a plate of hot bacon and eggs.

"So where's my plate?" Jackson asked.

"You said you weren't hungry," Christopher shot back.

"I assumed you would make my plate anyway. You know, for later," Jackson teased.

"You're ridiculous, and the kitchen is over there, by the way. I agree we should keep an eye on this guy. He is really pushing peace as the panacea for all the world's troubles," Christopher remarked thoughtfully.

"*Panacea*…I am going to take these big words as disrespectful. Now what on earth is a *panacea*?" Jackson asked with an exaggeratedly quizzical look on his face.

Christopher, choking on his coffee, replied with a smile. "You gotta stop. I almost choked to death. It means a cure-all, you country bumpkin."

"Well, college boy, just say that next time," Jackson said with a roll of his eyes.

Still smiling, Christopher made an abrupt shift. "Not to change the subject, but what should we do about John Barnes? I know he did well on the last mission, but between what happened in Brazil and his temperament, he just doesn't seem like a good fit for Omega."

"I think he should be sent packing," Jackson said very seriously. "The guy is trouble, Christopher."

"So what's the story? Why such strong negative feelings about this guy?"

Jackson got up from the sofa, muted the television, and moved into the kitchen to start making his own breakfast. He attempted to collect his thoughts on the problem named John Barnes before he spoke. "It was about eight years ago in Afghanistan where I saw the real nature of John Barnes," he finally began. "We were a part of the same task force, just different teams. We were running a combined op to capture a high-value target who had been ghosting both groups. My team catches the guy, but we allowed Barnes and his men to do the interrogation.

"An hour or so later, one of my guys runs up to me and says he heard gunshots and now the target is dead. But that's not the worst of the story. Barnes had apparently lined up the man's family and shot them one by one until the man told us what we needed to know, then he shot the man, too. I tried to get him investigated, but it turned into his people saw one thing, and my guys saw something else. John Barnes is a killer and has no moral compass."

"Wow, that's a lot to comprehend. I still don't know why he shot that guard in Brazil. I'm not sure if the guy even saw us."

"That's what I am telling you. Barnes is a nut job. He got into special operations thinking it was some sort of video game. He has zero internal conflict with killing someone, which is an indication of his dangerous mental state."

"I'll speak with Gabriella to discuss reassignment options for Barnes, but in the meantime, you need to keep your composure when you're near him," Christopher instructed. "Speaking of trouble…" He winced as he picked up his ringing cell phone. "Hello," he answered while mouthing to Jackson that it was Gabriella. "Yeah, he's here with me. We're roomies now," he said with a laugh. "Thanks for setting up this apartment. I figured you had a hand in me landing this place. Really? Okay, we'll be there. Bye." He hung up the phone.

"What's up? And by *what's up*, I mean I don't want to hear about another mission or problem somewhere in the world. I only want to hear you say that Gabriella just called to see how old Jackson is doing today," Jackson teased.

"It seems that we are going to get a good glimpse of Mr. Draven Cross. His first stop on his world domination tour—"

"That's not funny," Jackson interrupted.

"Anyway, he plans to meet with President Rodgers and speak at the United Nations. Omega has been offered up to beef up his security detail.

We have to meet Gabriella at the Pentagon in a few hours," Christopher explained.

"Man, are you serious? Forget surviving until Jesus returns in seven years. You guys are gonna kill me before next week."

"You're so dramatic, Jackson, old man. I swear you should've been an actor. I mean, you have to be the luckiest person on the planet. This is the perfect time to roll into an easy mission like guarding a politician. Plus it gives you the chance to figure out if this guy is the 'Antichrist,' as you described him."

"I consider myself blessed, not lucky. Secondly and almost as important, am I going to have to wear a suit and tie?" Jackson questioned in an aggrieved tone.

"Yep, no flannel or beer when working with dignitaries. I got you covered. I know a place on the way to the Pentagon where we can pick up a suit for you. I just hope the guy is still in business—or more accurately, still there."

CHAPTER 9

Gemma was right to dread the post-Draven speech media blitz. Her phone had not stopped ringing since the moment Draven concluded his remarks. She was surprised, though, that the first leader seeking an audience with Draven was the president of the United States. Draven expected the U.S. president to be a significant obstacle to his political goals, but after hearing the VIP treatment President Rodgers had in store for him, Gemma remembered Draven saying, "I guess the world is mine." The first stop on the "coronation tour," as Gemma called Draven's series of meetings and engagements with world leaders and influencers after his speech, was the United Nations.

Draven was pleased to see a media frenzy as he disembarked through the international terminal of JFK International Airport in New York, ahead of his U.N. speech. A mere twenty-four hours before, he had been preparing to give what he saw as the speech of his life. Now he was poised to take the world as his own.

"Gemma, you have done unexpectedly well. I can feel the world's anticipation of my next move," Cross said, the compliment a rarity.

"Thank you, sir."

Stopping suddenly, the EU president demanded, "Where is my security detail?"

"Sir, we have our usual four men from the EU tonight, but President Rodgers has offered up an elite U.S. military unit to augment our security personnel during your visit to America. He is also sending *Air Force One* to pick you up after your speech at the U.N. in the morning."

"I am almost impressed by the hospitality, but Rodgers is no fool," Draven responded cynically. "He is likely hedging his bets—trying to use my political stardom to ensure himself a second term. No matter. I will accept his flattery, nonetheless." The disappearances forced Draven's NYPD escorts to negotiate a path to his Upper Eastside luxury hotel through abandoned and wrecked cars as well as looted, fire-ravaged buildings in the borough of Queens. Draven felt a tug in his mind, oblivious to the suffering around him. The shifting of his typically razor-sharp mental focus to thoughts beyond himself usually meant his spirit guide was close. Draven had learned over the years that a sudden loss of concentration often indicated the Prince of This World would soon speak into his mind regarding some pressing matter.

"Remember, the promise of peace is the key to the hearts of humanity. Tomorrow I will give you the world," the Prince promised.

"Finally, my talents and genius are rewarded," Draven said aloud, obviously excited.

"I am sorry, sir, what do you mean?" Gemma asked, confused.

"Nothing you would understand. Just ensure you've prepared a time for me to address the press after my speech. The world will want to hear from its leader," Draven ordered with satisfaction.

Gemma trembled at the thought of Draven ruling the world. Not for the first time, she thought perhaps her family had been right about Draven, that he represented something wicked.

Christopher and Jackson enjoyed the walk to the Crystal City Metro Station the next morning in the bracing fall air, chatting as if nothing in the world had really changed. However, Christopher's well-honed attention to detail did notice the absence of traffic and fewer people than usual moving about for a Monday morning in Crystal City. The harsh reality of the new world in which the two men found themselves living stared Christopher and Jackson in the face as they waited for the blue line metro train to arrive.

The metro department had installed a portable ten-foot wall down the entire length of the train platform. The wall had integrated sensor doors at intervals that aligned with the train doors, but those doors remained closed until the train arrived in order to prevent suicides. Signage every five feet or so urged, wait! don't jump. call for help.

"What a depressing world we now live in, my friend," Jackson remarked sadly.

"Yeah, I am afraid of what's to come," Christopher replied.

"I try not to think about what's next, what we're facing." Jackson pointed to the wall. "That's like something out of a nightmare."

The two men boarded through the automatic platform doors a few moments later and arrived at their next stop, the Pentagon City Mall, a little less chipper than when they had left the apartment that morning.

"I thought you said you were taking me to a tailor or something. This is a mall," Jackson accused.

"Patience, grasshopper. There is a method to my madness," Christopher responded, trying to inject a little humor after the depressing metro ride.

Jackson followed Christopher into the men's section of a larger department store, questioning the plan he was following all the way.

"Here, go try this on. What size shoes do you wear?"

"Size ten in sneakers, and where do you want me to change clothes, right here?"

"Sir, may I help you?" queried a female sales associate as she approached the two men.

"Sure, where can I change into this suit without being charged with a misdemeanor for public indecency?" Jackson asked sardonically.

"Follow me, sir," the young woman responded.

Christopher watched as Jackson followed the woman like a sulking boy following his mom on a school shopping trip.

A few moments later, an obviously uncomfortable Jackson emerged to stand in front of Christopher."Would you like me to do a turn, so you get the whole picture?" Jackson quipped.

"Nope, I can already see from just this point of view that we have a long way to go," Christopher responded in kind.

"Oh, now you're a funny man. Can we go? These clothes make me feel funny," Jackson whined.

"Yep. Our next stop is Mr. Lee. He is the method behind my madness."

As the sales associate placed Jackson's new suit in a garment bag, Jackson began to laugh and said, "I've got new church clothes, but no church to attend. That's ironic, don't you think, Christopher?"

"Well, a suit can be multipurpose, but I see the irony. Let's go so we're not late meeting Gabriella." Christopher led Jackson out of the mall and into a luxury hotel not far away. As the two men made their way across the marble-floored, crystal-chandeliered lobby, Christopher was heading toward a small tailor shop with a simple sign above the entrance that read, lee's suits.

"Hello, Mr. Lee, are you here?" Christopher called as he entered the tailor shop with Jackson.

"Yes, yes, I am here. Oh, Major Barrett, it's you. I am so glad to see you. Wait one second."

Christopher and Jackson watched as the older man turned the sign on his door from open to closed.

"Special customer deserve all my time. Please sit, sit…" Mr. Lee directed Jackson and Christopher to two small chairs in front of rows of varying patterns of cloth. "So how can I help you today, Major?" Mr. Lee asked.

"Mr. Lee, I brought a good friend to see you. He has an off-the-rack suit that needs your magic touch. Do you think you can help him out?"

"You military?" Mr. Lee asked, pointing to Jackson.

"Yes, sir, I am," Jackson replied.

"Come, follow me," Mr. Lee said, grabbing Jackson's arm and leading him to a grainy old photo on the wall behind the register. "You see?

Min-jun Lee was a warrior like you. I fought against the communist in Korea." The old man beamed with pride.

"It's an honor to meet you, sir," Jackson responded warmly.

"You know a custom suit is better than buying one in the mall." Mr. Lee made this statement as though anyone should certainly know it to be true.

"Well, you see…" Jackson flushed, embarrassed by his apparent fashion *faux pas*.

"It's okay, Mr. Lee. He's a hardworking man. He usually doesn't need a high-quality suit," Christopher explained, winking at Jackson.

As Mr. Lee grabbed the suit from Jackson and pointed him toward the changing room, Christopher noticed that the man was not his typical jovial self. Hoping to bring a smile to his face, he inquired, "Mr. Lee, where's Mrs. Lee and her famous tea cookies?"

"She gone. Disappear with the others," Mr. Lee replied somberly as Jackson emerged and stepped up on the tailoring block.

"I'm so very sorry, Mr. Lee. You doing all right? You need anything?" Christopher asked.

"I'm fine. Do you know why Mrs. Lee leave me here? I went to church, too, you know. Why am I here?" the man asked Christopher, his genuine confusion evident on his face and in his voice.

"I don't know, sir. I wish I could explain why you were left," Christopher told the puzzled man. He sat in silence as Mr. Lee applied his expertise to Jackson's run-of-the-mill suit and made it look like the man had been born in it.

"I am done. What do you think?" Mr. Lee asked Jackson.

"I think I look sharper than my mother-in-law's tongue," Jackson replied, laughing.

"Major, what does this mean?" Mr. Lee questioned a bit suspiciously.

"Sir, it just means that Jackson likes your handiwork. We have to go, but how much do I owe you today?"

"No charge, my friend, no charge. I am just glad to see you're still here…" The man paused, obviously not finished speaking. "Major…I lie. I know why I was left. I didn't really love Jesus, never knew Him. I just like to socialize at church. It looked good, you know," Mr. Lee confessed as the tears ran down his wrinkled cheeks.

"I am sorry, Mr. Lee, but I do believe what many people say. God is a God of second chances. Just pray for help. I know God will not let you down if you're really trying to find Him."

"Thank you, Major, and take care, Mr. Jackson. When you want a real warrior's suit, you come see me, okay?" Mr. Lee encouraged.

"Yes, sir, I will, and thank you again for your help," Jackson replied.

As the two men left the shop, Christopher looked back, wishing he could have said or done something for Min-jun Lee. He was a good man who was searching, like a lot of people, for answers as to what had just happened.

"Hey, let's just walk over to the Pentagon. I don't want to see that wall down in the metro ever again," Jackson asserted firmly.

"Sure. Let's get moving. We don't want to keep the boss waiting."

Christopher and Jackson entered Gabriella's office and stood in front of her desk like two schoolboys called to the principal's office while she finished typing on her computer.

"What took you guys so long? You just live in Crystal City," Gabriella questioned.

"Christopher was getting me fixed up with some new clothes for this next thing you've signed our names to," Jackson answered.

"Ahh, that's sweet of Chris to help you expand your wardrobe beyond the outdoor recreation look," Gabriella said teasingly.

Laughing, Jackson responded, "Yeah, I guess flannel and tactical pants don't fit in with every crowd."

Gabriella chuckled as she threw a set of bath towels at Christopher and Jackson. "Here you go, guys. I didn't know what else to get you for a housewarming gift."

"Oh, you're a funny little thing there, Gabby," Jackson responded.

"*Little thing* and *Gabby*? You'd better watch yourself, Jackson. I am not afraid to smack you even in your fragile condition," Gabriella warned as she rose behind her desk.

Jackson howled with laughter. "I bet you could take a gator's dinner."

"Wow, are you two through acting like a dysfunctional set of siblings?" Christopher asked.

"Excuse me, *Major* Barrett. I am sorry to take some of your precious time with humor. What's got you in such a bad mood today?" Gabriella asked.

"Nothing. Could you just tell me about my assignment babysitting the savior of the world?" Christopher questioned, his disdain for the task evident in his tone.

"I told you—" Jackson began.

"Savior of the world… I am guessing you mean Draven Cross. So you're not a fan of his explanation for the disappearances, I take it, Chris?" Gabriella questioned, interrupting Jackson.

"I am still evaluating all possibilities, unlike Jackson or you. This guy is not even a head of state yet, and he's commanding this type of attention. My gut says that cannot be good considering the rapture just occurred," Christopher explained.

"The rapture! You must be joking, Chris. Mr. Cross presented scientific evidence that we are not alone in the universe, that an alien force took religious fanatics out of our world. I have some reservations about that part of his analysis, but his argument makes sense to me," Gabriella defended, moving in front of her desk to face Christopher.

"What I have is a growing belief, my friend. Keep in mind that my refusal to believe in the rapture before this event has cost me much."

"Hey, um, I can leave you two alone, if you want?" Jackson offered. "Seems you've got some stuff to work out."

"Real funny, Jackson," replied Christopher. "I just have one more thing to say. Just a few days ago, we saw millions of people disappear simultaneously. And now I am just supposed to believe the word of some rich guy that aliens popped up from nowhere because religion has been stopping humanity from achieving universal peace? I am more inclined each day to admit the truth of the Bible, as hard as that is for me. The Bible speaks of a man who would appear during a time like this promising peace, but who would actually be far from peaceful. I am not saying Draven Cross is the Antichrist, but I am not buying into him yet, either." He then slammed himself back into his chair.

Gabriella leaned forward to look Christopher right in the eyes. "Fair enough. I've also heard all the Sunday school stories regarding the end of the world. I believe in science, and the solutions science produces. I will evaluate Mr. Cross and come to my own conclusions. Now that we are all fired up, your mission is a simple one. You will fly out of Andrews Air Base tonight on *Air Force One* and integrate within Mr. Cross's security detail. Your point of contact is Gemma Sutherland, Mr. Cross's executive assistant. Any questions?"

"Yeah, one. Why *Air Force One*?" Jackson queried.

"President Rodgers is extending America's hospitality to the man that has captivated the world," Gabriella answered.

"Well, that's kind of like a man allowing another man to take his wife on a date, just because the other fella's wife is less attractive," Jackson retorted.

Christopher rolled his eyes, saying, "I'll take the Southern Aristotle here and get the team ready."

"What? Does that not make sense to y'all?" Jackson asked, clearly dumbfounded.

"No!" Christopher and Gabriella shouted in unison.

Gabriella added, "In any case, I will follow up with you two after, Mr. Cross' White House visit tomorrow afternoon. Just make sure you keep him safe." She addressed her final remark to Christopher. "And don't let Jackson talk to him."

"Heeeeey," Jackson protested.

"No promises," Christopher said over his shoulder as he exited the room with Jackson.

As the major and the sergeant major stood in the vast, bustling U.N. building lobby, Jackson was pensive as they waited to link up with Gemma Sutherland.

"You feeling okay, man?" Christopher asked.

"I'll make it, thanks to the wrap around my ribs and some strong painkillers in my system. By the way, how do I look?" Jackson asked.

"Out of place and uncomfortable," Christopher responded dryly.

"Awesome, I am nailing the look I was going for today. Just so you know, I have Barnes and the rest of the guys waiting in the SUVs, just in case. Heads up, I think Ms. Sutherland is coming our way."

Christopher was taken aback by the Junoesque figure of the woman walking toward them, from her perfectly coiffed blonde hair and piercing blue eyes to her expensive shoes. It was easy to see why Draven Cross had made her his assistant, but he wondered if there was more to the relationship. Her striking looks caused eyes all across the expansive lobby to track her every step.

"Good morning, gentlemen. I am sure today will be quiet and without incident. Let me introduce you to Agent Mitch McDougal, the head of security for the EU president," Gemma Sutherland offered calmly.

Agent McDougal looked like the poster child for guys who did nothing but work in the gym on making their arms bigger, and nothing else. The suit he was wearing looked like it was about to bust at the seams around his biceps while dangling loosely around his seemingly nonexistent legs. A large earpiece topped off the look. "So, Barrett, you're in charge of the military team," the agent stated more than asked.

"Yes, I am," Christopher agreed.

"Look, you gents just stay in the shadows, and this will be an easy assignment for you," Agent McDougal instructed.

"Not a problem, Mr. McDougal," Christopher responded.

Gemma stepped between the two men, offering her hand to Christopher. "Thank you, Major Barrett. Mr. Cross and I will see you later today for our departure."

"The pleasure is all ours, ma'am," Jackson said, bowing deeply at the waist.

As Christopher watched Gemma Sutherland and Agent McDougal leave for the U.N. General Assembly hall, Jackson and he headed backstage, where they would be positioned while Cross spoke. For the first time since the disappearances, Christopher noticed a buzz of excitement as people moved into the large hall for Draven's speech.

Laughing, Christopher said, "You're always putting on a show, Jackson, the funny guy, Williams. I am guessing that was an English accent you were shooting for back there with Ms. Sutherland."

"It would be boring without me around. And I think Agent McDougal doesn't like Americans. Just sayin'," Jackson stated with feigned nonchalance.

"It would seem that way, but we have more important things to worry about today. Just keep your eyes open. I didn't realize Cross was speaking to the entire U.N. General Assembly. Anything can happen," Christopher stated, looking concerned.

Draven felt exhilaration coursing through his body. He was lost in his thoughts as the outgoing U.N. secretary-general Maximilian Aguilar of Uruguay read through his biographical information. In a matter of moments, Draven felt that he would steal the hearts and minds of the world. Everything was happening just as the Prince of This World had predicted; humanity as a whole was enthralled by him. Though he expected the outcome promised by his spirit guide, it was still hard to fathom that the U.N. secretary-general had so easily pledged his support for Draven to become the head of the U.N. Of course, in exchange, Aguilar wanted assurances that he would become the next president of Uruguay as well as a hefty "campaign donation," but Draven saw these things as leverage to use against Aguilar in the future. Draven felt intoxicated by the power in the room and the realization that, by this time tomorrow, he would have achieved his lifelong goal of ruling the world.

Draven entered the stage to a thunderous ovation from the nations of the world. He received the applause for minutes, basking in the glow before repeating his previous speech regarding the disappearances. He ended the address as guided by the Prince of This World when he exhorted Draven to "bring them to you."

"In conclusion, I challenge this great institution to live up to its preamble. For too long, this organization has not unified the world, but rather allowed the strong to dictate conditions for living to the weak. It is time for all of us to unify under the banner of peace and one humanity."

Draven finished by saying, "It's in this spirit of peace that this body and all it represents has inspired me to action. I have personally donated sufficient resources to Israel so that rebuilding their sacred temple can begin immediately as a symbol of my commitment to peace. Additionally, on behalf of the EU, I am proud to announce today that a formal peace process with Israel and its neighbors will begin shortly at the Hague. I hope that the rest of the countries of the world will follow the EU's lead and let the age of peace on Earth begin in the Middle East today. Thank you for your time and may *peace* reign on Earth."

Christopher watched as the General Assembly of nations stood to their feet and all but formally crowned Draven Cross the ruler of the world.

"Well, that seals it for me," Jackson asserted, tongue in cheek. "That guy *is* the Antichrist. I should just shoot him here and now."

"I'm not sure that would be wise. I can say this, though. I have little faith in what I think anymore. Let's head out to the vehicles. That speech sent chills down my spine," Christopher said.

"Yeah, I feel dirty after hearing him speak in person—or maybe it's just this suit."

"More likely the suit. Let's go."

As Christopher watched Draven Cross exit the U.N. building, he felt intimidated by the man and fearful for what he perceived Draven might represent. The Holy Spirit, as Christopher now conceded to call the still, small voice, said, *"But the Lord is faithful, and he will strengthen you and protect you from the evil one."* Christopher locked eyes with Draven for only a moment just before the man climbed into his waiting SUV. The look reminded him of a lion stalking its prey on the nature channels.

"I will ride with you, Major Barrett, if you don't mind," Gemma said.

Still feeling strangely uncomfortable about being so close to Draven, Christopher was startled by what Gemma said. But he replied, "That will be fine. I see Agent McDougal is with Mr. Cross, so all seems well. Let's go."

"I'll ride up front," Jackson offered. "You can ride in the back with Ms. Sutherland."

As the convoy of SUVs departed to JFK airport, Christopher felt an overwhelming sadness. A chilly late-fall rain only added weight to his mood after listening to Cross speak. The major watched throngs of people cheering and snapping pictures on smartphones in hopes of catching a glimpse of Draven Cross, a man the world knew only on the surface. Draven had promised the world peace after the greatest disaster in recorded history, and it seemed the world was willing to accept this man, no matter the cost.

"It's astonishing, the reaction he generates, is it not?" Gemma asked.

"I would say more disconcerting than anything, ma'am," Christopher responded flatly.

"Please, call me Gemma."

"Okay, Gemma. What's the story on Mr. Cross?"

"Hmm, you're direct, aren't you? I would rather not discuss my employer at the moment. I will only say that he is a man who always gets what he wants. Today, it was the world."

"The other gentlemen that got into the SUV opposite Mr. Cross… who was that?"

"Is there not an American idiom that says curiosity killed the cat, Major Barrett?"

"Please, call me Christopher. And, yes, that expression might be fitting here. But indulge me if you would, Gemma. It's the military training in me. I always like to understand my surrounding environment."

"I heard you were sharp, potentially rash, but perceptive," Gemma remarked thoughtfully.

"Who provided you with that assessment?" Christopher asked, curious.

"Christopher, I work for what is easily the most powerful man in the world. There is little to nothing I cannot find out, if necessary."

"I'll keep that in mind, but do you think you could answer my question, or will you continue to evade the topic of the mystery man?"

Gemma grew somber and stared out the window as they drove several blocks, leaving Christopher to sit silently, awaiting her reply. After a while, she said, "He is Evan Mallory, one of the most powerful political and religious influencers in the world."

"Why does that name sound so familiar?"

"Evan is the patriarch and chief architect of the twenty-first-century church movement. He began with a small church and built an international brand, the Interfaith Religious Centers. The religious centers, based predominately in major metropolitan areas, drew praise from many due to their power in uniting various religious faiths in one worship complex," Gemma explained.

"That makes sense now. I've seen that guy with all kinds of politicians the world over. You think he is looking for a job with Mr. Cross?" Christopher wondered aloud.

"I expect he will be a more frequent visitor, if that answers your question."

"It does. But I have one more question, if you don't mind."

"I don't believe this will be the last question you will ask, but go ahead."

"So what's your angle with Mr. Cross?"

"There is a straightforward answer. I have always been nothing more than Mr. Cross's executive assistant. I was an intern at his large biotech firm near London while I was a student at Oxford. The rest is history, as you Americans say."

"I take it you're not happy with your employment situation?" Christopher probed.

"I thought the previous question was your last," Gemma remarked pointedly.

The convoy slowed, causing Christopher to look out the window and away from the elegant and astute Gemma Sutherland. The vehicles had passed through the security perimeter of JFK airport and were now on the tarmac heading toward *Air Force One*.

"Thank goodness, I am saved from further interrogation by our arrival," Gemma murmured with a laugh.

Smiling, Christopher replied, "I was just making conversation."

As Christopher and Gemma's SUV pulled up to allow the occupants to disembark, Christopher watched Draven salute a young Air Force officer standing at the bottom of the staircase leading to *Air Force One*. He thought, *What arrogance.*

"A final word of wisdom, Christopher. Fire is useful until you get too close," Gemma warned. "Meaning, know that Mr. Cross is useful, but there are limits to what you want to know about him. No one is ever who they seem to be, especially Mr. Cross and Evan Mallory."

With those words, Gemma quickly went up the staircase, leaving Christopher and Jackson at the bottom on the rain-soaked pavement.

"How did things go?" Jackson asked. "I am guessing she spilled the beans on old Saint Cross."

Chuckling, Christopher answered, "No, she played her cards close regarding our two new acquaintances, Draven Cross and Evan Mallory."

"I think I can guess who they are based on Rev's journal notes. It's hard to imagine being so close to such evil," Jackson proclaimed.

"I hope you're wrong," Christopher muttered grimly.

Evan Mallory, at fifty-five years of age, knew star power when he saw it, and Draven Cross reeked of it. He was grateful the man had finally accepted his request to meet with him, but he never would have guessed the meeting would have occurred on *Air Force One*, en route to meet the president of the United States. Evan knew his only goal today would be departing this meeting as an advisor to Mr. Cross.

"Evan, it is a pleasure to finally meet you," Draven greeted him.

"Sir, the pleasure is all mine," Evan responded warmly.

"So tell me about yourself and how you used religion to amass such respectable wealth and fame. I know the story, but I am always intrigued to hear firsthand accounts."

"Gentlemen, would you like anything to drink or eat?" a flight attendant asked before Evan could begin his story.

"A sparkling water for me," Draven replied. "Evan, care for anything?"

"No, I'm just fine," Evan answered.

"Hardly. He will have the same," the EU president told the flight attendant. "I can see the nerves in you, Evan. Trust me, today is going to be a great day for both of us."

The flight attendant left to prepare the drinks as Evan shuffled and adjusted his suit in a stately seat across from Draven.

"Now, please continue," Draven requested.

"Yes, sir. My story is a simple one, but I feel it extraordinary at the same time. My father was an English businessman that moved to the U.S. when I was a small boy. He built his small financial consulting firm into, as you likely know, one of the largest in the world. The big break for my father stemmed from religion. When I was around eight years old, we started attending this little community church that was really more of a networking club. My dad told me often, 'Religious wholesomeness sells in America, Evan.'"

"I'm sure it helped that your mother comes from a wealthy banking family, but please continue," Draven said, enjoying the look of surprise cross Evan's face at his comment.

"I see you've done your homework," Evan remarked, eyebrows raised.

"That is why I am the most powerful man in the world. Just continue your story."

Draven's words were definitely more of a command than a request, and Evan was momentarily thrown by the sudden flatness of his tone. "Yes, so, where was I? Oh, yes. I didn't understand at the time, but my father attended a church full of business and financial leaders with religious beliefs that were surface deep at best. Once I left for college, which was only a formality in my father's eyes to provide the credibility I'd need to run his business, I had a desire to merge business and religion. I decided if I could sell people on the idea that all one needs from religion is to be charitable and generally decent while tying a business model into that concept, well, I just knew I would have something.

"Telling people each week and in conferences and books that they were already good, but they just needed to believe, no matter what faith they chose—well, I became a wealthy man," Evan finished, sitting back in his seat satisfied that he had "sold" his worth to Draven. Stymied by Draven's silence, he added, "I'm sorry if I was a bit longwinded."

Draven finally spoke. "No apologies needed. I think you found the intersectionality of the business world and spirituality a potent combination in this world."

"I'm glad my spirit guide told me to reach out to you months ago, but I thought the Prince of This World was wrong when you never responded," said Evan a bit timidly.

"How delightful! So you're familiar with the Prince of This World?"

"Oh, yes! He is the one that told me to focus on teaching only prosperity and to diminish the difference in various religions and focus on them all pointing to the same God."

"Well, to be frank with you, Evan, I had no intention of ever reaching out to you. However, our mutual spiritual advisor told me that it would be profitable for me to extend an invitation to meet. I mean, really…all that drivel about prosperity starting with seeing yourself as prosperous and that goodness comes from providing charity for your fellow man is a balm for the masses, but it's utter nonsense," Draven said scornfully, seemingly now disinterested in his guest.

Evan, embarrassed by Draven's blunt remarks about his work, was at a loss for words.

"Come now, Evan. I know you don't actually believe your own dogma, especially considering you've witnessed the scope of the power that the Prince of This World commands," Draven added, his face mirroring his disbelief. When Evan still failed to speak, Draven emitted a burst of mocking laughter as he realized that Evan did indeed believe in his self-made religious tenets. "This is too great, Evan. I think you have been pushing your silliness around the world for so long that you believe it. Today, however, that stops. You are just fortunate that a real higher power sees value in you that I cannot, and he has assured me that your false religion will be the perfect compliment to my government. Otherwise I would never have given you a second glance," he stated disdainfully, staring into Evan's eyes intently.

Evan was shocked to realize that he felt almost helpless as he sat listening to Draven state unequivocally that he would now serve Draven. Internally, Evan fought against what Draven was expressing; his pride in his own work and fame rose up within him at Draven's arrogant tone. He struggled, asking himself whether this was indeed the job he wanted, serving the leader of the world? But all the questions in his mind survived only briefly, and he came back to himself just as Draven was summing up his role in the soon-coming government of the world.

"So it's settled. You will serve as my image bearer, using your false religion to spread my ideas and concepts on what peace will mean in this new era. I cannot bring peace to the world without people seeing the commonality with their fellow man and living under my control unknowingly. And as much as I don't believe religion is a real thing, I can see how it has the power to pull large groups of people into a single vision," Draven commented pragmatically.

"Excellent, sir. I am grateful and honored to be in your service," Evan replied, surprised by the subservient tone of his own voice.

"Now to sharpen my government's teeth, starting with the largest military prize of them all—the United States military."

Something about Draven's calculating words lit a quiver of unease in Evan's chest.

As his chief of staff entered his office, President Rodgers was just finishing a conference call with trusted allies in the Pentagon regarding a plan he was about to pitch to Gabriella—a project he'd been working on ever since listening to Draven Cross's speech a few days ago.

"Sir, *Air Force One* has just landed at Andrews, and Mr. Cross is en route via *Marine One*. Dr. Costa is also waiting outside," the man informed him.

"Thanks, please send in Gabriella."

Moments later, the president heard his door open and then Gabriella's greeting. "Good afternoon, sir."

"Hello, Gabriella. I see that our boys took care of Mr. Cross."

"Yes, sir, it went as expected. I guess that's why I am surprised you wanted me to attend your meeting with Mr. Cross."

"Honestly, Gabriella, my motives are self-serving—or perhaps more for our country—for having you here today," President Rodgers replied. "Please take a seat. I want to urge you to take a job, but hear me out first."

When she heard "take a job," Gabriella's stomach rolled nervously as she seated herself on the large couch next to the president. She was experiencing the same feeling she used to get when talking with her now-deceased dad as a child. "Sir, have you lost confidence in my ability to lead Omega Group?" Her dismay was evident.

"No, quite the contrary, Gabriella. Your success and my knowledge of your upbringing make you the ideal candidate for this assignment."

"Please explain, sir."

Laughing as he slapped his knee, President Rodgers continued. "You're all business and very analytical, just like your father. Okay, I want to 'offer' your talents as an intelligence officer and security expert to Draven Cross for what I expect to be his new role at the U.N. I have reservations about what Mr. Cross plans, and I want to be able to make informed decisions for our national security."

"When you say 'new role at the U.N.,' I am guessing you have some insight that leads you to that conclusion? Do I understand you correctly, Mr. President—you want me to be a spy?"

"Yes, I do have some insight you're not privy to regarding Mr. Cross. And, yes, Gabriella, spying is precisely what I want you to do for your country," President Rodgers stated firmly, standing to pace back and forth in front of his desk.

"First, what about Omega Group? But even more to the point, sir, what makes you believe Mr. Cross is a threat to the United States? He seems in all of his actions so far to be a champion of peace."

"That's what worries me, Gabriella. I have already expressed my wife's views—no, now my views—on what we just experienced, the rapture. If I am willing to accept that much of what the Bible has to say, I must be willing to believe the rest."

"Sir, are you telling me that you seriously think that Draven Cross is the Antichrist?"

"No, I am not willing to place such a horrible label on this man yet. However, as a recent convert to Christianity, I am on watch for the man who will fit that bill. Draven Cross may be indeed a man of peace, but he could also turn out to be just the devil in disguise, no pun intended. This makes placing you on the inside of his organization vital. You will have access to his plans and intentions. You will see through his public persona and help discover anything that might be detrimental to this country, ahead of time," President Rodgers concluded as he sat down behind his massive desk.

"What makes you think he would even accept me on his staff in the role you're offering?" Gabriella asked skeptically.

"He is a man who always wants to be surrounded by the best, and I can think of no one better in the field of intelligence tradecraft."

"Well, can I think it over? I mean, who will take the leadership role of Omega Group?"

The office door opened, and the president's chief of staff announced, "Sir, Mr. Cross just landed on the South Lawn. I will announce him in ten minutes."

"Thanks," the president acknowledged. "Gabriella, don't worry about Omega. This is your next job. Major Barrett will lead Omega and report directly to me. You need to figure out this guy as much as I do. My self-serving interest in your taking this assignment is, first, that I need someone I trust, someone who will earn his trust on the inside. You're that person. But secondly, it is my earnest hope that being in this precarious position will in some way lead to your receiving Jesus Christ as your personal savior," he confessed, his honest affection for her very evident on his face.

"Against my better judgment, I accept your proposition. But I have doubts about this, sir. We could lose credibility in the international community if my cover is blown. I have even more significant misgivings that working for Draven Cross will change my thoughts regarding God," Gabriella replied firmly.

"For our country's sake, I appreciate your willingness to go along with my plan, despite your misgivings. For your sake, all I ask is that you keep an open mind to the things of God, Gabriella. It is an arduous challenge for those of us that trust above all things the physical and explanatory world to consider the things of God as being real. But if the last few weeks have not even opened your mind to the possibility that God could be real, then I wouldn't consider you a critical thinker."

"Thanks for the guilt trip on God via reasoning, sir," Gabriella returned dryly.

"You and I go back a long way. I just want the best for you, Gabriella," President Rodgers said, assuring the woman he had known all her life.

Chapter 10

Draven Cross entered the Oval Office with all the pomp and false humility President Rodgers expected.

"President Rodgers, it is a real honor to visit you here at the White House. I appreciate your generous hospitality in flying me here in *Air Force One*. I may decide to keep it. I am jesting, of course. But, sincerely, it is a tremendous honor to be here," Draven gushed, as he posed for the U.S. and international media contingent to snap a few photos to record his first meeting with a significant world leader.

"I am glad you feel welcome here in our great country," Rodgers replied.

Before anyone else could speak, the chief of staff addressed the journalists. "Thank you, ladies and gentlemen. President Rodgers and Mr. Cross will now hold a closed-door meeting." Then he promptly and efficiently ushered the entire contingent out of the Oval Office and closed the door firmly as he, too, departed the room. President Rodgers barely waited for the click of the Oval Office door before launching into questioning the intentions of Draven Cross.

"Rumor is you'll be living here on a more permanent basis as the U.N. secretary-general," President Rodgers began as he moved to his seat behind his desk.

"My, and I thought I was a shrewd businessman. Straight to the point, as you Americans are fond of saying in such settings as we find ourselves today. Well, let me introduce and then dismiss my confidants before we get to the heart of today's visit."

Draven introduced Evan Mallory as his political advisor and Gemma as his personal assistant, before asking them to wait outside the Oval Office.

President Rodgers eyed Draven as his staff members departed, leaving Gabriella and him alone with the would-be ruler of the world.

"That's an interesting start to assembling your staff, but I am assuming you're just getting started. Evan Mallory has an impressive Rolodex of power players around the globe, not to mention a 'spiritual platform' to congeal the masses. A smart move, Mr. Cross," President Rodgers remarked.

"Please, call me Draven, and I am impressed with your assessment of my first key selection. While I think it may be premature to say I will be the next U.N. secretary-general, I like the way you're thinking, Mr. President."

"Thank you, but I think for now I prefer to call you Mr. Cross. As far as using religion to secure political power, your attempt will be nothing new."

"As you like, Mr. President. I would like to speak to you in private, but I am willing to permit Dr. Gabriella Costa to remain if you wish."

"I see you're well informed, Mr. Cross," returned President Rodgers, acknowledging Draven's use of Gabriella's full name without introduction. "Gabriella, please feel free to make whatever comments you wish before I ask you to step out of the meeting."

"It is a pleasure to meet you, Mr. Cross," she greeted. "Your track record of peace and charity precedes you. I wish you the best going forward, sir."

"Thank you, Gabriella. I am sure our paths will cross again. Your reputation as a professional and leader within the U.S. Intelligence Community is impressive."

The two men stood as Gabriella excused herself from the meeting.

President Rodgers felt like he had Draven pegged—a populist, or more accurately, an opportunist with the wealth and connections to take advantage of a disaster-ridden world. As the Oval Office door closed once again, President Rodgers addressed the man directly and somewhat coldly. "So what do you want, Cross? I've been in politics long enough to know that you always size up the toughest opponent first. I am guessing you see America as the primary challenger to your plans."

Draven laughed aloud before answering, "I like you, Rodgers. You're like a cowboy dressed up in a suit. You're still the fighter pilot blazing the sky with a massive ego and the notion that America's ideology is the best in the world. You think that as the American president you have me figured out, right? That I need you?" He matched the American president's tone.

"Well, at least you know where I stand. What about you, Mr. Cross? Exactly what are your plans for the immediate future?" President Rodgers asked bluntly.

"I expect to be announced U.N. secretary-general, and then I expect the support of world leaders like yourself to help me usher in universal peace on Earth," Draven returned expansively.

"Really? You think you're going to achieve universal peace through the U.N.?" President Rodgers' face reflected his humorous disdain for the idea.

"I guess the better question to ask, President Rodgers, is who will be able to stop me?" Draven responded with a steely look in his emerald eyes.

The dark edge to Draven's last remark shook Rodgers to his core. It seemed Draven was not at all intimidated by the setting. President Rodgers pondered that perhaps Draven Cross *was* the biblical Antichrist if his announced objective was to lead the world down a primrose path of peace. The president also knew he'd better stop "fighting this fish" for now before he broke away and viewed the U.S. as a clear and present danger.

"Well, I see no reason to oppose you at the moment. You have the majority, if not all, of the world's support. My question still remains regarding what you're pushing for regarding America by speaking with me first before other world leaders," President Rodgers said, attempting to disarm the man.

"That's simple, Mr. President. I need America to lead the way in denuclearizing and supplementing the U.N. with conventional arms and personnel," Draven stated matter-of-factly.

"Do you really think that, of all the nations in the world, the American people are just going to allow me to turn over our military might to the U.N.? I mean, even with the current state of the world, that will be an impossible sale to Congress," President Rodgers replied with astonishment.

Draven loved outmaneuvering those in power; moments like this were pure pleasure for him. "I don't think so, Mr. President. I've already taken the liberty of speaking, via a conference call, to your congressional Gang of Eight, and they have unanimously agreed that it's time America stopped solving the world's problems. It's time to lead from the back—at least, that is how your Speaker of the House put it."

President Rodgers tried to hide the quivering fury rising within him. Draven had been playing with him this whole time. He was being made a fool by not only the pretenious Draven Cross but the elected officials of his own country. *God help us*, was the only coherent thought he could muster. "I see. So really this meeting is just to feel me out, in a manner of speaking. You just want to know if I'm going to be friend or foe."

"Precisely. So whose side of history will you choose today, Mr. President?" Draven queried, steepling his hands beneath his chin while leaning forward in his seat toward the American president.

Rodgers's fighter pilot instincts told him he was outnumbered and low on fuel. *It's better to fly for safety and live to fight another day than die on a fool's errand*, he thought. He was smart enough to know that if Cross could reach Congress without him, he needed to move wisely and deliberately. "Obviously I choose to be in the camp of Draven Cross. I even want to make a strong recommendation for your future intelligence chief—Dr. Gabriella Costa." He stood up and extended his hand to Draven.

"I am glad your ability to see the big picture was not left behind in the cockpit of your F-16. I accept your recommendation for my intelligence chief and look forward to your pledging support for my world peace initiative, Mr. President," Draven said smugly, ignoring the extended hand.

"Once you're announced as the U.N. secretary-general, I will begin the process of allocating our military resources to your new organization."

The office door clicked open, and Rodgers saw his chief of staff's head appear around the edge. "Sir, my apologies but I needed to let you, both of you actually, know that the U.N. General Assembly, at the behest of Secretary-General Aguilar, just voted to make Mr. Cross the next secretary-general."

"Please excuse me. As you can imagine the world will be expecting my reaction to this 'shocking' news. President Rodgers, when should I expect your announcement about our discussion?" Draven asked, a smile barely concealing his thinly veiled sense of triumph.

"I'll schedule a press conference by this time tomorrow. Dr. Costa will be in New York by the end of the week," President Rodgers responded, working hard to hide his gut-level distaste for the man.

"It has been a pleasure, President Rodgers. Trust me, America's support and yours will not go unnoticed by the U.N. I will send *Air Force One* back to you once I arrive in New York today." The supremely confident man exited the room, throwing a quick, "Cheers," over his shoulder toward the president on his way out of the Oval Office.President Rodgers fell into his chair in the now empty and seemingly meaningless Oval Office, sickened by the encounter. He feared that America and the world were about to suffer much at the hands of a monster who had sold his soul to the devil. Pressing the intercom button on his desk, he told his assistant, "Send in Dr. Costa, please."

Christopher was glad to be in his shared apartment and away from Draven Cross. He grew restless watching evening news stories of clean-up efforts and human-interest stories on post-disappearance normalcy. He couldn't shake the feeling of dread that had swept over him after making eye contact with Draven. The breaking news announcement that Cross had been chosen as the secretary-general of the U.N. did little to soothe his misgivings about the future. He needed to know what was coming next for the world. He addressed Jackson, who was sprawled out on the couch.

"Hey, you've still got Rev's Bible and journal, right?"

"You know I do. I've been poring through them both every chance I get," Jackson responded.

"So besides believing that Draven is the Antichrist, what do you think is on the horizon based on what you see in there?"

"In one word: judgment," Jackson replied grimly, sitting up on the couch as he turned off the TV.

"That bad, huh? Is there anything we can do to prepare, to get ahead of these upcoming judgments?"

"I've been studying to figure that out. The short answer is, I see very little we can do to prepare to stay safe. The Bible, in Revelation, doesn't provide precise timelines for everything that will happen, but I can share what I see in broad terms. A lot will happen over the next seven years, but I'll give you the near-term, fifty-meter targets."

"Okay, let the end-of-the-world school begin," Christopher intoned pompously.

"Your sense of humor is terrible," Jackson said as he reached for Rev's journal and Bible, which he now claimed as his own. "Leave being funny to professionals like me. Anyway, the pain will come in three waves with seven judgments each. If Old Saint Cross announces a seven-year peace pledge with Israel and convinces the rest of the world to agree to the same, then the clock starts ticking based on what I see in here."

"The clock? Do you mean the seven years of tribulation?"

"You got it. The signing of a seven-year peace treaty with Israel marks the official start of the tribulation, also known as Daniel's seventieth week, from Daniel 9:27. I believe the first seal unleashing the rider on the white horse as the Antichrist has already been opened—when Draven was announced as the U.N. secretary-general. Revelation 6:1–2 describe the rider of the white horse using diplomacy and the promise of peace to establish his one-world government. Sound familiar?" Jackson asked with a sarcastic expression.

"I am hooked so far," Christopher replied guardedly.

"Rev marked verses in the Bible that give brief descriptions of what the opening of each of the following seals, trumpets, and bowl judgments will bring on the world. I'll sum up the first four seals and riders, then you need to study the rest yourself. A big takeaway for me right now is how Rev noted in his journal that God would show the world grace even during this outpouring of His wrath," Jackson said, leafing through Rev's journal.

"How?"

"Well, for starters, each of these waves of punishment builds on each other. It seems there are brief lulls between each judgment to allow for repentance—an opportunity that some will take, but most will refuse. The seal judgments are bad, the trumpets are badder, and the bowls are the baddest."

"Did you really just say bad, badder, and baddest?" Christopher asked, laughing. "If I didn't know you, I would never guess you're a fully qualified physician's assistant. Country grammar at its best, you goofball."

"Whatever. You get the point. It's gonna suck. You should be figuring this out from your own perspective, college boy," Jackson retorted, throwing a couch cushion at Christopher's head.

"Hey, watch it. I'm sorry, but what you said was funny. Anyway, keep going."

"The second seal sets the red horse and rider across the world that introduces a great war. The fallout from the war opens the third seal, and a black horse and rider will strike the world, which brings famine and further economic crisis. The fourth seal culminates in the natural results of a massive war, death. The pale rider and the three previous seals will claim over a billion lives and, sadly, many will enter into an eternity forever separated from God," Jackson finished, his face serious.

Christopher was no longer laughing, either. The somber description of the future to come was terrifying. A thousand-yard stare flashed across his face as he sat in silence, the daunting task of figuring out how to survive foremost in his mind.

"I could go on, but I suggest you study for yourself what's coming. The bottom line? Everything including the kitchen sink will be thrown at the world," Jackson concluded, standing to go to his room.

"Awesome. I had the chance to avoid all this, but I refused to see the truth," Christopher said glumly.

Jackson stopped in the hall leading to his bedroom, saying, "Hey, man, don't go down that road. We all missed the boat. God is gracious enough to allow us to have the chance to come to Him, even now in the midst of suffering, if we will only ask Him. Don't wait too long to make things right with God, Christopher. You had no promise of tomorrow before all this started, but you for sure don't now."

"Jackson, I know I need to surrender in this one-sided battle I'm waging against God, but I honestly don't know how to let go of the pain of the past. I've been angry with God for so long I can't remember anything else," Christopher confessed.

"Pain is a prison that Jesus died to release all of us from. If you would just walk out of the holding cell you've made for yourself, you would find the peace with yourself and God that you're craving. Look, you've never made excuses in your professional career, so why are you making excuses personally for trusting the only one that has always been there for you—God?" Jackson asked sincerely.

"I get it, Jackson. I really do, but life is not so black and white, even for me who has seen more evidence of God's existence in the last few days than I know how to acknowledge. But I do understand that we're facing a life-and-death battle for the next seven years."

"No, I'm not sure you do, Christopher. What you need to do is get over your little woe-is-me toddler temper tantrum of believing the pain hurts too bad to accept the only lifeline we have in this situation. Just don't wait too long, man. In our line of work, and now with the dawning of the tribulation, each day will only get harder. And more dangerous. I'm gonna get some sleep. Wake me in the event of some kind of crisis," Jackson said drily.

"Now whose sense of humor is horrible?"

Tapping first, Gabriella eased back into the Oval Office, only to find President Rodgers standing with his arms folded across his chest, staring out into the late-afternoon rainstorm.

"You wanted to speak with me, sir?" she said softly, seeing from his demeanor the heavy burden that sat on this man's shoulders.

"Yes, come in, Gabriella, and have a seat," President Rodgers invited, ushering her to a chair in front of his desk. "Mr. Cross has accepted my recommendation for you to become the head of intelligence in his new role as secretary-general of the U.N."

"I didn't know the U.N. had an intelligence division, nor that Draven Cross was the secretary-general of the U.N. That must have been some discussion going on in here," Gabriella replied, shocked.

"Our brief meeting confirmed for me more than you understand at this point. Cross was voted in by the U.N. General Assembly minutes ago on the endorsement of Aguilar. In the meantime, you and I will execute our plan to stay ahead of this man. There seem to be no limits to his power," President Rodgers stated direly.

"Yes, I can see the value of having insight into his future plans. I will hesitantly admit that Mr. Cross's rapid ascent in power and authority has me questioning some of the recent descriptions of him that I've heard, of the biblical nature. So explain the plan, sir."

"As we speak, a selection of our nuclear ICBMs are being transported to a remote location in Alaska, just in case they're needed. Mr. Cross wants the world to denuclearize and send military forces to the U.N. under his control. I can only imagine why he is seeking to disarm the world, but in the same breath arm himself," President Rodgers related drily.

"What? Are you really going along with that plan, sir? I mean to denuclearize and reduce our military strength seem to place this nation in a very vulnerable position." Gabriella, astounded by what she had just heard come out of the president's mouth, struggled to comment without sounding disrespectful of the man's office.

"Gabriella, I would never willingly sell our nation down the river. However, it seems that others in our government already made a deal with Cross before his ever walking in here today. As a result, I am politically isolated, at least for now. I have a feeling a few other countries are not going to just lie down for Cross. We will plan and hope that a war doesn't erupt over this. I'm hoping that you can now see the significance of his acceptance of you into his inner circle." The president leaned forward on his desk as he looked at her.

"Yes, I can. When do I have to report to New York?"

"You start later this week. I'll hold a press conference tomorrow afternoon, saying we support peace and are committing forces to the U.N. to ensure the stability of the world from a centralized government. This is political suicide for me, but I don't really see the country as we know it surviving to the next election cycle anyway. I want Omega Group to head to the Alaska site to ensure everything goes well with our hidden nukes."

"I am on it, sir. And, Mr. President, I hope this goes without saying, but I won't let my country or you down in this new role," Gabriella promised.

"I've never worried about your commitment to this country or even to me, my dear Gabriella. I worry about your soul. Listen to me for a second. I know that you believe in science and logic, but don't be blind to all that the Bible is saying about these historic moments you're now tied to. Please don't allow yourself to be swayed by Draven Cross. I have a feeling he's only beginning to demonstrate his power," President Rodgers stated sadly.

"I can promise only to be open-minded, but thanks for caring. I'll report in at least once a week via this, a quantum communications device," Gabriella said with a smile as she placed the device in his hand. "It's part smartphone, part computer, and virtually impossible to hack. Christopher and Jackson will each have one, and I'm leaving this one with you. The one I'm taking can be my farewell gift from Omega Group."

"Godspeed, Gabriella. I will be praying for you."

Christopher burst into Jackson's room. "You'll never guess the message I just got from Gabriella."

"Man, this better be something serious, like the end of the world is happening, or I am going to shoot you," Jackson replied.

Christopher laughed. "The world *is* ending according to you. Anyway, it's about our next mission. Gabriella wants to talk about it in person, but not at the Pentagon. She's coming over here."

"What, here? To discuss a mission? Man, I have a feeling this is going to be something crazy."

"Get dressed. She should be here any minute."

"Sure thing, Chris. Anything in particular you want me to wear?" Jackson asked as he threw off his blanket, exposing his hairy arms and legs.

"Oh, man, I swear you're the missing link. Just wear some clothes, you freak," Christopher said over his shoulder as he covered his eyes and fled the room.

About an hour after sending Chris the text saying she was on her way over, Gabriella stood knocking on the apartment door. Though she could hear a noise inside, she had been knocking and waiting for several minutes, freezing in the twilight, when Jackson finally opened the door.

"Hello, ma'am. Welcome to our humble abode. Please enter," Jackson invited with an outflung arm.

"Geez, what took you guys so long to open the door…and what's that smell?" Gabriella asked, nose wrinkling.

"Oh, Chris, as you call him, has been vacuuming and is burning some incense. He has a foot-odor problem and didn't want to offend you," Jackson replied with a wink.

"Is that Gabriella?" came the loud inquiry from Christopher in the back of the apartment.

"Yeah, it's me, swamp foot," Gabriella called back, followed by loud laughter shared with Jackson.

Swamp foot? Christopher thought. *What's that all about?* "Okay, I'll be there in a minute," he replied aloud.

Jackson had brought Gabriella a bottle of water and seated himself in the lone chair in the living room, leaving Christopher to sit next to Gabriella on the couch.

"Chris, you didn't have to clean up or mask your foot-odor problem for me," Gabriella murmured with fake sweetness.

Jackson choked on his water and laughed so hard he nearly fell out of his chair.

"Is that what you were told? It's the country boy over there with the foot and other odor problems. I was just trying to save you from his stench."

Jackson, still laughing, said, "Listen, there are two of us living in this small apartment. I would say the stench is half yours and half mine."

"I would say your math is half wrong," Christopher retorted.

"Well, I can see you two are getting along just fine, but a woman's touch would be nice," Gabriella asserted, placing her water bottle on the floor after looking around pointedly but failing to find either a coffee table or end table. "I came to tell you the fallout from the president's meeting with Draven."

"Look, if you expect me to wear a suit and babysit this guy on a permanent basis, I quit right here and now," Jackson burst out, reclining in the chair.

"Do you want to hear me out, Jackson, or just keep making wrong guesses about why I came here this evening?" Gabriella questioned acerbically.

"Proceed, ma'am," Jackson replied with mock penitence.

"Thanks. President Rodgers, like Jackson, believes there's a strong possibility Draven Cross is the Antichrist. He wouldn't say it as explicitly as I just did, but I know that's what he's implying. So after Congress sold the country down the river to Cross, he's hedging his bets by sending some of our nukes to a black site in Alaska."

"What? Slow down," Christopher demanded, grasping his head.

"You heard me right. Apparently, Cross called the Gang of Eight and worked a deal for their support of his plan for world peace, namely, America denuclearizing and supporting the U.N. militarily. The Gang of Eight, Jackson, are the leaders in Congress, particularly for intelligence matters. But practically, they hold power over what gets passed and what doesn't," Gabriella elaborated.

"I am glad you read my mind, but I was trying to hold my questions until the end," Jackson teased.

"So let me get this straight. President Rodgers is sending nukes to Alaska to hide them from Cross, then—with the approval of Congress—destroying the rest and sending conventional military assets to work for the U.N.," Christopher clarified, disbelief etched in every line of his face.

"Yes, and the president has asked me to work for Cross to spy on him—I've agreed," Gabriella reported, her face grim with purpose.

"What? You're going to willingly go work for the devil?" Jackson asked, his disapproval clear.

"Yeah, I agree with Jackson. That is crazy, Gabriella. You don't know enough about this guy. He seems like he could be ruthless to get what he wants."

Gabriella stood and moved to the raised fireplace hearth, obviously agitated by the pushback from Chris and Jackson to the plan to which she had agreed. Her frustration clear, she said forcefully, "First, we don't know who Draven Cross will be as a leader, but I'm willing to bet he is not hiding red skin, horns, and cloven feet—so he's probably not the devil, Jackson. Next, having a spy in his inner circle is America's best chance of figuring out his moves and how they might harm our nation. So get on board, guys."

Christopher changed his tone immediately. "I can see you didn't come here to hear our thoughts on this plan, Gabriella, so what does this have to do with Omega Group?"

"Chris, you're the new Omega Group commander with direct reporting to the president. He wants you guys to make sure the nukes sent to Alaska remain secure and ready should the need arise. That's your only mission for the foreseeable future."

Jackson pushed the recliner back up and stood, saying, "Okay, I've sat here long enough being quiet. First off, 'I told you so' about Cross feels so right about now, but I won't say it. Secondly, Gabriella, you have a lot of nerve acting like it's no big deal to jump into the unknown abyss that is Draven Cross. That guy is the Antichrist. I don't care what the president, Christopher, or you think. On top of that, missy, we care about you! Bad as I hate to admit it, that's a fact. We don't want to see you hurt or, even worse, dead, especially before accepting Jesus as your Savior."

Gabriella suddenly crumpled. As the tears started, she began to tremble. Both Christopher and Jackson moved to her side, and somehow all three of them ended up embracing.

She was the first to find her voice. "What the heck is wrong with me, guys? In my desperation to find out who Draven really is, have I accepted a suicide mission?"

"All I know is that we both care about you and about our country. At the moment, it seems that both of you are in serious danger," Christopher said gravely.

"Gabriella, if he catches on to your being a spy, there is no telling what he will do to you…or to America," Jackson warned.

Gabriella pulled away from the embrace, saying, "I know, Jackson, but I need to find out whether he is the brilliant, logical person that I've always wanted the world to have as a leader or the Antichrist of the Bible." She paused, then added, "Look, before I go, here are two quantum communications devices. You will be able to securely communicate with me and the president with these. They are GPS, Glonass, and Beidou enabled, solar powered and indestructible for the Jackson types. It makes your smartphone look like a string and cup."

"Uhh, quantum what? Please tell me I can still play games on this thing," Jackson begged.

"Don't worry, country boy, I'll teach you how to use this tech marvel," Christopher promised.

Gabriella and Christopher both laughed."The bottom line is, you have the most secure and capable mobile phone on the planet. I will so miss you two knuckledraggers," Gabriella said, hugging both men before gathering her belongings and heading for the door. Christopher followed her and stopped her with a hand on her arm before she could open it. She turned back to face him, and they stood close in the entryway as he spoke.

"Promise me you'll be careful…please. If you feel your cover is blown, just send us the word. We will get you out, I promise."

Gabriella rose to her toes and kissed Christopher on the cheek before saying, "I know, Chris."

Christopher walked with her to her car then stood watching outside his apartment complex as she drove out of the parking lot. As he watched her taillights disappear into the chilly night, he hoped that God would at least hear this one prayer. "Lord, please keep her safe."

As *Air Force One* soared out of the DC metro area and up the eastern seaboard back to New York City, Draven was strategizing his next move in the American president's meeting room aboard the executive aircraft.

"Evan, I need you to prepare the following resolution, as my first official act as secretary-general. I want a resolution pledging seven years of peace with Israel, guaranteed by all nations within the U.N. I also want to begin the groundwork for a single global currency. On the surface, it will be heralded as a measure to shore up the ongoing economic turmoil from the disappearances. However, it will also begin to provide me with more control over the world. Lastly, Evan, prepare to meet with all the major religious influencers and leaders in the world to move the world toward a singular faith, orchestrated by me. I will announce ahead of your conference, in Rome preferably, my full support for this interfaith movement. We need not waste the momentum this crisis has afforded me. I want to solidify my hold on the world immediately."

"Draven, I'm glad that you brought—" Evan began but was interrupted.

"Excuse me, did you just refer to me by my first name?" Draven asked, getting up out of his seat and moving to stand in front of Evan.

"Yes, I just assumed it would not be an—" Draven again stopped Evan from speaking, this time by holding up a hand. "I am better than you, Evan, in every conceivable way. What would ever possess you to think we were equals or even friends? If you value your pathetic role in my service, then never assume anything for me. I will tell you exactly what to do, and you will execute it to perfection. If you fail me, you will only make that mistake once. Now apologize to me for causing me to lose my temper with you."

"Sir, please accept my sincerest apologies for insulting you by insinuating that I could possibly be a peer," Evan begged, sounding as though he might burst into tears.

Without acknowledging Evan's words Cross turned his attention to Gemma. In a demeaning tone, he demanded, "Please tell me that you have arranged for my first press conference as secretary-general to take place on this flight."

"Yes, sir, the press is ready for you at your leisure," Gemma replied calmly.

"Have you figured out exactly who Dr. Gabriella Costa is? I want to ensure that Rodgers is not sending me some washed-up, tenured bureaucrat," Draven spat.

"No, sir, I am not prepared to detail anything beyond what I initially provided you regarding Dr. Costa for the earlier meeting with President Rodgers."

"You vex me, Gemma. In one breath you seem brilliant, and then in the next moment you fall flat on your lovely face. Get it together and provide me an answer by the time this plane lands in New York City. I will meet with the press in five minutes. Both of you, leave me now. I need to collect my thoughts."

As Evan and Gemma hurried out of the presidental suite of *Air Force One*, Draven sought his spiritual guide for assistance. *"Prince of This World, what should I do next?"*

"Consolidate power," the Prince replied in Draven's mind.

"Exactly what I thought," Draven agreed.

He stepped out of the presidental suite, ready to draw the world closer to him.

"Ladies and gentlemen, I will be brief in my remarks here, as I am overwhelmed with the support by world leaders for me to lead the U.N. through this next chapter in the aftermath of the horrible disappearances. I will have several announcements regarding resolutions and plans for the days ahead, but I want to thank President Rodgers and the American people for leading the way. President Rodgers stated that America will denuclearize and provide additional military resources to the U.N. to help further the peacekeeping role this great organization champions.

"Additionally America has graciously provided me with *Air Force One* to use in my service to the U.N. I will take only a couple of questions now," Draven said, almost magnanimously.

"Herb Katz, from the *Boston Reader*, so you really believe that an alien power took all the religious folks, including children, out of the world because they were the problem?"

"I believe that a forgotten power, alien in that sense, did, in fact, remove the harmful religious element from our world for humanity to unify and achieve our potential," Draven agreed.

"You mean unify peacefully, with enhanced military capabilities under your leadership of the world?" Katz said, drawing ire from the press pool for asking the second question.

Draven chuckled at the brazen confidence of the reporter but did not fall into the trap of his question. "I admire your instincts, young man. You have great potential. My role right now is to lead the U.N. and convince the world leaders that peace is our only hope for a better tomorrow."

Gemma quickly inserted, "There will be no further questions for the secretary-general," as Draven headed back to the secretary-general suite of the newly acquired *Air Force One*.

Chapter 11

As Christopher and Jackson made their way to the Pentagon on Friday morning to finalize plans for securing the nuclear black site in Alaska, they were greeted by a red-orange dawn sky over the Jefferson Memorial tidal basin. Christopher couldn't help but see the contrast between the beautiful dawning of a new day and the carnage left behind from the rapture. Looted and burned cars were littering the streets, making the regular D.C. morning commute a thing of the past as fewer and fewer drivers attempted to navigate around crews working to clean up the mess and collect the dead.

In the distance, at Regan National, the end of a taxiway had become a graveyard for twisted airplanes. The rapture had been instantaneous but a nightmare for those caught in its wake. Christopher dreaded the thought that God's judgment of the world was only beginning.

As Jackson and Christopher's ridesharing service passed the numerous office buildings adjacent to the Pentagon, Christopher almost sensed the regularity of a routine business day, as the parking lots were full of cars. However, he knew they just bore witness to the rapture. Many of the cars hadn't been moved since that day and were a physical manifestation that some had been taken and some left, but all had been affected by the event.

"You guys have a good day," offered the rideshare driver as

Christopher and Jackson exited the vehicle in the north parking lot of the Pentagon.

"Be blessed," Jackson returned, drawing an unaffected nod from the driver as he pulled away. "What? I hope the guy is blessed today, perhaps coming to believe in Jesus, like me," he added in response to a surprised look from Christopher.

"No, I am just shocked at the transformation in you, from ignorance of Jesus to curiosity, and now a passion for your belief in Him."

"I can't explain it myself. I just wish I had made the decision to accept Jesus into my life as Lord before the rapture."

"I am starting to feel the same," Christopher confessed as they walked through the security line at the Pentagon.

"Coming from you, that statement is shocking," Jackson responded, eyebrows shooting skyward.

Gabriella's rideshare arrived earlier than expected at the U.N. headquarters in midtown New York City. Traffic was less hectic than usual for a Friday morning in the Big Apple, but with so many people gone and still missing, she quickly realized her early arrival was due to the disappearances. The city had suffered population losses just like every other city, but it seemed to her that New York City had also lost the energetic and optimistic feeling that defined the city and its inhabitants.

As she walked toward the U.N. entrance, she noticed a group of Hasidic Jewish men forming what looked like a protest behind barricades nearby. They carried signs in what looked like Hebrew script. While it wasn't bizarre to see Hasidic Jews in New York City or a demonstration near the U.N., it was their manner of dress that caught Gabriella's attention— they had donned what looked like burlap coats over their traditional black pants. At one point, Gabriella met the eyes of the man she guessed to be the leader of the group—a taller, slender man who was rallying the others like a coach does before a big game.

Dismissing the gathering as she mentally prepared for her own "game," she entered the U.N. lobby. If she were honest, she had to admit to herself that she was worried about whether or not she was up to the task she'd been given and also about whether or not Draven Cross was a wolf in sheep's clothing.

Gemma Sutherland approached Gabriella almost as soon as she entered the building. "Good morning, Dr. Costa. I am glad to see you're punctual, as we have a full-day scheduled."

"Oh, you startled me, Ms. Sutherland. I didn't expect to meet you in the lobby. And, please, call me Gabriella."

"As you wish, Gabriella. But as I said, we have a tight schedule for today. Please follow me. And call me Gemma."

Gemma led Gabriella by building security, handing her U.N. credentials with a photo already attached as they entered a bank of elevators leading them to the executive floor.

"How did you get my most recent CIA photo for these credentials?" Gabriella asked.

"I merely called Langley and had the digital copy sent to the badging office. You will soon realize that Mr. Cross has unlimited resources."

Gabriella's apprehension about being exposed as a spy for the American government rose as Gemma spoke of the far-reaching powers of Draven Cross. *What on earth have I gotten myself into?* she wondered fretfully.

"Here we are. Your office is the one down the hall in the far-right corner. You will need to be in the secretary-general's office for an introductory meeting in ten minutes. His office is at the end of this hall through the double-glass doors, in case you couldn't guess.

"One final thing, Gabriella. Always try to stay ahead of Draven, as it's better to be at the right hand of the devil than in his path," Gemma advised before heading off to her own alcove outside the double-glass doors leading to the purgatory awaiting Gabriella.

Gabriella had no idea what to make of Gemma's last statement, or the drop of formality in using Cross's first name, but if it had accomplished anything, her training at the "Farm" had prepared her to handle working in this environment. She thought back to the words of her favorite instructor, a Cold-War-era CIA veteran, as she stared out of her office window across the East River toward Long Island: *"Remember the Moscow Rules. They will save you in countless situations."*

Draven had wasted little time in removing any items adorning the secretary-general's office that were of cultural significance or that spoke of the legacy of his predecessors. He opted for a clean, modern motif with neutral beige walls, several mahogany-colored leather upholstered chairs, and two large leather sofas in the chasm that was his new office. Most prominent in the room was the massive, handcrafted British rosewood executive desk that carried an almost black luster in the wood. He had insisted that his desk align directly with the entrance to his office—he had every intention of imposing himself instantly on all who entered.

During the relatively few hours he had been secretary-general, Draven had found endless delight in watching people lose their confidence and nerve in his office. *Highlighting people's weaknesses is pure pleasure*, he thought to himself while lecturing Evan Mallory.

"Evan, let me enlighten you on the way forward for the world—the process I will use to build a new world from the old. I call this plan Project Babylon. You play a crucial role in my vision. The Interfaith religion you created will serve as a compliment to my political and economic plans, thus bringing the entire world under my stewardship. I expect you to have the Global Economic and Governance Forum of the ten world leaders I've provided you finalized by Monday. It is critical that the world accepts Project Babylon."

"Sir, it is an honor to serve you. Your vision will bring the world to a place of unimagined prosperity. Everything is on track for the leaders' conference, though President Rodgers was upset about *Air Force One* and your announcement of American support before he had the opportunity to address the nation," Evan replied.

"Ha, that old fool should be glad I didn't make the White House my new headquarters," scoffed Cross.

"I will also announce the U.N. backing of Interfaith as a step to unite diverse groups and best foster peace as compared to other spiritual mediums," Evan continued.

"Evan, did you just call this organization the U.N.?"

"Yes, sir. I was not aware that you had changed—" Evan was interrupted by Draven swearing at him.

"I have yet to understand what the Prince of This World sees in you. You will either keep up with me or I will find a replacement for you. I don't care what our mutual spiritual mentor says. By the end of the day, the U.N. will be known as the Unified Earth Organization, U.E. for short. 'One world and one people, striving for peace' is our mantra. You should have sensed the need for that change without my having to articulate it," Draven continued, swearing at Evan in dismissal as he buzzed Gemma's intercom for Gabriella.

Gabriella overheard swearing emanating from the office as Evan Mallory, red-faced and sweaty, stormed off to his office adjacent to hers.

"You can enter now. Please leave your phone with me; we'll run a security scan on it during your meeting," Gemma told Gabriella.

"Scanning my phone…this is a first," Gabriella replied, carefully schooling her face so as not to reveal the trepidation this pronouncement caused.

"Standard procedure for new hires," Gemma replied, looking sympathetically into Gabriella's eyes before motioning her to enter Draven's office.

Gabriella felt a shiver run down her spine and beads of sweat forming on her palms and forehead as Draven Cross eyed her from behind a giant desk as she stopped inside the doorway of the secretary-general's office. Her mind was racing. *What if security personnel discover my phone is an encrypted communicator? I could be floating in the East River by lunch.*

Calm down and pay attention—you are in the lion's den and need your wits about you, she admonished herself as Draven motioned for her to be seated in a deceptively uncomfortable leather chair in front of his desk.

"Good morning, Gabriella," Draven greeted her. "It's a pleasure to finally have someone of your intellect and talent aboard my staff."

"Thank you, sir. It's a great opportunity and privilege to work with you toward achieving a better world," Gabriella returned calmly.

"Yes, it is a privilege to work toward such a noble goal. So tell me, how did a trained spy who has conducted numerous clandestine operations around the world end up sitting in front of me?"

"I am not sure why you would think I am a trained spy," Gabriella responded, trying to remain calm as she tried to ascertain whether her cover had already been blown.

"Let's not play games, Gabriella. I have your entire dossier and operational history right here in front of me." Draven made a show of throwing the files across the desk at Gabriella. He smiled, revealing his snow-white teeth, as Gabriella looked at the documents with stunned dismay. Her face, however, gave away nothing of her feelings.

"I don't see how my past affects my present employment, sir."

"Oh, but it does, my dear. I have every intention of your using all those skills the American government taught you and that Ivy League intellect to help me ferret out my enemies—all those who seek to undermine my vision for global peace." Draven's silky voice held a thread of underlying steel.

"And who would those enemies be, sir?"

"Let's start with your former boss, President Rodgers. I have this feeling that the old dog is trying to come up with a few new tricks. Tell me, would that be a correct assessment?" Draven queried pointedly.

"Sir, President Rodgers is a man who wants peace. He is seeking your goodwill, which is one reason for my appointment to work with you," Gabriella replied, hoping to deflect away from her allegiances and to reinforce Draven's vision.

Draven stood and walked behind Gabriella, causing her to whirl around to face him looking down at her.

"You are fooling only yourself, Gabriella. You believe in intellect, reason, and the hope that a leader with the right ideology will usher in the world of your dreams. You're wrong. It's the use of power to exploit the weaknesses of people and systems that will create the world you desire. I will identify enemies to my goals, and you will provide me with weaknesses to crush them. Do you understand?" Draven demanded as he hovered over Gabriella.

Gabriella felt almost no control over herself as she stared into Draven's intense green eyes. She heard herself respond affirmatively but realized there was no emotion behind the response, as if she were not the one speaking.

"Welcome to the team. I expect a complete report by Sunday evening outlining the foibles of each of the ten leaders that will be attending next week's conference. That's all for now," Draven said in dismissal as he once again seated himself behind his desk.

Gabriella walked out of Draven's office in a daze and shook her head, trying to clear her mind and get her new boss's gaze out of her mind. As she sat down at her desk with her hands bracketing her face and became lost in thought, Gabriella realized with certainty that she was intellectually outmatched by Draven. She stared at her quantum communicator on the corner of the desk. A sticky note had been attached, merely saying she was okay. However, Gabriella knew she was far from good. Her brain would not be enough to keep her alive as a spy in the ranks of Draven Cross. She breathed aloud the words that had been running incessantly through her mind for the last several days. "What have I gotten myself into?"

As Christopher and Jackson made their way into the Omega Group office spaces in the Pentagon, both men stopped at the sight of John Barnes intently "working" at a classified information computer terminal.

"Oh, hey, how's it going?" John greeted them, quickly logging off the computer and standing as Christopher approached the terminal.

"You tell me, John. What are you doing here so early in the morning?" Christopher asked.

What Christopher did not realize about John Barnes was he always sought to benefit himself in any situation. His early arrival to the Omega Group offices and snooping through classified files was Barnes's way of finding something he could use in the future.

"Yeah, I've never thought of you as particularly industrious," Jackson added.

"That's funny, Jackson, considering I'm on the same elite team as you," Barnes spat back.

"That's enough," Christopher ordered, moving in between the two men.

"You're right. I'm going to grab some coffee," Jackson explained, staring Barnes down as he left the room.

"John, I was hoping to have this conversation later, but that little exchange is just further evidence that you're not a good fit for Omega," Christopher said.

"What? You're kicking me off Omega because I don't play well with Jackson? This is ridiculous," Barnes said, shoving a chair in palpable anger.

"Look, you're emotionally out of control. Starting with Brazil, your constant flare-ups with the team sergeant, aka Jackson, and the way you just handled this news is final confirmation. It all tells me you're a walking liability, which in our line of work is unacceptable. I have serious doubts that anything is going to improve, so effective today, you're reassigned to SOCOM headquarters," Christopher ordered.

"I always heard you were a Boy Scout, Barrett. I'll one-up your reassignment—I'm retiring. But trust me, you will regret this move." Barnes punched a wall next to Christopher before grabbing his backpack and leaving the Omega Group offices.

"Hey, did I just see Barnes walking out of here?" Jackson asked, reappearing with two cups of coffee.

"Yep, I just sent him packing," Christopher replied.

"Oh, that's a shame," Jackson muttered, not even trying to hide a big, toothy grin.

"It's not funny, Jackson. Barnes was crazy, but he's a skilled operative. We will miss his talent in the days ahead."

"Whatever, man. That dude should have never been here. He was a turd that just wouldn't flush. So what do we need to do for this mission?"

Christopher and Jackson were planning for the security mission at the nuclear black site in Alaska, with other members of Omega filtering in and out of the room, when Christopher's quantum mobile device vibrated, meaning a new message had been delivered. The display read: *"Package from Susan destroyed in 15 minutes."*

"Jackson, take over. I've got to step out for a few minutes," Christopher ordered before darting into Gabriella's old office. He hit identify on his phone's display, which would close the quantum key distribution loop between his device and the sender, in this case dubbed Susan, aka Gabriella. The system checked near instantaneously for eavesdropping or "hacking." Hacking a quantum system required some level of measuring, which would produce a detectable anomaly, causing the transmission of a sender's message to fail.

Christopher's device was correctly identified and provided the encryption algorithm to decrypt the incoming message. The security on each phone was ensured by limiting the time quantum information could be stored on the device. Christopher knew it would be impossible to penetrate the network as long as no one got to the actual human sender, which made him wince as he thought about one of the owners—whom he knew and cared about—of this technological marvel being discovered in her role as a spy.

Gabriella's now decrypted message read, *"Draven is a frigid and power hungry person. I am not saying he is the AntiChrist, so don't say 'I told you so' just yet. Make sure you and Jackson watch the U.E. press conference in about an hour. Big announcements to be made today. Take care. I will be in touch."*

U.E.? What does that mean? Christopher wondered. He typed out a brief message telling Gabriella that the team would be flying out to Alaska later that night and that he would watch the U.N. meeting, assuming U.E. must be a typo. He headed back to the planning room to finish up so he and Jackson could tune in to the press conference in Gabriella's old office.

"Everything all right?" Jackson asked, observing his boss through narrowed eyes.

"Yeah, I think so, but let's wrap this up and get everyone out of here. We have a press conference to watch," Christopher replied.

"Oh, man, don't tell me that was a message from Gabriella. Every time, I mean *every* time we hear from that woman, it leads to something crazy, like me wearing a suit or babysitting the devil."

Chuckling, Christopher responded, "You're ridiculous. I can't believe you're still going on about wearing a suit. You would think a country boy like you would enjoy dressing up."

Jackson laughed, saying, "Dressing up where I grew up did not require a suit, just a clean button-up shirt, jeans, and maybe a pair of boots if you're feeling sexy."

Christopher belly laughed before replying, "I've got nothing to say to that."

Evan Mallory took the podium in the now U.E. press room to deliver his first address as the U.E. deputy. Surrounded by story-hungry journalists, Evan exuded more confidence than he did in consultation with Draven. He needed this moment to be flawless in order to show his new boss that the Prince of This World was right for causing their paths to cross.

"Ladies and gentlemen, I want to begin today's press briefing with an essential administrative note. Effective immediately, the United Nations will be known as the Unified Earth Organization, or U.E. for short. This decision centers on Secretary-General Cross's vision to bring the world together under the banner of peace and harmony in the wake of the global disappearances.

"The first official resolution passed under the first U.E. secretary-general's tenure, signed just this morning, is ratification of a seven-year peace treaty with Israel by all U.E. countries, an extension of the EU peace treaty with Israel. Additionally the secretary-general has formed an exploratory committee to expand the Interfaith spiritual movement toward a unifying organized faith that encompasses all religious beliefs and several other economic initiatives to be discussed with world leaders early next week.

"Lastly, the headquarters of the U.E. will relocate from New York City to a yet-to-be-determined location. Mr. Cross feels that for too long the Western world has benefited from and corrupted this organization while failing to help the truly needy of the world. I will provide further details on the relocation of the U.E. at a later date."

Evan closed the press briefing by fielding questions from the "U.E." press pool with a confidence Gabriella had not seen in the man before. The reporters seemed enthralled by his message, in a manner that was similar to the reception Draven received when speaking. As she watched Evan exit the press room with a renewed vigor, her only thought was that it appeared this odd duo was destined for greatness.

Evan was the last member of the fledging U.E. secretary-general's staff to enter Draven's office, and he was greeted by unexpected applause from Draven.

"Bravo, old man. You have a rare gift to be brilliant when it counts, which is on a big stage," Draven complimented as he replayed the press briefing.

Evan beamed with pride as he took his seat at the eight-seat conference table that had been recently placed in the vast office space.

"Gemma, please bring up the Project Babylon presentation," Draven directed as he moved in front of the conference table where Gemma, Evan, and Gabriella were seated. A large screen dropped down behind him from the vaulted ceiling. "Well, my dear colleagues, we are off to an excellent start to making the world indeed a global village. I plan to fill out my senior staff next week during the leadership conference to help finalize Project Babylon, my plan for a one-world government," he said with a prideful smile.

"Project Babylon will be executed in three phases. We are currently in the first phase, consolidation of the world's power. The disappearances helped push my agenda and leadership to the forefront, speeding my process of gaining control of the world. What I imagined would take years to complete has been accomplished in just a little over a month. Evan, I want you to solidify Interfaith as the 'social balm' for an ailing world. I need you to get this done within the next three months. In our current phase, I want you to push the world toward one religion, centered on my political objectives."

"Great idea, sir. I will have a plan on your desk before the leadership conference," Evan responded.

"Phase 2 will be eliminating rivals. This elimination will focus not only on competing leaders but also governance systems. Evan's moving toward a one-world faith is but one element to ensure the leadership of the world is headed by me. In the days ahead, I plan to move the economic system to a single currency and consolidate each nation's government under the authority of the U.E., and ultimately myself."

"So what rivals to this plan are you expecting, sir?" Gabriella questioned.

"A simple question you should be able to answer, Dr. Costa. However, I'll entertain your query. My rivals will come in the traditional fashions—political, economic, and the conservative religious sects. If the world is to have peace, we must plan to marginalize any resistance to our plans," Draven stated firmly.

"That's an interesting vision, but it doesn't come across as peaceful, but rather authoritarian." Gabriella drew deep stares from the others in the room.

"Gabriella, I take your challenging naivety as a symptom of your American upbringing. The bottom line is, as the first and only world leader that can bring universal and lasting peace to this planet, I am willing to take stern measures to bring humanity to its full potential. I suggest you come to support my plans rather than second-guessing them," Draven expressed with a sharp-edged tone that stilled the room.

Gabriella merely nodded in agreement, fearing she might have been dragged out of the room by security had she spoken another word.

"Now, where was I? Oh yes, governance of the world reborn in my image is the final phase. I plan to lead from a new global headquarters built upon the ancient ruins of Babylon. This resurrected Babylon will be a city that the merchants of the world will swoon after, making the financial district here in New York City a distant memory. Babylon City will become a pilgrimage, a spiritual destination for the peoples of the world. Just imagine all of humanity finally worshipping together with the supreme power of this world, physically manifested in a city like no other.

"In closing, I will ensure that nothing stops this grand strategy from becoming a reality. This is the world that everyone has dreamed of. I am the leader that the world has always sought. We will rule the world and bring humanity to its destiny with an iron fist wrapped in a velvet glove," Draven declared with a decidedly fiendish flash in his green eyes.

When the others in the room clapped—either from fear or genuine zeal—Gabriella joined them to keep from arousing Draven's suspicion, but she felt nothing. She had long dreamed of a world united, not blinded by differences. However, the cost the world was about to pay seemed steep. Draven would rob the world of freedom while being praised by the masses. As she headed to her office more confused than anything else, she had the thought that perhaps President Rodgers and Jackson were right about the man whose presence she had just left.

Chapter 12

As they packed the final "tough boxes" full of equipment for the Alaska mission, Christopher could tell by Jackson's constant huffing that the U.E. press conference was bothering him.

"What's up? Why all the sighs?" Christopher asked, his hands stilling over the box he was packing.

"Oh, nothing, I'm okay. Just thinking about what Mallory said," Jackson returned dejectedly.

"And…?"

Jackson inhaled loudly then sat down opposite Christopher on a desk in the now-empty Omega Team room. "For starters, Draven's signing of a covenant for seven years of peace with Israel will satisfy the prophecy found in Daniel 9:27, marking the official start to the tribulation."

"I'm listening," Christopher encouraged.

"It is also interesting that the U.N. headquarters is moving—"

"You mean, the U.E. headquarters," Christopher interrupted.

"U.E., U.N., whatever. I want to know what's behind the move," Jackson asserted.

"That's easy enough. Remember, we have an insider on Draven's staff."

"I realize that, but each message Gabriella sends puts us all at risk. I think for now it's best to wait for her to contact us," Jackson said, crossing his arms and staring off into the emptiness of the room.

"So we are at the beginning of the timeline for the end-times, right?"

"You need to—"

"I know—study. But just tell me," Christopher said, cutting off a visibly irritated Jackson again.

"I was going to say study, but who knows when you will study the Bible? Well, I suppose we, or better said I, know that Draven is the Antichrist already. However, he won't be fully manifested as the Antichrist until the midway point of the tribulation. We have forty-two months before the great tribulation, which Jesus described in Matthew 24:21: 'For then shall be great tribulation, such as was not since the beginning of the world to this time, no, nor ever shall be.' Jesus was describing the forty-two months after the abomination of desolation, mentioned in Matthew 21:15, that will take place under the leadership of the Antichrist in the rebuilt temple in Jerusalem."

"So we are in the first forty-two months of the tribulation."

"You got it, slick," Jackson confirmed. "As we've already discussed, according to Revelation 6:1, Jesus has opened the first seal, which is where John saw the Antichrist on a white horse. Draven is conquering the world with peace, but it's all a setup. But this is just the calm before a massive storm. The opening of the second seal in Revelation 6:3–4 will unleash global war. Then the best we can hope for is survival until Christ Jesus returns. You really should crack open a Bible, college boy."

"Wow, you have really been studying all of this," Christopher said thoughtfully.

"There is a ton of information regarding the tribulation, a term that's now our reality. I've been reading not only Rev's journal but articles on the Internet and the ultimate guide, the Bible itself, on the topic. It's sad to see how much truth was available but deemed nonsense by folks like me." Jackson dropped his face into his palms.

"Nothing we can do about that now. We just have to focus on survival. Do you think this Alaska mission will play a part in the coming war," Christopher inquired?

"I don't know, but we need to have a plan. Our days in the U.S.

military are likely numbered. I know I won't serve Draven Cross as a solider," Jackson replied, grabbing a sizeable black rifle case as he moved to the team room exit.

"I'm with you there. I might not see the Antichrist in Draven Cross yet, but I can't see serving him, either. Alaska may prove to be our final U.S. government assignment," Christopher said sadly, turning off the lights as they went out the door.

Gabriella was exhausted after yesterday—her first day as a double agent. Thankfully it was Saturday. She donned her robe and stood to stare out the floor-to-ceiling windows in her luxury apartment bedroom with a Sutton Place address, mere minutes away from the U.E. building. The view should have been an exhilarating testament to her professional ascension. However, across the East River, Roosevelt Island was being transformed into a collection point for disappearance victim's vehicles, reminding Gabriella of how she had acquired the job.

She watched the endless trailers of ownerless cars being brought to large lots of land being cultivated to hold relics from a world that was lost. She saw the reality of the situation where millions had been taken by God or some alien power, leaving the world and her search for answers and hope in one man, Draven Cross. *What a difference a month can make in a person's perspective on career success*, she thought bleakly.

Departing her apartment for a casual working weekend at the U.E. building, Gabriella was confused but focused on finding a way to stay ahead—at least, as best she could—of Draven. While a part of her was awestruck to be working for arguably the most brilliant mind on the planet, she also saw in Draven characteristics that elicited fear in her heart. She couldn't shake the suspicion that her friends might be right about Draven Cross being the Antichrist and, even worse, that God did exist and she had missed a chance to have a relationship with Him.

As Gabriella completed the half-mile walk and entered U.E. plaza, she saw the same group of Hasidic Jewish men dressed in what could best be described as burlap overshirts protesting near barricades. The tall wisp of a man she presumed to be the leader of the burlap gaggle was intriguing. The leader seemed to be calling out to bystanders, angering most, but persuading others to talk with his followers nearby. She drew closer to find it was not protesting but rather preaching projecting from this man with the penetrating tone and clear enunciation.

"Brothers and sisters, hear the words of the true and living God—the God who sent His only Son, Jesus the Christ, into this world to die for our sins. It is not too late to come to know the one true Prince of Peace, the wonderful counselor, who is named Jesus. You should not trust the promises of peace that come from the institutions of man. Look instead to the assurances of the Bible."

While some cursed the man, it seemed to Gabriella that his words drew many to his colleagues who appeared to be praying and weeping with those who heeded his voice.

"That is a strange message coming from a Hasidic Jew," Gabriella said as the preacher took a break and passed her as he moved toward his friends.

"I was blind, but now I see. Jesus was the Messiah. *Yahweh* has shown my brothers and me the truth, and we have felt compelled to tell the world without ceasing about Jesus. My name is Samuel, and your name is?"

"Gabriella Costa. I work at the U.E. You know, that institution you're bashing out here."

"Well, I am sorry for that Gabriella, as the U.N. is becoming a perversion of the principles it supposedly represents. The world will suffer under the fist of the man who now leads the organization," Samuel replied confidently.

"It's U.E. now, but those are strong words about an organization and man you know little of," Gabriella retorted, surprised by her defense of a man she didn't trust.

"I am part of a voice that cries out to the world from the wilderness.

My brothers and I call the world to Christ Jesus in this final season. You, Gabriella, have questioned the character of Mr. Cross. You have wrestled with trusting your intellect and reason over the evidence of the living God of Heaven rapturing His Church. It is not too late to accept the gift of salvation that Jesus offers. Know that your position places your very life and soul in danger. Choose wisely where you place your faith. It's either Jesus or your belief in Draven Cross."

"What? How did you know? I mean, what are you saying to me?" Gabriella shouted at Samuel's back as he walked back to his position and began preaching again, leaving her shaken and unanswered.

Jackson was mesmerized by the rugged beauty of the Canadian Rockies displayed below the commercial jet streaking toward Anchorage, Alaska, the gateway to the remote nuclear black site. While he was grateful to have found the saving grace and mercy of God through His Son Jesus, he struggled with how he had failed his family. Hot tears streamed down his face as the snow-capped peaks brought his wife Sarah to mind, as she had asked him a thousand times to take her to Alaska. Despite his quiet sobs, Jackson still heard the soft, peace-filled voice of the Holy Spirit as it flooded his mind, saying, *"Give all your worries and cares to God, for He cares about you."*

"It is so hard, Lord. I let my family down. I lost them because my priorities were others before them," Jackson said as he sensed the presence of God in his mind.

"Oh, my son, who of you by worrying can add a single hour to his lifespan? Therefore do not worry about tomorrow, for tomorrow will worry about itself. Today has enough trouble of its own. Remember, Jackson, the eyes of the LORD are on the righteous, and his ears are open to their cry."

"Hey, are you all right?" Christopher asked, dropping into a nearby seat and reaching over to touch the shoulder of his friend, who was slumped over in his chair.

"Yeah, man, I'll be fine. I was just thinking about my family and talking with the Lord," a red-faced Jackson said, sitting up to face Christopher.

"I am sorry, man. Do you want me to leave you alone for a while? I just had a thought for a plan to survive the next seven years, but we can talk later," Christopher offered, getting up to return to his seat.

"No, please stay. I could use a good laugh and some distraction."

"Laugh? What? Do you think I can't come up with a good survival plan?" Christopher asked, feigning offense.

"Just pulling your overly sensitive leg. Lay your plan on me, brother."

Smiling, Christopher began. "All I came up with, truth be told, is that we need a new base of operations. If what you're saying is true about global war, coupled with the fact we are heading to a secret site to guard nukes, then heading back to D.C. is the last thing we should do after this mission."

"There is a lot of truth in that statement. You're absolutely right—D.C., or any major city, won't work. I have a feeling nukes will be in play during this global war. This war, the second seal judgment, is the foundation for some horrible postwar fallout judgments. The Bible is clear that within the first four seal judgments, one-fourth of the population left on this planet will be dead, which places the death toll well above a billion people. It makes the words of Jesus in Matthew 24:22 all the more real: 'If those days had not been cut short, no one would survive, but for the sake of the elect those days will be shortened.' Just accept Jesus, Christopher. Let the pain go. Trust me, life is uncertain now. Stop resisting before you make an eternal mistake."

"Don't push me, Jackson. I understand that things are not looking good for any of us right now, but it's not easy to just let God take over my life, my thoughts, to forgive the hurt."

"It is that easy to surrender to God, but I will keep praying for you. As far as surviving the next seven years, my family's homestead in Alabama will probably be a good basing option. I'm gonna sleep on the details. Wake me when we reach the polar bear city."

"I will let you have your beauty rest, princess, but we need to finalize how we are going to survive," Christopher said, pushing the now-outstretched legs of Jackson off the seats as he headed back to his row.

"Watch it, or I will leave you out of the final plan," Jackson threatened, smirking and pulling his ball cap down over his eyes.

Gabriella's encounter with Samuel added to her paranoia of the future. How did he know her internal struggles with Draven's character? It couldn't be possible that God was speaking to her through Samuel. She rationalized Samuel's seeming intuition regarding her reservations about Draven as him just projecting his hostility toward her employment with the U.E.

As she sat behind her desk to start working on the list Draven had demanded for the global leaders' conference in two days, her quantum communicator vibrated, signaling a message had arrived. The display read: *"A package from the Eagle will be destroyed in 15 minutes."* Her first thought was, *Ugh, that is a poor cover for POTUS.* While she could wait the fifteen minutes for the quantum device to automatically erase the message, Gabriella loved the autokill feature, which—with the user's biometric data, in this case a thumbprint—instantly turned the device into an expensive paperweight.

President Rodgers's message read, *"Gabriella, I've arrived unannounced into New York ahead of the global leaders' conference. If you're available, message me, and I will respond with where we can meet. I would like to gain your insight into the recent announcements by the U.E. and that snake, Cross."*

Gabriella wiped the message from her device after responding to President Rodgers, laughing at his attempts to work incognito. Sure enough, her phone chirped a few moments later with directions to meet the president at seven o'clock that evening at a small steakhouse in Hell's Kitchen. *Well, I had better get to work. Who knows what tonight holds in store?*

As the chartered commercial plane taxied to a secluded section of Ted Stevens International Airport in Anchorage, Christopher walked back to wake Jackson.

"Wake up, old man. We're in the polar bear city."

"What…really? Man, I didn't realize how tired I was. Wait…is that snow on the ground?" Jackson shouted as he pressed his face against his window to see the snow-covered tarmac awaiting the Omega Team.

"Yeah, that's snow. Surprise, surprise. Snow in Alaska in mid-November. Put on your big boy pants and jacket. You'll live," Christopher replied drily.

Several SUVs with dark-tinted windows and emergency flashers sat at the bottom of the staircase as the frigid Arctic air rushed through the open cabin door.

"Dude, really. I knew it was going to be cold in Alaska, but I am getting frostbite before I even set foot outside," Jackson grumbled.

"Look, suck it up. You have some of the best winter gear available. I hope you're not going to complain the whole time we're here," a laughing Christopher said over his shoulder.

"I just might," Jackson replied with a pursed face.

As the other men of Omega began filing off the plane and into the SUVs, a single, hulking figure bundled in a large mountaineering parka waited outside the lead vehicle.

"I am guessing you're Major Barrett and Sergeant Major Williams," the human mountain greeted, extending a hand, which looked like a bundle of bananas, to Christopher and Jackson.

"Yes, I'm Sergeant Major Williams, but call me Jackson. I am guessing you're missing from the local circus."

Laughing, the man replied, "Nah, my momma just knows how to grow 'em big. I'm Chief Master Sergeant Jim Petty, but please call me Jimbo. I'm in charge of the site's security."

"Please excuse the comedian on my team, Chief. It's a pleasure to meet you, Jimbo. Just call me Christopher. I am guessing we still have a little traveling to do before we reach the site."

"Roger that. We should get going. We have Blackhawks waiting for us at Elmendorf Air Base, just outside of Anchorage. From there, it's a two-hour flight into the Alaska Range, then we'll drive an hour from the helipad to the site location," Jimbo explained.

"Man, this little excursion just keeps getting better and better. Seems to me I remember a television show about some folks being stranded forever in the middle of nowhere starting out with a theme song that said something about a three-hour tour," Jackson said, smarting off.

Smiling at Christopher, Jimbo asked, "Is he always so motivated?"

"You have no idea. We can get to know each other over the next few hours, but let's head out. We're losing daylight standing here."

Over the next five hours (instead of three, due to bad weather), Christopher and Jackson learned that Jimbo was from Sioux City, Iowa, and had been raised on a hog farm that supported a local processing plant. He measured six feet and seven inches and weighed in at a solid 240 pounds of pure muscle. With golden-blonde hair and blue eyes, Jimbo was the poster child for an all-American farm boy. He had joined the Air Force after high school in search of adventure and became a pararescueman, or PJ as they're colloquially known. Christopher could see in Jimbo Petty the makings of a great new ally for the troubled days ahead.

Gabriella arrived a little late to the steakhouse as the disappearances had created complete havoc in the already unpredictable New York City traffic patterns. As she entered the restaurant, she laughed to herself at the disguise President Rodgers had donned for their dinner meeting.

"May I help you?" the maître d' asked.

"I see my party has already arrived," Gabriella replied, pointing to an elderly gentleman with a flowing white wig. "I'll just join him, thanks." The restaurant the president selected was luxurious but had an older-era charm with exposed wooden beams in the ceiling, elegant white-linen table coverings, and the subtle notes of fine cigars in the air. Laughing as she was seated, she teased, "You've got to be kidding me, sir. You look like a senile grandpa that got lost in his pajamas. If it were not inappropriate, I'd take a picture of you and sell it to the tabloids."

"I get it, I would never pass as a CIA field agent, but it has all these people fooled," President Rodgers retorted.

"Anyway, it's good to see you, sir. The first few days with Draven have been interesting, to say the least."

Putting up a hand to halt her speech, the president said, "Hey, let's order food first. I am starving." He signaled their waiter, who moved immediately across the room to their table.

"Good evening. It will be my pleasure to serve you this evening. What may I bring you tonight?" the waiter asked.

"Ladies first," Rodgers replied.

"I will have your center-cut filet mignon, medium, and a baked potato with butter." Gabriella couldn't help but tack on with a grin, "My grandfather will have the steak salad."

"Grandpa will have the porterhouse, medium rare, with the steak fries," the president quickly corrected with a grin of his own. As the waiter departed, he said, "Now fill me in on what Draven has been planning."

"Well, you've heard of the name change for the former U.N., but really that was just an element of what Draven calls Project Babylon."

As they ate, Gabriella detailed Draven's three-phase plan of consolidating world power and ruling the world. She even relayed her encounter with the group led by Samuel in the U.E. plaza earlier in the day.

"I would be lying if I said I was shocked by what you've told me tonight. In my opinion, Draven is, without doubt, Gabriella, the man the Bible calls the Antichrist."

"Sir, I get that the plan sounds very authoritarian, but it's hard to contemplate Draven is the Biblical Antichrist. I can't even say Antichrist without wanting to smack myself for saying something so ridiculous. No, I see Draven moving toward what countless non-Antichrist leaders before him have done, which is taking power for himself. We need to prepare to fight him, sir."

"My dear Gabriella, your heart is leading you to the truth, but your intellect is in the way. Your soul is screaming God exists, He raptured His Church, and you work for the worst leader the world will ever witness, but you're trying to suppress the evidence with logic. If the detailed encounter with this man named Samuel today doesn't resonate with you that God is trying to reach you, well, then I fear for you." The president's concern for her was evident in his tone.

"I want to encourage you to continue to challenge your own mind as well as the assertions that there is no way God exists. Start opening your thinking to the genuine possibility that God is at work in the world around us. If I may be quite honest with you, your issue is pride, plain and simple. You see your intellect as superior to perhaps everyone—well, everyone not named Draven. You've been carrying an arrogance that you know everything into each argument presented for God, believing that there is no way God could exist. The world around us should tell you that for all your education, you have missed the most precious knowledge any of us can ever receive, namely, that God is real and you—in fact, we all—need Him," President Rodgers concluded as he signaled for the check.

Gabriella began to tear up, unable to challenge the assertion—for the second time today—about her hesitance to accept God. And both encounters had provided such clear insight into her struggle between reason and God.

"Look, I won't accept Draven's plan lying down. I am taking the Lord with me into that meeting on Monday. I'll play along, but if the opportunity to bring this man down presents itself, I am taking the shot,"

President Rodgers stated emphatically and he stood and handed the waiter a wad of cash.

"Nice move, paying in cash. Doesn't leave a named trail. You seem like you could survive as a field agent. However, there is one thing that's been bugging me all night. How did you get away from your Secret Service agents?" Gabriella asked, standing as the president placed her jacket around her shoulders.

"Oh, that! Well, take a look around," Rodgers replied.As Gabriella watched, every other diner in the restaurant stood to escort the president and Gabriella out of the restaurant."The owner is a lifelong friend, so we had this intimate space all to ourselves tonight," President Rodgers explained with a smile.

Laughing, Gabriella replied, "You're a smooth operator. I wish you the best on Monday." They exited the restaurant into a brisk, cold wind.

"Yield to your heart, Gabriella. You're missing things all around you that will point you to God. I am trying to pound the same message home to my daughter. Tonight and earlier today should reinforce my point with you. Take care, and I'll be in touch," President Rodgers promised, climbing into a waiting SUV and leaving Gabriella alone with her thoughts in the cold.

Gabriella felt overcome with emotion as she jumped into her rideshare car. She would be a fool to deny that Draven was not who he portrayed himself to be to the world. She also couldn't dismiss her incredible encounter with the stranger named Samuel, when he had detailed the war between her mind and emotions. Gabriella wanted a clear sign from God that he was reaching for her, which seemed outrageous even to her. As the car stopped at a light, she noticed a streetlight pole covered in missing/looking for person posters of disappearance victims.

As she exited the vehicle at her apartment, Gabriella challenged the God of the Universe. "If You exist, show me who Draven really is," she demanded expectantly, while still doubting God would answer.

CHAPTER 13

Security was tight ahead of Monday morning's global leader's conference at the U.E. headquarters. Draven felt a surge of energy and the strong presence of his spiritual guide coursing in his thoughts. *"You don't need to sell your plan. These men will be your servants as pride fills their hearts. Place your trust only in me,"* the Prince of This World said clearly in Draven's mind.Cross felt ready to make the world his and trample anything or anyone who got in his way. "Gemma, the world leaders' photo with me will happen in the next ten minutes, correct?"

"Sir, we are missing a couple of leaders. I've already spoken with—"

"Spare me the excuses. Let me guess...President Rodgers and former U.N. Secretary-General Aguilar. Well, those two should get over the fact that I will usher in an era of peace they only dreamed of achieving. If they are not here in five minutes, we will take the picture without them," Draven said imperiously, moving toward the elevators.

"Yes, sir, understood," Gemma responded quietly.

"Sir, hold up, I'll ride down..." The elevator door promptly closed in the face of Evan Mallory. "It's a big day, Gemma. Everyone is excited," Mallory said, in an attempt to maintain his dignity despite the insult he had just received.

"Yes, sir. It's a big day," Gemma said flatly, noticing Dr. Costa heading for the elevators. "Oh, glad to see you, Gabriella. Could you please pass the message to the secretary-general that President Rodgers is detained in traffic and won't make the photo with the other leaders?"

"I'll handle that, Gabriella," Evan Mallory said as he held the door to the elevator open. When the elevator doors opened to the U.E. lobby, Evan was shocked to see the photographers already snapping photos of Draven and the world leaders, minus President Rodgers, and him.

"Evan, you're late, and I wait for no man," Draven said as the group moved to a conference room adjacent to the main foyer of the U.E. building. As everyone settled in, President Rodgers made a fashionably and purposefully late entrance, his presence bringing relief to many in the room when they realized that the U.S. would participate. Draven produced a fake smile as the two men moved to greet each other.

"I was beginning to worry about you, old man. I'm glad you could make it, though it's a shame you missed the historic photos. I am sure we could add you in later if you'd like," Draven offered, extending a hand to President Rodgers.

"Amazing the traffic you can encounter in this city," President Rodgers replied. "Before I forget, I was wondering where the bill for *Air Force One* should be dropped off."

"I'll just deduct it from your military contributions to the U.E. How does that sound, President Rodgers?" Draven said silkily.

"Shall we get down to business, Mr. Secetary-General?" President Rodgers asked, none-too-subtly avoiding Draven's extended hand as he moved toward his seat.

"A man always focused on business… I respect that attribute of yours. Yes, let's get on with our business. I think you will be inspired before the day is over, President Rodgers."

"Well, let's see how the day goes first," Rodgers responded from his seat at the large conference table before turning to nod to Gabriella, who was seated along the wall with the staff members of the various leaders.

Christopher felt an uneasiness about the mission Omega was performing in Alaska. As he nursed a cup of coffee in the base command post, he was glad to see the sun emerging after being hidden by a massive snowstorm for the last several days. Christopher planned to get out today to see the base his team was supposed to defend, hoping that would calm his nerves to some degree.

"Good morning, Jimbo. Quick question for you. Do you think we can head out this morning in the SUSVs to take a look at the perimeter of the site? I would like to get the know the area better, but the recent weather has stopped me," Christopher said as Jimbo entered the command post with Jackson.

"What is an SUSV?" Jackson asked.

"Small Unit Support Vehicle—it's used for Arctic environment military operations. It's also known as the 'big thing,' as you called it when we rode here in it from the helipad a few days ago," Christopher remarked sarcastically.

Answering Christopher's question, Jimbo said, "You read my mind. I'll go warm up a vehicle. Who knows how long this weather will hold? The last few days are more the norm than today during this time of year up here." He then left the warm command post to get a vehicle ready for travel.

"I was starting to wonder whether the sun was ever going to show its face again. It was dark when we showed up, and it's been snowing like we're in a snow globe for the last two days. To top that off, it's so cold, Jack Frost called in sick," Jackson grumbled as he nursed a cup of coffee.

Laughing, Christopher asked, "What does that mean where you're from?"

"It means it's too cold for me to be far from a heater," Jackson drawled with pretend gloom.

"That's too bad because you're coming with me. Remember the last recon I went on in Brazil?"

"You're right. I'll bring some coffee," Jackson retorted, smiling.

"Thanks for the vote of confidence in my recon abilities."

Jimbo entered the room along with a blast of cold air. "You guys ready to see some wild Alaska?"

Draven, utilizing to his advantage the information he had received beforehand on each of the ten leaders present, worked his way around the table, appealing to individual egos and eccentricities as he unfolded his plan for control of the world.

"Distinguished guests, you've been handpicked to join me in restoring the world after the devasting events of the past month. I ask that this week you all take a more in-depth look at the message you will soon be presented, looking for the opportunity not only for the world but for each of you and the part of the world you represent here today. I hope each of you will be inspired to share my vision of bringing the world to a level of prosperity and peace never before known to mankind.

"I foresee that within the next three months, the globe will be ruled by our centralized government, which will consist of ten regions ruled with semi-autonomy by a regional ambassador, or king, if you will. If you accept my plan, each of you will be made the ruler of your own area of the world—under my authority, of course.

"I call this plan Project Babylon. I chose the name *Babylon* since it was one of the most advanced civilizations the world has ever known. Throughout history, Babylon has been written about with awe and reverence, a history that we will recapture as we inspire the world within this new era for humanity. It is a project in the sense that it will take dedication and a rigorous process that we will define this week. The conclusion of our venture, once fully manifested, will bring the world under one government," Draven said, pausing briefly in an attempt to detect any resentment among the world's most powerful political leaders who were seated around the large conference table.

Intentionally choosing his first pawn by playing on the former U.N. secretary-general Maximilian Aguilar's sense of pride, Draven began to paint a picture for Aguilar of power beyond his wildest dreams. "Maximilian Aguilar, please stand," he said, and the group watched a hesitant Aguilar rise to his feet and move away from his seat at the table to stand in front of Draven. "My dear friend, you graciously paved the way for my ascension, stepping down from a seat of power, when most men would not have done so. You are a man of destiny who sees the potential of lasting peace and prosperity my leadership represents. Therefore upon the establishment of our universal government, you will be the first named U.E. Regional Ambassador. I bestow upon you the title Ambassador to the Unified South American Nations, which will include all of Central and South America."

"Sir, I am at a loss for words." Aguilar fell to his knees and praised Draven without hesitation.

Draven made no attempt to stop the overly emotional response from Aguilar. He merely began walking around the conference room, bestowing similar titles on the leaders present, listing the regions and countries that would be under the rule of each ambassador, flawlessly reciting all the information by memory. He enhanced his control over the influential group by conferring each of the titles in the future ambassador's native language, down to each person's unique dialect. Before long, the appointed ambassadors were bursting with pride, just as Draven's spiritual guide had predicted.

He continued in a magnanimous tone, saying, "The Unified African Nations will consist of all the nations on the African continent and the island of Madagascar, led by the representative here from Nigeria. The Unified Russian Nations, led by the representative here from Russia, include Russia, Mongolia, Estonia, Latvia, Lithuania, Ukraine, Georgia, Azerbaijan, Kazakhstan, Uzbekistan, Kyrgyzstan, Tajikistan, Turkmenistan, Afghanistan, and Turkey.

"The Unified Asian Nations are comprised of China, Taiwan, the Korean Peninsula, Japan, Vietnam, Laos, Cambodia, Thailand, Malaysia, Singapore, Indonesia, Papua New Guinea, and the Philippines, led by the representative here from China. The Unified Indian Nations, led by the representative here from India, include Sri Lanka, all Indian Ocean islands, Nepal, Bhutan, Bangladesh, and Myanmar. The Unified Nordic Nations will be led by the representative from Denmark and will include Denmark, Norway, Sweden, Greenland, Finland, and Iceland. The Unified European Nations, led by the representative from Germany, include Germany, France, Switzerland, all Central and Eastern European nations, Spain, Portugal, Italy, and Greece. The Unified British Commonwealth Nations, led by the representative here from Great Britain, include the United Kingdom, Australia, Tasmania, New Zealand, Ireland, and all Atlantic Ocean islands.

"The Unified Arabian Nations will be led by me," Draven said in Arabic. "My region will be unique, as it will hold the world seat of power in a location yet to be disclosed and include Israel, Iraq, Lebanon, Jordan, Syria, Iran, and the entire Saudi Arabian Peninsula."

Draven made a grand show of concluding his announcements of future titles and holdings for the exuberant room of leaders, coming to stand near the seat of the American president. He spoke in English once again. "President Rodgers, please stand."

Gabriella watched nervously as President Rodgers casually stood and buttoned his suit jacket, much less animated than his peers before him.

"Last and certainly not least, President Rodgers, the esteemed leader of these United States of America. I know you're a man that cares deeply about his country and ensuring your legacy as a great American president. You have been such a tremendous example of leadership for the world during your many years of global service. I was truly touched by your sentiment of hospitality upon my ascension to the world stage. It is with great honor and pride that I bestow upon you the title of Ambassador of the Unified American Nations, which include the United States of America, Canada, Mexico, all the Caribbean islands and the remaining Pacific islands." Smiling broadly, Draven delivered this pronouncement as though conferring an incredible honor.

"I am speechless," Rodgers stated flatly, quickly lowering his eyes to prevent Draven from seeing how revolted he was by the man. He hoped the schemer interpreted his minimal response as the result of being thunderstruck instead of the disdain he was trying so hard to mask.

President Rodgers was glad that Gabriella had "supplied" Draven with his idiosyncrasies being pride and love of country. It allowed him to better maneuver in his understanding of Project Babylon.

"Your silence is expected. There is no need to say anything. It is quite apparent that you are overcome by the honor I have bestowed upon you," Draven said silkily, gesturing for President Rodgers to be seated before concluding with the same chilling words he had spoken to each leader before him. "Your service is to me. You will do as I ask to ensure peace for all."

President Rodgers did not respond, but Draven seemed satisfied that the American president was so overcome with emotion that he couldn't acknowledge him.

Gabriella felt distant from the meeting, more like an observer looking through a two-way mirror than one seated in the conference room. She noticed that President Rodgers seemed agitated and more cognizant than the other leaders sitting around the table. She only hoped he was not being drawn in by Draven's pomp and circumstance.

Jackson felt a lump of pain rising to his throat as he took in the commanding view of untouched Alaskan wilderness beauty high above the secret nuclear missile base. He knew his wife Sarah would have loved the endless expanse of snow-capped peaks and sprawling forest. He prayed he would see her face again someday.

"Awesome view, right, Jackson?" Christopher pointed out.

"You called it," Jackson replied.

"Yeah, this is my favorite vantage point of the base," Jimbo said, handing out two pairs of high-powered binoculars. "Okay, so as you guys can see, the base is located in a U-shaped valley right at the base of this mountain. There…" he pointed to the snow-covered main road, "…is the only way vehicles can enter the base's footprint. As you probably remember, the road deadends at the helipad ten miles southeast of here. What you didn't see or know is, the road is surveilled every hundred meters by cameras and infrasound equipment, meaning we know if something is coming. In addition, antipersonnel and tank mines are placed at selected points along the road."

"Wow, that seems a little aggressive for one road," Christopher stated.

Jimbo replied, "Well, think about what this base holds and our purpose here."

"What about the boundaries for this place?" Jackson asked.

"The helipad marks the southern boundary, protected and hidden by the ridgeline of that granite mountain you see in the distance. Over there..." Jimbo pointed to the west, "...is a 100-mile-long glacier-fed river that eventually dumps into the ocean. We monitor the shore on both sides via motion-activated cameras and laser fields over sixty kilometers both directions of flow. To the east, about twenty kilometers out, you will see a line of black spruce trees that serve as the eastern boundary, guarded by a series of motion-detecting sensors, infrasound detectors, and laser fields placed randomly through the trees. Finally, the plateau we're standing on makes up the northern border of the base, extending another fifteen kilometers north from here. It's marked by the mountain range you see, which continues deep into the heart of Alaska and is protected by the same technologies as the other borders. The bottom line, gentlemen, is that it would be nearly impossible to find this place or get here without us knowing."

"I am impressed by the security and the remoteness. I just hope you're right about no one being able to get here," Christopher said grimly.

Jackson spoke up, a look of concern on this face. "The one big error in picking this place that I can see is where we are standing. I mean, the base sits in a large U-shaped bowl. A few explosive charges in the right place could bring this entire mountain down on the launch areas." He pointed to the towering solid granite mountain face looming over the base below.

"You're right, Jackson," replied the chief master sergeant. "But the location and the weakness you highlight are why the base was built here."

"What do you mean?" Jackson queried, apparently puzzled.

"When the ICBMs launch, the heat and vibration from the launches will break this mountain apart and bury this base, thus hiding the fact that it ever existed. We can remotely deploy the missiles once we are given the launch command by the president," Jimbo explained.

"I got it. That makes sense," Jackson agreed, both surprised and relieved.

"I just hope we don't have to find out if the design works," Christopher said quietly.

Rodgers had been silently praying for strength to resist Draven's manipulation as he watched leader after leader blindly falling into the pit of an unknown future with the ravenous wolf named Draven, despite his portrayal of himself as a sheep. He was grateful that God had protected him and allowed him to seem disingenuous to Draven thus far. Now he just needed to discover all he could about Project Babylon, as he was convinced Draven Cross had to be stopped at all costs.

"It is an honor to be counted as one of the world's top leaders and to have the opportunity to hear firsthand your plan for ushering in this era of world peace you've described. However, I think we all would like to hear further details on how you plan to do that, Mr. Secretary-General," President Rodgers remarked carefully.

Thankfully Draven assumed the American president's insistence on hearing the details of Project Babylon to be his agreement to serve him.

"Such enthusiasm from our most distinguished leader! Well, ladies and gentlemen, let me elaborate on what I aim to accomplish this week with you all. By the end of the week, the path to universal peace will be solid…and well funded," Draven said with a smile, drawing laughter from all those present in the room, except Gabriella and President Rodgers.

As the Project Babylon presentation she had seen days ago was brought up on a giant video screen, Gabriella met Rodgers's eyes as he gave her a reassuring smile. She breathed a sigh of relief that he had played his role well enough that Draven appeared to believe he was a loyal supporter of whatever was coming.

Draven stood, confident that he had in the palm of his hand the nine most influential world leaders, poised to serve him in his one-world government. It was in this moment of prideful reflection that the heavy feeling came to his mind, indicating that the Prince of This World was about to speak to him.

"You've won their prideful hearts. Now bind them to the plan with economics and religion," the Prince said in Draven's heart.

"The primary task for the remainder of this week will be building the process to achieve a single global economy, driven by one currency. My vision is to one day move to a cashless society based on the single currency, but first things first," Draven asserted, bringing up an infographic that outlined his economic plan. "As you can see, the disappearances have forced the international financial system into a recession. The estimates of damage caused by this event are nearing tens of trillions of U.S. dollars. My economic plan will eliminate foreign exchange transactions and hedging costs, and a single currency will reinvigorate stalled world trade and improve the efficiency of global capital allocation, which for too long has resided with only a few nations in this room. The near-term benefit will be a fast allocation of resources the world needs to rebuild, thus speeding up the global recovery process.

"We will move to three currencies initially and transition to a single currency over the next three months to prevent economic panic. China's yuan will be the currency for Asia, including Russia, the Indian subcontinent, the Indian Ocean islands, and Australia and Oceania. The euro will be the currency of choice for Europe and the African continent. Finally, the United States dollar will be the currency for all of North, Central, and South America," Draven finished.

All of the ambassadors except Rodgers applauded the economic plan. The American president knew he had to voice his displeasure, and his mind raced as he strove to speak in a manner that wouldn't raise Cross's suspicions.

"If I may make a comment, Mr. Secetary-General?" Every eye in the room immediately focused on Rodgers.

"Yes, please," Draven acknowledged.

"While I do believe there are some significant benefits to the plan you laid out, I have two primary concerns. First, I think it will be a tough sell to get the American people to sign off on moving to one currency if that currency is not the U.S. dollar. A lot is at stake if the dollar is not the reserve currency for the world. Second, what do you plan to do about resistance to forming your one-world government? I mean, that is the only way a single global currency would ever work," President Rodgers said, trying to keep his voice as meek as possible, hoping Draven would tell him more about his plan to control the world.

"While I think we all appreciate and can see the genuine concern you have for such a bold and aggressive economic plan, I believe your thinking highlights why the world craves a one-world government. While it is understandable up until today, your entire focus is only on the American people," Draven responded, unspoken censure in his tone.

"You're absolutely right, and it always will be in some shape or form," President Rodgers returned, interrupting Draven.

"Yes, I can see your passion. As I was saying, for too long the world has revolved around the political, cultural, and economic policies of the United States of America. A one-world government will ensure that everyone in the world has a voice in government. The buying power for citizens in the poorest nations will be the same as in your great nation, Mr. President," Draven replied forcefully, only to be cut off once again by President Rodgers.

"At what cost, Secretary-General?"

"The cost. That answer gets to the heart of your secondary concern. In any revolution or dramatic paradigm shift, sacrifices will need to be made. Based on the support I've received thus far in this room, I don't anticipate much resistance. I see the job of each of you in this summit, who have sworn allegiance to me and this plan, is to leave here this week prepared to carry forth our shared goals. If need be, President Rodgers, threats to global peace will be isolated and eliminated. Does that answer your concerns?" Draven intoned icily, which spoke volumes.

"Yes, sir, it does. I believe everything is crystal clear now," President Rodgers replied quietly, working hard to keep his face neutral, knowing he mustn't tip his hand.

"Excellent. America is a vital element in the world to come," Draven responded, seemingly assured of the American president's cooperation.

President Rodgers avoided Gabriella's eyes. She didn't know what to make of the economic plan or the president's body language. She was looking forward to the end of the day so the two of them could communicate over the quantum devices.

Jackson was enjoying the postcard-worthy scenery as he rode back down the mountain with the chief master sergeant and the major. His heart was focused on living out whatever time he had left on Earth in a way that was pleasing to God. He had found such joy and peace in his daily study of the Bible and Rev's journal. He prayed multiple times a day for Christopher to come to salvation before it was too late, and with Gabriella now working for a man he considered to be the Antichrist, Jackson prayed she would also come to have a relationship with Jesus Christ sooner rather than later.

"Hey, you guys mind me asking you a question?" Jimbo queried as he drove the lumbering SUSV back down to the base.

"Go for it," Major Barrett responded.

Chief Master Sergeant Petty said, "What do you guys think happened last month? I know what the new secretary-general has the world believing, but do you guys agree or what?"

"I think it was the rapture of the Church," Sergeant Major Williams replied before the major could even consider how he wanted to answer.

"That's interesting," Jimbo said. "I've also come to accept that to be the best explanation for what happened."

"Really?" Jackson asked. "What makes you think that?"

"The short answer is, I've become a believer in Jesus Christ. You wanna hear the longer version?" Jimbo asked with a smile.

Christopher gave up on responding since the subject had instantly made him uncomfortable anyway.

"Let's hear it, brother," Jackson responded enthusiastically. "I love hearing these stories."

"Okay," the chief replied. "Well, my parents took my siblings and me to church all the time growing up, but it was something we did just because that's what everyone in my small town did. You know, going to church was critical to the family's social standing. We never talked about God or salvation or anything related to daily living with God. We just went to church. I just assumed that I was a good guy and going to heaven one day. Once I left home, I never went to church and never really thought about God. Well, the rapture happened, and I was in shock like everyone else. I called home to check on my parents to see if they had disappeared. My mom answered the phone, crying and rambling on about them being left behind and she didn't understand why.

"I was just plain confused when we finished our call. I saw my parents as good Christians. They're honest, hardworking people that never did anything wrong, so I didn't understand how they could have been left behind, as my mom believed. That question started my search for the truth, which led me to the Internet and some famous pastor's teachings on salvation, having a relationship with Christ, and the rapture. I prayed to receive Jesus' salvation in my apartment before I left for this mission."

"So if you don't mind me asking, how did your parents take the news? You know…that they had never really accepted Jesus as their personal Savior?" the sergeant major asked thoughtfully.

"It's a work in progress. I think I'm more close to convincing my mom than my dad. He's a proud man and refuses to look at any of the materials I've given them. He tells my mom that if their pastor and friends are still here, then it couldn't have been God. I don't know, man. I pray and worry about them, but what can you do?"

"Well, I will pray for them with you," Williams promised.

"Thanks, Jackson. That means a lot to me. Well, it looks like we're here," the chief master sergeant said as he parked the SUSV in front of the command post where they had started the day.

Major Barrett didn't say anything as he jumped down from the vehicle and walked off to the living quarters.

"Did I offend him or something?" the chief asked.

"No, don't mind him. Christopher is having a hard time coming to accept God in his life. We just need to pray for him," the sergeant major answered.

"Hey, would you want to start a Bible study here on the base? I mean we have nothing but time to kill, right? And who knows? Maybe we can get guys like Christopher to accept Christ."

"That's an awesome idea. I'm in," Jackson responded enthusiastically.

Chapter 14

Draven Cross was proud of what he had been able to accomplish during the opening day of the summit. All of the critical political influencers in the world had agreed to his vision for the future, but what was even more significant was that they had accepted his authority over them. As he listened with the rest of the group to the final economic brief on the impacts and steps required to ensure Project Babylon's financial success, he knew he would rest well tonight knowing that his future was bright. As the presentation concluded, he rose to speak.

"Please allow me to thank the World Bank and International Monetary Fund for outlining the steps we will need to take to achieve a better financial future. As we prepare to close out a long but fruitful day, I'd like to cover a few final items," Cross began.

"First, during the remainder of the week, we will focus on smaller breakout sessions between your political and economic advisors and my team for the purpose of outlining a schedule of your upcoming responsibilities, namely, the contributions of military arms to the newly established Global Peace Assurance Directorate here at the U.E."

Rodgers interrupted, "Yes, sir. I was pleased to once again provide so much capability to the U.E., but could you describe for everyone's edification what the Global Peace Assurance Directorate is meant to accomplish?"

"For the sake of everyone's evening plans, I will simply say that this directorate has the teeth to ensure peace amongst nations here on Earth. My Global Peace Assurance forces are a departure from the lackluster U.N. peacekeepers who were woefully under-resourced, trained, or equipped for any mission. U.E. Global Peace Assurance soldiers will be able to isolate and destroy any threat to the peace we are striving to achieve. Is that clear enough for you, President Rodgers?" Draven asked sharply.

"Yes, Mr. Secretary-General, it is quite clear for all of us, I am sure," President Rodgers responded dryly.

"Good. In closing, please note the time on your schedules for your one-on-one meeting with me this week. In this meeting, I will provide you with refined guidance on your future role and my expectations. Then our summit will conclude on Friday with a briefing on bridging the religious and political elements of the world. Thank you for your support and best efforts in making the world a place of peace and harmony for all of humanity. I will see you all soon. Good night."

Gabriella watched as many of the world leaders quickly moved to thank and congratulate Draven on Project Babylon and their expected roles. She saw President Rodgers, Aguilar, and the Nigerian president talking in their own little huddle, and she wondered what the obviously tense men were discussing. President Rodgers shook hands with the other two men and called Gabriella over to him as they walked away.

He started talking when she was close enough to prevent others from hearing their conversation. "What a day. I have a raging headache from listening to all the lies and watching everyone fawn all over Draven. I will send you a couple of messages tonight regarding what I plan to do over the next few months, based on what I heard here today. Stay safe, and keep me in the loop if you hear anything regarding America or me. I meet privately with Draven on Friday, right before the closeout briefing."

"I will keep you updated, sir, but today has me worried. I mean, am I mistaken or did everyone here today just willingly accept Draven Cross taking over the world? What politician have you ever known to just accept giving up power without at least a token protest?" Gabriella asked.

"Something tells me that Draven has dirt on everyone in this room and has placed enough fear into most of them, minus me, that they are afraid to challenge him, at least right now. Don't get me wrong, Draven has an extraordinary ability to appeal to people, which in my mind indicates the real power behind the man—Satan. I know I've already told you that, as far as I'm concerned, he's the Antichrist."

Gabriella tried to hide a grimace. "Sir, don't you think that's a bit far-fetched? Look, I agree he is an egomaniac bent on world domination, but really? The devil hiding in the bushes? Let's just devise some way to sabotage his economic and military objectives."

"Just expect a message from me later tonight. I am not planning to just take Draven's fleecing of America lying down," President Rodgers replied before heading out of the conference room and across the U.E. lobby.

Gabriella was worried as she watched Rodgers leave. He seemed resigned to picking a fight with Draven over his policies. She knew enough about Draven to realize that if she couldn't dissuade Rodgers to abandon that plan, Draven would destroy the man and America just to prove a point. As she entered the elevator that would take her to her office, she felt helpless. It appeared she was in an impossible situation that had no analytical or logical solution. As Gabriella sat at her desk and prepared to send a message to Christopher and Jackson, she heard her mother's voice echoing in her mind—giving advice that had irritated her as a child. *"Gabby, you need to realize that you can't outthink every problem. Sometimes you need to accept help. God's strength, a power that can help you overcome any problem, is available only after you surrender the problem to Him."*

Gabriella had no idea how she was going to keep Draven Cross from considering President Rodgers and America as his enemy, but she knew she had to try. Perhaps God *was* the answer.

The major needed to clear his head after listening to the chief master sergeant and the sergeant major talk. He walked to the smoker's shack, a small three-sided shed that offered just enough shelter to encourage those on the base who still participated in the unfashionable habit of smoking to gather inside for fellowship and indulgence. No matter the temperature it was rarely empty, so Christopher was grateful to find himself alone in the seatless shed so he could think in solitude about his ongoing conflict with God.

Hearing Jimbo's story made his own dilemma all the more real. Though the chief's parents had lived with a superficial religious understanding of what being a Christian meant and were now facing the consequences for their crime of ignorance, Christopher saw an easy fix for them—they just needed to receive the truth. For himself, the answer was not so black and white. His rebellion against God had a long history. He already knew enough about Christianity to understand God was real and to realize that salvation rested on establishing a relationship with God through accepting Jesus as his Savior, but Christopher's loss of loved ones in his early life had created a resentment that made him resistant to a relationship with God despite all he knew. However, no matter how angry he was with God, the major could no longer deny that he needed that same God to whom he had thrown up his fist in defiance if he hoped to survive the tribulations ahead.

The war within Christopher's heart and mind were a burden that weighed on him deeply, a battle he would lose for eternity if he chose to continue fighting God. He worried about what steps God would take to bring him to surrender. He remembered his grandmother saying, "God has a way of getting our attention. Sometimes it's more painful than we want, but He will get our attention." A part of Christopher wished something dramatic would happen that just allowed him to accept God's gift of salvation. He wondered how many times he would get to cheat death before he lost his life. At the thought of dying without "getting things right with God," as his grandmother would say, he shivered—or maybe he was just getting cold.

The major's quantum communicator vibrated in his parka pocket, indicating a new message had arrived. The display read. *"You have a new package from Susan. You have 15 minutes to access this message before it is destroyed."* Christopher pressed the authenticate button and began reading the news from Gabriella. The further he read, the more troubled he became.

"Chris and Jackson, I hope you're both staying warm in Alaska. Things are moving quickly here. Draven continues to consolidate world power. His vision for the emerging new world political order is named Project Babylon. For the sake of brevity, just understand that his plan is a centralized world government with ten regions governed by leaders handpicked by Draven himself and considered to be loyal to him. Rodgers is one of the ten, so Draven's wrong about at least one of the ten.

"The president concerns me. Between what he has you guys doing and his growing hatred for Draven, I think he's driving us toward a conflict. I am open to any suggestions to head him off, but I can't even think straight most days. I am struggling to determine God's influence in our lives, in my life, this whole rapture thing, and my search for some sort of scientific, logical explanation for all that is happening.

"Well, it's late here, and I am exhausted. President Rodgers told me in an earlier message that he plans to reach out to you two, but wouldn't tell me for what. If you would just give me a heads up on what he discusses with you, I would be grateful. I am worried, guys. I think he believes he can take down Draven, but I am not so sure of that.

"Take care, my Arctic Warriors, from the sassy woman stuck with the devil (haha). That's just to rile you up, Jackson."

As Christopher finished reading the message, his phone vibrated again with a message from the Eagle. He also saw Jackson quickly moving toward him among what looked like some soldiers eager for a smoke break.

"Hey, did you read Gabriella's message?" Jackson asked.

"Yeah, I just finished, but let's head into the barracks to have this conversation." The major nodded to the two smokers who entered the small shed.

"Okay. I also got an email from President Rodgers," the sergeant major replied quietly.

"Me, too. Let's go in here," Christopher answered, opening the door to a large barracks bay lined with cots and sleeping bags.

"So what do you make of that message from Gabriella? It sounds like she's in trouble."

"Yeah, I think she's overwhelmed. Gabriella wants to be able to think up a solution for everything—so not being able to solve the emerging problems between Draven Cross and the president are going to eat at her. Add to that the fact that Cross is running intellectual laps around her, and Gabriella is being forced way out of her comfort zone," Christopher replied tersely. "On the other hand, the Project Babylon one-world government sounds like trouble for the good ole U.S. of A. I think you were right in saying our days with the U.S. military are likely numbered."

"Man, I am telling you, Draven Cross is the Antichrist and he is establishing his global kingdom. The next thing we should be concerned with is the coming global war that's described in *Revelation 6:3–4*, which is the opening of the second seal judgment. From the looks of this base and the effects the Bible describes postwar, I think nukes are going to be in play. The tribulation will accelerate quickly from the breaking of the second seal forward, and as we say in our line of work, the environment will become 'non-permissive' for Christians. In time, Draven and his followers will kill everyone who claims to be a follower of Christ," Jackson asserted. His confidence shook the major.

"I think the time is quickly coming to work on the plan for occupying our new base of operations in Alabama, don't you think?" Christopher questioned.

"Absolutely. My family homestead in Alabama will be perfect. It's remote and has a small airstrip."

"We can talk about the details later," Major Barrrett said, lifting his device to display the letter. "For now, let's see what the president wants." Jackson stepped closer to Christopher so they could both read the message on one screen while pressing the button on his communicator to erase the president's message.

"Boys, I hope the polar bears haven't chased you off. I wish I could say things are getting better here, but they're not. Gabriella has likely already told you about Project Babylon, so I will spare you that discussion. What she doesn't know—and I don't want you guys to say anything to her yet—is that I am planning to conduct a massive military strike against Draven, his assets, and those that are following him within the next three months. I've been working on this since I heard his first speech. Gentlemen, I will not go down in history as the American president who allowed some two-bit thug to destroy our way of life without a fight.

"I have little faith or trust in the U.S. intelligence services, much less the other leaders in our nation, after the willingness of so many to go along with Draven Cross's stripping of our military power and sovereignty. So what I am asking of you tonight is that you head into the fray once again. The nukes will be safe until we are ready to strike. I need your talents elsewhere.

"I've gotten word from a couple of other leaders here with me in New York that Cross is building his new HQ somewhere in Iraq. I want you to fly to Israel and link up with our old friend Defense Minister Benjamin Havid. See if the Israelis have some insight into Draven's plans in the region. I know most of Israel is infatuated with the peace ceremony and the rebuilding of their temple, but Havid has signaled that he has his doubts about Draven's intentions, which is good enough for me.

"I am sending the C-39XER jet to Anchorage tonight so you guys can fly out tomorrow. That will put you there ahead of next week's scheduled peace signing ceremony with Draven Cross at the embassy in Jerusalem. Godspeed, and I will be in touch. The Eagle."

Jackson thoughtfully said, "If, as the president believes, Draven Cross is the Antichrist, then no matter what we throw at him militarily, he won't be defeated until Jesus' second coming. God, please help us."

"I agree we need some help because I have no ideas at this point on keeping the U.S. out of a war with Draven Cross's growing regime," Christopher responded.

Draven could not have scripted a better week. Project Babylon had been a rousing success, and the nine leaders he had selected had accepted his plan with no resistance. Of course, the fact that Rodgers had not tried to fight him made him wary. While the American political infrastructure had made it easy to push his agenda, he was reasonably sure there must be some of the fighter pilot spirit left in Rodgers. He had to be sure the old dolt was not trying something; he needed someone inside his inner circle.

His thoughts were interrupted by Gemma's voice coming through his intercom. "What is it? I told you I was not to be disturbed for the next two hours," he snapped harshly.

"I know, sir, but security says they want you to meet a Mr. John Barnes who's been downstairs in the lobby demanding an audience with you. He says he knows America's secrets," Gemma explained.

"So I work for security and you now, Gemma? Get rid of this mental patient. It's likely all he wants is my autograph or something. And don't disturb me until President Rodgers arrives for his meeting. Is that understood?"

"Okay, sir, but he told security he used to work for Omega Group," Gemma added smoothly.

"Interesting. Okay, have security bring him up. I will give Mr. Barnes the chance to persuade me not to put him in jail," Draven muttered irritably.A few minutes later, John Barnes was escorted into Draven's office by two large U.E. security officers.

"Good morning, Mr. Barnes. I understand you have a dire need to meet with me. So I hope, for your sake, that this interruption to my time is worth your efforts," Draven said sharply, staring coldly at John Barnes.

"Mr. Secretary-General, by the end of our discussion, you will hire me. I think you should ask your security to leave the room. The information I have is sensitive," John Barnes stated confidently.

"Bold statement, Mr. Barnes. Just know that if you fail to deliver or if you attempt any malfeasance here today, your error will cost you your life. Leave us," Draven ordered the security officers.

John Barnes turned and watched as the two security guards closed the glass doors of Draven's office behind them, drawing high-powered handguns as they stood watching the meeting.

"I have something for you." Barnes opened his suit jacket and looked down to retrieve the item from an inside pocket. His hand froze when he heard a stern warning from the man he'd come to see.

"Easy, Mr. Barnes. I may seem like a harmless politician, but if you wish to live to see tomorrow, slowly retrieve whatever you're looking for in that pocket," Draven commanded.

As Barnes raised his head, he was surprised to see Draven holding a gun, and shocked to see the red laser dot dead center on his shirtfront as he glanced down where the gun was pointing.

"I can assure you sure, sir, I am no threat to you, and that gun is not necessary," Barnes replied cooly, slowly pulling a small USB flash drive from his suit jacket and holding it up in one hand.

"What's on the drive, Mr. Barnes?"

"In my hand, I hold the operational plans for President Rodgers's military strike against the U.E., including the locations of several undeclared nuclear weapons on a remote base in Alaska."

"My, my. That would be worth an offer of employment. How did you come by this information?"

"I recently quit Omega Group after seeing the writing on the wall for the American military and the devaluing the nation held for soldiers like me. But before I left the group, I discovered these plans and downloaded them from a classified database in the Omega Group office."

"Ah, you were fired. I am guessing for being a bit of a rogue as well as brash. And now you're selling state secrets to who you assume will be the highest bidder. A risky maneuver, Mr. Barnes, coming to me first. Your assumption that I will not have you killed for being a traitor may have been premature," Draven answered, racking back the slide on the handgun.

"Sir, please, I am telling you the truth," Barnes pleaded, raising both hands.

"Gemma, dear, please bring your laptop into my office," Draven said into his intercom, the handgun still pointed at Barnes.

"Oh my God, sir," Gemma exclaimed as she entered Draven's office to find John Barnes, shaking hands raised, with a bright red laser dot on his chest.

"Calm yourself, my dear. I am just in the middle of an intense employment interview with Mr. Barnes here. Please take the flash drive from Mr. Barnes, pull up a chair next to me, and open the flash drive. If what Mr. Barnes described to me is located on the device, he has a job. If it is not… Well, my dear, Mr. Barnes will hate my employment rejection process," Draven said, smiling.

Gemma was shaking like a leaf in the wind as she walked over to John Barnes and took the flash drive from him. She pulled up a chair from the conference table in Draven's office and plugged the flash drive into a USB port. "Sir, what should I be looking for on here?" Her voice wasn't quite steady when she spoke.

"Mr. Barnes, please tell Gemma the name of the operation," Draven instructed.

Barnes said, "The only folder on the drive is named Operation Eagle Storm."

"Eagle Storm…that is a ghastly and sophomoric name," Draven said, laughing. "Gemma, is that the name of the file you see?" His hand was unwavering as he held the gun on Barnes.

"Yes, sir, it is," Gemma confirmed.

"Great. Open it, then leave the office and send in the U.E. security officers," Draven ordered.

Gemma clicked open the file and quickly made her way out of the office, flushed and sweating, waving the security detail into the office without speaking.

"Gentlemen, I want you to kill Mr. Barnes if I give the word," Draven said starkly. He then turned his attention to Gemma's laptop and the open Operation Eagle Storm folder. He quickly pored over President Rodgers's directives to dispatch and secure several nuclear weapons on a remote base in Alaska. The files even contained a Presidental Security Memo to his coconspirators, namely, the Nigeran president and former U.N. secretary-general Aguilar, who both had been named future ambassadors by Draven earlier in the week. Anger exploded in Draven's chest, and he swore out loud.

"Well, here is what I am prepared to offer you, Mr. Barnes, for your efforts to ensure global peace and prosperity," Draven Cross said when he calmed himself enough. "Effective immediately, you will be named the U.E. Special Activities Unit Commander. I will empower you to only one end, which will be the rooting out and elimination of threats to the U.E., myself, or my interests. I will plan a meeting with you later today along with my head of intelligence, Dr. Gabriella Costa, whom I am sure you know."

"Thank you, sir," Barnes replied. "However, I don't know if it would be wise to bring in Dr. Costa. I don't know if she was even aware of the operation against the U.E., but she may tip off President Rodgers."

"Mr. Barnes, you're alive only due to your penchant for having a weak moral consistency that serves my needs, not to be a critical thinker on my staff," Cross replied disdainfully. "Get out of my office, and coordinate with Gemma for the details of our meeting later today."

"Yes, sir," Barnes said before departing with the security guards.

Once the office doors closed, Draven sought the counsel of his spiritual mentor. He shouted, "Prince of this World, what should I do with this information? I feel I should kill President Rodgers and his henchmen where they stand right now!"

"No, this will serve my purposes. You will play along with their ruse until my appointed time. Remember to trust and serve only me," came the message from the Prince to Draven's thoughts.

"Fine," Draven shouted, "but they will pay for their disrespect toward me."

Gabriella was heading to Draven's office to provide some information he'd requested ahead of his meeting with President Rodgers when she saw John Barnes heading toward the elevators. The sly wink he sent her way as he boarded the elevator made her blood run cold. She hurried over to Gemma's desk to figure out why John Barnes, a former Omega Group soldier, was in the U.E. HQ.

"Gemma, why was John Barnes here today?" Dr. Costa asked, working hard to sound only mildly curious.

"He met with Draven earlier saying he had American secrets to share," Gemma answered.

Gabriella was unable to form an immediate response, her mind instantly jumping to the worst case scenario: that Barnes had somehow discovered she was a spy for Rodgers.

Gemma's intercom buzzed, and she heard Draven's voice on the other end.

"Find Gabriella. Tell her I am ready for her report," Draven directed.

"I will send her in momentarily, sir," Gemma replied. After she disconnected from the intercom speaker, she turned to Dr. Costa and, appearing genuinely frightened, whispered," Draven was going to kill Mr. Barnes if he had been lying, so I am guessing Barnes told him something of value. The man is starting to scare me, Gabriella."

"Yeah, we should get together some time after work and discuss our interesting work environment. In the meantime, just be strong and try to stay on Draven's good side. Speaking of which, I'd better get in there before you get in trouble."

"Thanks, and be careful," Gemma cautioned.

You have no idea how careful I am trying to be, Gemma, Gabriella thought as she entered Draven Cross's office.

Jimbo was a little worried and voiced as much as he drove Jackson and Christopher to the helipad for their flight to Anchorage and then Israel. "Guys, I know you can't tell me all the details, but it seems risky to be working against the most powerful man in the world. You could be walking into an ambush," he warned.

"I know, Jimbo, but right now we all still work for the president of the United States, and he is trying to figure out just what Draven Cross is up to," Christopher replied.

"I already know what he's up to," Jackson said assertively. "Nothing good."

"I agree," Jimbo said. "Mr. Cross is my number one candidate for being the biblical Antichrist."

"Look, before you two both get into the spiritual ramifications of who we're dealing with, let me just say, remember that you could be wrong. Draven could just be a slick politician who is trying to destroy our country," Christopher replied reasonably.

"Yeah, and fish might not be wet in the water, but the evidence says they are. The same thing goes for Saint Cross. The evidence says he's the Antichrist," Jackson stated forcefully.

Laughing, Christopher responded, "Jackson, I can't even do the country boy logic thing with you right now. I am just saying let's focus on what we can control, like getting the requested information back to the president and then getting back here and finishing this job."

"I will be praying for you guys. And don't worry. I will keep everything and everybody in order while you're gone," Jimbo said as the SUSV pulled up to the Blackhawk helicopter waiting to ferry them to Anchorage.

"Thanks, brother," Christopher replied. "We'll let you know when we're heading back. Take care."

"Yeah, thanks, man. Keep us in your prayers. The Middle East isn't exactly a vacation spot," Jackson said, closing the door to the SUSV and running for the helo.

Chapter 15

As Gabriella was completing her update on the U.S. military capabilities that were soon to be under Draven Cross's authority, he began to smile as if he knew something that she wanted to know but did not have access to.

"Sir, is there something funny I am missing right now?" Gabriella asked.

"Perhaps, but really I have just been savoring the thought of what must be going through your mind right now after seeing John Barnes leave my office."

"John Barnes was here today? I must have missed him, as I was working in my office all morning," Gabriella replied, consciously stilling her nerves.

"It's a shame you missed him. No matter, you will get a chance to catch up later today when he comes back to discuss his first mission as the U.E. Special Activities Unit Commander."

"The Special Activities Unit? What exactly does this unit do for the U.E.?"

"Oh, the same sort of things you Americans had your Omega Group doing across the globe. The difference here will be John will work to meet *my* goals, not America's. Tell me what you know about Operation..." Draven was cut off as his office door was flung open by Evan Mallory, with Gemma close on his heels.

"Sir, I told him you were in a meeting, but he walked in anyway," Gemma explained.

Gabriella was grateful for the ruckus since it prevented Draven from finishing his likely life-threatening question.

"It's okay, Gemma. Today seems destined to have me at its mercy," Draven replied with apparent resignation as Gemma departed, closing the doors behind her.

"Sir…you've got to…" Evan Mallory stopped when Draven held up his hand.

"This had better be good. I don't have time for any of your foolishness, Evan. I am in the midst of preparing for my final future ambassador meeting. President Rodgers is my most critical appointment, and we meet within the hour," Draven threatened silkily.

"Sir, it's important." Evan grabbed the remote from Draven's desk and turned on the large flat-screen television mounted on the adjacent wall, selecting the all-news network's coverage of a breaking event. "You see, sir, this is coming out of Israel."

"Yes, Evan, I can clearly see it's an event in Israel, but what do you think I need to look at? Why am I watching news coverage of two old men sitting next to the Wailing Wall? I swear you're daft. Get out of my office."

Just as Draven finished chiding Evan, the newscaster began describing what had been happening since the appearance of the two men and growing crowd near the Wailing Wall. Evan raised the volume as Draven's interest was caught by the two men being enhanced on his screen by high-definition broadcasting.

"Ladies and gentlemen, if you're just joining us, we have a potential terrorist situation or violent protest ongoing right now at the Wailing Wall in Jerusalem. The situation seems to be in a state of flux. The two men you now see on your screen reportedly appeared at the Wailing Wall around two o'clock in the afternoon local time in Jerusalem. They have yet to speak or move, but several eyewitness accounts credit the men with killing or incapacitating a few dozen security forces who have tried to remove them from the Wailing Wall. Now we take you to Jerusalem to a local field correspondent who is with a tourist who was visiting the Wailing Wall when the two men appeared," the anchor concluded.

"Yes, I am here with a gentleman on vacation from the United States of America. He was within fifty feet of the Wailing Wall when the two men appeared, and the subsequent attacks occurred. Sir, could you describe to us what you saw here today?" the field correspondent requested.

"Sure, well, I and my wife Jean were about to head back to our tour bus after visiting the Wailing Wall when all of a sudden we heard screams and saw people running everywhere. Well, Jean yells at me to get down because she thought it was one of them terrorist attacks or something, but I just stood there videoing everything with my phone."

"So can you describe how the two men attacked the security forces?" the field correspondent queried.

"Well, they're two older fellas, but they seem young and strong at the same time. I mean you guys can probably see their beards and them having no shoes, but their clothes and eyes were the weirdest things to me. I think they're wearing like potato sacks or burlap or something, and it looks like they're covered in ashes. Those eyes though made me feel like a child again—you know, like when your mom knows you did something wrong and you can't stand to look her in the eye. Those guys were looking right down to my bones," the tourist said.

"What about the attack, sir, what type of weapons did they have?" the field correspondent asked.

"I can't say I saw a weapon. The security folks ran toward them, and those old men didn't move a limb. They just opened their mouths and didn't say anything, but the security folks just dropped where they stood. It was the craziest thing I ever saw." The man's shock was evident in his tone.

"Well, there you have it, one man's perspective on an idyllic day turned tragic. I am sending the story back you in New York," the field correspondent concluded.

Evan turned off the TV and looked at Draven as if expecting some sort of praise for informing him of the events in Israel. Gabriella felt awestruck as she reviewed in her mind the tourist's accounting and the camera images of the fallen security forces and the two unwavering men. Draven, however, was enraged.

"Get out of my office, both of you. Now!" Draven Cross shouted.

Evan and Gabriella quickly moved out of Draven's office, leaving him to his angry thoughts.

Draven swore aloud and slammed his fist on his desk. "What is going on today? I don't need a detractor ahead of the historic peace accord with Israel in a few days. Give me something to work with here," he said into the void of his office.

"Those men are enemies who will be dealt with in due time. I am working all things to my glory. You need only trust me and follow my instructions. We will deal with the American president and these two interlopers when my timing is right," the Prince of This World replied into Draven's mind.

Cross calmed himself and regained his composure, comforting himself with the words of his spiritual master. "I will obey, my lord. I will trust you," he promised.

"Sir, President Rodgers is here," said Gemma's voice over Draven's intercom. "Should I send him in now?"

"Yes, send him in. And set up a meeting with John Barnes, Gabriella, and Evan for immediately following," Cross ordered.

The C-39XER was just as comfortable and fast as Christopher remembered from his recent trip to Afghanistan. He and Jackson covered the nearly 6,000 miles from Anchorage to Tel Aviv in less than nine hours. As the nimble jet taxied into a private hangar at Ben Gurion International Airport, Christopher noticed the familiar face of the retired general who was now the Minister of Defense, Benjamin Havid. The major hoped this trip would be uneventful and pleasant, but conducting a military operation in the Middle East was always fraught with uncertainty.

"Shalom, my dear Christopher," Havid greeted, kissing both of the major's cheeks.

"Shalom, Minister Havid. I would like to introduce you to my team sergeant, Sergeant Major Jackson Williams," Christopher replied.

"Shalom, Sergeant Major. But, Christopher, where is Rev? I had hoped to see him."

"Sir, we lost Rev almost two months ago now during a mission."

"I am sorry, my friend. But as you know, not many in our line of work reach the point of a peaceful retirement. Come, let us depart. You are staying at my home, and we shall feast and talk tonight, yes?" Minister Havid was smiling from ear to ear as the brisk winter wind whipped through his salt-and-pepper hair.

"You're too kind, Minister Havid. We really appreciate the hospitality," Jackson replied.

"Please, call me General. I only took this job to keep an eye on the politicians. My heart is still a warrior's heart," Havid said with a smile.

"Sounds great, General. Let's roll," Christopher urged.

As "General" Havid's caravan made its way along Highway 1 toward Jerusalem, Christopher noticed that Rev had been right in his evaluation three and half years ago when he'd projected it would take Israel seven years to clear all the remnants of war from their borders. *But Rev would likely have quickly pointed out to me that it was not his assessment, but God's. I sure do miss that old firebrand, but even more than his physical presence, I sure do wish I had his spiritual guidance right about now,* Christopher mused.

President Rodgers had prayed for both wisdom and prudence ahead of his final meeting with Draven. He felt he might have been too brash in the corporate meeting and had been trying to come across as more of a team player ever since, while secretly continuing his plans to bring Draven down. Maybe Gabriella had been correct in her view that the world would eventually see Draven Cross for the autocrat he was, but President Rodgers's instincts told him the man was the Antichrist and had to be stopped. As he entered the office and caught a glimpse of the man who was now the *de facto* ruler of the world, he felt his blood pressure rising.

"Good morning, President Rodgers. I've been looking forward to this meeting all week, as I view your support essential to securing a global peace," Draven said in greeting as he directed Rodgers to be seated in a chair in front of his desk.

"I appreciate your trust in America and me. America stands ready to defend the world against tyranny," President Rodgers returned.

"Interesting choice of words, Mr. President. It almost seems to me that you view my plans as an assault on freedom. Liberty, the quintessential value you American's love to boast about having and continuously try to define for all the world, is at the heart of all that I aim to accomplish. I think it was your famed Abraham Lincoln who said it best, though I'm paraphrasing, 'We all desire liberty, but in using the same word, we do not all mean the same thing.' I am defining liberty, President Rodgers, for everyone in the world going forward, including America. I suggest you get comfortable with that thought," Draven stated flatly.

"So what you're saying is that the most powerful influencer in the world system will be you—is that correct, Mr. Secretary-General? That doesn't sound so benevolent. It really sounds more like dictator speak 101," President Rodgers replied, struggling to keep his tone level.

"As I've explained to all the other ambassadors this week that sat where you're currently seated, I expect loyalty. I realize that you lead one of humanity's greatest nations, but America's ideology and, quite frankly, ego must take a back seat for the greater good. Going forward, the U.E.—or as you correctly surmised, I—will be the leader of the international system," Draven Cross stated firmly.

"What is it that you desire from America and from me, beyond loyalty?" President Rodgers asked.

"America has been excellent in leading the way toward global peace by allocating ten percent of its military capabilities to the U.E. This contribution ensures the U.E. will be equipped to defend against aggression in the future, a claim the former U.N. could never make. I expect that this level of support to any of my plans will continue."

What about your mandate to the nuclear nations to turn over all nuclear weapons to the U.E.…what peaceful objective would the U.E. have for those, Mr. Secretary-General?"

"I am destroying them. It will be one of my greatest contributions to the peace of the world—complete denuclearization. I am a shoo-in for this year's Nobel Peace Prize," Draven bragged.

"To be completely honest with you, Mr. Secetary-General, it's hard for me to believe that the unprecedented amount of military power being made available to you will lead to prolonged peace and not war. Let's be realistic. I was briefed by your new lackeys in my government that we are turning over all personnel, equipment, and command structures located at our three largest Army, Air Force, and Naval bases—not the mention our nukes. Despite my appeals and pressures within Congress and the Supreme Court, my country is moving forward with the wholesale shuttering of our military. Your demands have effectively destroyed America's military. Who could we attack even if we wanted to?"

"Precisely, Mr. President. All the great nations of this world are doing exactly as the United States military has done, which guarantees the peace that people want. You're blind to the need for the necessary changes in how the world will be governed going forward. Thus, the leaders of your country are helping move the world toward a better future. Within a month, the U.E. will be the most powerful organization in all of human history. No one will dare challenge the peaceful initiatives that we have developed here this week. As a result, everyone will enjoy the peace and freedom that has been only a dream until now."

"That will be true only *if* they obey *your* vision for freedom," President Rodgers stated flatly.

"Tread carefully, President Rodgers. Your challenges are not unnoticed and make me question your loyalty to the U.E., and more importantly to me," Draven warned.

President Rodgers paused, feeling foolish for getting into a squabble with Draven. He must maintain the element of surprise if he was going to destroy Cross. However, his disgust of all things Draven bubbled to the surface too often. *I need to calm down, focus, and stay on track. But whether he knows it or not, Cross just showed his hand in one regard—he needs only a month to implement his game plan.*

"I am speaking to you, President Rodgers. I expect acknowledgment," Draven demanded, now standing.

"I apologize, Mr. Secretary-General. I am sure a man of your intelligence can understand how hard this transition is for the great nation of America and for me personally. Rest assured, however, that I fully support your plan for the future and will not impede the U.E. or your leadership," President Rodgers said, extending his hand as he came to his feet.

"Excellent. Let us hope for America's sake—and for your sake—that you're a man of your word. Meeting adjourned," Cross said dismissively, ignoring the outstretched hand.

"Okay, *Draven*. Until we meet again," President Rodgers replied before turning to leave.

Cross fumed at not being able to gun down President Rodgers where he stood for his insolence, but he was held back by the Prince of This World, who told him the timing was not right. Draven knew that in a month America would be too weak to protest the death of their president in the face of the military might he would gain. "Gemma, send in Gabriella, John Barnes, and Evan in ten minutes."

Christopher looked out the car window in disbelief. Jerusalem had changed drastically since his last visit three and a half years earlier. The Israeli nation's newfound wealth, stemming from the discovery of massive energy reserves and Israel's unquestioned military strength, had transformed the country into a foreign investment and global commerce hub. While Israel, like any country, had always had morally questionable areas and unspoken practices, large billboards for gentlemen's clubs and an entertainment district in Jerusalem now lined Highway 1. Israel may have always been a "Jewish state," but Christopher knew that, like other countries, the faith of many Israelis was only surface deep. Still, the wanton materialism and hedonistic atmosphere he saw today were not what Christopher would have ever guessed to witness within the nation of Israel.

Noticing Christopher's face as he gazed out the car windows, General Havid said, "Israel is changing, my friends, and not for the better. We've completely abandoned Yahweh for Draven Cross—just like our ancestors when they longed to return to the whips of Egypt instead of trusting in the power of Yahweh in the wilderness. You know, some religious scholars here are even trying to link Mr. Cross to the Davidic line in an attempt to proclaim him as the long-awaited Messiah. I, however, believe he is far from our Messiah, a topic we can discuss over dinner."

"Yes, sir, I was going to say this is certainly not what I expected to see on my first trip to the Holy Land," Jackson remarked, his surprise evident in his voice.

"Holy Land…ha! This land is holy only due to memories. The good news is that Yahweh will soon make all things right again, and the eternal city will shine anew for all humanity," General Havid assured them.

The three men were silent during the remaining short drive to the northern outskirts of Jerusalem. General Havid's home was located within an exclusive alcove near the Ramat Givat Ze'ev neighborhood. He had bought three lots to build a secure and private retreat that overlooked the Old City and most of Jerusalem.

Jackson broke the silence. "Your security presence is impressive. No one would get in here without you knowing."

General Havid laughed as the convoy pulled into his circular driveway and one his staff members quickly opened the vehicle doors for the general and his guests.

"Gentlemen, please excuse me. I must get a quick update on a situation at the Wailing Wall and then I will join you for dinner. My home is your home," Havid graciously offered before walking away with several members of his staff in tow.

Jackson immediately moved toward a scenic backyard overlook using a well-manicured garden path. "Would you look at that? God is so good, my friend," the sergeant major said as he looked at a setting sun behind the ancient Old City.

"It's incredible," Christopher agreed.

"Just wait! In seven years, this place is going to get a renovation like nothing you've ever seen, when the good Lord returns," Jackson assured Christopher.

"I hope I survive to see it," Christopher muttered darkly.

Gabriella had hoped President Rodgers would stop by her office after his meeting with Draven Cross. Instead she watched him storm by her door without even a second glance. Now she had to endure a meeting with a likely agitated Draven, the potentially traitorous John Barnes, and the enigma named Evan Mallory. If Jackson was right about Cross, the rapture, God…everything…then Gabriella wasn't worried about surviving to see the second coming of Jesus because her job was going to kill her first. Her intercom buzzed, and she heard Gemma's voice.

"Gabriella, Mr. Cross is ready to meet with you and the others in his office."

"Thanks, Gemma, on my way," Gabriella responded. She grabbed her coffee mug and was gathering her notes for the meeting when her quantum communicator pulsed, signaling a new message had arrived. She pulled the device from her suit jacket and read the display, which indicated Rodgers was the sender. She hurriedly pressed authenticate and quickly skimmed the screen.

"Gabriella, I am sorry I did not stop by your office, but I want to put as much distance between us as possible. Long story short, I plan to execute a preemptive military strike against Draven Cross within a month. I hope you soon discover the truth about him for yourself, but I will not allow him to destroy our country. I'll be in touch."

"Gabriella, they're waiting for you," Gemma said urgently, standing in Gabriella's office doorway.

"Yes, sorry. I'm on my way," Gabriella replied with a small smile. As she walked the short distance to the secretary-general's office, she felt a strong sense of foreboding—like a great tragedy was about to unfold, and she couldn't do anything to prevent it.

"Well, I'm glad you could join us, Gabriella. I hope this meeting didn't inconvenience you," Draven said with obvious sarcasm.

"No, sir. My apologies for being late. I was getting a refill of coffee," Gabriella said as she took her place at the conference table.

"Listen up. Today has been an incredibly trying day for me. I need you all to leave here prepared to execute my orders with precision and without excuse," Draven ordered sharply. "John, I want you to track down and present options for decimating the emergency command bunkers for all of the new ambassadors. Additionally I want you to provide me with a brief no later than six o'clock tonight on the persons needed to fill your team and any resources you will require. Acknowledge your understanding of those orders," he said curtly.

"I understand, sir, but what about Operation—?" John Barnes was cut off abruptly by Draven.

"Shut up, you imbecile. Granted this is a U.E. security staff meeting, but not everyone here needs to know everything. Just execute your orders and report to me when complete. Get out and get started," Cross demanded.

"Yes, sir," replied a red-faced John Barnes before rapidly exiting the office.

"Gabriella, I am still trying to figure out just how much to trust you. So let's put your loyalties to the test. I need you to provide me with the known and secret locations of the U.S. president's crisis command and control bunkers. You will also supply John Barnes's newly formed unit the intelligence they need to mitigate potential threats to my plans. Lastly, to test the limits of your loyalty, I need you to provide John and me with the daily whereabouts of Omega Group for the next month. Frankly, I don't trust you or President Rodgers, and until I see a reason to change my mind, I want to be able to hold hostage your mentor Rodgers and his best weapon, his beloved Omega Group."

Gabriella fought hard to subdue the trembling that began deep inside—she was also surprised by a strong urge to cry. Her mind raced. *Is there no way out of this situation? What did John Barnes tell him about Omega? Think quickly!* She said out loud, "Sir, those requests are beyond the bounds of my employment. You're asking me to betray my country when America poses no risk to you or the U.E."

"You will not question my authority. I'll deem who is my enemy and who isn't. Gabriella, your concern at this moment should be your own life instead of others," Draven directed.

"I have your orders, sir. Is there anything else you have for me?" Gabriella questioned, standing to leave.

"My dear, tread lightly. No one is too valuable to replace. Sit down. You will stay until you are dismissed," the secretary-general commanded imperiously. "Evan, you will head to Rome this weekend in preparation for the World Religious Leaders Conference next week. I expect that, by the end of next week, you will have solid momentum toward unifying the world with the Interfaith dogma. One last thing for you to jot down, Evan. I want you to keep an eye on those two old men at the Wailing Wall. I don't want them to overshadow my accomplishments in the coming days. Finally, as you both know, I'm flying out on Sunday for the Israel Peace Treaty signing ceremony on Tuesday. I will be addressing the Knesset on Monday, followed by a meeting with the Israeli prime and foreign ministers. Evan, expect me to 'surprise' the conference later in the week, which should bolster your efforts. Do either of you have any questions regarding your assignments?"

"No, sir. I am excited about this upcoming week, sir. The world is about to turn a corner to a new day in its history," Evan replied enthusiastically.

"Gabriella, anything puzzling you?" Draven inquired.

"No, sir. What I need to do is evident."

"Excellent. Meeting adjourned. Let's bring peace to Earth."

Chapter 16

General Havid walked out into his lush garden to join Christopher and Jackson amongst the fragrant juniper trees overlooking the postcard-worthy view of Jerusalem that his estate commanded.

"The eternal city is a beautiful place, yes?" Havid asked.

"Yes, sir, it is. I can't wait to see what God does with it in a few years. I am sorry, sir. Forgive my religious zeal. I am a new convert," Jackson confessed.

"No need to apologize, my friend. I believe you're referencing the Bible New Testament book of Revelation, chapter 21 and verse 11, which says, 'Having the glory of God. Her light was like a most precious stone, like a jasper stone, clear as crystal.' I hope Yahweh allows me to see this remaking of my beloved Jerusalem," General Havid replied earnestly. "Ah, but before that day, we will feast tonight. Come, the food is ready, and we can continue talking." He directed Major Barrett and Sergeant Major Williams into his home.

Christopher was reminded of his childhood as he walked into an understated but elegant dining room. He could sense the room had been given a woman's touch in a past era. The table held enough food to feed all of Omega Group and still have leftovers. His grandmother had prepared similar feasts each Sunday after church, often inviting other church members to their home to share the meal. He remembered hearing her regularly say, "It's hard to hate somebody when you're sharing a good meal together." He immediately felt right at home, and he confessed with a grin, "This looks amazing, sir. I can't wait to eat."

"I agree," Jackson seconded.

"You've come at the right time, as tonight is my weekly Shabbat dinner. We will start with a celery root and parsnip soup with caramelized garlic, followed by lamb meatballs in swiss chard and chickpea stew, complemented by a beet, pomegranate, and tomato salad or cauliflower couscous if you prefer. The final touch will be a slice or two of my wife's famous orange, polenta, and marzipan cake," the general replied.

As General Havid's staff heaped steaming Israeli delights on their plates, Christopher asked, "Sir, will your wife be joining us tonight?" Instantly the serving staff stilled.

"No, my friend, she will not," General Havid replied. You see, she is dead."

"I am so sorry, sir. Please forgive me."

"No need for apologies, Christopher. You did not know. I lost my beautiful Abagail many years ago to cancer. We never had children, so my love of country and work became my obsession."

"This food is amazing, sir," Jackson complimented, so involved in enjoying the meal that he had utterly missed Christopher's *faux pax.*

General Havid laughed. "I am happy to see you enjoying the food. Please, eat to your heart's content, my friends."

As the men ate, they shared stories of military valor in days gone by, but General Havid's tone changed once the meal was finished.

"Gentlemen, I would ask we take our coffee and tea into my study, as there are a few pressing matters I wish to discuss with you in more seclusion."

"Lead the way, sir," Christopher said, standing.

"Excellent. Follow me. There is much to discuss tonight," General Havid replied gravely.

Gabriella was glad that Draven Cross and Evan Mallory were going to be out of the office for the next week. She needed some time to resolve the battle between her mind and God and determined to accomplish that task before the weekend was over. She had invited Gemma out to dinner later that evening, assuming the secreatry-general's assistant shared her feelings about Draven Cross and might want the opportunity to vent. However, Gabriella knew enough and had been trained well enough not to divulge too much too soon, so she would let Gemma take the lead in any conversation about their demanding employer. Glancing at her watch, Gabriella realized she'd have to hurry to keep from being late for dinner with Gemma. The disappearances had made getting a cab or rideshare harder and more expensive given the shortages of people, cars, and gas.

Gabriella left her apartment and headed toward U.E. plaza, as there was a cab stand in the square. As she approached the plaza, light snow began to dust the area beautifully, the first snow of the season. She saw the cab stand was empty and pulled out her phone to text Gemma she'd be late and to select a rideshare service when she was startled to hear a voice close behind her.

"Why do you still disbelieve in His presence?" Samuel asked quietly.

"My goodness, you scared me. That's a super creepy way to approach someone. What did you say?" Gabriella asked.

"Was it not predicted, 'For the Lord himself will come down from heaven, with a loud command, with the voice of the archangel and with the trumpet call of God, and the dead in Christ will rise first. After that, we who are still alive and are left will be caught up together with them in the clouds to meet the Lord in the air. And so we will be with the Lord forever'?" Samuel continued, as if he didn't hear her, nor cared about her reaction to him.

"What does that mean, Samuel? And why are you out here so late? Look, just stay away from me, okay?" Gabriella looked at her phone, hoping to see a notification that her rideshare was close.

"I am sent by the one you seek and who seeks you, the true and living

God—the God of Abraham, Isaac, and Jacob…the God who so loved the world that He sent His only Son to die for its redemption. You need no further proof of whom you work for. You know in your heart that he is the son of perdition, the Antichrist. Gabriella, you must choose to accept the salvation Christ Jesus offers you before it's too late."

With those words, Samuel started walking away from Gabriella, heading to the subway. He seemed either driven by a higher purpose or mentally deranged. Gabriella was having a hard time deciding which at the moment.

"Where are you going?" Gabriella called after him.

"I have been called for a time like this with thousands of other brothers to proclaim the hope that Christ Jesus offers this fallen world, even now in the world's darkest hours. I am being compelled by the Holy Spirit to preach the gospel around the world. So I don't know where I am going, but I do know who I am serving. It's time you answer those questions for yourself, Gabriella. Where are you going? Who are you serving?" Samuel answered as he looked back over his shoulder at her while still moving forward.

Gabriella was watching him walk down into the subway station when a honking from her rideshare made her jump.

"You getting in or what, lady? I don't have the gas or time to be messing around," the rideshare driver shouted through his open window.

Gabriella climbed into the back seat. As the car sped off toward dinner with Gemma, she began to cry as she realized that God had answered the prayer she had prayed after her secret meeting with President Rodgers a week ago. *I guess God is real*, she admitted to herself. *Now what?*

Secretary-General Draven Cross's arrival in Israel had been turned into a national holiday. He was met by the prime minister of Israel and his wife at the airport, at the head of a long red carpet lined with soldiers holding alternating Israeli and United Earth Organization flags, the latter being the same flag his predecessor had used for the U.N. With camera's flashing and the TV news cycle entirely focused on this event, the secretary-general felt an incredible sense of pride in the future he was creating.

"Mr. Secretary-General, welcome to Israel on the eve of this historic moment," the Israeli prime minister greeted warmly.

"Thank you for the kind welcome. It has been an honor to be able to secure a peaceful future for Israel." Draven shook the prime minister's hand, before turning to raise their joined hands aloft in a gesture of solidarity for the cameras.

Once they were in the car, Draven's mind was abuzz with the possibilities this week held for him. As the convoy made its way from Ben Gurion to the King David Hotel in Jerusalem, he read sign after sign proclaiming him to be the king of the World, even a few as the Messiah of Israel. His pride told him nothing could stop him now—he had claimed the world.

As they entered General Havid's study, Christopher looked around the room with admiration. The walls were adorned with photos, plaques, and citations that spanned many years—all the things you'd expect to find from a distinguished military career. But it was the framed undergraduate and graduate degrees in Jewish studies from Tel-Aviv University that caught his eye. It seemed that the famed "Israeli warrior" had once been on the path to becoming a rabbi.

General Havid's pacing caught the major's attention. He watched the seasoned special operations veteran moving around his office like a caged animal trying to escape.

"Sir, what's wrong? You have seemed beside yourself all evening," Christopher questioned.

"Please sit," the general replied, directing Christopher and Jackson to a large leather sofa. "I think we all need to sit for this discussion." General Havid sat behind his book-littered desk for only a moment before standing to pace again, stopping to peer between the wooden slats on the closed French doors securing the study.

"Tell me, gentlemen, what do you think of Draven Cross?" he asked, glancing around as if he were expecting to find someone standing behind him.

"Well, shoot, that's pretty easy, sir. He's the Antichrist of the Bible. I am not sure if y'all here in Israel are tracking that information, as it's in the back of the Bible," Jackson explained, somewhat apologetically.

"Really, Jackson. I swear I should just leave you at home more often. The Tanakh, or Hebrew Bible, consists of the Torah, Nevi'im, and Ketuvim—so to break it down into country boy language, the Tanakh ends where the Christian New Testament begins," Christopher chided.

"Outstanding, Christopher," General Havid said sadly. "I thought for a moment there you were a Jewish studies student. But, Jackson, many of us here in Israel have studied the New Testament, including the end-time prophecies. In fact I have always felt in my heart that it was a distinct possibility that we Jews missed our Messiah, that Jesus Christ was the one we had been looking for all along." Christopher gave a quick shake of his head toward Jackson, daring him to say a word, as it looked like Jackson was about to comment on General Havid's observation regarding who Jesus was to the Jews.

"Alas, I buried these thoughts of the Messiah and Yahweh, and everything became just meaningless rituals until three and a half years ago. You remember what happened here during that time, don't you, Christopher?"

"Yes, sir. It was when the Russian-led coalition of nations invaded Israel," Christopher replied.

"Exactly. I remember what Rev told us as we looked out over the destruction of the enemy in the Valley of Jezreel. I believe he said that the invasion had been foretold in the book of Ezekiel and that it would take us seven years to clear the nation of the remnants of that invasion. Rev's words shook me awake. I've spent the last three years researching the Messiah, Israel's future, and what that invasion meant. Gentlemen, tonight I will share my conclusions with you," General Havid announced.

"Well, lay it on us, sir," Jackson encouraged, earning a longsuffering gaze from Christopher.

Laughing, the general replied, "You have an interesting way with words, Jackson."

"You could say that again and still be correct, sir," Christopher agreed.

"Yes, well, here are my conclusions and my biggest fear. First, I agree with Jackson's assessment of Draven Cross. After evaluating the evidence presented since his emergence on the global political scene, he is my leading candidate to be the Antichrist. Next, I believe we, Israel, are on the brink of entering what the Tanakh called Daniel's 70th Week, or in common Christian terminology, the tribulation. I believe this 'spirtual week' begins with next week's signing of the covenant of peace between the world, represented by Draven and Israel. Finally, I have come to the undeniable decision that the man named Jesus Christ was the Messiah Israel had long awaited and missed. On this topic of the Messiah, I have read the New Testament over and over again. Finally yielding to the tug on my soul, I accepted Jesus as my personal Lord and Savior last week," General Havid confessed, finally sitting down behind his desk.

"That is awesome news!" Jackson blurted out. "Well, at least the part about accepting Jesus as your Savior."

"I am glad you've been able to confide what's obviously been bottled up for a while, and I am honored to hear it first, but what was your fear?" Christopher asked.

Tears streaming down his plump cheeks, the general said, "I fear for what the Bible declares the next seven years will be like—a time about which Jesus said if it were not cut short, none would survive. Christopher, I am afraid of the horrors to come, knowing it could have been avoided. And I realize I am helpless to protect the nation and people I love so dearly. I am concerned about how long I will be able to serve Israel given my commitment to serve Christ Jesus. You both realize that the prime minister and many in Israel feel that Draven is our savior, the man who has finally secured peace for the Jews. But since I don't believe that's who he is, I am in an impossible situation."

"Sir, there is much to discuss with you, and thankfully I brought the best guides for getting us through the days ahead." Jackson pulled Rev's journal and Bible from his backpack. "I say we have one of your staff brew some of that strong coffee you folks have in this part of the world, and then you and I have a talk tonight," he offered comfortingly.

"Yes, I would like that. I would like that very much," General Havid said.

Gabriella arrived at the restaurant in the Little Italy neighborhood frustrated but excited all at the same time. She was glad that Gemma was running late as well, so she would have a few moments to process her thoughts. *I feel like I've at least been given clear guidance and the answer to my most significant question over the last few months. Is God real? I'm going with, yes, God is real. But I'm still not sure about Draven being the Antichrist. If he is the Antichrist, can I work for him and still believe in God and remain in God's good graces? I just have so many questions.* Suddenly a laugh erupted from deep within. She knew without a doubt what the one dependable spiritual advisor in her life would have to say about all of this. She'd be hearing a big *I told you so* from Jackson Williams.

She knew that no matter what she chose regarding working for Draven or leaving the U.E., her days, like so many others, were numbered.

"Would you like to order anything, or can I get you a drink?" the waiter asked.

"No, I'll wait for my friend… Oh, here she is. We will need a few moments, thanks," Gabriella answered, watching as the waiter returned to an empty booth in the nearly empty restaurant—a common sight since the disappearances.

"I am sorry for being late," Gemma Sutherland apologized. "It took forever to catch a cab from my apartment."

"No problem. I just got here myself. I hope this place is good. It's one of the only restaurants in this area that's still open. But by the looks of things tonight, I'm not sure how much longer they'll survive," Gabriella remarked sadly.

"I am sure it will be fine. I am just grateful to get out of my apartment and talk with someone."

"Do you want to order a meal?"

"How about we just order some appetizers and wine?" Gemma replied. "I am not really hungry. I just want to nibble a bit and talk."

"Sounds like a plan," Gabriella agreed.

"Great. You order while I run to the loo."

This could be an excellent opportunity to find out more about Draven Cross, if Gemma's lips get loose with wine. There are a few things I need to know, Gabriella thought. She called the waiter and said, "Waiter, could you please bring us a bottle of Merlot?"

As the sun began to rise above the Judean hills surrounding Jerusalem, Christopher crept back into the study, only to find the general and the sergeant major still deep in conversation. Christopher had given up listening to the two talk about the rapture, the looming tribulation, and the Antichrist named Draven Cross around midnight last night.

"You two are still talking," he remarked. "I am impressed by your stamina."

"Oh, Christopher, I feel like a small boy again listening to my Abba recite the Scriptures," General Havid replied enthusiastically. "There was always so much passion in my Abba's voice that the messages seemed to come alive. Jackson's description of the timeline of the events that lie ahead was the same. I feel energized. Rev lives through his journal and his disciple Jackson."

"I'm glad you're feeling better about your decision regarding Christianity," Christopher replied.

"Yes, I am, but more importantly, I can now envision a way to serve Yahweh for however long He allows me to remain in service of the defense of Israel. I believe what Jackson has told me, that a little more than three years from now Draven Cross will manifest himself as the Antichrist to the world and defile the sacred temple that will soon be completed."

"And what will this vision of yours entail, sir?" Christopher asked as he poured a cup of coffee for himself.

"It will be guys like us who undermine Cross's efforts to rule the world. We are going to take it to the man—literally," Jackson explained.

"Now I wish I had stayed up last night. Are you two really serious? You think we are going to thwart the plans of a man that is potentially described in the Bible? Jackson, you know that if Draven Cross is who you claim he is that he will remain in power until Jesus' second coming in seven years. Not to mention, Cross commanded that each nation contribute ten percent of its military capabilities to the U.E. We are outgunned and outmanned," Christopher stated unequivocally, sitting down on the sofa as he sipped the overly sweet coffee.

"Oh, what a lack faith you have, Christopher," the general said, eyes gleaming with zeal. "Yes, it is foolish to try to attack the enemies of God head-on. But, my friend, we are covert warriors, neurosurgeons on a battlefield, skilled in precision to achieve a maximum effect. We will aim for targets that glorify our new government, the Kingdom of God, and produce a thorn in the side of Draven Cross. If we can't stop him, we can at least make his road bumpy."

"I love it. When can we start?" Jackson asked enthusiastically.

"I don't love it. This is not some movie where the good guys overcome evil and walk into the sunset having learned some profound lesson. No, plain and simple, the next seven years will be about survival. If what the Bible, Rev, Jackson, and every other Christian theologian who ever studied this time says is even half correct, I would be shocked if any of us live seven more years. I am not even sure I want to do any fighting on God's side. You know, God and I are not on the best terms right now," Christopher replied.

"Have you not dedicated your life to helping countless others who don't even know your name or care if you've served your country?" General Havid asked pointedly. "You have protected nameless people from the horrors of war and suffering. Yet now, knowing you will soon not have a nation to defend but will still have skills and abilities to protect the weak, you would selfishly only hide somewhere hoping for the best? That is not living for the purpose Yahweh has deemed for your life, Christopher—that purpose being your call to be a warrior. I told you this much upon our first meeting. God will use our rebellious and resentful hearts, which led to us being left behind from the rapture, to now serve Him during the final seven years of history as we know it. We must give all we have, even our lives, for Christ Jesus who died to provide us with eternal life. If I die, so be it, but I will not cower in hiding.

"Christopher, I cannot tell you anything that will heal your heart, that will make the pains of this world pass away. What I will say to you is your obsession—yes, obsession—with holding on to things that have long passed is a poison, a poison that has blinded you to the reality that Yahweh has continuously cared for you. Yahweh has relentlessly sought after you without growing weary, despite your rebuffs. There is little assurance that any of us in this room will live to see the moment when Christ Jesus' foot strikes the nearby Mount of Olives in seven years. However, we can be assured that a decision to live for Him, to trust Him as our Savior, gives us eternal life, while a decision against Him provides eternal damnation. It's your choice, my young friend, and it's that simple."

"Thanks, sir, for your candor. I am—" The older man cut him off. "Stop trying to explain your relationship with God to everyone but the person who matters, you. Enough. I will know your decision when you know, as well as everyone around you. Now, let's eat and enjoy the remainder of this weekend since I feel next week will prove to be fateful." General Havid buzzed for his staff to bring food and drinks.

Gemma arrived at the table to find a glass full of Merlot and a tempting antipasto platter awaiting her. "This looks divine, Gabriella. It's like you read my mind," she said as she picked up her glass.

Gabriella smiled. "It's good to be able to bond with the only other woman on the senior staff. Draven Cross doesn't seem like a man who's too in touch with women-equality issues," she said, testing the waters.

"If you only knew the half of it, Gabriella. Mr. Cross puts on this air that he is dedicated only to the service of others, but he is by far the most selfish and egotistical person you will ever meet," Gemma said, refilling her wineglass.

"I am sure you have seen a lot in your years of service to Mr. Cross. He seems a bit rough in the way he handles matters sometimes," Gabriella remarked, striving for an informal tone.

"That's an understatement. Mr. Cross forced his father out of Cross Industries, the chemical company started by his grandfather. Draven felt his father's business model was too narrow and lacked significant political influence, so he convinced the board of directors to fire his father as CEO and place him in charge instead."

"Wow, his technique was harsh, I guess, but it's hard to argue with the results. Cross Industries is a multibillion-dollar biotech company with branches into seemingly every sector of business," Gabriella responded as she reached over to fill Gemma's glass for the third time.

"It's due only to his ruthless business practices. Mr. Cross has forced the closing of more business deals through extortion or violence than I can even recount. Those that have crossed him and dared stand up for themselves have lost everything, sometimes including their lives. His only goal has been to get to where he is now, ruling the world no matter the cost. I even heard a rumor that he killed someone close to him as a child because of some perceived slight," Gemma reported, red in the face. She added, "I think this needs to be my last glass. The stress of this job has me feeling a little light in spirit tonight."

"I just have to ask…why have you stayed? I mean, you're smart, beautiful, you could have a different path in life." Gabriella left the question hanging. To her shock and horror, Gemma's face crumpled and tears flowed, followed by deep, quiet sobs. "Gemma, get ahold of yourself. What's wrong? What did I say?"

"I loved him, Gabriella. That's why I stayed around Draven for so long at first. I thought that if I gave myself to Draven and did what he said, he would love me. I saw myself becoming his wife. The reality is, Draven just used me, and I grew too scared or proud or something to leave him. My family thought he was the devil himself. I grew up in a Christian home. My parents tried several times to get me to stop working for him. They gave up after I responded rudely to them after skipping a family function to be with Draven as he closed out yet another business deal."

"I'm sorry, Gemma. I thought there might have been a personal reason you stayed around for such harsh treatment, but I had no idea it was that personal," Gabriella said apologetically.

"Ah, look at me…a sobbing, drunk mess. It's okay, Gabriella. I realized after seeing Draven with several women that he saw me only as a plaything. I've pushed my revulsion for him deep inside. I get paid well and don't have to endure half of what you and the others go through. My only regret is, I never got a chance…" She trailed off, crying bitterly.

"You never got a chance to make up with your parents before the disappearances," Gabriella finished for her.

Gemma simply nodded.

"Let me ask you one more question. Do you think it's possible that Draven is the biblical Antichrist? I am sure you've heard those rumors," Gabriella queried.

"I would say he is the leading candidate, if not the devil himself.

Gabriella, you have no idea how evil Draven can be when he wants something."

"That's an interesting way to describe the man," Gabriella remarked as she signaled the waiter for the bill.

"We only accept cash. The credit card system is still messed up since the disappearances," the waiter told her.

"That's fine," Gabriella answered, paying in cash.

As the two women departed the restaurant and stood in silence on the street, waiting for their respective rideshares to arrive, Gabriella could tell Gemma wanted to say something.

"I hope you'll forgive me for losing my head a bit tonight. I'll blame it on the wine. It's just that I don't have anyone to talk to anymore. My family is gone, and I lost my friends years ago due to Draven. Thanks for just listening," Gemma said timidly.

Gabriella felt a little guilty for exploiting Gemma's weakness just to get information that would help with her own decision-making process. "It's okay, Gemma. I will always be here for you. Remember, misery loves company," she quipped with a laugh as Gemma's rideshare pulled up.

"Take care," Gemma called over her shoulder. "I'll see you on Monday."

"Yep, I'll be there," Gabriella said, waving as Gemma drove off into the night.

God, thank you for hearing me and giving me the answers I need to make a decision to believe in You. I just need some help on the process, but I know just the person I need to talk to…Jackson Williams, Gabriella thought as she pulled out her quantum communicator and stepped into her rideshare.

Chapter 17

As the buzz of a Monday morning began around the Israeli capital, Draven Cross reflected upon the lavish attention the Israeli government had showered upon him since his arrival. The weekend had been a nonstop tour of parties and fawning from politicians and his favorite indulgence, licentious men and women. He attributed his festive weekend to an emerging aspect of Israel's increasingly secular business and political culture after its windfall in energy wealth. The blue skies of a crisp early winter day only added to Draven's optimism as his convoy made the short two-kilometer drive from the King David Hotel to the Knesset for a speech before the Plenum.

Draven was glad for reports of a promising start to the World Religious Leaders Conference in Rome. However, he was troubled by the increasing number of stories about the two mysterious older men who had been appearing all over Israel since the Wailing Wall incident. No one knew where they were staying, how they moved around, or when and where they would appear next.

As Draven's door opened in front of the Knesset, he was greeted by not only the usual political luminaries but also a boisterous Israeli public, many of whom had brought signage proclaiming Draven to be the savior of Israel. He stood at the top of the steps leading into the historic Knesset to bask in the crowd's apparent adoration. He waved animatedly, which sent the people into an elated frenzy before he disappeared into the building.

Cross moved quickly toward the Plenum Hall, greeted by clapping and cheering the entire way. When he entered the hall, the whole assembly rose and applauded. As he prepared to speak, one thought was uppermost in his mind: *I am Israel's Messiah.*

"Ladies and gentlemen," he began. "I am nearly overcome by the warm and heartfelt welcome you've provided me over the last few days. I hope it didn't cost too much to round up that crowd outside." Laughter spread across the hall. "I assure you I jest, my dear friends. Sincerely, I am very appreciative of the welcome I've received. Today is not just another historic moment. No, today is a moment without historical comparison, for today marks the first of many steps toward real peace on Earth.

"Since the inception of the Jewish state in the early twentieth century, Israel has faced numerous trials and tribulations, all of which you've overcome. The latest threat to Israel's existence occurred only three and a half years ago in the form of a savage and unwarranted attack. Those days, however, are no more. Today I stand as the spokesman for the entire world, echoing a sentiment from Red Square to the White House, from the West Bank to Tiananmen Square, and all points in between. The message is that the world wants to be a friend to Israel and not a foe."

The Plenum Hall reverberated with shouts of praise and applause in response. Draven stepped back from the lectern and joined in the applause, motioning for the Israeli leader to join him on the dais, and the cheers grew even louder. It was as if the building itself had come alive and was cheering.

Draven Cross raised his hands as he prepared to conclude his remarks and join the Israeli president and prime minister for the official signing of a peace treaty between Israel and the U.E., ensuring Israel's security for the next seven years.

"Yes, this is a moment for celebration. While the document I am preparing to sign outlines only seven years of guaranteed security, let me say now that Israel's safety will extend far beyond the boundaries of this treaty. Thank you, and may peace reign on Earth," Draven finished.

The Israeli president and prime minister waited for Draven Cross to join them at a table with a blue velvet covering that had the Star of David emblazoned on one end and the U.E. symbol in front of Draven's seat on the other end. The treaty was placed before each leader for a signature one at a time. Once the signing was completed, the men stood in unison as cameras flashed and cheers rose like the crashing of waves, but only Draven heard the words of the Prince of This World in his mind. *"I am well pleased in you. All your enemies will bow before you. Today I give you the world."*

Christopher, Jackson, and General Havid had departed Jerusalem early to avoid the crowds descending on the city in hopes of seeing Draven Cross sign the peace agreement and dedicate the new temple. While Christopher was focused on the upcoming meeting with the Israeli intelligence services and President Rodgers's request of them to discover Draven Cross's new U.E. headquarters, the sergeant major and the general were completely enthralled by the significance of the secretary-general's visit.

"This is really something. I mean, to be in Israel watching the signing of the temporary peace treaty between Israel and the Antichrist is amazing. Praise God for allowing me to see His holy Word come to pass," Jackson said, watching the televised signing of the peace accord on a small television in General Havid's SUV.

"I love your enthusiasm, Jackson, but I feel today is also a sad day in Israel's history. We have aligned ourselves not with Yahweh, but with His sworn enemy," General Havid remarked with a sad smile as he watched Draven Cross stand with Israel's president and prime minister, their joined hands raised high in the air in triumph.

"You know, sir," Jackson said, "it's funny how once I understood just how much God loves me, He was no longer some distant, angry grandfather playing whack-a-mole with my entire life. My entire outlook changed. Rev's journal and my experience over the last couple of months have opened my eyes to see just how real God is. As the Bible says in John 14:17: 'The Spirit of truth. The world cannot accept him, because it neither sees him nor knows him. But you know him, for he lives with you and will be in you.' It was not until I saw my need for Christ through the Holy Spirit that I was able to realize how real and good God has been in my life."

"Ah, yes, I feel the same way. I could not see all that Yahweh had already done for Israel and me until I accepted the truth of His Word and Holy Spirit. However, what is this whack-a-mole analogy?" General Havid asked. "I am not familiar with this." Laughing, Christopher replied, "It's a game involving a rubber mallet hitting the heads of moles that pop up through a game board. Jackson is saying he thought God was always punishing us through diseases, crime, and all the bad things of this world—like He was playing a game."

"Oh, I understand now," the general said. "We're here, gentlemen. Welcome to the Israeli Ministry of Defense. The objective is for you to hear our assessments on Cross's Middle East activities and then for you to head out to Iraq tonight to observe for yourselves why we believe a particular area near ancient Babylon will be his headquarters. Before we get out, please leave all your electronic devices in the vehicle. They are not allowed inside the Ministry of Defense."

Christopher and Jackson had powered off their communicators when they entered Israel, so they just placed them in their backpacks and left them behind in the SUV.

"I am sure this recon will go a lot better than Christopher's last one did because I am going this time," Jackson teased as the men walked into the building.

"We will see," Christopher replied.

After a long day of waiting for the peace accord and temple ceremonies to begin, due to the time difference, Gabriella sat contemplating what the eternal ramifications of the peace treaty between Israel and world would be, if any. *God, I'm grateful that You responded to my questions about Your existence. Now I just need confirmation that Draven Cross is the Antichrist before I make a decision to accept Jesus as my Savior.* She caught herself and smiled. *Even in accepting Jesus Christ as a real part of life, I am using a rigorous analytical plan—I really do need some help.*

"Why are you still here watching this event?" Gemma asked as she entered the U.E. executive conference room.

"Primarily because it's my job, but also because it is a very historic moment. I guess I could ask you the same. How was the rest of your weekend? I haven't seen you around the office today," Gabriella said.

"I'm curious, too, truth be told, despite my abhorrence for the man. My weekend was good. In many ways I felt like a weight had been lifted off my shoulders after our dinner. I actually dug out my old Bible and read a little."

"That is interesting, but hold that thought," Gabriella said as John Barnes entered the conference room.

"Good evening, ladies. I see the boss is out there winning the hearts and minds of the world," John Barnes observed happily.

"In a manner of speaking, he is. What brings you to the office so late? I figured you'd be painting the town red with your new larger salary," Gabriella replied sarcastically.

"The night is still young, but business brought me here, mainly to find you. Where is Omega right now and have you finished identifying the locations of the U.S. secret command and control sites?" Barnes asked.

"You have no shame, do you? I mean, one day you're working for your country, and the next you're aiming to destroy it," Gabriella mused.

"That's funny, considering who's providing me with the intel. In any case, boss's orders. So do you have the information or do I need to report to the secretary-general that you're late?" Barnes queried snidely.

Gabriella tossed a manila folder across the table, which contained legacy command and control sites, all of which she knew would never be used, and the one identified by the public due to its annual "Santa tracking" outreach activity. Gabriella hoped she could get away with providing only the partial truth in delivering what Draven Cross had asked of her.

"I don't see any information on Omega's location. Where is Omega?" Barnes insisted.

"The last information I had through intelligence channels—as you know, I don't work for the U.S. government anymore—was that Omega was likely in the Middle East," Gabriella replied.

"Really? The Middle East is the best you can come up with?" Barnes asked skeptically.

"Look, that's why they're Omega Group, okay? You should appreciate the unpredictability of tracking Omega personnel," Gabriella answered, keeping her tone conciliatory.

"Well, if you get details of their location, shoot me a message. They're likely in Israel for the peace treaty ceremony. I am flying out later today to check the security around the new headquarters project near Babylon, and then to Rome to meet up with the boss and Evan for the last few days of the preacher conference, or whatever they called it. I will catch you, pretty ladies, later," Barnes said in farewell before leaving the conference room.

"He's is such a vile pig, and none too bright, I might add," Gemma observed with obvious disgust.

"Yes, he's the sneaky, always-taking-care-of-number-one type of guy," Gabriella agreed, pulling out her quantum communicator, which appeared to the casual observer to be a cell phone, thinking to herself, *It's two thirty in the morning here, so it should be nine thirty in the morning in Israel. I am sure the guys are moving around. I wonder why Jackson hasn't responded to my last message.* She typed a short communication: *"Draven has Barnes and his new team of mercenaries searching the globe for you. Please be careful. As for his intent when he finds you, I can only guess. He is heading to Babylon, Iraq. I can confirm that as the new U.E. headquarters. Don't go to Babylon, as Barnes's team will be there. Please confirm receipt of this message."*

Once she sent the message, Gabriella continued watching the coverage of Draven Cross in Israel.

"You okay, Gabriella? You look like something is bothering you," Gemma commented.

"I'm fine. Just worried about some old friends," Gabriella replied.

"I'm sure they're okay. You do know it's late, right? I'm heading out soon," Gemma said with a smile.

"Yeah, they're most likely fine…I hope," Gabriella replied pensively.

Draven's procession was thronged by his fans as they made their way to the Temple Mount in the Old City. He read sign after sign calling him a hero and the champion of Israel, but his favorite thus far was the numerous signs with the Star of David above his name followed by "Messiah" and a question mark. Draven Cross was nearly bursting with pride as the vehicles rolled to a stop.

Flanked by Israeli Defense Forces, dignitaries, and a huge press corps, Draven walked from an access road toward the Temple Mount, which had been excavated. The wooden frame on the new construction soared skyward above the masses below.

Television commentators had begun describing the scene to their worldwide audiences, with the all-news network securing the honor of providing a simulcast transmission, which was not only displayed on large monitors to the masses around the Temple Mount but also streaming around the world via the Internet. The Jewish religious elite were in place at the Temple Mount, where a deep-purple sash hung between two columns. The sash was emblazoned with two bowing cherubims, their wings touching at the center point, similar to the cover for the Ark of the Covenant. A select group of Jewish high society took their seats with Draven Cross and the officials arriving on the dais.

The two chief rabbis, one Ashkenazi and one Sephardi, overseers of the Chief Rabbinate of Israel, opened the ceremony with remarks and prayer. Cross's comments were to follow before the purple sash was cut. Although sacrifices had already begun on a temporary altar nearby, the ribbon cutting was to mark the official opening of the temple construction project.

Just as Draven stood to speak, a fierce wind blew across the Old City and engulfed the Temple Mount, pushing some of the VIPs out of their chairs and sending hats flying. As the wind ceased, two older men suddenly appeared behind the purple sash—now torn in two within the framework of the rising temple of God.

The voice of the taller man rang out across the assemblage as he addressed Draven Cross. "You will not speak at this holy site today, son of perdition. Woe to you, Israel, for you have denied the true and living God. You have played the role of a harlot with the beast, leaving the God of Abraham, Isaac, and Jacob. The commands of the LORD your God were given to your forefathers. Is it not written that if you obey God, He will be your God and walk among you? Did He not break the bonds of Egypt from around your stiff necks and allow you to walk with your head high among the nations? You are a stiff-necked people who have greatly offended the true and living God, with whom there is no equal."

Utter silence fell across the adjacent Old City and Temple Mount in response to the booming pronouncement of the first witness. Even Draven ran from the dais toward his security detail. The vast throng stood in shock as the man continued while his shorter companion stood quietly beside him.

"You missed the signs of the Messiah, whose name is Jesus, whose name is the name above all names. We will proclaim His glory for 1,260 days, to be a witness against your hypocrisy, Israel, and to urge you to repent of your sins against God."

"Who do you think you are?" Draven Cross shouted in a moment of courage.

"Silence, evil one, for your very breath is at the mercy of *El Shaddai*.

Today is not yours, but belongs to the God of Heaven," the shorter witness bellowed authoritatively.

With this proclamation, Draven clutched his throat and fell to the ground. Security forces rushed to his side before carrying him from the Temple Mount to his vehicle, which sped off.

The shorter witness continued. "We are two olive trees and two lampstands, which stand before the Lord of the earth. We proclaim God's glory and authority. A weary world should listen now to the decree of the LORD. It will not rain again in Israel until God allows. We are unmovable until our time is complete."

The two men walked toward the staircase that led to the Wailing Wall plaza below, where they had first appeared, parting the crowds and security forces, as God had done to the Red Sea thousands of years before. After descending, they seated themselves in front of the ancient temple wall as the people of Israel formed a broad but distant semicircle around them. Israeli security forces called out to the men to surrender or face death. However, the two servants of God sat in complete silence. As a squad of policemen advanced and aimed their weapons, the two men stood, causing the policemen to stop their advance momentarily.The police captain called out, "This is your last warning." But his threat was met only with silence. "Open fire," the captain shouted. As the rifle reports rang out, seemingly announcing the demise of the two self-proclaimed witnesses, an intense wave of heat and flame engulfed the entire squad. As the intense flames consumed the policemen, reducing them to ashes, the two witnesses of God sat down again as if nothing had happened.

Observers and security forces alike ran away in fear, their shrieks and cries heard all over Jerusalem as a result of the impressive display of power by the God of Israel.

Christopher was impressed as usual with the methodical and cerebral approach to intelligence collection the Israeli's undertook to discover

Draven Cross's plans. It seemed that General Havid had orchestrated a plan to recruit a source in the construction firm from Dubai that had been awarded a recent significant contract from the U.E. That contract was in fact for the building of the U.E.'s new home, near the ruins of ancient Babylon in Iraq.

"So as you can see, we are confident of the location for the new U.E. headquarters. I think your mission is complete," General Havid said confidently.

"Wow, that was a great rundown, but…" Christopher stopped as the doors to the small, isolated meeting room flew open and a frantic staffer rushed into the room.

"What is the meaning of this disruption?" General Havid demanded.

"My apologies, sir, but Secretary-General Cross was attacked at the temple ceremony, just moments ago," the staffer replied, touching a button on the desk near General Havid. A flat screen descended from the ceiling, and the staff member changed the channel to the event coverage on the all-news network.

"If you're just joining us, we're continuing our coverage from Israel. Moments ago, Secretary-General Draven Cross was rushed to Hadassah University Hospital in Jerusalem where his status is unknown after being attacked by two unidentified males. The two men then proceeded to attack several policemen near the Wailing Wall, where they remain. We have footage of the attack, but we wish to offer a word of caution to sensitive viewers due to the graphic nature of the content," the anchor warned.

Christopher, Jackson, Havid, and the aide watched in awe as the two men proclaimed their condemnation of Israel and their allegiance to God. While it was clear one of the men had told Draven he could not speak, it was unclear just exactly how they had attacked him. The most chilling scene was the fire that engulfed the policemen; the cameras had zoomed in and enhanced the footage, focusing on the two men. A flame had appeared to come from out of their mouths, or perhaps just near them—it was hard to tell precisely, but the end result was clear.

"Please tell me I am not the only one who knows who these two guys are," Jackson said excitedly.

Christopher and General Havid both looked at each other in obvious puzzlement.

"Man—" Jackson began in disbelief, but he was cut off by Christopher.

"I know, I know, I need to study my Bible," Christopher agreed before Jackson could finish his chiding.

"Well, at least that message is getting into that thick skull of yours," Jackson joked.

"Gentlemen, perhaps we should finish this conversation in my office upstairs," General Havid suggested, directing Christopher and Jackson out of the conference room and toward a bank of elevators, hitting the button for the twelfth floor when they entered the first available car.

Gabriella and Gemma both stood watching in horror as Draven was being carried off the Temple Mount after a tense exchange with two men who called themselves messengers from the God of Israel.

"Do you think he's dead?" Gemma asked.

"I don't know, but we'd better start trying to figure out what just happened. I'll call Evan…never mind, he's calling now. Call the staffers on the ground and find out Draven's status," Gabriella directed Gemma as she answered the call from Evan Mallory.

"No, Evan, we don't know if he's alive or dead. Well, we're trying, but he took most of the staff with him, minus Gemma and me. Wait! I said wait, Evan! Gemma's trying to tell me something," Gabriella explained as Gemma passed her a note.

The note read, *"Draven is alive and mad. He's being evaluated at Hadassah University Hospital. Expect taskings to follow shortly."*

Gabriella relayed the message to a relieved and overly dramatic Evan. "Yes, I am sure we will exact justice for the attack. Okay, I've got to go. Good-bye, Evan."

“Who are those two men?” Gemma asked.

“I’m not sure, but they have just made themselves a deadly enemy, that’s for sure. The only thing we can do now is await further instructions,” Gabriella responded thoughtfully.

Draven Cross wished he could yell and scream at the medical attendants caring for him. Instead he was limited to pushing and shoving people away. He gestured an unmistakable demand for pen and paper. A junior U.E. staffer handed Draven her pen and pad and watched him write furiously.

“I am fine, minus not being able to speak. Someone tell me, are those two old fools dead?” Draven wrote.

The female staffer began writing something back to Draven, who ripped the pen and pad from her hands.

“I am unable to speak. My hearing is fine, you twit,” Draven scrawled angrily.

“My apologies, sir. The two attackers are still alive and killed several policemen according to Israeli reports,” the staffer responded hastily.

“I am leaving this horrible country. Make sure my plane is ready to depart. We’re heading to Rome,” Draven wrote before grabbing his suit jacket and storming out of the hospital, leaving a stunned crowd of doctors and nurses in his wake.

General Havid instructed his aides to wait in the reception area outside his office as he closed the door.

“Now, Jackson, tell us what you know of these two men who attacked Mr. Cross today,” the general requested.

“Boy, oh, boy, what a trip this has been. I can’t believe y’all don’t know who those two men are,” Jackson said with disbelief.

“Well, we don’t, so just tell us,” Christopher instructed shortly.

"I believe those two men are none other than the prophets of God described in Revelation 11. If you consider the whooping they put on old Saint Cross and his cronies, then add in their message, you have all you need to identify them. Dressed in sackcloth to indicate mourning, they will prophesy God's glory to a fallen world and tell mankind about the cure to the fatal disease of sin. But sadly, the world will reject their message. The two prophets will be a shining light in this dark time, and the world will hate them," Jackson explained.

"What can I do with them?" General Havid asked. "The prime minister will demand their removal from the Wailing Wall. This is the second time Israeli lives were lost."

"You can do nothing. Remember, gentlemen, the witnesses said God numbered their days to 1,260. Their demise will be at the hands of the Antichrist, and not until the Word of God says so," Jackson informed his friends.

"Sir, my advice to you is to take what Jackson says is going to happen as fact. The best thing you can do is try to keep the people at a safe distance," Christopher counseled.

"Fine, I will do my best to convince the prime minister and others to stay away, but I feel that I will lose that fight. We need to get you two on your way to Iraq." Havid pushed a buzzer to summon his executive assistant. Before the man arrived, he continued, saying, "I have arranged for you to fly into Baghdad this evening, where you will connect with one of our best Mossad agents, Gilana Edri. She will help you get near Babylon so you can conduct your reconnaissance mission. I wish you well and will be in touch after the mission."

"Thanks, sir," Christopher replied. "We really appreciate your help and hospitality."

"Yes, sir, thank you," Jackson added.

"My friends, we have only just begun our journey. May Yahweh bless you and keep you on the journey ahead. Now go," General Havid urged. "We all have a mission before us to accomplish."

Christopher cast one last longing look back over his shoulder at the stately old warrior as the door to the office closed before he and Jackson were led back to the vehicle that had brought them to the Ministry of Defense. Christopher hoped that General Havid was right—that their journey together had only begun, as he longed to find a positive wave in the midst of the sea of disaster around him. He needed something or someone to trust, because he had let himself down too many times to be trusted any longer.

CHAPTER 18

As Evan Mallory looked out from the foyer balcony of the Palazzo Caelum, an ancient Roman palace located along the banks of the Tiber, pride swelled within him. Grand imams and ayatollahs intermingled with priests, preachers, and rabbis; men and women were all chatting amicably, a pleasing testament to Evan's efforts throughout the week of the World Religious Leaders Conference. Leaders from every significant faith rallied around the Interfaith vision Evan had laid out for them throughout the week—a religious creed stating that God is within all of mankind and, despite revealing Himself in different ways to various cultures, He is the same God to everyone.

The attack on Draven by the two religious fanatics served only to bolster among the spiritually influential crowd gathered below Evan that the world needed one faith. He had even made plans to exploit the attack on Draven, as suggested to him in a dream last night by his spiritual guide, the Prince of This World. So when the unquestioned leader of Shia Islam, after hearing about the attack in Israel, told the entire session, "The world needs one faith, centered on the unity and peace found in all spiritual expressions, to bring us together and not apart," he and many of the others at the conference were shocked.

"Gentlemen, I want to thank you for the heartfelt outpouring of concern and well wishes for the secretary-general, who was savagely attacked yesterday. The great news is that he will be joining us within the hour to conclude this historic conference. Please finish your refreshments and make your way to the conference hall. We will open the morning with communal prayers, invoking the spirits of the universe to grant us a successful close to our meeting," Evan announced grandly before making his way into the main foyer.

Gabriella grew more concerned about what Christopher and Jackson were up to in Israel given the bizarre exchange between Draven and the two witnesses, a moniker given to them by the media. President Rodgers's latest message only drove home the point that he was looking for a reason to attack Draven. She sat at her desk, wearing the same clothes she had put on thirty-six hours earlier, staring at the American president's most recent communication.

"Gabriella, I know you're in a tough situation, but I wouldn't have asked you to do the job if I didn't believe you were up to it. I have been purposefully keeping communications between us at a minimum to protect you as well as the mission I feel must be accomplished, which is stopping Draven Cross at all costs. Right now, I have Christopher and Jackson in Israel working to find the location of the new U.E. headquarters. I know I could have asked you, but I also needed to get a feeling for whether General Havid is the trusted ally I hope he is, and my prayers have been answered. The boys are on their way to the suspected new U.E. headquarters site now.

"I pray that you will decide one day soon to make Jesus Christ Lord over your life, that you will finally surrender that fifty-pound brain of yours to its creator. I don't believe we will ever meet face-to-face on this side of eternity again, but please know I care for you like a father and it has been a privilege to serve our nation with you. I will send you a message before any attack to give you a chance to shelter. Just try to stay away from that new HQ. It is my earnest and heartfelt prayer that we will meet in Heaven one day. Your devoted friend, President Rodgers."

Tears welled up in Gabriella's eyes as she sat at her desk helpless to prevent the seemingly inevitable war and worried about the future for herself and her friends Christopher and Jackson.

"God, please help us," was all Gabriella could muster as sobs rose up from somewhere deep within and the tears spilled over to flow unchecked down her cheeks.

Christopher and Jackson's travel had been strictly commercial and comfortable. However, the major's attention was quickly caught outside the small passenger terminal at Baghdad International Airport. Seeing the familiar, small, poorly maintained vehicles driving around wildly, he knew things were about to become a lot more uncomfortable. Fight-or-flight response kicked in as a tall, raven-haired, fair-skinned woman wearing a brown abaya and matching *al-Amira* accompanied by a muscular man in a black *thawb* and sandals approached him and Jackson as they stood near a taxi stand.

"Get ready for a fight," Christopher told Jackson. "Potential trouble coming right at us."

"I'm always ready," Jackson retorted, but Christopher knew he was paying attention.

The woman paused about ten feet from Christopher and Jackson and stared, while the man kept coming toward them.

"General Havid sent us to take care of you," the man said in a thick accent. "We should go."

"General Havid told us that we were meeting a woman. What's your female friend's name?" Christopher questioned as Jackson moved to the left side of the man.

"Her name is Gilana Edri. You know women cannot speak to a strange man in public here without drawing attention, so please let's go," the man urged nervously. "Now."

"Okay, we will go with you, my friend, but just know if you try anything, you're losing a kidney," Jackson warned, poking the man with the butt of his field knife as they followed him to the woman.

Christopher and Jackson followed the odd couple away from the airport terminal and into the parking lot, toward an antiquated van.

"Okay, that's far enough. Before we get in that van, let's see some ID," Jackson instructed, pushing the man against the van, drawn knife in hand.

"Relax, Sergeant Major Williams," the woman said, holding up an Israeli Defense Forces identification card. "My name is Gilana Edri, the lead Mossad agent in Iraq. This is my lieutenant, Uri Hadad. I obviously could not approach you or speak in such a public place."

"My apologies, ma'am, but I'm sure you understand. By the way, please call me Jackson."

"Yes, our apologies. I think we should have better coordinated the recognition signal before you departed Tel Aviv," Christopher added, extending his hand to Gilana and Uri.

"No hard feelings," Uri replied. "It's part of the business."

"We can kiss and make up later. Let's get going," Gilana urged. "We need to get to Babylon before it gets dark."

"Now there's some fire that could get you going in the morning. Gilana reminds me of that little firecracker back home named Gabriella," Jackson said quietly to Christopher.

"Get in before Gilana beats you down," Christopher said, throwing a duffel bag at Jackson.

Gabriella tried calling both Christopher and Jackson's communicators, but voicemail picked up each time. She was desperate after receiving Barnes's message that he had arrived at Babylon and was assessing the security situation. She had a feeling that Christopher and Jackson were heading right into a trap set by Barnes, so she tried calling again. Still nothing.

"Ugh, why are you not answering?" she shouted.

"You okay? I heard you from down the hall," Gemma asked a moment later as she poked her head into the office.

"I'll be fine, just trying to reach some friends," Gabriella responded.

"Well, I'll leave you, but just so you know, Mr. Cross is about to speak in Rome. He will be heading back to New York with Evan right after his speech."

"Thanks. I'll meet you in the conference room in a few minutes," Gabriella promised.

Gabriella tried calling Christopher and Jackson one more time, but there was again no answer, so she decided to send them another message, warning them of the danger at Babylon.

She wrote, *"I don't know why you've had your communicators off for the last twenty-four hours, but don't go to Babylon. I'm sure that's where President Rodgers has you guys going, but don't go. Call me when you get this message."*

Sighing as she laid her quantum communicator on her desk, she went to the conference room to watch Draven Cross address the World Religious Leaders Conference. She could do nothing else now but hope for the best as evening approached in the Middle East.

Draven had been shaken by the power displayed by the two witnesses at the Temple Mount. He had never in his life been confronted by a person or a situation that had caused such fear to rise within him, but he had been comforted by the Prince of This World this morning in a lucid dream. *"You will have your revenge against the two agents of our enemy. Use the attack to push the world toward one religion."*

As Cross moved to the podium to address the religious leaders, he grabbed his throat as he tried to shut the thought of the two witnesses out of his mind. The applause of the audience died down as they saw him, for the first time since his ascension, appearing to be vulnerable.

"I am honored to stand before you today. As the world witnessed yesterday, two religious fanatics claiming to be representatives of God attacked me. The men released a still unknown incapacitating agent into the air, and I took the brunt of the weapon as I stepped forward to protect the audience gathered for the Temple ceremony."

Applause erupted after hearing Draven's account of the events. With feigned humility, he gestured for the crowd to be silent and continued his speech.

"Despite the cowardly and unprovoked incident yesterday, I still believe spirituality has a place in our society. However, unyielding religious dogma and traditions are unacceptable. My spirits were buoyed yesterday in my hospital room upon learning from Mr. Mallory that this conference of religious leaders has unanimously agreed to converge all of the world's traditions under a single faith, an Interfaith vision." The crowd roared in approval.Draven allowed the applause to proceed for a few moments before finishing his speech. "The last two months have been difficult. The losses we have experienced can never be forgotten. Yet I see many bright spots for our future. The global economy is stabilizing. I am proud to have led the other world leaders into the implementation of bringing the world markets under three currencies and ultimately a single currency, thus preventing a crushing global recession. I hope to announce shortly an initiative to centralize the governance of the world to further reduce the chances of war or exploitation in this time of unprecedented change. Cleanup around the world will likely to continue for some time. However, I am pleased to see new construction projects emerging from the rubble of the past.

"We will not let the gloom and doom of a few religious fanatics and critics prevent us from achieving universal peace. The efforts made here over the last week will have a lasting effect on generations to come. I salute you for moving past petty differences in leading the world toward a better place. Thank you, and may peace reign on Earth." Draven Cross waved to the now united world faith clergy.

On his way out of the conference room, Cross told Evan, "My

consolidation over all elements of societal power is nearly complete. All that's left now is to eliminate the American-led conspirators, and that will be accomplished soon enough."

Christopher had slept during the entire trip from Baghdad to Hilah, Iraq, a city near the ancient ruins of Babylon and the Mossad's safe house location. The fresh smell of pita bread and hot shawarma flooded the van, making the major realize it had been hours since he had last eaten.

"Hey, sleeping beauty," Jackson said. "You want shawarma? We're making a pit stop before going to the safe house. We only have a couple of hours before sundown."

"Sure, I'm starving. Where are Gilana and Uri?" Christopher asked.

"They're across the street in that little restaurant, picking up food. They suggested we stay in the van and out of sight considering we stand out like a baboon's butt."

Laughing, Christopher replied, "I don't think I'll ever get used to your remarkably unique way of expressing yourself. Look, here come Gilana and Uri."

The pair jumped in the van and quickly took off, Uri's eyes glued to the rearview mirror.

"What's up? Is someone after us?" Christopher asked.

"No, but we did learn that a small team of Westerners who were dressed like soldiers, according to the store clerk, arrived at the construction site earlier today. Security has been light the last few weeks, to say the least, so we're worried that someone knows you guys are coming," Uri responded.

"We'll need to consider this reconnaissance plan again before we do anything else," Gilana said.

Uri zipped along Highway 8 and the mighty Euphrates River before exiting across from a large artificial lake constructed by the long-deposed Iraqi dictator Saddam Hussein. He brought the vehicle to a stop near the gate of a two-story earthen private home, with a towering six-foot mud-brick fence enclosing the property.

"Wait here," Gilana instructed as she and Uri exited the vehicle, moved through the gate, and walked away into the compound in opposite directions.

Christopher and Jackson watched as the orange disk of the sun began sinking toward the horizon, leaving everything coated in the deep red-orange of a desert sunset.

"Let's go, move quickly," Gilana ordered, tapping on a van window.

Christopher and Jackson slipped out of the van and into the small but well-furnished safe house. While the Israelis had gone to great lengths to blend in with the few neighbors on the outside, the inside of the safe house had a couple of sofas, large flat-screen television, and several Western-style beds.

"You folks sure know how to rough it," Jackson teased.

Uri laughed. "There is no need to suffer while doing your duty."

Christopher had already found the stairs leading to the roof, a common feature of many Middle Eastern homes. As he came out onto the rooftop, he was awestruck by the view the safe house afforded him. Across the lake, the ongoing construction of the new U.E. headquarters was clearly visible. The distant ancient ruins of Babylon were stunning against the backdrop of the sun sinking below the horizon of the Euphrates.

The major found himself hoping that tonight went smoothly. He wished that the last two months had been a bad dream, that he was in Iraq, preparing to rescue a journalist from ISIS instead of trying to locate the headquarters of the new leader of the world. Gilana's voice broke into his thoughts.

"You should get some rest. It's impossible to know what tonight holds."

"I'll be down in a second," Christopher replied, watching the last shimmers of sunlight dance off the ruins of Babylon and hoping for the best.

From the climate-controlled comfort of the U.E. security and operations center located in Saddam's former summer palace, which overlooked the entire Babylon complex, John Barnes watched darkness settle over the installation of passive infrared motion sensors near a potential outer wall breach. A vein along the side of his head bulged as he remembered his arrival earlier today at the U.E. HQ construction site. He had found the local security forces foreman sleeping and had angrily kicked the legs out from under the man's chair, causing him to yelp as he scrambled to get to his feet.

"Get up, you lazy dog!" Barnes yelled. "You people are all the same. I should kill you for sleeping. You do realize how important this construction site is, don't you?"

"Sorry, sorry, sir, but everything is good," the foreman had assured in broken English.

"We will see. Get in the truck!" Barnes screamed, cursing the man roundly as they drove around the site. "Stop here. What is that?" He pointed to a large mound of dirt that sat along the outer wall of the complex. "And tell me we have some sort of surveillance on that area," he intoned threateningly.

"No need for surveillance. That is the place where the construction teams bring in their dirt," the man responded.

Barnes slapped the man across the head and cursed him, telling him to fix it.

He had called Gabriella earlier to find out if she could pinpoint Omega's location in the Middle East. She'd responded that she didn't know any more than she had already told him, but Barnes couldn't shake the feeling that they were coming to this site. He had to be ready.

"Tell those men to hurry up out there, or they will answer to me. I want that job done before dark. I want to be ready for any visitors we might have," Barnes said.

Christopher had gotten only a few restless hours of sleep before Uri came into the room where he and Jackson were bunked to wake them. "Time to plan and get ready to go, my friends."

Jackson, as usual, was snoring.

"How can you sleep like that? I mean, you're out like a light when we could be heading off to our deaths," Christopher questioned, poking his sleeping friend.

"You should know better than anybody why I can rest and be at peace. Let me jog your memory. 'He who dwells in the secret place of the Most High shall abide under the shadow of the Almighty. I will say of the Lord, He is my refuge and my fortress; My God, in Him I will trust.'"

"Psalm 91, Rev's favorite Bible chapter, especially before a mission," Christopher said.

"Exactly. No matter what happens tonight, I know who's with me, even after this life. That's a great comfort, my friend. Now stop worrying. We will be fine.

Without responding to Jackson's optimism, Christopher followed him out to the living room where Uri and Gilana had laid out a large map of the construction site. Without even asking how the two had slept, Gilana jumped right into the planning for their mission.

"Okay, so here are my thoughts for tonight. We drive to Highway 8 across from the man-made lake. Once there, Christopher and Jackson, you two will walk toward a large mound of dirt that covers the outside wall." She pointed to a spot on the map as Christopher uploaded the grid coordinates to his GPS device. "I will then drive Uri to a drop point near the Ishtar Gate. Uri's job will be to serve as a second set of eyes and an emergency distraction, if needed. I will stay with the vehicle here." She pointed to a second location along the tourist road to Babylon. "I'll monitor the radio and provide quick extraction, if needed. You have two hours on target and then must head back to the van. Any questions?"

"How will Uri create that distraction, if needed?" Christopher asked.

"Follow me," Gilana said, walking into what looked like a breakfast nook and pushing on the wall, which swung open to reveal a hidden room.

She turned to her partner and said, "Uri, grab the Doorbell." Christopher and Jackson watched as Uri walked into a small arsenal and grabbed a U.S. AT4 recoilless rifle, also called the Doorbell.

Jackson walked into the room after Uri, saying with a laugh, "I am happier than a hog that fell into the slop trough by himself. I'll take one of these and two of these." He grabbed a G36 rifle and two antipersonnel claymore mines.

"Why the mines?" Gilana questioned.

"Well, if somebody tries to rush us while we are up on that hill, they will get a nasty surprise, won't they?" Jackson answered.

"Does everybody have what they need for weapons?" Gilana queried as she handed out radios, night-vision goggles, and binoculars.

"Yep, let's roll," Christopher said.

Major Barrett took the moonless night as a sign of favor for this mission. Gilana waved the two men off, their black tactical clothing allowing the pair to become one with the inky black night. He and Jackson, per the plan, would maintain radio silence until they neared the link-up point, unless compromised. Two clicks across the radio meant Uri was in place, three meant Christopher and Jackson were set, and four clicks indicated Gilana was ready.

This is too easy, Christopher thought as they crossed over the near side of the artificial lake, closest to Babylon. They had just heard the two clicks over the radio from Uri and expected to hear Gilana any moment. In the distance, the summer palace and main excavation site were brightly lit. The large pile of dirt covering the outside wall loomed in front of the two covert warriors.

Man, I hate night-vision devices. This green glow makes me feel sick, Christopher thought as they reached the base of the dirt pile, which thankfully was dry. Jackson held up four fingers, which Christopher acknowledged with a nod. Jackson signaled that he was going to put in the claymore mines in front of the dirt pile on the Babylon side, so Christopher quietly climbed to the top of the heap, low crawling the last five meters to the top so that he could cover Jackson below. The two seasoned special ops soldiers were able to work in silence using only hand signals and battle-tested operating procedures.

Through high-powered binoculars, Christopher studied a quiet and motionless construction site. Only a few guards were active about a kilometer away at the summer palace. Jackson had moved down the outer wall access road about fifty meters from the dirt pile to place one of the claymores, and Christopher saw that he was running back toward the mound.

As Jackson made his way to the left side of the dirt pile about ten meters below Christopher, he clicked the radio three times. Now all they had to do was observe from their respective vantage points then meet Gilana at the link-up point. Things were going well for a change.

John Barnes could not sleep and made his way to the operations center at around one in the morning to see if anything was going on. He walked in to find the guards asleep and a blinking red LED light on the security control panel, indicating one of the passive infrared motion detection sensors had been tripped. Yet no one was responding in the operations center.

Barnes pulled his pistol from its holster and shot the same sleeping foreman in the head. The loud boom from the shot startled the other two guards awake, only to see death staring them in the face as John Barnes squeezed the trigger on his pistol twice more, killing the other two guards. He hit the blood-soaked alarm button, flooding the complex with light and sirens.

"We have intruders near the dirt pile," Barnes said into his radio. "Load up and find out who they are." He spat on the dead men before exiting the control tower and running down the stairs to a truck filled with his U.E. special activities unit personnel. "Let's go," he ordered his men via radio. "It's likely the American Omega Team, so be on your guard." He thought, *I've got you now, Christopher.*

Uri broke the radio silence of the past hour by transmitting, "Shots fired!"

Jackson responded, "The shots were not directed at us, but this place is lit up like the fourth of July."

"Trouble—two trucks inbound, headed right for us. Uri, get that distraction going," Christopher said urgently.

Christopher and Jackson watched as the two trucks sped across the construction site, closing quickly on their location. The vehicles would be within firing range in less than a minute.

"Uri, shoot the—" Christopher's radio transmission was broken by the loud concussive explosion of a fuel truck back near the summer palace, and the bright flash from the blast whited out his night-vision goggles.

"I am on my way to you guys," Gilana transmitted.

Christopher watched as one truck turned around to head back toward the summer palace, while the other vehicle kept coming. Jackson held the claymore detonator in his right hand. As the truck approached Jackson's firing mark along the road, the unique crack of the claymore mine resounded in the complex and Christopher watched as the vehicle lurched to one side and then rolled several times before coming to a stop. Christopher's goggles, operating once again, confirmed what he already knew: everyone in that truck was dead.

"Jackson, let's go!" Christopher shouted into the radio.

"I am way ahead of you. I'm heading toward Gilana's light already," Jackson answered.

Christopher jumped and slid down the hill and began running to the dirt tourist road and the safety of Gilana's van. Jackson was a few meters in front of him when he heard the gunfight erupt between what he assumed was Uri and the guards who had turned around.

Gilana pulled up in a cloud of dust, screaming at Christopher and Jackson to get in the van.

"We need to get up there and help Uri," the major shouted back as he jumped in the back of the van.

"No, we must go. The U.E. called for reinforcements from the Iraqi national police. Listen, you can hear the police sirens," Gilana replied as she sped away from the ruins of Babylon and toward Highway 8.

"You can't leave a man behind, Gilana," Jackson said, punching the console in front of him. "That's not how we operate." Gilana slammed on the brakes, causing the van to slide to a screeching halt under a highway light on the access ramp to Highway 8. "You have no idea how hard it is for me to leave the man I love to his death, but Uri knew the risks, as do you. Don't lecture me on my duties. No one is above the mission—no one. If you two are caught along with Uri, it could lead to disaster for both our countries," she said harshly, tears streaming down her half-silhouetted face.

"Where are we going?" Christopher asked.

Gilana replied, "I am taking you to Al-Mafraq, Jordan, and the King Hussein Air Base. Uri and I established the air base as our non-permissive environment escape and evasion airport. An aircraft will be waiting for you there. I will contact General Havid to make all the necessary arrangements once we get out of this area." All three occupants were silent as the van made its way up Highway 8 toward the infamous MSR Tampa from the distant Iraqi Conflict of the early 2000s. Christopher didn't even know where to begin. Gilana had lost more than just a fellow soldier. He and Jackson had confirmed only that this location held significant value to Draven and the U.E. *The fight for survival is already a grind*, Christopher thought. *There is no way any of us will make it until Jesus returns.*

"Cease fire, boys. I think we got 'em," John Barnes instructed the guards and the Iraqi national policemen advancing toward the location of suspected Omega operatives who had returned fire for the last fifteen minutes. "What? It was only you back here? I could have sworn you were someone else, and that you had a whole army with you," he spat to the wounded and dying man. Bending to grab Uri by his sweat-soaked and blood-matted hair, he barked, "Who do you work for, and why are you here?"

Uri, defiant to the end, spat bloody phlegm in John Barnes's face with his last bit of strength.

Barnes swore and shot Uri twice in the chest. "Check him for something that will identify who he worked for. Give me a name…something," he said, wiping his face.

"He's clean, boss. Nothing on him," a U.E. special activities unit member responded.

John Barnes swore aloud. He had thought for sure the attack had been perpetrated by Omega. He knew he had to find that team, as they posed a credible threat to the U.E. and Draven Cross. "All right, boys, get a few hours of sleep. We're heading back to New York tomorrow," he ordered, pulling out his cell phone to call his boss.

Chapter 19

Draven Cross was sleeping peacefully when Evan Mallory burst into the presidential quarters aboard the aircraft now known as *U.E. One*.

"Sir, I am sorry to wake you, but something horrible has happened at the Babylon-alternate headquarters site," Evan reported. "I have an urgent call from Barnes."

"Evan, why do you always expect me to handle your inbox, instead of you?" Draven asked disgustedly as he grabbed the phone from Evan's hand and said into it, "What do you want, Barnes?"

John Barnes described what had taken place and related his fear that the attackers had been Omega.

"Well, that is troubling, John, but I do like the way you handled the situation. I am sure the next security force will take their jobs more seriously. Don't worry about Omega. It seems Gabriella has been straightforward, though I must admit her candor surprises me. Yes, I will see you in New York," Draven said, ending the phone call.

"Sir, is everything okay?" Evan asked worriedly.

"Yes, everything is going fine. It seems that a group of Islamic fundamentalists attacked the Babylon construction site. Barnes proved to be every bit of the savage I thought he was, which demonstrates his usefulness. In any case, we will discuss this matter in further detail in New York. Get out of my room and turn off the light as you leave, Evan," Draven barked.

Christopher woke to find Jackson driving and Gilana counting out what looked like a large sum of U.S. currency. He asked, "What's going on?"

"I've been driving while you've been getting your beauty rest," Jackson replied dryly.

"Thanks for the obvious, Jackson, but I meant why the money," Christopher replied.

Still counting out the money, Gilana answered, "It's to make sure we don't end up in an Iraqi or Jordanian prison. We're about ten kilometers from the Iraqi border crossing."

"Man, how long was I out?"

"About twelve hours. I left water and a sandwich in the seat next to you," Jackson said.

"Thanks. You heard from Gabriella or General Havid?" Christopher said through a mouthful of some sort of meat sandwich.

"Gabriella, no. General Havid, yes," Jackson replied. "He has secured the C39XER at King Hussein Air Base and said he's convinced the prime minister to leave the two witnesses alone…for now."

"That's great news about our ride, but bad news on the other fronts, I guess."

Gilana shoved two wads of hundreds into two different sacks and threw one sack in the back of the van with Christopher as a road sign indicated it was five kilometers to the Tarbil Border Crossing and six kilometers to Al Karamah Border Crossing, Jordan.

"Listen to me carefully," Gilana stated calmly. "Jackson, wrap your keffiyeh around your head and mouth and put on your sunglasses now. When we reach the border crossing, I'll get out and talk with the guard. No matter what, stay in this van. Christopher, stay down until we tell you it's safe.

"If I am detained, drive through the crossing and then run off the road just short of the Jordanian crossing so you're not shot. The Jordanians will be more likely to detain you than the Iraqis. Give them the other sack of money and then tell them to call General Havid. If this doesn't go well, we will all be joining Uri soon."

"Lord, I know You're going to be with us right now," Jackson said as he pulled up behind a car being inspected at the Iraqi checkpoint.

Gilana got out with one of the money sacks, while Jackson kept one foot on the clutch and the other hovering over the gas pedal, ready to make a dash across the Iraqi border if required. The head guard waved over two other men, all of them peering into the bag and then back at Gilana.

"I don't think they're buying it. Gun it, Jackson," Christopher said, peering over the front seat.

"Just have a little faith. If we go now, there is no guarantee any of us make it out of here alive. Sit tight and stay low," Jackson directed coolly.

After a few tense moments of talking, Gilana jumped back into the van. She said tersely, "Drive, and don't make eye contact with any of them. Stay out of sight, Christopher."

Jackson shifted into first gear and crept across the Iraqi border, sweat soaking his clothing as he gripped the steering wheel tightly. The Iraqis moved from the roadway and waved the van through. Just as they were crossing the border, an Iraqi guard jumped in front of the van, causing Jackson to hit the brakes hard, slamming Christopher against the front seat.

Gilana lowered her window, yelling at the guard angrily in Arabic.

"Should I drive through?" Jackson mumbled.

"No," Gilana shouted without turning to face Jackson. "Give me the other sack of money."

From the back of the van, Christopher slid the sack into Gilana's outstretched hand, and she threw it at the guard's chest, who flashed a toothy grin, showing rotted teeth.

"*Yalla imshi*," the guard yelled at Gilana, smacking the van with a free hand.

"Drive. Now. I hope your God is watching because we are out of money," Gilana muttered through clenched teeth.

Jackson prayed the entire kilometer to the Jordanian border crossing, which seemed to be a million miles away. Gilana stayed in the vehicle this time, displaying a fake document claiming she was a Jordanian citizen who had been conducting humanitarian aid in Iraq for the last month.

While the guard scoured Gilana's document, another guard with a dog walked around the entire vehicle and paused for what seemed like an eternity to stare at Jackson. After the guard with the dog signaled to the head border agent an all-clear sign, the guard waved them through.

They drove another five kilometers past the border crossing before anyone spoke.

"Thank you, Jesus! Whew!" Jackson exclaimed, breaking the silence.

"I thought for sure bullets were going to rip through this van any moment, and that would be that. I need some water. I am sweating to death back here," Christopher complained, throwing off a pile of blankets.

"God must have been watching over us," Gilana asserted.

"He always is, and He is always ready to help, my friend," Jackson assured her as the group passed a road sign that read al-mafraq 276 kilometers. "Three more hours until we are heading home. Thank you, Jesus," he shouted again.

As *U.E. One* taxied to its hangar in a remote section of JFK International Airport under the first rays of a new day, Draven Cross finished his coffee, secure in his thought that the world was under his influence. As the cabin door opened, he was pleased to see a red-carpeted staircase and Gemma Sutherland awaiting him at the bottom of the stairs.

"Gemma, you always know how to welcome me back from a business trip," Draven greeted as she opened the door to his limousine.

"I do my best, sir," Gemma commented calmly. "I'm sure you're eager to get to work."

"Yes…where is Evan?" Draven looked out his window to see Evan conversing with the flight crew and leisurely making his way down the staircase. He shouted impatiently out his window, "Evan, if you plan to ride with me, move with a sense of purpose."

"I'm sorry, sir. I just thought it would be good to commend the flight crew on your behalf for doing such a good job over the last few days," Evan explained as he climbed into the limousine and seated himself across from Gemma and Draven.

"Evan, they're paid…well…to take me wherever I want and whenever I want. I don't need to thank them any more than I do every two weeks."

"My apologies, sir," Evan replied timidly.

"Sir, here are a few of the most interesting news articles from across the globe while you were in transit overnight," Gemma said, handing the secretary-general a folder of selected news articles.

"Evan, have you seen this? I am being defamed by these religious nuts around the world. What are you and your Interfaith followers doing to combat this dribble?" Draven asked, handing Evan copies of the *Die Welt* and *The Times*, which carried stories of mass Christian rallies led by men of the former Jewish faith in opposition to a Draven-run U.E.

"Sir, I was traveling with you. How could I have seen these articles?" Evan asked nervously.

"I realize where you were in time and space, Evan," Draven spat sharply. "However, you were also aboard the most technologically advanced aircraft in the world. I've said this before. Stay ahead of me, Evan, or you will find yourself fired." He turned to Gemma and said, "I want to have a security staff meeting within the next two hours. I'm ready to discuss the final planning to consolidate my power."

"Sir, John Barnes is en route from Iraq to New York right now. Shall we patch him in for the meeting?" Gemma inquired.

"Yes, I have a special mission for Barnes, one that requires his savagery." Draven's smile of anticipation looked positively evil.

Christopher laughed as he watched Jackson sleeping on top of a stack of cargo boxes in the "executive terminal"—aka a storage warehouse—at the King Hussein Air Base as Gilana made the final arrangements for their departure. *I declare that man can sleep anywhere at any time—a skill I wish I could imitate.*

"Okay, the plane has been fueled and your flight plan's cleared with the Jordanians. This is where we say good-bye," Gilana said firmly.

The major said, "I just wanted to tell you how sorry I am about Uri. I know what it feels like to lose someone you love."

"I appreciate your words, Christopher. The good news is that I will get to say good-bye. General Havid was able to secure Uri's body from the Iraqi government. The claim was made that he was radicalized and his wealthy family wanted to bury him at home. A cargo plane is being flown from Israel to Baghdad to pick him up as we speak," she answered softly.

"That's good news. Well, thank you for everything. I hope we get the chance to work together again in the future," Christopher replied as he kicked the boxes where Jackson was sleeping.

"Hey, what's going on?" Jackson asked.

Gilana laughed at Jackson as he struggled to regain coherent thought.

"Jackson, get up. It's time to go," Christopher answered before walking out of the warehouse toward the C39XER on the tarmac.

"Gilana, thank you. I'm so sorry about Uri. Will you be okay here?" Jackson queried.

"*Leich l'shalom*, which means 'go toward peace.' I wish you both the best. I will be fine. I have a commercial flight home later tonight," Gilana replied with a sad smile.

"God bless you, my friend." Jackson ran to catch up with Christopher.

Christopher prepared to send President Rodgers a summary of his findings on his communicator as they departed the Middle East, but he found himself once again with more questions than answers regarding God, faith, and his future survival.

Gabriella dreaded having Draven back at the U.E. headquarters; she felt confident he would find some way of blaming her for what had happened at Babylon. She couldn't be sure until she spoke with Christopher and Jackson, but the incident had all the hallmarks of those two in action. Gemma had given her a phone call from JFK that Draven had arrived and wanted to have a security staff meeting, and she really had no idea what to expect.

President Rodgers's latest message indicated that he planned to attack the U.E., or more precisely Draven, in two weeks, based on updated intelligence from the field. "From the field" was likely Christopher and Jackson, but she had no idea how to slow down this train heading for sure disaster. Surely God would intervene and stop President Rodgers from thrusting the world into a global war—at least, that was her hope.

"Ma'am, the secretary-general just arrived," a staff intern told Gabriella.

"Thanks," Gabriella replied. *Well, time's up. The best I can hope to do is warn everyone of any trouble Cross is throwing their way*, she thought as she placed her communicator on her desk and made her way to Cross's office.

Somewhere over the Arctic Circle, closing in on Anchorage, Alaska, Christopher's mind was consumed with reaching Gabriella, especially given the mission he had just completed for the president. However, the present view drowned out his worries, at least momentarily. The vast dark horizon before him seemed to be dancing as he watched the red and green glow of the northern lights lapping around the sky in front of the plane. Charlie Smith, the lone C39XER pilot, had invited Christopher up to the cockpit for the show.

"Amazing, right?" Charlie said across his headset to Christopher.

"I am at a loss for words that would even begin to describe how amazing this view is right now. I also want to thank you, Charlie. I know you've been tasked to fly us at a moment's notice around the world," Christopher replied.

"No worries. It's a pleasure to support you guys. Plus, it keeps me focused on something that keeps me sane. You know, those disappearances were something else."

"You prior military?"

"Yeah, I did a stint in the Air Force as a fighter pilot. I even flew in the first Gulf War. Got out of the service after that and started flying for the Agency, in and out of some interesting places. I retired a few years ago, but I maintain a contract flying for various government programs. It gives me flexibility and keeps me flying—the best things in life for a rolling stone former fighter pilot," Charlie responded with a smile.

Christopher liked Charlie's down-to-earth approach to life. He could only imagine the places the fifty-something Agency man had seen during his career. In a hushed tone, he asked, "So where were you when it happened?"

"If you mean the disappearances, I was right here in this seat, flying a test flight with my copilot Tim Johnson. We were about halfway between D.C. and Miami when I looked over at Tim, who was smiling and happy like always—he was the best guy. Well, the next thing I see is his headset drop into a pile of his clothes. I think the plane nosedived about a thousand feet before I was able to shake that image from my mind and regain control." Charlie's voice sounded almost haunted.

"Wow, that sounds about how my disappearance day went, besides pulling myself and sleepyhead Jackson back there out of the Potomac."

"I was floored when I landed in Charleston, South Carolina, to find out that my experience was only one of millions around the world."

"You lose anybody significant?" Christopher asked.

"Nah," Charlie replied. "I divorced a long time ago, right as I was going into the CIA. I tried tracking down my ex-wife just to see if she was still around. I couldn't reach her, so who knows if she was taken or just caught up in the immediate aftermath and died?"

"I lost my wife—actually, she and her parents were taken,"

Christopher said, thinking back to that fateful morning at the farmhouse as he watched the dazzling light show before him.

"I'm really sorry about that, sir. What do you think happened to all those people?" Charlie asked, his confusion evident.

"Please, call me Christopher, but we've finally reached the core question, Charlie. I think all those people, including millions of children and special-needs folks, are in Heaven right now. I have zero doubt about that. Whether I will ever get there is another question," Christopher answered soberly.

Charlie appeared to be engaged in a radio-checkpoint update and almost disinterested in Christopher's explanation. Then he said, "Sorry about that. Yeah, I've heard that theory from a few folks over the last couple of months. It's the most logical thing I can seem to wrap my head around. I mean, Cross's whole alien intervention thing sounds too clean-cut, you know? It's like he took what so many already accepted—that aliens exist and interact with us—and just fed it to the world."

"So do you believe in God now, Charlie? I mean, have you accepted Him into your life as your personal Savior?" Christopher asked.

"No, I've never been one for religion or God or anything like that. However, I would be lying if I didn't admit that my interest in the supernatural has peaked in the last couple of months. The Christian explanation of things just makes the most sense to me for some reason. I mean, if I were God, I would come to get my people before punishing everybody who has willfully chosen to reject me. I just don't know enough about God to make a decision."

"Let's change that," came the voice of Jackson from the dark cabin behind Charlie and Christopher.

"Ahh, we've awakened the sleeping preacher, Charlie," Christopher said with a laugh.

"You'd better listen, too… Wait a second. The sky looks like a bunch of fireflies are having a square dance," Jackson remarked in wonder.

Laughing again, Christopher said, "Charlie, welcome to my world."

Gabriella was shocked as she watched Draven Cross enter the conference room. The man's eyes appeared to shimmer with energy. The trip to the Middle East seemed to have energized the megalomaniac global leader. She sensed that Draven viewed the mishaps overseas as playing out in his favor. The rage she had expected from him was replaced by an even scarier outpouring of optimism.

"John, can you hear me?" Draven asked.

"Yes, sir, loud and clear," Barnes replied.

"Excellent. Where are you, my good man?" Draven inquired, causing everyone in the room to look at each other in surprise over his mood.

"Sir, we are crossing the Mediterranean as we speak, about 400 kilometers from Rome," Barnes answered.

"That's good to know. Stay tuned, as you will likely need to divert to a new destination soon," Draven said. Then he turned to the others in the room and said, "Well, my esteemed inner circle, what a few days we've had, right? Those two idiots in Jerusalem attacked me, and the world's religions are set to become a single faith controlled by me. One win for me, one win for the enemy, but I am about to break the stalemate.

"Gabriella, I was pleased to learn that your loyalty to me and the U.E. vision of global peace are unquestioned. John tells me you were actively assisting him in the Middle East, and your daily reports on President Rodgers and the Omega Group have been well received, despite your inability to pinpoint Omega's location. You can't win them all, right, dear?"

"Thanks, sir. I have tried to do all I can to show my commitment to your mission," Gabriella replied, drawing a brief but intense stare from Gemma.

"Yes, your efforts are commendable. However, the time has come to put down the final vestiges of the old world and its power system. I have consolidated the world leaders around my vision of the future and will not have it undermined by outliers who desire to promote the old way of thinking." He turned to Mallory and asked, "Evan, what is the status of the U.E.'s military capabilities as of this morning?"

Evan clicked a few buttons on his laptop and brought up an infographic on the large television monitor hanging on the wall at the end of the table, which displayed various military installations around the world. "Sir, based on your mandate that every member state of the U.E. brings ten percent of its military capabilities under U.E. authority, including all nuclear weapons, we are well positioned for any form of dissent. We have over two million personnel located at U.E. military installations, which were claimed from the host nation for our purposes. The future regional ambassadors have done a tremendous job in pushing the countries that will be under their authority to turn over personnel and hardware to the U.E."

"How much resistance have the ambassadors met in their regions, and how many nuclear weapons do we have?" Draven inquired.

"Varying levels of dissent were present in each member state," Evan answered. "Resistance came in the form of simple resignations of military leaders, legislative bodies attempting to remove heads of state, and—in a few isolated cases—violent demonstrations. Again, the regional ambassadors were able to stamp out resistance and maintain order, albeit using diplomacy, as they are not in charge of their regions as of today.

"The nuclear weapons have been a bit more of a challenge. Per your orders, we have retained about twenty-five Russian and Chinese nuclear weapons. As heads of their respective states, the future ambassadors from Russia and China have made available to you the launch authorization codes for these particular weapons. The remaining weapons are being stored temporarily at central holding areas in Kazakhstan, Russia, and the United States until Babylon comes online, where they will be dismantled."

"I have to say, Evan, you've almost impressed me with your oversight of the regional ambassadors and the religious leaders," the secretary-general said. "However, I will not destroy the remaining nuclear weapons. I will leave them at the holding sites in the event I need them."

"I am doing my best, sir, and we will do as you wish regarding any weapons systems at your disposal," Evan agreed.

"Sir, it seems to me that you're preparing for war. My only question is, with whom?" Gabriella asked.

"Very astute of you, Gabriella. Thank you for providing a segue to the conclusion of our meeting. Despite Evan's report, he was inept in reporting everything correctly."

"Sir, but I—"

"Silence," Draven said, cutting him off. "As usual, Evan, you got the job only halfway done, and I'm left to clean up the mess, as always. While the regional ambassadors have done well in suppressing the open resistance, I have insight into a vast underground movement led by some influential leaders. I plan to launch a preemptive strike against these subversive groups at a date that will be disclosed to everyone later. After we stamp out this resistance, I will enable the regional ambassadors to take control over their regions, and me the world.

"John, I want you to divert to the hidden base of the resistance leader you previously identified to me and destroy whoever and whatever you find there. Your confirmation that the base has been destroyed will initiate the attack against the remaining resistance network. The U.E. staff and everyone here, minus Evan, will not be notified of our new headquarters location until we are safely on the way to that location."

"Sir, I thought Babylon was going to be our new headquarters," Gabriella said, hoping to gain something she could relay to the people who were depending on her.

"That's what I want everyone to think. It's merely an alternate location, which I publicly announced, so the resistance would tip its hand. I am playing chess, Gabriella, and everyone else is playing checkers." Draven ended the meeting curtly, saying, "You're dismissed, and be prepared to depart for the new headquarters at a moment's notice."

Chapter 20

Gabriella didn't know where to start or what to do given everything she had just learned from Draven Cross. She raced back to her office and sent a group message from her communicator to President Rodgers, Christopher, and Jackson.

"I don't have much time. Long story short, Cross is preparing for war against an undisclosed resistance to his leadership—though I think we all know who that is. He is fully prepared to use nuclear weapons. Also, the new U.E. HQ is NOT at Babylon, which is being prepared instead as some sort of logistics node. You can reach me by phone in an hour, as I will be at my apartment packing. Godspeed."

Once the message was on its way, Gabriella left her office, heading for the elevators.

"Interesting meeting," Gemma mused, walking into the elevator with Gabriella.

"Terrifying is more how I would describe it," Gabriella replied.

"I am wondering if it was wise for me to disclose such personal information to someone who so easily sells out her country," Gemma said as the elevator doors opened to a busy U.E. lobby.

"Look, Gemma, we are all playing a game that's for keeps. I have been doing just enough to keep myself alive, nothing more and nothing less. What lies are you telling to keep your job and status? I certainly haven't sold out my country, nor would I put you in harm's way. Good day," she said curtly, turning her back on Gemma as she headed toward the lobby exit.

"Gabriella, wait, please. Look, I was out of line, okay? I am just on edge since it seems like World War III is looming over our heads. Please accept my apology," Gemma pleaded. "You're the only friend I have that I can trust."

"I get it, Gemma. You'll just have to believe me when I say that I am not your enemy. I've got to go to my apartment and pack a few things. If anyone is looking for me, you know where I am and have my number," Gabriella said before heading out onto the sidewalk. "I hope somebody calls me back," she mumbled under her breath as she jumped into a ride-share car.

As Christopher dozed on and off, he caught snippets of Jackson and Charlie's conversation regarding God, the rapture, the tribulation, and—what was most important to Jackson—salvation. Charlie had been so enthralled by Jackson's story of how he had lost everything a couple of months ago but had found renewed hope in Christ Jesus that the plane was left on autopilot for hours.

"I have to say, Jackson, you make a compelling case for me to ask Jesus to be my personal Savior, as you say. I've never had much use for religion before and have never really been exposed to any religion, much less Christianity. I've always felt that Christians above all others were arrogant in their view that Jesus was the only way to God, that their worldview was the only logical answer. Yet after two-plus hours with you, I can't find an argument against Jesus," Charlie confessed, checking the instruments and preparing the C39XER for final approach into Anchorage.

"That's great news! So you're ready to have Jesus take control of your life—similar to the way you're controlling this fancy plane?"

"I am. I mean, what do I have to lose at this point? It seems to me, based on your outline of the next few years, that things are about to ratchet up a notch or two in the pain department. There's no better time than now, but I'll be honest—I have no idea how to ask Jesus to save me."

"Your decision to follow Christ Jesus is awesome! Let me help you with a prayer, but remember—it's not this prayer or any ritualistic formula that will save you here today, Charlie. It's your repentance of living a life of sin and your faith that Jesus' death on the cross redeems you back to Him as you place your life in Jesus' hands. You can pray something like this: Lord Jesus, I've kept You out of my life. I know that I am a sinner and that no matter what I try, I cannot save myself. I'm no longer running from You or ignoring Your invitation for help in life. By faith, I ask for your forgiveness and gratefully receive your gift of salvation. I trust you as my Lord and Savior. I believe you are the Son of God who died on the cross for my sins and rose from the dead on the third day. Thank you for bearing my sins and giving me the gift of eternal life. Come into my heart, Lord Jesus, and be my Savior. Amen." Charlie repeated the prayer after him.

Jackson was enthused, embracing the pilot. "Charlie, did you mean what you just prayed? If you did, that's it, man. You just joined the family of God. Welcome to the eternal Kingdom of Jesus Christ."

"Wow, it feels weird, but in a good way. Who knew getting saved at 50,000 feet could feel better than anything else I've experienced up here? What now? I mean, do I need to do something else?"

"No, that's how simple it is to receive Jesus as your Savior. I have a spare Bible I can give you, and I'd recommend you start reading the four gospels to get a better understanding of who Jesus Christ is and what He came to accomplish. I'll email you the links to a few commentaries and other resources that will help you understand more about what you'll be reading."

"Sounds great. Let's get you boys into Anchorage."

"Congrats, Charlie," Christopher said.

"Thanks," the pilot responded. "It feels good to know I am right with the man upstairs." That *congrats* was all Christopher could muster up after watching yet another person go from foe to friend of God. The major was beginning to abandon hope that he could ever summon the resolve to surrender in his fight with God. He felt hollow, knowing he needed God in his life right now, but still too afraid to let go of his pain. He thought of what Erin would have said to him wanting to give up, for all of eternity. "God, bring me to a place where I can meet You and surrender," he quietly prayed.

Gabriella quickly opened her apartment door, tossing her purse toward the couch so she could answer the incoming call from President Rodgers.

"Hello, sir. It's good to hear from you. I'm glad you got my message. Cross is planning a decisive offensive strike at a yet determined time and location. No, I don't know the headquarters location, but I do know I'll be there—so think carefully about how you want to conduct a strike. It's not too late, sir. Millions, if not billions, of lives are on the line. Yet you have resigned yourself to war as the only policy option. No, sir…respectfully, you need to hear me out. If Cross is who you think he is, will a war stop him? Exactly, sir…you don't know. Look, just go along with him for now to gain more time to figure out how to bring him down. If you attack him or if he attacks the U.S., there is no turning back. Next week? Why are you accelerating the attack timeline? Have you heard nothing I've said? Hello? Hello?"

Gabriella screamed with frustration and threw the sophisticated quantum communicator against a distant wall. She couldn't prevent the tears from streaming down her cheeks or the sobs welling up from deep inside, and she collapsed in an emotional heap on her living room floor.

"God, why? What are we supposed to learn from all of this?" she screamed. Receiving no answer, she continued to sob as what little energy she had faded away, and a restless sleep overtook her.

As the sun began to appear just above the horizon of the snow-covered Chugach Mountains surrounding Anchorage, Christopher's communicator buzzed for the first time in days. "We must have cleared 10,000 feet. I just got a voice message from Gabriella to call her," he remarked quietly to Jackson, who was now seated next to him in the passenger cabin.

"Yeah, I got the same message. I wonder what's up. Whatever it is, it doesn't sound good," Jackson said glumly.

"I'm calling her now. It's midmorning in New York," Christopher said thoughtfully.

When she answered, he was shocked to hear the defeat in Gabriella's voice. She described both Rodgers's and Cross's plans, and they both agreed that President Rodgers felt a fatalistic sense of duty to go down fighting if he was going to be the last American president in history.

"Okay, I'll contact you in a couple of days from here in Alaska. Just do your best to give us a heads up if you find out where the initial strike is going to take place. Be careful, bye," Christopher admonished as a cold rush of frigid air filled the cabin when the door was opened.

"Well, how bad is it?" Jackson asked.

"It's bad, but let's discuss it with Jimbo on the way back to the base. We need to have a plan going forward—things are about to go from bad to worse." He waved an arm in greeting toward the massive Jimbo waiting for them on the tarmac.

"Okay, but give me a minute to wrap up things with Charlie. I'll meet you in the truck," Jackson replied.

"You got it."

Charlie was going through his postflight checks when Jackson entered the cockpit.

"Hey, brother. I just wanted to check in with you before we head off into the unknown. I just wanted to reemphasize that you're saved. You belong to Jesus forever now," Jackson assured his new brother in Christ.

"I know," Charlie replied calmly. "I'm not worried about the future."

"How do you know? I mean, I am glad you do, but you've only been saved a few hours."

"God told me He was never leaving me. I don't mean He came and sat in the copilot's seat and told me that out loud...but He did just kind of tell me in my head. It's weird, you know?"

Laughing, Jackson replied, "Man, do I? I don't think I will ever get used to that still, small voice that's in my head sometimes. One other thing, where do you live or where are you based when you're not on call for us? I mean, I'm fairly certain you weren't just sitting in Israel waiting around."

"Well, I have a house outside of Nashville, Tennessee, but I am never there. I have flexibility in where I am based as long as I can be reached anytime. For example, when you were running around in the Middle East, I just flew over to Bulgaria and spent my downtime with an old buddy." Charlie went quiet, and his face grew red, almost like he was embarrassed.

"What's wrong, Charlie?"

"My buddy is a black marketeer, among many other things. I guess I can't hang out with him anymore, huh?"

"I would say that, in my not-so-expert opinion, you should hang out with him just to get the chance to share the good news of Jesus with him. I am not saying you do everything he does, especially if it's wrong, but Jesus made it His mission to hang out with sinners, and I for one am glad He did," Jackson replied.

"Amen to that," a laughing Charlie agreed.

"I'll be in touch," Jackson promised.

"You know how to reach me," Charlie replied warmly.

John Barnes and his U.E. Special Activities Group or SAG, as Barnes had begun referring to his paramilitary organization, arrived in Anchorage, Alaska, about eight hours after the target they sought, though they didn't know it. Draven Cross had ordered Barnes to destroy a secret U.S. military base as the opening salvo against a global rebellion against the U.E. He hoped he would have the opportunity to eliminate the Omega Group in the process, and he was particularly looking forward to making Jackson and Christopher suffer before they died. The mere thought of their demise brought a smile across to his face.

"Boss, I've got some bad news. The helicopter pilot says the weather is too bad farther north to move us into position tonight. We'll have to leave in the morning," a SAG troop reported.

"No matter," Barnes replied. "I can wait another day or so to finish my work against the country and organization that betrayed me." Christopher walked into the base operations center to find Jimbo and Jackson talking with a few other Omega guys and base personnel sipping coffee.

"Good morning, you want some coffee?" Jackson asked.

"Yeah, thanks, bro, and good morning to you guys, too. Hey, can I talk with Jimbo and you in that little office over there?" Christopher pointed to a briefing room adjacent to the base operations monitoring station.

"Lead the way," Jimbo said.

Christopher closed the blinds and shut the door as Jackson and Jimbo sat down. "I've been thinking, guys. If Jackson's prediction that the second seal is about to be opened with this great war that President Rodgers and Cross are edging toward, then we need an exit strategy."

"I am ready to hear the plan, but I just want you to know that I am sticking with you until the end. So don't get some crazy idea that you're leaving me like an old truck that's beat up and barely running," Jackson remarked drolly.

Laughing, Christopher said, "Why would I want to leave you anywhere? I would miss all the entertainment provided free of charge by your crazy country sayings."

"So what's the plan, Christopher?" Jimbo inquired.

"It's simple," the major said firmly. "First, for the safety of all the guys, we disband Omega effective today. Jackson has made appeals to all nine of those guys out there about Christ, and not one of them has shown any interest. I am open to them joining us, but they need to know what they are getting into and then make a final decision. If they decide they don't want to be a part of our survival plan, then we fly them out of here tonight and wish them the best of luck serving under Draven Cross."

"I have my doubts, but I am guessing there's more, right?" Jackson asked.

"Yep, I was just pausing to gather my thoughts," Christopher replied. "After we get the guys out, we three stick around until the president gives the word to launch the nukes, then we make our way to Alabama to your family's homestead, Jackson. From there, I think we implement yours and General Havid's plan to be a thorn in Draven's side until we meet our end. I can't tell you what to do, Jimbo, but the invitation to join Jackson and me is open."

"I like the plan, minus sending those guys out there into Cross's clutches. I mean, the talent in that room could create some havoc in this world," Jackson stated worriedly.

"First, count me in, but I agree with Jackson about the Omega soldiers being disbanded. You're creating a lethal insurgent force," Jimbo stated firmly.

"Glad to have you, Jimbo. I was hoping you were going to follow Jackson and me around for a while. I understand your concern, but if these guys don't believe in the message Jackson has presented, that alone makes them potential insider threats against us and our future missions. I am not sending them off without a choice, so I think we need to proceed."

The chief said, "Well, to be fair, using your own criteria for an insider threat, Christopher, you shouldn't be coming with Jackson and me. You don't believe in the message of the Bible, so who's to say you won't sell us out at some point to save yourself?"

"You have a lot of nerve, Jimbo," Christopher yelled.

"Okay, easy fellas," Jackson said. "Let's not get our underwear in a knot here. Look, Jimbo has a valid point as far as not being hypocritical. However, you need to come to a decision for salvation freely and clearly. I also know you would never sell out Jimbo, me, or anyone else on our team, so I have no fear about that. The bottom line is that you need to get right with God, but I see your point about Omega. I support you, brother."

Jimbo spoke up. "I didn't mean to offend you. I just want you to accept Christ Jesus into your life. I support the plan. I'll gather the men for a final briefing from Jackson and start to get the birds en route up here in case some guys decide to leave." He headed out the door.

Christopher was still hot about Jimbo's insinuation and merely nodded his approval. Jackson waited until the door closed before speaking.

"Look, man, that's a good dude right there and a trusted brother. Yeah, he was a little blunt, but he meant no harm. Let's get out of here and see if we can get a few of these stubborn boys like yourself saved," Jackson said, placing a steady hand on Christopher's shoulder as they headed to the door.

"Wait. Thanks for being here for me. It means more than you know," Christopher said.

"No problem. Now let's go. We have a lot to do in a short time."

John Barnes and his men were sitting in a nearly empty executive terminal lounge at Anchorage International Airport, awaiting word on whether a contact within a helicopter tour company would be able to get them close to the secret base location.

A man whom John assumed to be the helicopter pilot approached and asked, "Are you, John Barnes?"

"Yes, I am. I am guessing you're the guy that's going to take us to the grid location my deputy provided you."

"Well, here's the thing, chief. That's government-restricted air for about seventy-five square kilometers. If I go up there, who knows what will happen? For the money provided, I can't see us doing business."

Barnes looked at his deputy, nodding to indicate that he should clear the lounge of all the civilian passengers. He kept his gaze on the pilot as he heard the brief struggle of businessmen being forced out of the lounge by his men. As he listened to the doors close after the last person, leaving him alone in the room with the pilot, he pulled a semiautomatic pistol from his concealed holster and pressed it to the pilot's temple.

"What are you doing? You're crazy!" the pilot shouted.

Barnes struck the man in the temple with the butt end of the pistol, causing the man to fall to his knees in pain. Then he shoved the gun barrel to the pilot's head and racked a round into the chamber. "This is how this little trip is going to work. You're going to take my team and me to the precise location I desire for the amount you've been given, or you will never leave this room alive."

"Okay, okay. Calm down. Just don't shoot me. We can leave in two hours," the pilot said nervously.

"Go," Barnes ordered, pulling the man up off the floor and shoving him to the door.

The rest of the U.E. SAG group came back into the room laughing, enjoying the show of force by their leader.

"Get your gear ready," John Barnes ordered. "We're leaving in two hours." He pulled out his phone and dialed Gemma's desk. "Gemma, tell the boss to expect a message from me this time tomorrow morning, saying the mission is complete." He hung up the phone, smiling.

Christopher stood in the back of the operations center with Jimbo as Jackson told the soldiers of Omega Group that a decision had been made at the highest levels to disband the team. Jackson shared his personal story of learning about Jesus' gift of salvation through Rev's journal after the disappearances. After describing the loss of his wife and daughters, the sergeant major appealed to the men to trust Jesus because He would never leave them and would provide an inexplicable sense of peace and hope in life's most difficult moments.

Christopher glanced at Jimbo. Tears streamed down his cheeks as he listened to the warrior preacher attempt to persuade these lethal soldiers to become warriors for Jesus.

As Jackson finished his message, the major watched a few of his soldiers leave the operations center, emotional but unconvinced of their need for Jesus as their personal Savior. A couple of soldiers lingered to talk with Jackson, whom they had all come to respect almost in a father-figure type role. But in the end, only Jackson, Christopher, and Jimbo remained.

"I tried my best, guys. I really thought those last two were ready," Jackson said sadly, voice hoarse and eyes red.

"You did your best, Jackson," Jimbo said to him. "Accepting Jesus Christ as the Lord of your life is an individual thing. Jesus only asks us to tell the world about the good news, to present the truth of the gospel and pray that those who are blind to the truth will see it for themselves. I have faith that there is still hope for those nine men to find Jesus before it's too late. Keep your head up. You've done all that could be asked of a person and more."

Christopher said, "I agree with Jimbo. You can't force someone to accept Jesus. If Jesus didn't force people by sword or threat, then we certainly can't."

"I was hoping and praying *you* would give your life to Jesus tonight, Christopher. I'll just keep praying. Okay, when do these boys head out of here?" Jackson queried.

Jimbo replied, "The birds are on their way here right now to pick them up. The only one who'll still be here besides the three of us is one of my contracting guys, named Max, who will make sure the systems for launching the nukes continue running."

"The good news is that, within a week, we'll be out of here and on our way to Alabama," Jackson asserted optimistically.

"Speaking of our departure, I am going to have a helo positioned at the pad down the road so we'll have a way out of here with the contractor when the time comes," Jimbo explained.

"You can fly a helicopter," Jackson said sarcastically.

"Yes, I can. I spent my early pararescue years hanging out with some of the MH-53 pilots from the 20th Special Operations Squadron down in Hurlburt Field when we still had MH-53s. I got the itch to fly and took lessons on the weekends and my free time. Now is there anything else you want to know, nosey?" Jimbo responded.

"No, I just wanted to make sure that y'all weren't counting on me to fly us anywhere," Jackson said, chuckling.

"It never crossed my mind," Jimbo replied, shooting a wily look at Christopher.

"Good thinking, Jimbo, on staging a ride out of town for all of us," the major said. "The auto-launch feature is a plus. At least we don't have to wait around for the return-to-sender nukes I am sure will be heading this way after the launch."

"Yep, by the time those nukes go off, we'll be in Anchorage," Jimbo said.

"Sounds to me like it's going to be a quiet couple of days. I'm gonna go check on those guys in case anyone has questions," Jackson said on his way out of the room.

Christopher said, "Hey, Jimbo, about earlier—" The big man cut him off. "No need for apologies. I was wrong for trying to push you or cast your indecision for Christ in a negative light. *I* apologize."

"Thanks, man, and welcome to the new Omega," Christopher replied.

"Glad to be with you, brother," Jimbo said as the two of them made their way to the living areas.

Because of the message Gemma had passed along from John Barnes, Draven was as giddy as a young schoolboy on the last day of school before the summer holiday. He had instructed Gemma to have planes ready to fly the nonessential staff within three hours to a holding location in Amsterdam, where they would await orders to move to the new head-quarters. He also directed that the security staff should prepare to depart tomorrow morning at ten o'clock aboard *U.E. One*. Now in the solitude of his office, he sought the council of the Prince of This World.

"My great leader, show me how I should execute vengeance on my enemies. Please give me a vision for the future," Draven begged, speaking into the void of his office.

Draven felt like he was suddenly falling through a vast chasm that had opened in his office. He attempted to scream, but no sound came from his mouth. He landed on his knees before the stairs of a grand temple where a radiant light, so intense that he could not look up or move before it. He looked away from the temple light and saw an innumerable crowd all kneeling, facing the temple. He felt he was in the presence of awesome power—no, a real god—and he attempted yet again to ask for help. "Please help me, Prince of This World."

He was instantly pulled back into his office, where he felt the Prince speak into his mind.

"This is the future of the world. All will worship me, the god you have always sought and desired. You need only trust me, and all that you deserve will be given to you."

"Oh, thank you, my lord. I am grateful to serve you and will make our enemies suffer," Draven promised aloud.

Evan, having learned to knock before entering Cross's office, rapped twice more before cracking the door open. "Sir, are you here? There is trouble out of Israel again with those two witnesses," he reported.

"Come in, Evan. What is going on now with those two old fools in Jerusalem?" Draven responded impatiently.

Evan entered and turned on the television, bringing up the ongoing coverage of the two witnesses' most recent speech.

"If you're just joining us, we're taking you to Jerusalem where two yet-to-be-identified men have been speaking—or preaching, as some say—multiple times each day from the Temple Mount since the signing of the peace treaty between the U.E. and Israel. It seems that moments ago, the two men made a proclamation of plagues striking Israel. We go now to breaking live coverage of what we anticipate to be a response by the Israeli government that may turn violent. Let's listen as the two militants confront an Israeli government spokesperson," the anchor concluded.

"Gentlemen, why do you continue to hold this sacred site hostage? You've threatened to withhold rain from our nation and now, you promise plagues. This doesn't portray either you or your God in a very positive light," the Israeli representative accused, drawing laughter from the crowd.

The taller of the two witnesses spoke in a deeply resonant voice, causing the crowd to move back from the barriers and the man. "He who has ears to hear let him hear. You would not accept John the Baptist, claiming he had demons. You would not accept the Messiah, the Lion of Judah, saying he was a drunkard and a friend of sinners. Yet now you accept the beast, the son of perdition, who will make you drink from his winepress of sorrow and despair. The world must repent of its iniquities, must turn away from its sinful desires, and seek the forgiveness and salvation of the true and living God of Israel and Heaven." He finished and sat down.

The second witness stood up and said, "God looks at the heart while men look at outward appearances. The world leader you believe to be pure and righteous is corrupt and hollow inside. This man is like a new tomb, gleaming on the outside, but that shiny exterior hides corruption and death underneath. *El Shaddai* knows the hearts of men and, as He did to the pharaoh before you, He will turn your hearts over to hardness."

"Yes, we have heard all of this before. The Israeli government demands…" Mid-sentence the Israeli spokesman fell to the ground, writhing in pain as large boils broke out all over his face and body.

"It is unwise to mock Elohim," the taller witness warned as the second witness moved to his side.

The two witnesses boldly proclaimed together, "Hear what the God of Abraham, Isaac, and Jacob says. Since you mock the Lord your God, may the waters of this land become bitter until we, the two servants and lampstands of God proclaim their restoration. Turn your hearts away from sin and hardness and yield to the salvation and life found in Jesus Christ." The two men seated themselves once again and remained motionless as the crowd began to disperse.

"As you, our viewers, have seen, these two men have perpetrated yet another horrific attack and made threats of terrorism against the nation of Israel. We will continue to monitor the ongoing situation in Jerusalem and update you with any breaking news. Thank you for watching the all-news network."

Evan turned off the television, expecting Draven Cross to swear at him for bringing such a bad report, but the secretary-general appeared unexpectedly calm.

"I see the two old men wish to continue defaming me," Draven said. "No matter. I have been promised by our universal spiritual guide that I will have my revenge against these enemies in due course. My only regret is signing that agreement with Israel. Otherwise, I would drop a nuclear bomb on the Temple Mount. Anyway, on to more pressing matters. I need you to ensure that all the security staff is ready to be in the air by ten o'clock tomorrow morning. I would hate for someone to be left in New York City."

"I understand, sir. I will make all the arrangements," Evan promised.

"Good. All I need now is that message from Barnes in order to be sure we have wiped out all the political relics of the past. Tomorrow should bring a clean slate to work with, Evan. Leave me," Draven ordered imperiously.

CHAPTER 21

John Barnes searched the navigation system, looking for a valley about five kilometers away from the northern ridgeline behind the secret U.S. base. The sun was beginning to set, and they needed to be on the ground before darkness fell so they could maximize the night hours to accomplish this mission. Feeling anger well up in his chest at the thought that they might be lost, he finally saw the destination arrow populate on the GPS screen.

"Put us down there," he ordered the pilot, who landed in an open space in the forest about half a kilometer away from the destination that Barnes had initially selected. "You will wait here until we return. In fact give me the keys."

"Really? You're leaving me without a way to turn on the heat," the pilot responded incredulously.

Barnes threw the man an extra assault pack. Laughing, he barked, "I suggest you make yourself comfortable in that sleeping bag. It's rated for survivability down to minus twenty degrees Fahrenheit." He then turned to his team. "Pack up, boys, and let's go. We've got a little over five clicks to cover before sunup," he commanded, leading his hired special operatives into the darkness.

Jimbo returned from a security patrol to find Christopher and Jackson in the operations center, watching a special news report coming from Israel regarding the "terror" attack by the two witnesses and the growing number of Christian rallies being led by Jewish men.

"Everything looks good out there. Due to our limited personnel here now, I had to take down the north ridge passive security system. We don't have anyone to monitor or respond to that sector. Though it's a risk, it's one I'm willing to take since it would take strong mountaineering skills to get to the top of that ridge due to the terrain," Jimbo explained.

"I am just glad the missile field and that large north granite face are a good half a kilometer away from us. If that face ever falls in an earthquake or something, it's going to create a monster avalanche. But I guess that was the point of building the base in this location, right?" Jackson remarked.

"You're right," Jimbo confirmed. "When we let our nukes go, Mother Nature will take over."

"Today has been a long day. Our former teammates arrived safely in Anchorage, and the security front looks clear, so it's lights out for this soldier," Christopher said.

"I think I'll turn in, too," Jackson agreed.

"Well, I am going to check in with Max—to make sure he is good to go for the night. I'll see you in the morning," Jimbo told them.

"Good night, don't let the polar bears bite," Jackson warned.

Christopher said, "It never stops, does it?"

"Never," Jackson replied with a laugh.

The march through the forests had been more challenging than John Barnes had expected, but thankfully he had enough guys with mountaineering experience to make it to the top of the north ridge slightly ahead of schedule, with about forty-five minutes of darkness left. They had just enough time to place the charges along the ridgeline to destroy the sleeping base below.

The lack of response to the team climbing up the ridgeline made him wonder if this was, in fact, the right place. John Barnes shuddered at the thought of reporting to Draven that the American base had been a decoy.

"Okay, guys, let me know when you have all your charges in place. We will move back down the mountain to our last rally point and then set them off. We'll do a flyover to make sure the job was done—worst case, we land and do some cleanup." Barnes received nods of acknowledgment from all thirteen of his men and watched as they disappeared along the ridgeline to place the explosives.

About thirty minutes later, the job was done and the U.E. SAG operatives were moving back down the mountain about 800 meters from the ridgeline summit.

John Barnes retrieved the radio-transmitter detonator from his assault pack. "Well, men, nothing to do now but start us a well-paid war," he commented, pressing the detonator button.

Christopher had a hard time sleeping. He kept having dreams of being back in the special forces selection course, where falling asleep and being caught could lead to being dismissed from the class. Every time he fell asleep, he would dream he was being told to wake up.

He had donned his heavy winter jacket and snow pants and was preparing to make his way outside when he noticed that Jimbo and Jackson were missing. Christopher figured they were in the operations center, probably drinking coffee. Yet when he left the living quarters, he saw Jimbo and Jackson talking outside.

"What's going on?" Christopher asked.

"Oh, man, I hope we didn't wake you. We finished getting dressed out here trying not to. It's strange. Neither one of us could sleep. I was telling Jimbo it's like the Holy Spirit kept slapping me in the face. I can understand how them disciples must have felt when Jesus asked them to pray all night because I am so tired right now I could sleep all day," Jackson said.

"Yeah, I kept dreaming my mom was coming in to wake me up for school. I never did fall sound asleep. Let's head up to check on Max and then do a quick security sweep. Then maybe we'll all be able to sleep for a few more hours," Jimbo suggested.

"I like the way you think," Christopher agreed, though he didn't confess to the other two that he'd also been unable to sleep well.

"Amen to the patrol and to going back to bed," Jackson chimed in.

As the three of them were nearing the operations center, they heard the loud cracking of rock and what sounded like explosions.

Max burst out of the operations center about forty meters in front of them, screaming for them to run, having just activated the missile-launch sequence. In a panic, he was now running for his life down the trail.

"My God, an avalanche!" Jimbo yelled.

As the men made their way toward two snow machines about ten feet away, Christopher stopped and looked on in horror as two ICBM nuclear-armed weapons streaked through the early dawn sky with their fiery tails.

"God help us, we're at war!" Christopher screamed to Jackson and Jimbo, who were frantically trying to start the snow machines.

"Hop on! Let's move!" Jimbo ordered.

Jackson had just gotten his snow machine started, picked up Max, and was following close behind Christopher and Jimbo as they raced to the trail that led to the helicopter pad. The machines were, however, no match for the impressive display of power unleashed by the avalanche.

The major felt the coolness of the air being pushed in front of the avalanche and heard the deafening roar of the snow and debris now mere meters away. As the first wave of snow mass tumbled over Jackson and Max, Christopher saw Jackson say something before the sound was cut off abruptly. He felt sudden panic and dread of the fate that was coming down upon them. He tried to remember his mountaineering training, of what to do in an avalanche. He knew he needed to try to "swim" to stay above the surface of the snow, if possible, but as the snow mass engulfed him, he felt like the snow had turned into cement. Sure that this was it for him, Christopher's only coherent thought was that he had not given his life to Christ.

U.E. One, carrying Draven Cross and his security staff, was making its way across the Atlantic to Rome and Palazzo Caelum, where the World Religious Leaders Conference had been held. Draven was quite satisfied that the palace would be an ideal location for the new U.E. global headquarters. An aide interrupted his musings to say that John Barnes was on the phone. Once John confirmed that the base had been destroyed, Draven—delighted by the report—immediately ordered military strikes against targets in Uruguay, Nigeria, and the United States.

"I want one-megaton nuclear weapons directed at Aguilar's home in Uruguay's capital, the Nigerian leader's home outside of Lagos, and also New York City, Los Angeles, NORAD, and the White House. The remainder of the nuclear weapons under my control will be held in case our forces encounter heavy resistance in the days ahead," Draven directed.

Without thinking, Gabriella jumped up from her seat and slapped Draven Cross—the most powerful leader in world history, a man who held her life in his hands, and possibly the biblical Antichrist. "How could you? How could you? You have killed millions of innocent people, you monster!" she screamed as Evan and security forces pinned her to the floor.

"Let her go, gentlemen. I would have been concerned if that had not been her response. She just lost her father figure in President Rodgers, her closest friends within Omega Team, and her homeland. Though the vitriol directed at me is misplaced, it is understandable. I am sure that, given time, Gabriella will apologize as she comes to understand why today's actions were necessary to bring about the peace future generations will now enjoy," Draven said magnanimously.

"I will never forgive you. You're pure evil," Gabriella spat before storming out of the conference room and collapsing into one of the press pool seats.

She wept bitterly for her friends, who were now gone. She cried for a country she loved that would never be the same, and she cried for herself. She knew she was lost now, without much hope, working for an evil dictator who might well be the Antichrist. As she stared out into the dark blue waters of the Atlantic Ocean below her, she prayed. "God, I don't know if you're even listening to me, but please help me to find You. I am all alone, but I don't want to serve that monster. Help me, and please don't forget me."

Christopher was surrounded by darkness, and his breathing was labored. He felt pain all over his body. He enjoyed the silence that invaded his mind and almost laughed at the thought that his impending death was going to be easier than he had envisioned. As the blood from a head wound flowed across his face, he uttered a simple three-word prayer that he hoped he lived to make good on. "I surrender, God."

CPSIA information can be obtained
at www.ICGtesting.com
Printed in the USA
LVHW051726240719
625184LV00001B/1